HENRY ROTH was born in 1906 in New York City and moved to New England in 1945, first to Boston and then to Augusta, Maine, where he became a water-fowl farmer. CALL IT SLEEP was published in 1934 and reissued in hardcover in 1960. In recent years new articles and stories by Roth have appeared in *Commentary, Midstream, The New Yorker,* and *Atlantic Monthly.* Upon the Avon publication of CALL IT SLEEP in paperback in 1964, Alfred Kazin wrote:

Perhaps now CALL IT SLEEP will at last reach the wide audience it deserves, for the book has for thirty years been one of the underground classics of psychological fiction. Since Roth brought this book out thirty years ago, there have been many novels of Jewish life in this country; none has ever gone so deeply as CALL IT SLEEP, with so much tremulous honesty, into the pain and ardor of family relationships. A sensitive boy's growing up, that much-handled subject, here becomes only one strand in the complex web of the parents' tense life with each other and of their immigrant strangeness in a new world. CALL IT SLEEP is one of those rare novels that unite the indistinct inner world and the external world of brutal fact into a single composition made lyrical by its intense truthfulness alone. It is "faithful," as no other novel on the subject ever has been, to profound, exalting, and unbearable facts. Roth has been silent ever since this book came out thirty years ago; perhaps this silence has been the cost of so much solitary effort. But this book has never been forgotten by those who had a chance to read it.

November 1983

With *[best wishes?]*,
C——

CALL IT SLEEP

HENRY ROTH

Afterword by
WALTER ALLEN

 A BARD BOOK/PUBLISHED BY AVON BOOKS

AVON BOOKS
A division of
The Hearst Corporation
959 Eighth Avenue
New York, New York 10019

Copyright 1934 by Henry Roth
Copyright Renewed © 1962 by Henry Roth
Afterword reprinted by arrangement with Michael Joseph, Ltd.
Published by arrangement with Sidney B. Solomon
Library of Congress Catalog Card Number: 60-13694
ISBN: 0-380-00755-x

First Bard Printing, October, 1964

BARD TRADEMARK REG. U. S. PAT. OFF. AND IN
OTHER COUNTRIES, MARCA REGISTRADA, HECHO EN
U. S. A.

Printed in the U. S. A.

WFH   31   30   29   28

To

EDA LOU WALTON

CONTENTS

PROLOGUE

*(I pray thee ask no questions
this is that Golden Land)*

THE small white steamer, Peter Stuyvesant, that delivered the immigrants from the stench and throb of the steerage to the stench and the throb of New York tenements, rolled slightly on the water beside the stone quay in the lee of the weathered barracks and new brick buildings of Ellis Island. Her skipper was waiting for the last of the officials, laborers and guards to embark upon her before he cast off and started for Manhattan. Since this was Saturday afternoon and this the last trip she would make for the week-end, those left behind might have to stay over till Monday. Her whistle bellowed its hoarse warning. A few figures in overalls sauntered from the high doors of the immigration quarters and down the grey pavement that led to the dock.

It was May of the year 1907, the year that was destined to bring the greatest number of immigrants to the shores of the United States. All that day, as on all the days since spring began, her decks had been thronged by hundreds upon hundreds of foreigners, natives from almost every land in the world, the joweled close-cropped Teuton, the full-bearded Russian, the scraggly-whiskered Jew, and among them Slovack peasants with docile faces, smooth-cheeked and swarthy Armenians, pimply Greeks, Danes with wrinkled eyelids. All day her decks had been colorful, a matrix of the vivid costumes of other lands, the speckled green-and-yellow aprons, the flowered kerchief, embroidered homespun, the silver-braided sheepskin vest, the gaudy scarfs, yellow boots, fur caps, caftans, dull gabardines. All day the guttural, the high-pitched voices, the astonished cries, the gasps of wonder, reitera-

9

tions of gladness had risen from her decks in a motley billow of sound. But now her decks were empty, quiet, spreading out under the sunlight almost as if the warm boards were relaxing from the strain and the pressure of the myriads of feet. All those steerage passengers of the ships that had docked that day who were permitted to enter had already entered—except two, a woman and a young child she carried in her arms. They had just come aboard escorted by a man.

About the appearance of these late comers there was very little that was unusual. The man had evidently spent some time in America and was now bringing his wife and child over from the other side. It might have been thought that he had spent most of his time in lower New York, for he paid only the scantest attention to the Statue of Liberty or to the city rising from the water or to the bridges spanning the East River—or perhaps he was merely too agitated to waste much time on these wonders. His clothes were the ordinary clothes the ordinary New Yorker wore in that period—sober and dull. A black derby accentuated the sharpness and sedentary pallor of his face; a jacket, loose on his tall spare frame, buttoned up in a V close to the throat; and above the V a tightly-knotted black tie was mounted in the groove of a high starched collar. As for his wife, one guessed that she was a European more by the timid wondering look in her eyes as she gazed from her husband to the harbor, than by her clothes. For her clothes were American—a black skirt, a white shirt-waist and a black jacket. Obviously her husband had either taken the precaution of sending them to her while she was still in Europe or had brought them with him to Ellis Island where she had slipped them on before she left.

Only the small child in her arms wore a distinctly foreign costume, an impression one got chiefly from the odd, outlandish, blue straw hat on his head with its polka dot ribbons of the same color dangling over each shoulder.

Except for this hat, had the three newcomers been in a crowd, no one probably, could have singled out the woman and child as newly arrived immigrants. They carried no sheets tied up in huge bundles, no bulky wicker baskets, no prized feather beds, no boxes of delicacies, sausages, virgin-olive oils, rare cheeses; the large black satchel beside them was their only luggage. But despite this, despite their even less than commonplace appearance, the two overalled men, sprawled out and smoking cigarettes in the stern, eyed them curiously. And the old peddler woman, sitting with basket of oranges on knee, continually squinted her weak eyes in their direction.

The truth was there was something quite untypical about their behavior. The old peddler woman on the bench and the overalled men in the stern had seen enough husbands meeting their wives and children after a long absence to know how such people ought to behave. The most volatile races, such as the Italians, often danced for joy, whirled each other around, pirouetted in an ecstasy: Swedes sometimes just looked at each other, breathing through open mouths like a panting dog; Jews wept, jabbered, almost put each other's eyes out with the recklessness of their darting gestures; Poles roared and gripped each other at arm's length as though they meant to tear a handful of flesh; and after one pecking kiss, the English might be seen gravitating toward, but never achieving an embrace. But these two stood silent, apart; the man staring with aloof, offended eyes grimly down at the water—or if he turned his face toward his wife at all, it was only to glare in harsh contempt at the blue straw hat worn by the child in her arms, and then his hostile eyes would sweep about the deck to see if anyone else were observing them. And his wife beside him regarding him uneasily, appealingly. And the child against her breast looking from one to the other with watchful, frightened eyes. Altogether it was a very curious meeting.

They had been standing in this strange and silent manner for several minutes, when the woman, as if driven by the strain into action, tried to smile, and touching her husband's arm said timidly, "And this is the Golden Land." She spoke in Yiddish.

The man grunted, but made no answer.

She took a breath as if taking courage, and tremulously, "I'm sorry, Albert, I was so stupid." She paused waiting for some flicker of unbending, some word, which never came. "But you look so lean, Albert, so haggard. And your mustache—you've shaved."

His brusque glance stabbed and withdrew. "Even so."

"You must have suffered in this land." She continued

gentle despite his rebuke. "You never wrote me. You're
thin. Ach! Then here in the new land is the same old
poverty. You've gone without food. I can see it. You've
changed."

"Well that don't matter," he snapped, ignoring her sympathy. "It's no excuse for your not recognizing me. Who
else would call for you? Do you know anyone else in this
land?"

"No," placatingly. "But I was so frightened, Albert.
Listen to me. I was so bewildered, and that long waiting
there in that vast room since morning. Oh, that horrible
waiting! I saw them all go, one after the other. The shoe-
maker and his wife. The coppersmith and his children
from Strij. All those on the Kaiserin Viktoria. But I—I remained. To-morrow will be Sunday. They told me no
one could come to fetch me. What if they sent me back?
I was frantic!"

"Are you blaming me?" His voice was dangerous.

"No! No! Of course not Albert! I was just explaining."

"Well then let me explain," he said curtly. "I did what
I could. I took the day off from the shop. I called that
cursed Hamburg-American Line four times. And each time
they told me you weren't on board."

"They didn't have any more third-class passage, so I
had to take the steerage—"

"Yes, now I know. That's all very well. That couldn't
be helped. I came here anyway. The last boat. And what
do you do? You refused to recognize me. You don't know
me." He dropped his elbows down on the rail, averted his
angry face. "That's the greeting I get."

"I'm sorry, Albert," she stroked his arm humbly. "I'm
sorry."

"And as if those blue-coated mongrels in there weren't
mocking me enough, you give them that brat's right
age. Didn't I write you to say seventeen months because
it would save the half fare! Didn't you hear me inside
when I told them?"

"How could I, Albert?" she protested. "How could I?
You were on the other side of that—that cage."

"Well why didn't you say seventeen months anyway?
Look!" he pointed to several blue-coated officials who
came hurrying out of a doorway out of the immigration
quarters. "There they are." An ominous pride dragged at

his voice. "If he's among them, that one who questioned me so much, I could speak to him if he came up here."

"Don't bother with him, Albert," she exclaimed uneasily. "Please, Albert! What have you against him? He couldn't help it. It's his work."

"Is it?" His eyes followed with unswerving deliberation the blue-coats as they neared the boat. "Well he didn't have to do it so well."

"And after all, I did lie to him, Albert," she said hurriedly trying to distract him.

"The truth is you didn't," he snapped, turning his anger against her. "You made your first lie plain by telling the truth afterward. And made a laughing-stock of me!"

"I didn't know what to do." She picked despairingly at the wire grill beneath the rail. "In Hamburg the doctor laughed at me when I said seventeen months. He's so big. He was big when he was born." She smiled, the worried look on her face vanishing momentarily as she stroked her son's cheek. "Won't you speak to your father, David, beloved?"

The child merely ducked his head behind his mother.

His father stared at him, shifted his gaze and glared down at the officials, and then, as though perplexity had crossed his mind he frowned absently. "How old did he say he was?"

"The doctor? Over two years—and as I say he laughed."

"Well what did he enter?"

"Seventeen months—I told you."

"Then why didn't you tell them seventeen—" He broke off, shrugged violently. "Baah! You need more strength in this land." He paused, eyed her intently and then frowned suddenly. "Did you bring his birth certificate?"

"Why—" She seemed confused. "It may be in the trunk—there on the ship. I don't know. Perhaps I left it behind." Her hand wandered uncertainly to her lips. "I don't know. Is it important? I never thought of it. But surely father could send it. We need only write."

"Hmm! Well, put him down." His head jerked brusquely toward the child. "You don't need to carry him all the way. He's big enough to stand on his own feet."

She hesitated, and then reluctantly set the child down

on the deck. Scared, unsteady, the little one edged over
to the side opposite his father, and hidden by his mother,
clung to her skirt.

"Well, it's all over now." She attempted to be cheerful.
"It's all behind us now, isn't it, Albert? Whatever mistakes
I made don't really matter any more. Do they?"

"A fine taste of what lies before me!" He turned his
back on her and leaned morosely against the rail. "A
fine taste!"

They were silent. On the dock below, the brown
hawsers had been slipped over the mooring posts, and the
men on the lower deck now dragged them dripping from
the water. Bells clanged. The ship throbbed. Startled by the
hoarse bellow of her whistle, the gulls wheeling before
her prow rose with slight creaking cry from the green
water, and as she churned away from the stone quay
skimmed across her path on indolent, scimitar wing. Behind the ship the white wake that stretched to Ellis Island grew longer, raveling wanly into melon-green. On
one side curved the low drab Jersey coast-line, the spars
and masts on the waterfront fringing the sky; on the other
side was Brooklyn, flat, water-towered; the horns of the
harbor. And before them, rising on her high pedestal
from the scaling swarmy brilliance of sunlit water to the
west, Liberty. The spinning disk of the late afternoon
sun slanted behind her, and to those on board who gazed,
her features were charred with shadow, her depths exhausted, her masses ironed to one single plane. Against
the luminous sky the rays of her halo were spikes of
darkness roweling the air; shadow flattened the torch she
bore to a black cross against flawless light—the blackened
hilt of a broken sword. Liberty. The child and his mother
stared again at the massive figure in wonder.

The ship curved around in a long arc toward Manhattan, her bow sweeping past Brooklyn and the bridges
whose cables and pillars superimposed by distance,
spanned the East River in diaphanous and rigid waves.
The western wind that raked the harbor into brilliant
clods blew fresh and clear—a salt tang in the lull of its
veerings. It whipped the polka-dot ribbons on the child's
hat straight out behind him. They caught his father's eye.

"Where did you find that crown?"

Startled by his sudden question his wife looked down.

"That? That was Maria's parting gift. The old nurse. She bought it herself and then sewed the ribbons on. You don't think it's pretty?"

"Pretty? Do you still ask?" His lean jaws hardly moved as he spoke. "Can't you see that those idiots lying back there are watching us already? They're mocking us! What will the others do on the train? He looks like a clown in it. He's the cause of all this trouble anyway!"

The harsh voice, the wrathful glare, the hand flung toward the child frightened him. Without knowing the cause, he knew that the stranger's anger was directed at himself. He burst into tears and pressed closer to his mother.

"Quiet!" the voice above him snapped.

Cowering, the child wept all the louder.

"Hush, darling!" His mother's protecting hands settled on his shoulders.

"Just when we're about to land!" her husband said furiously "He begins this! This howling! And now we'll have it all the way home, I suppose! Quiet! You hear?"

"It's you who are frightening him, Albert!" she protested.

"Am I? Well, let him be quiet. And take that straw gear off his head."

"But Albert, it's cool here."

"Will you take that off when I—" A snarl choked whatever else he would have uttered. While his wife looked on aghast, his long fingers scooped the hat from the child's head. The next instant it was sailing over the ship's side to the green waters below. The overalled men in the stern grinned at each other. The old orange-peddler shook her head and clucked.

"Albert!" his wife caught her breath. "How could you?"

"I could!" he rapped out. "You should have left it behind!" His teeth clicked, and he glared about the deck.

She lifted the sobbing child to her breast, pressed him against her. With a vacant stunned expression, her gaze wandered from the grim smouldering face of her husband to the stern of the ship. In the silvery-green wake that curved trumpet-wise through the water, the blue hat still bobbed and rolled, ribbon stretched out on the waves. Tears sprang to her eyes. She brushed them away quickly, shook her head as if shaking off the memory, and looked

toward the bow. Before her the grimy cupolas and towering square walls of the city loomed up. Above the jagged
roof tops, the white smoke, whitened and suffused by the
slanting sun, faded into the slots and wedges of the sky.
She pressed her brow against her child's, hushed him with
whispers. This was that vast incredible land, the land of
freedom, of immense opportunity, that Golden Land.
Again she tried to smile.

"Albert," she said timidly, "Albert."

"Hm?"

"Gehen vir voinen du? In Nev York?"

"Nein. Bronzeville. Ich hud dir schoin geschriben."

She nodded uncertainly, sighed . . .

Screws threshing, backing water, the Peter Stuyvesant
neared her dock—drifting slowly and with canceled momentum as if reluctant.

BOOK I
The Cellar

I

STANDING before the kitchen sink and regarding the bright brass faucets that gleamed so far away, each with a bead of water at its nose, slowly swelling, falling, David again became aware that this world had been created without thought of him. He was thirsty, but the iron hip of the sink rested on legs tall almost as his own body, and by no stretch of arm, no leap, could he ever reach the distant tap. Where did the water come from that lurked so secretly in the curve of the brass? Where did it go, gurgling in the drain? What a strange world must be hidden behind the walls of a house! But he was thirsty.

"Mama!" he called, his voice rising above the hiss of sweeping in the frontroom. "Mama, I want a drink."

The unseen broom stopped to listen. "I'll be there in a moment," his mother answered. A chair squealed on its castors; a window chuckled down; his mother's approaching tread.

Standing in the doorway on the top step (two steps led up into the frontroom) his mother smilingly surveyed him. She looked as tall as a tower. The old grey dress she wore rose straight from strong bare ankle to waist, curved round the deep bosom and over the wide shoulders, and set her full throat in a frame of frayed lace. Her smooth, sloping face was flushed now with her work, but faintly so, diffused, the color of a hand beneath wax. She had mild, full lips, brown hair. A vague, fugitive darkness blurred the hollow above her cheekbone, giving to her

17

face and to her large brown eyes, set in their white ovals, a reserved and almost mournful air.

"I want a drink, mama," he repeated.

"I know," she answered, coming down the stairs. "I heard you." And casting a quick, sidelong glance at him, she went over to the sink and turned the tap. The water spouted noisily down. She stood there a moment, smiling obscurely, one finger parting the turbulent jet, waiting for the water to cool. Then filling a glass, she handed it down to him.

"When am I going to be big enough?" he asked resentfully as he took the glass in both hands.

"There will come a time," she answered, smiling. She rarely smiled broadly; instead the thin furrow along her upper lip would deepen. "Have little fear."

With eyes still fixed on his mother, he drank the water in breathless, uneven gulps, then returned the glass to her, surprised to see its contents scarcely diminished.

"Why can't I talk with my mouth in the water?"

"No one would hear you. Have you had your fill?"

He nodded, murmuring contentedly.

"And is that all?" she asked. Her voice held a faint challenge.

"Yes," he said hesitantly, meanwhile scanning her face for some clue.

"I thought so," she drew her head back in droll disappointment.

"What?"

"It is summer," she pointed to the window, "the weather grows warm. Whom will you refresh with the icy lips the water lent you?"

"Oh!" he lifted his smiling face.

"You remember nothing," she reproached him, and with a throaty chuckle, lifted him in her arms.

Sinking his fingers in her hair, David kissed her brow. The faint familiar warmth and odor of her skin and hair.

"There!" she laughed, nuzzling his cheek, "but you've waited too long; the sweet chill has dulled. Lips for me," she reminded him, "must always be cool as the water that wet them." She put him down.

"Sometime I'm going to eat some ice," he said warningly, "then you'll like it."

She laughed. And then soberly, "Aren't you ever going down into the street? The morning grows old."

"Aaa!"

"You'd better go. Just for a little while. I'm going to sweep here, you know."

"I want my calendar first," he pouted, invoking his privilege against the evil hour.

"Get it then. But you've got to go down afterwards."

He dragged a chair over beneath the calendar on the wall, clambered up, plucked off the outworn leaf, and fingered the remaining ones to see how far off the next red day was. Red days were Sundays, days his father was home. It always gave David a little qualm of dread to watch them draw near.

"Now you have your leaf," his mother reminded him. "Come." She stretched out her arms.

He held back. "Show me where my birthday is."

"Woe is me!" She exclaimed with an impatient chuckle. "I've shown it to you every day for weeks now."

"Show me again."

She rumpled the pad, lifted a thin plaque of leaves. "July—" she murmured, "July 12th . . . There!" She found it. "July 12th, 1911. You'll be six then."

David regarded the strange figures gravely. "Lots of pages still," he informed her.

"Yes."

"And a black day too."

"On the calendar," she laughed, "only on the calendar. Now do come down!"

Grasping her arm, he jumped down from the chair. "I must hide it now." He explained.

"So you must. I see I'll never finish my work today."

Too absorbed in his own affairs to pay much heed to hers, he went over to the pantry beneath the cupboard, opened the door and drew out a shoe-box, his treasure chest.

"See how many I've got already?" he pointed proudly to the fat sheaf of rumpled leaves inside the box.

"Wonderful!" She glanced at the box in perfunctory admiration. "You peel off the year as one might a cabbage. Are you ready for your journey?"

"Yes." He put away the box without a trace of alacrity.

"Where is your sailor blouse?" she murmured looking

about. "With the white strings in it? What have I—?" She found it. "There is still a little wind."

David held up his arms for her to slip the blouse over his head.

"Now, my own," she said, kissing his reemerging face. "Go down and play." She led him toward the door and opened it. "Not too far. And remember if I don't call you, wait until the whistle blows."

He went out into the hallway. Behind him, like an eyelid shutting, the soft closing of the door winked out the light. He assayed the stairs, lapsing below him into darkness, and grasping one by one each slender upright to the banister, went down. David never found himself alone on these stairs, but he wished there were no carpet covering them. How could you hear the sound of your own feet in the dark if a carpet muffled every step you took? And if you couldn't hear the sound of your own feet and couldn't see anything either, how could you be sure you were actually there and not dreaming? A few steps from the bottom landing, he paused and stared rigidly at the cellar door. It bulged with darkness. Would it hold? . . . It held! He jumped from the last steps and raced through the narrow hallway to the light of the street. Flying through the doorway was like butting a wave. A dazzling breaker of sunlight burst over his head, swamped him in reeling blur of brilliance, and then receded . . . A row of frame houses half in thin shade, a pitted gutter, a yawning ashcan, flotsam on the shore, his street.

Blinking and almost shaken, he waited on the low stoop a moment, until his whirling vision steadied. Then for the first time, he noticed that seated on the curbstone near the house was a boy, whom an instant later, he recognized. It was Yussie who had just moved into David's house and who lived on the floor above. Yussie had a very red, fat face. His big sister walked with a limp and wore strange iron slats on one of her legs. What was he doing, David wondered, what did he have in his hands? Stepping down from the stoop, he drew near, and totally disregarded, stood beside him.

Yussie had stripped off the outer shell of an alarm-clock. Exposed, the brassy, geometric vitals ticked when prodded, whirred and jingled falteringly.

"It still c'n go," Yussie gravely enlightened him. David

sat down. Fascinated, he stared at the shining cogs that
moved without moving their hearts of light. "So wot
makes id?" he asked. In the street David spoke English.

"Kentcha see? Id's coz id's a machine."

"Oh!"

"It wakes op mine fodder in de mawning."

"It wakes op mine fodder too."

"It tells yuh w'en yuh sh'd eat an' w'en yuh have tuh
go tuh sleep. It shows yuh w'ea, but I tooked it off."

"I god a calenduh opstai's." David informed him.

"Puh! Who ain' god a calenduh?"

"I save mine. I godda big book outa dem, wit num-
buhs on id."

"Who can't do dat?"

"But mine fodder made it," David drove home the one
unique point about it all.

"Wot's your fodder?"

"Mine fodder is a printer."

"Mine fodder woiks inna joolery shop. In Brooklyn.
Didja ever live in Brooklyn?"

"No." David shook his head.

"We usetuh—right near my fodder's joolery shop on
Rainey Avenyuh. W'ea does your fodder woik?"

David tried to think. "I don't know." He finally confessed, hoping that Yussie would not pursue the subject
further.

He didn't. Instead "I don' like Brownsville," he said.
"I like Brooklyn bedder."

David felt relieved.

"We usetuh find cigahs innuh gudduh," Yussie continued. "An we usetuh t'row 'em on de ladies, an we usetuh run. Who you like bedder, ladies or gents?"

"Ladies."

"I like mine fodder bedder," said Yussie. "My mudder
always holluhs on me." He pried a nail between two
wheels. A bright yellow gear suddenly snapped off and
fell to the gutter at his feet. He picked it up, blew the
dust off, and rose. "Yuh want?"

"Yea," David reached for it.

Yussie was about to drop it into his outstretched palm,
but on second thought, drew back. "No. Id's liddle like a
penny. Maybe I c'n pud id inna slod machine 'n' gid gum.
Hea, yuh c'n take dis one." He fished a larger gear out of

his pocket, gave it to David. "Id's a quarter. Yuh wanna come?"

David hesitated. "I godduh waid hea till duh wissle blows."

"W'a wissle?"

"By de fectory. All togedder."

"So?"

"So den I c'n go opstai's."

"So w'y?"

"Cuz dey blow on twelve a'clock an' den dey blow on five a'clock. Den I c'n go op."

Yussie eyed him curiously. "I'm gonna gid gum," he said, shrugging off his perplexity. "In duh slod machine." And he ambled off in the direction of the candy store on the corner.

Holding the little wheel in his hand, David wondered again why it was that every boy on the street knew where his father worked except himself. His father had so many jobs. No sooner did you learn where he was working than he was working somewhere else. And why was he always saying, "They look at me crookedly, with mockery in their eyes! How much can a man endure? May the fire of God consume them!" A terrifying picture rose in David's mind—the memory of how once at the supper table his mother had dared to say that perhaps the men weren't really looking at him crookedly, perhaps he was only imagining it. His father had snarled then. And with one sudden sweep of his arm had sent food and dishes crashing to the floor. And other pictures came in its train, pictures of the door being kicked open and his father coming in looking pale and savage and sitting down like old men sit down, one trembling hand behind him groping for the chair. He wouldn't speak. His jaws, and even his joints, seemed to have become fused together by a withering rage. David often dreamed of his father's footsteps booming on the stairs, of the glistening door-knob turning, and of himself clutching at knives he couldn't lift from the table.

Brooding, engrossed in his thoughts, engrossed in the rhythmic, accurate teeth of the yellow cog in his hand, the thin bright circles whirling restlessly without motion, David was unaware that a little group of girls had gathered in the gutter some distance away. But when they began

to sing, he started and looked up. Their faces were sober,
their hands locked in one another; circling slowly in a ring
they chanted in a plaintive nasal chorus:

> "Waltuh, Waltuh, Wiuhlflowuh,
> Growin' up so high;
> So we are all young ladies,
> An' we are ready to die."

Again and again, they repeated their burden. Their
words obscure at first, emerged at last, gathered meaning.
The song troubled David strangely. Walter Wildflower was
a little boy. David knew him. He lived in Europe, far
away, where David's mother said he was born. He had
seen him standing on a hill, far away. Filled with a warm,
nostalgic mournfulness, he shut his eyes. Fragments of
forgotten rivers floated under the lids, dusty roads,
fathomless curve of trees, a branch in a window under
flawless light. A world somewhere, somewhere else.

> "Waltuh, Waltuh, Wiuhlflowuh,
> Growin' up so high,"

His body relaxed, yielding to the rhythm of the song
and to the golden June sunlight. He seemed to rise and
fall on waves somewhere without him. Within him a
voice spoke with no words but with the shift of slow
flame. . . .

> "So we are all young ladies,
> An' we are ready to die."

From the limp, uncurling fingers, the cog rolled to the
ground, rang like a coin, fell over on its side. The sudden sound moored him again, fixed him to the quiet, sub-
urban street, the curbstone. The inarticulate flame that had
pulsed within him, wavered and went out. He sighed,
bent over and picked up the wheel.

When would the whistle blow he wondered. It took
long to-day. . . .

II

AS FAR back as he could remember, this was the first time that he had ever gone anywhere alone with his father, and already he felt desolated, stirred with dismal forebodings, longing desperately for his mother. His father was so silent and so remote that he felt as though he were alone even at his side. What if his father should abandon him, leave him in some lonely street. The thought sent shudders of horror through his body. No! No! He couldn't do that!

At last they reached the trolley lines. The sight of people cheered him again, dispelling his fear for a while. They boarded a car, rode what seemed to him a long time and then got off in a crowded street under an elevated. Nervously gripping David's arm, his father guided him across the street. They stopped before the stretched iron wicker of a closed theatre. Colored billboards on either side of them, the odor of stale perfume behind. People hurrying, trains roaring. David gazed about him frightened. To the right of the theatre, in the window of an ice cream parlor, gaudy, colored popcorn danced and drifted, blown by a fan. He looked up apprehensively at his father. He was pale, grim. The fine veins in his nose stood out like a pink cobweb.

"Do you see that door?" He shook him into attention. "In the grey house. See? That man just came out of there."

"Yes, Papa."

"Now you go in there and go up the stairs and you'll see another door. Go right in. And to the first man you see inside, say this: I'm Albert Schearl's son. He wants you to give me the clothes in his locker and the money that's coming to him. Do you understand? When they've given it to you bring it down here. I'll be waiting for you. Now what will you say?" he demanded abruptly.

David began to repeat his instructions in Yiddish.

"Say it in English, you fool!"

He rendered them in English. And when he had satisfied his father that he knew them, he was sent in.

"And don't tell them I'm out here," he was warned as he left. "Remember you came alone!"

Full of misgivings, unnerved at the ordeal of facing strangers alone, strangers of whom his own father seemed apprehensive, he entered the hallway, climbed the stairs. One flight up, he pushed open the door and entered a small room, an office. From somewhere back of this office, machinery clanked and rattled. A bald-headed man smoking a cigar looked up as he came in.

"Well, my boy," he asked smiling, "what do you want?"

For a moment all of his instructions flew out of his head. "My—my fodder sent me hea." He faltered.

"Your father? Who's he?"

"I—I'm Albert Schearl's son," he blurted out. "He sent me I shuh ged his clo's f'om de locker an' his money you owing him."

"Oh, you're Albert Schearl's son," said the man, his expression changing. "And he wants his money, eh?" He nodded with the short vibrating motion of a bell. "You've got some father, my boy. You can tell him that for me. I didn't get a chance. He's crazy. Anybody who— What does he do at home?"

David shook his head guiltily, "Nuttin."

"No?" he chuckled. "Nothin', hey? Well—" he broke off and went over to a small arched window in the rear. "Joe!" he called. "Oh Joe! Come here a minute, will you?"

In a few seconds a gray-haired man in overalls came in.

"Call me, Mr. Lobe?"

"Yea, will you get Schearl's things out of his locker and wrap 'em up for me. His kid's here."

The other man's face broke into a wide, brown-toothed grin. "Is zat his kid?" As if to keep from laughing his tongue worried the quid of tobacco in his cheek.

"Yea."

"He don' look crazy." He burst into a laugh.

"No." Mr. Lobe subdued him with a wave of the hand. "He's a nice kid."

"Your ol' man near brained me wid a hammer," said the man addressing David. "Don' know wot happened, nobody said nuttin." He grinned. "Never saw such a guy, Mr. Lobe. Holy Jesus, he looked like he wuz boilin' up. Didja see de rail he twisted wid his hands? Maybe I oughta to give it to 'im fer a souvenir?"

Mr. Lobe grinned. "Let the kid alone," he said quietly. "Get his stuff."

"O.K." Still chuckling, the gray-haired man went out.

"Sit down, my boy," said Mr. Lobe, pointing to a seat. "We'll have your father's things here in a few minutes."

David sat down. In a few minutes, a girl, bearing a paper in her hand, came into the office.

"Say, Marge," said Mr. Lobe, "find out what Schearl gets, will you."

"Yes, Mr. Lobe." She regarded David, "What's that, his boy?"

"Mmm."

"Looks like him, don't he?"

"Maybe."

"I'd have him arrested," said the girl opening up a large ledger.

"What good would that do?"

"I don't know, it might put some sense into his head."

Mr. Lobe shrugged. "I'm only too glad he didn't kill anybody."

"He ought to be in a padded cell," said the girl scribbling something on a paper.

Mr. Lobe made no response.

"He gets six sixty-two." She put down her pencil. "Shall I get it?"

"Mmm."

The girl went over to a large black safe in a corner, drew out a box, and when she had counted out some money, put it into a small envelope and gave it to Mr. Lobe.

"Come here," he said to David. "What's your name?"

"David."

"David and Goliath," he smiled. "Well, David, have you got a good deep pocket? Let's see." He picked up the tails of David's jacket. "There, that's the one I want." And fingering the small watch-pocket at the waist. "We'll put it in there." He folded the envelope and wedged it in. "Now don't take it out. Don't tell anybody you've got it till you get home, understand? The idea, sending a kid his age on an errand like this."

David, staring ahead of him, under Mr. Lobe's arm, was aware of two faces, peering in at the little window in the back. The eyes of both were fastened on him, regarding him with a curious and amused scrutiny of men beholding for the first time some astonishing freak. They both grinned when the girl, happening to turn in their direction, saw them; one of the men winked and cranked his temple with his hand. As Mr. Lobe turned, both disappeared. A moment later, the gray-haired man returned with a paper-wrapped bundle.

"Here's all I c'n find, Mr. Lobe. His towel, and his shoit an' a jacket."

"All right, Joe," Mr. Lobe took the package from him and turned to David. "Here you are, my boy. Put it under your arm and don't lose it." He tucked it under David's arm. "Not heavy, is it? No? That's good." He opened the door to let David pass. "Good bye." A dry smile whisked over his features. "Pretty tough for you."

Grasping the bundle firmly under his arm, David went slowly down the stairs. So that was how his father quit a place! He held a hammer in hand, he would have killed somebody. David could almost see him, the hammer raised over his head, his face contorted in terrific wrath, the rest cringing away. He shuddered at the image in his mind, stopped motionless on the stair, terrified at having to confront the reality. But he must go down; he must meet him; it would be worse for him if he remained on the stair any longer. He didn't want to go, but he had to. If only the stairs were twice as high.

He hurried down, came out into the street. His father, his back pressed close to the iron wicker, was waiting for him, and when he saw him come out, motioned to him to hurry and began walking away. David ran after him, caught up to him finally, and his father, without slackening his pace, relieved him of the bundle.

"They took long enough," he said, casting a malevolent glance over his shoulder. It was evident from his face that he had worked himself into a rage during the interval that David had left him. "They gave you the money?"

"Yes, Papa."

"How much?"

"Six—six dollars, the girl—"

"Did they say anything to you?" His teeth clenched grimly, "About me?"

"No, Papa," he answered hurriedly. "Nothing, Papa. They just gave me the—the money and I went down."

"Where is it?"

"Over here," he pointed to the pocket.

"Well, give it to me!"

With difficulty, David uprooted the envelope from his pocket. His father snatched it from him, counted the money.

"And so they said nothing, eh?" He seemed to demand a final confirmation. "None of the men spoke to you, did they? Only that bald-headed pig with the glasses?" He was watching him narrowly.

"No, Papa. Only that man. He just gave me the money." He knew that while his father's eyes rested on him he must look frank, he must look wide-eyed, simple.

"Very well!" His lips stretched for a brief instant in fleeting satisfaction. "Good!"

They stopped at the corner and waited for the trolley . . .

David never said anything to anyone of what he had discovered, not even to his mother—it was all too terrifying, too unreal to share with someone else. He brooded about it till it entered his sleep, till he no longer could tell where his father was flesh and where dream. Who would believe him if he said, I saw my father lift a hammer; he was standing on a high roof of darkness, and below him were faces uplifted, so many, they stretched like white cobbles to the end of the world; who would believe him? He dared not.

III

THE table had been set with the best dishes. There was a chicken roasting in the oven. His mother was pouring the last of the Passover's lustrous red wine from the wicker-covered bottle into the fat flagon. She had been quiet till now, but as she set the bottle down in the center of the table, she turned to David who was watching her. "I feel something I don't know what," she said. "Troubled." She looked at the floor a moment, gazing mournfully at nothing; then turned up her palm as if asking herself, "why," and sighing let her hands fall again, as if unanswered. "Perhaps it is because I think my work is fated to be lost."

David wondered a moment why she had said that, and then he remembered. That man was coming, that man whose name had been on his father's lips for the last week—ever since he had gotten his new job. That man was a foreman. His father said that they came from the same region in far-off Austria. How strange it was that they should come from far away and find each other in the same shop, and find each other living in the same neighborhood in Brownsville. His father had said that he had found a true friend now, but his mother had sighed. And now she sighed again and said that her work was fated to be lost. David hoped that she would be wrong. He wanted to be like the other boys in the street. He wanted to be able to say where his father worked.

Soon he heard his father's voice on the stairs. His mother rose, looked about her hastily to see whether all was prepared and then went to the door and opened it. The two men came in, his father first and the other man after him.

"Well, here we are," said his father with nervous heartiness. "This is my wife. This is Joe Luter, my countryman. And that over there," he pointed to David, "is what will pray for me after my death. Make yourself at home."

"A fine home you have here," said the other smiling at David's mother. "Very, very fine," he beamed.

"It's livable," answered David's mother.

"A fine boy too." He eyed David approvingly.

"Well!" said his father abruptly, "Let's have some dinner soon, eh?"

While his father was urging Luter to drink some wine, David examined the newcomer. In height he was not as tall as his father, but as much broader, fleshier, and unlike his father had a fair paunch. His face was somehow difficult to get accustomed to. It was not because it was particularly ugly or because it was scarred, but because one felt one's own features trying to imitate it while one looked at it. His mouth so very short and the bow of his lips so very thick and arched that David actually felt himself waiting for it to relax. And the way his nostrils swelled up and out almost fatigued one and one hoped the deep dimples in his cheek would soon fill out. His speech was very slow and level, his whole attitude tolerant and attentive, and because of this and because of the permanent wreathing of his features, he gave one the impression of great affability and good nature. In fact, as it soon turned out, he was not only affable, but very appreciative and very polite and commended in very warm tones the wine and the cake that was served with it, the neatness of the house as compared to his landlady's and finally congratulated David's father on having so excellent a wife.

When supper was served, he refused to begin eating until David's mother had sat down—which embarrassed her since she always served the others first—and then during the meal was very considerate of everyone, passing meat and bread and salt before it was asked for. When he spoke, he included everyone in the conversation, sometimes by asking questions, sometimes by fixing his eyes upon one. All of which disconcerted David not a little. Accustomed as he was to almost silent meals, to being either ignored or taken for granted, he resented this forcing of self-awareness upon him, this intruding of questions like a false weave into the fabric and pattern of his thought. But chiefly he found himself resenting Mr. Luter's eyes. They seemed to be independent of his speech, far outstripping it in fact; for instead of glancing at one, they fixed one and then held on until the voice caught up. It became a kind of uneasy game with David, a kind of secret tag, to beat Luter's gaze before it caught him, to look down at the tablecloth or at his mother the very moment he felt these eyes veering toward him.

Conversation touched on many subjects, drifting from the problems of the printing trade and the possibilities of a union among the printers to the problems and possibilities (and blessings, said Luter with a smile) of marriage. And then from this land to the old land and back again to this. And whether David's mother kept a kosher house—at which she smiled—and whether David's father still had time to don phylacteries in the morning and what synagogue he attended—at which his father snorted, amused. Most of what they said interested David only vaguely. What did fascinate him, however, was the curious effect that Luter had on his father. For once that brusque, cold manner of his had thawed a little. A faint though guarded deference mitigated somewhat the irrevocable quality with which his voice always bound his words. He would ask at the end of a statement he had just made, "Don't you think so?" Sometimes he would begin by saying, "It seems to me." It was strange. It disturbed David. He didn't know whether to be grateful to Luter for softening the harsh, inflexible edge of his father's temperament, or to be uneasy. Somehow it was a little unreal to see his father expand this way, uncoil warily like a tense spring slowly released. And urged on by only a sympathetic look from Luter, to hear him speak of his youth, he, who was so taciturn and thin-lipped, whom David never could think of as having a youth, speaking of his youth, of the black and white bulls he had tended for his father (and try to hide a frown at the word, father, he, who never hid displeasure), how they had fed them mash from his father's yeast mill, how he had won a prize with them from the hand of Franz Joseph, the King. Why did Luter need to look that way to make his father speak? Why did Luter only need to say, "I don't like the earth. It's for peasants," to make his father laugh, to make his father answer, "*I think* I do. *I think* when you come out of a house and step on the bare earth among the fields you're the same man you were when you were inside the house. But when you step out on pavements, you're someone else. You can feel your face change. *Hasn't that happened to you?*" And all that Luter needed to say was, "Yes. You're right, Albert," and his father would take a deep breath of satisfaction. It was strange. Why had no one else ever succeeded in doing that? Why not his mother? Why not himself? No one except Luter.

His questions went unanswered. He only knew that when supper was over he wanted very much to like Luter. He wanted to like any man who praised his mother and guided his father into untrodden paths of amiability. He wanted to like him, but he couldn't. But that would pass, he assured himself. As soon as Luter came again he would like him. Yes, the very next time. He was sure of it. He wanted to. As soon as he got used to his eyes. Yes.

A little while after dinner, Luter got up to go. His father protested that he had just come, that he ought to stay at least another hour.

"I also have to work in the morning," Luter reminded him. "Otherwise I would stay. It's heaven compared to my landlady's." And then he turned to David's mother, and in his slow way, smiling, extended his hand. "I want to thank you a thousand times, Mrs. Schearl, I haven't had so good a dinner or so much to eat since my last uncle was married."

She reddened as she shook hands with him and laughed. "You've praised everything but the water you drank."

"Yes." He laughed also. "And the salt. But I was afraid you wouldn't believe me if I said their flavor surpassed all others."

And after exchanging "Good-nights" and patting David's head (which David wasn't quite reconciled to) he left.

"Ha!" his father exclaimed exultantly after he had gone. "I told you this cursed wandering from job to job would end. I'm working for Dolman's Press to stay. Now time may bring something—who knows. There are two other foremen there. I'm as good a pressman as any of them. I know more about that iron juggler than they do. Who knows? Who knows? A little money. In time I might even suggest to him that we try— Well! In time! In time!"

"He looks like a very decent man," said his mother.

"Wait till you really know him!"

And from Luter's departure to his bedtime, David never remembered spending so serene an hour in his father's presence. . . .

IV

"NOT a single one?" Luter was asking with some surprise. "Not in the old land either?"

The old land. David's thoughts turned outward. Anything about the old land was always worth listening to.

"Not one," his mother answered. "Nothing ever came to my hamlet except the snow and the rain. Not that I minded. Except once—yes. A man with a gramophone —the kind you listened to with ear pieces. It cost a penny to listen to it, and it wasn't even worth that. I never heard anything labor so and squawk. But the peasants were awed. They swore there was a devil in the box."

Luter laughed. "And that's all you had seen before you came here to this turmoil?"

"I've seen little enough of *it!* I know that I myself live on one hundred and twenty-six Boddeh Stritt—"

"Bahday Street!" Her husband corrected her. "I've told you scores of times."

"Boddeh Stritt," she resumed apologetically. He shrugged. "It's such a strange name—bath street in German. But here I am. I know there is a church on a certain street to my left, the vegetable market is to my right, behind me are the railroad tracks and the broken rocks, and before me, a few blocks away is a certain store window that has a kind of white-wash on it—and faces in the white-wash, the kind children draw. Within this pale is my America, and if I ventured further I should be lost. In fact," she laughed, "were they even to wash that window, I might never find my way home again."

His father made an impatient gesture. "Speaking of Yiddish plays," he said, "I did see one. It was when I stayed with my father in Lemberg, the days of the great fair. They called it the Revenge of Samson. I can see him yet, blind, but shaggy again, waiting his time against the pagans. It moved me greatly."

"For my part," said Luter, "I go to the theatre to laugh. Shall I go there and be tormented when life itself is a plague? No, give me rather a mad jester or the antics of a spry wench."

"I don't care for that." His father was brief.

"Well, I'm not mad about it either, you understand, but I was just saying sometimes when one is gloomy it does the heart good. Don't you think great laughter heals the soul, Mrs. Schearl?"

"I suppose so."

"There, you see! But listen, I have an idea. You know that the People's Theatre always gives Dolman the job of printing its placards. Well, it has a stage that is never empty of tears—at least one good death rattle is heard every night. And if you like that sort of play, why I can talk to the agent or whatever he's called and squeeze a whole month's pass out of him. You know they change every week."

"I don't know whether I want to." His father frowned dubiously.

"Why, certainly! It won't be any trouble at all. And it won't cost you a cent. I'll get a pass for two, you watch me. I wish I had known this before."

"Don't trouble about me," said his mother. "Many thanks, but I couldn't possibly go away and leave David here alone."

"Oh, that can be solved!" he assured her. "That's the least of your worries. But first let me get the pass." Luter left early that evening, before David was put to bed. And when he was gone, his father turned to his mother and said, "Well, did I make a mistake when I said this man was my friend? Did I? Here is one who knows how to express friendship, here as well as in the shop. Tell me, do I know a decent man when I see him?"

"You do," was the mild answer.

"And you with your fear of taking strangers into the house!" he continued scornfully. "Could you ever have a better boarder than he?"

"It isn't that. I'm glad to serve him dinners regularly. But I do know that most often it's better for friends to be a little apart than always together."

"Nonsense!" He retorted. "It's your silly pride."

V

TRINKETS held in the mortar of desire, the fancy a trowel, the whim the builder. A wall, a tower, stout, secure, incredible, immuring the spirit from a flight of arrows, the mind, experience, shearing the flow of time as a rock shears water. The minutes skirted by, unknown.

His mother and father had left for the theatre, and he was alone with Luter. He would not see his mother again until morning, and morning, with his mother gone, had become remote and tentative. The tears had started to his eyes when she left, and Luter had said "Come child, do you begrudge your mother the little pleasure she may get to-night?" David had stared sullenly at the floor, aware that a great resentment against Luter was gathering within him. Had not Luter been the agent of his mother's going? And now how dared he reprove him for weeping when she was gone! How did he know what it felt like to be left alone? It wasn't *his* mother.

"Now you look just like your father." Luter had laughed. "He has just such lips when he frowns."

There had been something in his voice that had had a peculiar sting to it. Hurt, David had turned away and gotten out his box in the pantry in which he saved both the calendar leaves he collected and whatever striking odds and ends he found in the street. His mother called them his gems and often asked him why he liked things that were worn and old. It would have been hard to tell her. But there was something about the way in which the link of a chain was worn or the thread on a bolt or a castor-wheel that gave him a vague feeling of pain when he ran his fingers over them. They were like worn shoe-soles or very thin dimes. You never saw them wear, you only knew they were worn, obscurely aching.

He fingered one of his newly-found acquisitions. It was one of those perforated metal corks that the barber used to squirt perfumed water on one's head. One could blow through it, peep through it, it could be strung on a thread. He dropped it back into the box and picked up instead the stretched helix of a small window-shade spring. If one had these on one's feet instead of shoes, one might bound instead of walk. High as the roof; far away at once. Like Puss in Boots. But if the mouse changed back into an ogre inside the puss—just before he died—I'm a mouse—an ogre!— Then poor Puss would have swelled and swelled and—

Luter sighed. Startled, David looked up. I'm a mouse —I'm an ogre! The thought lingered. He eyed Luter furtively. Unaware that he was being watched, Luter had put down his paper and was staring ahead of him. Something curious had happened to his expression. The usually upturned, affable lines of his face either curved the other way now, downward, or where not curved were sharp, wedge-shaped at the eyes and mouth. And the eyes themselves, which were always so round and soft, had narrowed now, so narrow, the eyeballs looked charred, remote. His upper teeth gnawed the skin of his lips, drawing his face into a brooding frown. It worried David. A faint thrill of disquiet ran through him. He suddenly felt an intense desire to have someone else present in his house. It didn't have to be his mother. Anybody would do—Yussie from upstairs. Even his father.

Luter rose. David hastily dropped his gaze. Deliberate, brown-clad legs approached (what?) passed by him (he relaxed) stopped before the wall (peered over his shoulder) the calendar. Luter thumbed the leaves (black, black, black, red, black, black) held up a thin sheaf, and with puckered lips, stared at the date as though something far more intricate and absorbing than the mere figures were depicted there. Then he lowered the upturned leaves slowly, cautiously (Why? Why so carefully? They had only one place they could fall to) and rubbed his hands.

On his way back to the chair, he glanced down at the empty shoe-box between David's knees, emptied of everything except its calendar-leaves.

"Well!" His voice seemed amused, yet not entirely so,

as if crossed by a slight start of surprise. "What are those? Do you get them from there?"

"Yes." David looked up uneasily. "I save them."

"Yesterday's days? What do you want with them? To scribble on?"

"No. Just save."

"Chm!" His laughing snort sounded unpleasant to David. "If I had so few days as you have I wouldn't bother about them. And when you're as old as I am—" he stopped, indulged in a short chuckle that pecked like a tiny hammer— "you'll know that the only thing that matters are the days ahead."

David tried not to look resentful for fear Luter would accuse him again of looking like his father. He wished he would go away. But instead Luter nodded, and smiling to himself, glanced at the clock.

"It's time for you to go to bed now. It's long after eight."

He poured the various trinkets back into the box, went over to the pantry and stowed them away in the corner.

"Do you know how to undress yourself?"

"Yes."

"You'd better go in and 'pee' first," he advised, smiling. "How does your mother say it?"

"She says numbuh one."

Luter chuckled. "Then she's learned a little English."

After he had gone to the bathroom, David went into his bedroom, and undressed and got into his night-gown.

Luter looked in. "All right?" he asked.

"Yes," he answered climbing into bed.

Luter shut the door.

Darkness was different without his mother near. People were different too.

VI

IN THE bedroom where she had gone to tuck away the tablecloth, David heard the closet drawer chuckle softly close. And then,

"Alas!" came his mother's voice. "He has forgotten it." She reappeared, in her extended hand a parcel. "The present he was going to give them. He goes empty-handed now." She set it down on a chair. "I must remember to give it to him to-morrow, or perhaps he'll remember and return."

That Luter might come back disturbed David, he pushed the thought away. He had been looking forward to this evening when he would have her to himself until bed-time. It was the second theatre night. His father had gone alone.

She lifted the kettle of water from the stove, bore it to the sink and poured the steaming water into the basin.

She turned to look at him. "The way you watch me," she said with a laugh, "makes me feel as if I were per-forming black magic. It is only dishes I'm washing." And after a pause. "Would you like another little brother?" she asked slyly, "or a little sister."

"No," he answered soberly.

"It would be better for you, if you had," she teased. "It would give you something else to look at beside your mother."

"I don't want to look at anything else."

"Your mother had eight brothers and sisters," she re-minded him. "One of them may come here some day, one of my sisters, your Aunt Bertha—would you like that?"

"I don't know."

"You'd like her," she assured him. "She's very funny. She has red hair and a sharp tongue. And there's no one she can't mimic. She's not so very fat, yet in the sum-mertime, the sweat pours down her in torrents. I don't know why that is. I have seen men sweat like that, but never a woman."

"I get all wet under here in the summer." He pointed to his arm pits.

"Yes," said his mother with peculiar emphasis, "she did too. They told her once—but you never saw a bear?"

"In a book. There were three bears."

"Yes, you told me about them. Well, in Europe the gypsies—gypsies are men and women, dark people. They roam all over the world."

"Why?"

"It pleases them."

"You asked me about a bear."

"Yes. Sometimes these gypsies take a bear along with them wherever they go."

"Do they eat porridge?" He had said the last word in English.

"What's porridge?"

"My teacher said it was oatmeal and farina, you give it to me in the morning."

"Yes, yes. You told me. But I'm not sure. I know they like apples. Still if your teacher—"

"And what did the bear do?"

"The bear danced. The gypsies sang and shook the tambourine and the bear danced."

David hugged himself with delight. "Who made him?"

"The gypsies. They earned their money that way. When the bear was tired, people threw pennies in their tambourine— Now! I was telling you about your aunt. Someone told her that if she crept up behind the bear and rubbed her hands on his fur, she would stop sweating under her palms. And so one day while the bear was dancing—"

She stopped speaking. David had heard it too: a step outside the door. A moment later someone knocked. A voice.

"It is only I—Luter."

With an exclamation of surprise, she opened the door. Luter came in.

"I went away without my head," he said apologetically. "I've forgotten my gift."

"It's a pity you had to take all that trouble again,"

she said sympathetically. "You left it in the bedroom."
She picked up the parcel from the chair.

"Yes, I know," he answered, resting it on the table.
He looked at his watch. "I'm afraid it's too late for me
to go now. I couldn't get there before nine and then how
long can one stay, an hour."

David was secretly annoyed to see him sit down.

Luter opened his coat and with an expression of anxious
indecision on his face regarded David's mother. His eyes
had a brilliance and restlessness greater than usual. David
was again aware of the difficult curves of the man's face.

"Take your coat off," she suggested. "It's warm here."

"If you don't mind," he slipped it from his shoulders,
"Now that I have nowhere to go."

"Won't they be disappointed when they see you're not
coming?"

"No, they'll know that the black hour hasn't seized
me." He laughed. "Please go on with your work, don't
let me interfere."

"I was merely washing some dishes," she said. "I've
finished now, except for these pots." She picked up the
red and white can of powder in the corner of the small
shelf above the sink, shook some of it into a pot, and
rubbed the inside vigorously with a dish rag, stooping
over with the effort.

David, who was leaning from the side of his chair
could see Luter and his mother at the same time. Absorbed in watching his mother, he would have paid
little attention to Luter, but the sudden oblique shifting
of Luter's eyes toward himself drew his own gaze toward
them. Luter, his eyes narrowed by a fixed yawn, was
staring at his mother, at her hips. For the first time,
David was aware of how her flesh, confined by the skirt,
formed separate molds against it. He felt suddenly bewildered, struggling with something in his mind that
would not become a thought.

"You women," said Luter sympathetically, "especially
when you marry must work like slaves."

"It isn't quite so bad as all that. Despite the ancient
proverb."

"No," said Luter meditatively, "anything may be lived.
But to labor without thanks that's bitter."

"True. And to labor even with thanks, what comes of it?"

"Well," he uncrossed his legs, "nothing comes of anything, not even millionaires, but esteem gives the trumpeter breath—esteem and gifts naturally."

"Then I have my esteem," she laughed, straightening up and turning around as Luter arranged his mouth more firmly. "I have esteem that grows." She regarded David with an amused smile.

"Yes," said Luter with a sigh, "but everyone can have that kind of esteem. Still, it's good to have children." And then earnestly, "Do you know I have never seen a child cling so to his mother."

David found himself resenting Luter's comment.

"Yes, I'm sure you're right," she agreed.

"I think so," he said warmly. "Why, my cousin's children—the very relative I was going to visit to-night—they are home only when they sleep and eat. At night after dinner, they are up in some neighbor's house," he lifted his hand to emphasize the point, "playing with other children the whole evening."

"There are other children in the house," answered his mother. "But he seems to make friends with none. It has only been once or twice," she turned to David, "that you have been in Yussie's house or he here, has it not?"

David nodded uneasily.

"He's a strange child!" said Luter with conviction.

His mother laughed condoningly.

"Though very intelligent," he assured her.

There was a pause while she emptied the dishpan into the sink; the grey water muttered down the drain.

"He looks very much like you," said Luter with the hesitance of careful appraisal. "He has the same brown eyes you have, very fine eyes, and the same white skin. Where did you get that white German skin?" he asked David playfully.

"I don't know." The man's intimacy embarrassed him. He wished Luter would go away.

"And both of you have very small hands. Has he not small hands for a child his size? Like those of a prince's. Perhaps he will be a doctor some day."

"If he has more than hands."

"Yes," Luter agreed, "still I don't think he'll need

labor for his bread like his father, or even like myself."

"I hope not, but only God knows."

"Isn't it strange," he said suddenly, "how Albert has seized hold of the theatre? Like a drunkard his dram. Who would have believed it?"

"It means a great deal to him. I could hear him beside me gnashing his teeth at a certain character."

Luter laughed. "Albert is a good man, even though the other workers think him odd. It is I who keep the peace, you know." He laughed again.

"Yes, I do know, and I'm grateful to you for it."

"Oh it's nothing. A word here, a word there smooths everything. Truth is, I might not have been so ready to protect him, if I hadn't known you, that is, if I hadn't come here and been one of you. But now I take up his interest as though he were my own brother. It is not always easy with so strange a man."

"You're very kind."

"Not at all," said Luter. "You have repaid me. Both of you."

Picking up several dry utensils she crossed the kitchen to the pantry. There she pulled open the door, bent over and hung them on the nails inside. Luter's head tilted, his gaze flitting to her bosom. He cleared his throat with a pecking sound.

"But say what you will, Albert is—what shall I say, a nervous man—till you know him, of course. But I can see why you've never gone out with him anywhere," he ended sympathetically. "You're a proud woman with a great deal of feeling, no?"

"No more than anyone else. What has that to do with it?"

"I'll tell you. You see, Albert, well—" he smiled and scratched his neck, puzzled. "Even in the street, he behaves so strangely. You know better than I do. He seems to look for jeers in the faces of passersby. And when you go with him—I go with him every night—it's as though he finds some kind of pleasure walking behind a cripple or a drunkard or any kind of freakish person—I don't know what! One would think it made him feel safer. He wants people on the street to look at someone else. Anyone else, instead of himself. Even a water wagon or street gamblers give him this odd satisfaction. But why do I talk this way when I like him so much." He paused and laughed quietly.

David's mother looked at the dish towel, but made no answer.

"Yes," he chuckled, hurriedly. "I like especially the way he never speaks of Tysmenicz without leading in the cattle he once tended."

"Well, there weren't many things he loved more in the old land."

"But to love cattle so," Luter smiled. "All I thought of when I saw a cow was that it gave milk. Now when I think of Europe, and of my hamlet, the first thought that comes to me, just as his first thought is a cow or a prize bull, my first thought is of the peasant women. You understand?"

"Naturally, each has his memories." Having placed the last dishes in the closet, she drew a chair beside David's and sat down. On one side of the table sat Luter, on the other David and his mother.

"Exactly," said Luter, "Each one remembers what appealed to him, and I remember the peasant wenches. Weren't they a striking lot, in their tight checked vests and their dozen petticoats?" He shook his head regretfully. "One never sees the like here. It's a scanty soil from what one sees of it in Brooklyn and its women are spare. But in Sorvik they grew like oaks. They had blonde hair, their eyes blazed. And when they smiled with their white teeth and blue eyes, who could resist them? It was enough to set your blood on fire. The men never dazzled you that way?" he asked after a pause.

"No, I never paid much attention to them."

"Well, you wouldn't—you were a good Jewish daughter. Besides, the men were a worthless lot, vacant lumps with great shoulders and a nose on them like a split pea. Their women were wasted on them. You know," his voice was very earnest, "the only woman I know who reminds me of those girls, is you."

She reddened, threw back her head and laughed, "Me? I'm only a good Jewish daughter."

"I am not accusing you of anything else, but never since I have been in America have I seen a woman that so reminded me of them. Their lips were so full, so ripe, as if to be kissed."

She smiled curiously with one cheek. "God knows, there must be enough Austrian peasants even in this land. If Jews were let in, surely no one would bar the Slovaks."

Luter looked down at the ring he was twisting around his finger. "Yes, I suppose so. I have seen a few of them, but none I cared much about."

"You better look about a little more then."

Luter's face grew strangely sober, the lines about his nostrils deepened. Without lifting his head, his eyes slanted up at David's mother. "Perhaps I can stop looking."

She laughed outright. "Don't be foolish, Mr. Luter!"

"Mr. Luter!" He looked annoyed for a moment, then shrugged and smiled. "Now that you know me so well, why use the formal still?"

"Apparently I don't know you so well."

"It takes a little time," he admitted. His gaze roved about the room and came to rest on David. "Perhaps you would like some refreshments?"

"No, but if you do, I can make some tea."

"No, thanks," he said solicitously, "don't take the trouble. But I know what you would like—a little ice cream."

"Please don't bother."

"Why, it's no trouble. The young one there will go down for us." He drew out a coin. "Here, you know where the candy store is. Go get some tutti frutti and chocolate. You like it don't you?"

With troubled eyes David looked first at Luter, then at the coin. Beneath the table a hand gently pressed his thigh. His mother! What did she want?

"I don't like it," he faltered. "I don't like ice cream."

The fingers of the same hand tapped his knees ever so lightly. He had said the right thing.

"No? Tutti frutti ice cream? Candy then, you like that?"

"No."

"I think it's a little too late for him to have either," said his mother.

"Well, I guess we won't buy any then, since he's going to bed soon." Luter looked at his watch. "This is just the time I put him to bed last time, wasn't it, my David?"

"Yes," he hesitated fearful of blundering.

"I suppose he's sleepy now," Luter suggested encouragingly.

"He doesn't look sleepy," his mother, smoothed the hair back from his brow. "His eyes are still wide and bright."

"I'm not sleepy." That, at least, was true. He had never been so strangely stirred, never had he felt so near an abyss.

"We'll let you stay up awhile then."

There was a short space of silence. Luter frowned, emitted a faint smacking sound from the side of his mouth. "You don't seem to have any of the usual womanly instincts."

"Don't I? It seems to me that I keep pretty closely to the well-trodden path."

"Curiosity, for instance."

"I had already lost that even before my marriage."

"You only imagine it. But don't misunderstand me, I merely meant curiosity about the package I left behind. It must be clear to you that I didn't get what's in it for my relatives' sake."

"Well, you'd better give it to them now."

"Not so soon." And when she didn't answer, he shrugged, arose from the chair and got into his coat. "Hate me for it if I say it again, but you're a comely woman. This time though I won't forget my package." He reached for the door-knob, turned. "But I may still come for dinner tomorrow?"

She laughed. "If you still haven't tired of my cooking."

"Not yet." And chuckling. "Good-night. Good-night, little one. It must be a joy to have such a son." He went out.

With a wry smile on her lips, she listened to the sound of his retreating steps. Then her brow puckered in disdain. "All are called men!" She sat for a moment gazing before her with troubled eyes. Presently her brow cleared; she tilted her head and peered into David's eyes. "Are you worried about anything? Your look is so intent."

"I don't like him," he confessed.

"Well, he's gone now," she said reassuringly. Let's

forget about him. We won't even tell father he came, will
we?"

"No."

"Let's go to bed then, it grows late."

VII

ANOTHER week had passed. The two men had just
gone off together. With something of an annoyed laugh,
his mother went to the door and stood fingering the
catch of the lock. Finally she lifted it. The hidden tongue
sprang into its groove.

"Oh, what nonsense!" She unlocked it again, looked up
at the light and then at the windows.

David felt himself growing uneasy. Why did Thursdays
have to roll around so soon? He was beginning to hate
them as much as he did Sundays.

"Why must they make proof of everything before
they're satisfied?" Her lips formed and unformed a
frown. "Well, there's nothing to do but go. I'll wash those
dishes later." She opened the door and turned out the
light.

Bewildered, David followed her into the cold, gas-lit
hallway.

"We're going upstairs to Mrs. Mink." She cast a hurried look over the bannister. "You can play with your
friend Yussie."

David wondered why she needed to bring that up.
He hadn't said anything about wanting to play with Yussie. In fact, he didn't even feel like it. Why didn't she
just say she was running away, instead of making him
feel guilty. He knew whom she was looking for when she
looked over the bannister.

His mother knocked at the door. It was opened. Mrs.
Mink stood on the threshold. At the sight of his mother,
she beamed with pleasure.

"Hollo, Mrs. Schearl! Hollo! Hollo! Comm een!" She
scratched her lustreless, black hair excitedly.

"I hope you don't find my coming here untimely," his mother smiled apologetically.

"No, as I live!" Mrs. Mink lapsed into Yiddish. "You're wholly welcome! A guest—the rarest I have!" She dragged a chair forward. "Do sit down."

Mrs. Mink was a flat-breasted woman with a sallow skin and small features. She had narrow shoulders and meager arms, and David always wondered when he saw her how the thin skin on her throat managed to hold back the heavy, bulging veins.

"I thought I would never have the pleasure of seeing you in my house," she continued. "It was only the other day that I was telling our landlady—Look, Mrs. Schearl and I are neighbors, but we know nothing of each other. I dare not ask her up into my house. I'm afraid to. She looks so proud."

"I, proud?"

"Yes, not proud, noble! You always walk with your head in the air—so! And even when you go to market, you dress like a lady. I've watched you often from the window, and I've said to my man— Come here! Look, that's her! Do you see how tall she is! He is not home now, my picture of a spouse, he works late in the jewelry store. I know he will regret missing you."

David found himself quickly tiring of Mrs. Mink's rapid stream of words, and looking about saw that Annie was observing him. Yussie was nowhere to be seen. He tugged his mother's hand, and when she bent over, asked for him.

"Yussie?" Mrs. Mink interrupted herself long enough to say. "He's asleep."

"Don't wake him," said his mother.

"That's all right. I've got to send him to the delicatessen for some bread soon. Yussele!" she called.

His only answer was a resentful yawn.

"He's coming soon," she said reassuringly.

In a few minutes, Yussie came out. One of his stockings had fallen, and he trod on it, shuffling sleepily. He blinked, eyed David's mother suspiciously a moment, and then sidled over to David, "W'y's yuh mudder hea?"

"She jost came."

"W'y'd she comm?"

"I donno."

At this point Annie hobbled over. "Pull yuh stockin' op, yuh slob!"

Obediently Yussie hoisted up his stocking. David could not help noticing how stiff and bare the white stocking hung behind the brace on Annie's own leg.

"So yuh gonna stay by us?" asked Yussie eagerly.

"Yea."

"H'ray! C'mon inna fron'room." He grabbed David's arm. "I godda—"

But David had stopped. "I'm goin' inna fron' room, mama."

Turning from the chattering Mrs. Mink, David's mother smiled at him in slight distress and nodded.

"Waid'll I show yuh wod we god," Yussie dragged him into the frontroom.

While Yussie babbled on excitedly, David stared about him. He had never been in Yussie's front room before; Annie had barred the way as if it were inviolable ground. Now he saw a room which was illuminated by a gas lamp overhead and crowded with dark and portly furniture. In the middle of the floor stood a round glass-topped table and about it chairs of the same dark stain. A china closet hugged one wall, a bureau another, a dressing table a third, cabinets clogged the corners. All were bulky, all rested on the same kind of scrolled and finical paw. On the wall space above the furniture hung two pairs of yellowed portraits, two busts of wrinkled women with unnatural masses of black hair, and two busts of old men who wore ringlets under their skull caps and beards on their chin. With an expression of bleak hostility in their flat faces, they looked down at David. Barring the way to the window squatted a swollen purple plush chair, embroidered with agitated parrots of various hues. A large vapid doll with gold curls and a violet dress sat on the glass top of a cabinet. After his own roomy frontroom with its few sticks of furniture, David not only felt bewildered, he felt oddly warm.

"It's inna closet in my modder's bedroom." Yussie continued. "Jost wait, I'll show yuh."

He disappeared into the darkness of the adjoining bedroom. David heard him open a door, rummage about for a minute. When he returned, he bore in his hand a curious steel cage.

"Yuh know wat dis's fuh?" he held it up to David's eyes.

David examined it more closely, "No. Wot d'yuh do wit' it?"

"It c'n catch rats, dot's wot yuh do wit' it. See dis little door? De rat gizz in like dot." He opened a thin metal door at the front of the cage. "Foist yuh put sompin ove' hea, and on 'iz liddle hook. An' nen nuh rat gizzin. Dey uz zuh big fat rat inna house, yuh could hear him at night, so my fodder bought dis, an' my mudder put in schmaltz f'om de meat, and nuh rat comes in, an' inna mawingk, I look unner by de woshtob, an'ooh—he wuz dere, runnin' dis way like dot." Yussie waved the cage about excitedly, "An I calls my fodder an' he gets op f'om de bed an' he fills op de woshtob and eeh! duh rat giz all aroun' in it, in nuh watuh giz all aroun'. An' nen he stops. An nen my fodder takes it out and he put it in nuh bag an trew it out f'om de winner. Boof! he fell inna guttah. Ooh wotta rat he wuz. My mudder wuz runnin' aroun', an aroun', an after, my fodder kept on spittin' in nuh sink. Kcha!"

David backed away in disgust.

"See, I tol' yuh I had sumtin tuh show yuh. See, like dot it closes." He snapped the little, metal door. "We didn't hea' it, cause ev'ybody wuz sleepin'. Rats on'y come out innuh da'k, w'en yuh can't see 'em, and yuh know w'ea dey comin' f'om, dey comin' f'om de cellah. Dot's w'ea dey live innuh cellah—all rats."

The cellar! That explained it. That moment of fear when he turned the bottom landing before he went out into the street. He would be doubly terrified now.

"Wotta yuh doin?" They started at the intruding voice. It was Annie coming in. Her face was writhed back in disgust.

"Eee! Yuh stoopid lummox! Put it away. I'll call mama!"

"Aaa, lemme alone."

"Yuh gonna put it away?" she squealed.

"Aa, shit on you," muttered Yussie sullenly. "Can't do nuttin'." Nevertheless, he carried the cage back to the bedroom.

"W'y d'yuh let 'im show it tuh yuh fuh?" she demanded angrily of David. "Such a dope!"

"I didn' know wot it wuz," he stammered.

"Yuh didn' know wot it wuz? Yurra lummox too!"

"Now g'wan." Yussie returned from the bedroom. "Leave us alone."

"I will not," she snapped. "Dis is my frontroom."

"He don' wanna play witchoo. He's my frien!"

"So who wants him!"

"So don' butt in."

"Pooh!" She plumped herself in a chair. The steel brace clicked disagreeably against the wood.

David wished she could wear long pants like a man.

"Comm on ove' by de winder," Yussie guided him through a defile in the furniture. "We mus' be a fireman. We c'n put out de fire inna house." He indicated the bureau. "Yuh wanna?"

"Awrigh'."

"An' we c'n slide down duh pipe an' we c'n have a fiuh-ingine, an' nen I'll be duh drivuh. Yuh wanna?"

"Yea."

"Den let's make fiuh hats. Waid, I'll get some paper inna kitchen." He ran off.

Annie slid off the chair and came over. "Wot class yuh in?"

"1A."

"I'm in 4A," she said loftily. "I skipped a'reddy. An' now I'm duh sma'test one in my class."

David was impressed.

"My teacher's name is Miss McCardy. She's duh bes' teacher inna whole school. She gave me A. A. A."

By this time Yussie had returned bearing several sheets of newspaper.

"Wotta ya gonna do?" she demanded.

"Wotta you care!" he defied her. "We' gonna be fiuh-men."

"Yuh can't!"

"No?" Yussie inquired angrily, "Why can' we?"

"Cause yuh can't, dat's w'y! Cause yu'll scratch op all de foinichuh."

"We won' scratch nuttin'!" stormed Yussie whirling the newspaper about in frustration. "We gonna play."

"Yuh can't!"

"We will!"

"I'll give yuh in a minute," she advanced threateningly.

"Aa! Wodda yuh wan' us tuh play?"

"Yuh c'n play lottos."

"I don' wanna play lottos," he whined.

"Den play school den."

"I don' wanna play school."

"Den don' play nuttin!" she said with finality.

A large bubble of saliva swelled from Yussie's lips as he squeezed his face down to blubber. "I'll tell mama on you!"

"Tell! She'll give yuh a smack!" She whirled threateningly on David. "Wadda *you* wanna play?"

"I don' know," he drew back.

"Doncha know no games?" she fumed.

"I—I know tag an' I know, I know hide an' gussee'." Yussie revived. "Let's play hide an' gussee'."

"No!"

"You too!" he coaxed desperately. "C'mon, you too." Annie thought it over.

"C'mon I'll be it!" And immediately, he leaned his face against the edge of a bureau and began counting. "G'wan hide!" he broke off.

"Wait!" shrilled Annie, hopping off. "Count twenny!" David scurried behind the arm chair.

He was found last and accordingly was "it" next. In a little while the game grew very exciting. Since David was somewhat unfamiliar with the arrangement of the house, it chanced that several times he hid with Yussie when Annie was it and with Annie when Yussie was it. They had crouched together in barricaded corners and behind the bedroom door.

However, just as the game was reaching its greatest pitch, Mrs. Mink's voice suddenly called out from the kitchen.

"Yussele! Yussele, my treasure, come here!"

"Aa!" from somewhere came Yussie's exasperated bleat.

David, who was "it" at the time, stopped counting and turned around.

"Yussie!" Mrs. Mink cried again, but this time shriller.

"Can't do nuttin'," complained Yussie, crawling out from under the bureau. "Waddayuh want?" he bellowed.

"Come here. I want you to go down stairs for a minute."

Annie, evidently aware that the game was over for the time being, came out of the adjoining bedroom. "He has to go down?"

"Yea," diffidently. "Fuh bread."

"Den we can't play."

"No. I'm gonna go back tuh my modder."

"Stay hea," she commanded, "We gonna play. Waid'll Yussie comes back."

The voices from the kitchen indicated that Yussie had been persuaded. He reappeared, dressed in coat and hat. "I'm goin' down," he announced, and went out again. An uncomfortable pause ensued.

"We can't play till he comes back," David reminded her.

"Yes, we can."

"Wot?"

"Wotcha want."

"I don't know wot."

"Yuh know wot."

"Wot?"

"Yuh know," she said mysteriously.

That was the game then. David congratulated himself on having discovered its rules so quickly.

"Yea, I know," he answered in the same tone of mystery.

"Yea?" she peered at him eagerly.

"Yea!" he peered at her in the same way.

"Yuh wanna?"

"Yea!"

"Yuh wanna den?"

"Yea, I wanna." It was the easiest game he had ever played. Annie was not so frightening after all.

"W'ea?"

"W'ea?" he repeated.

"In the bedroom," she whispered.

But she was really going!

"C'mon," she motioned, tittering.

He followed. This was puzzling.

She shut the door: he stood bewildered in the gloom.

"C'mon," she took his hand. "I'll show yuh."

He could hear her groping in the dark. The sound of an unseen door opening. The closet door.

"In hea," she whispered.

What was she going to do? His heart began to race.

She drew him in, shut the door. Darkness, immense and stale, the reek of moth balls threading it.

Her breathing in the narrow space was loud as a gust, swooping down and down again. His heart throbbed in his ears. She moved toward him, nudged him gently with the iron slat of her brace. He was frightened. Before the pressure of her body, he retreated slightly. Something rolled beneath his feet. What? He knew instantly, and recoiled in disgust—the trap!

"Sh!" she warned. "Take me aroun'." She groped for his hands.

He put his arms about her.

"Now let's kiss."

His lips touched hers, a muddy spot in vast darkness.

"How d'*you* play bad?" she asked.

"Bad? I don' know," he quavered.

"Yuh wan' me to show how I?"

He was silent, terrified.

"Yuh must ask me," she said. "G'wan ask me."

"Wot?"

"Yuh must say, Yuh wanna play bad? Say it!"

He trembled. "Yuh wanna play bad?"

"Now, *you* said it," she whispered. "Don' forget, you said it."

By the emphasis of her words, David knew he had crossed some awful threshold.

"Will yuh tell?"

"No," he answered weakly. The guilt was his.

"Yuh swear?"

"I swear."

"Yuh know w'ea babies comm from?"

"N-no."

"From de knish."

-*Knish?*

"Between de legs. Who puts id in is de poppa. De poppa's god de petzel. Yaw de poppa." She giggled stealthily and took his hand. He could feel her guiding it under her dress, then through a pocket-like flap. Her skin under his palm. Revolted, he drew back.

"Yuh must!" she insisted, tugging his hand. "Yuh ast me!"

"No!"

"Put yuh han' in my knish," she coaxed. "Jus' once."

"No!"

"I'll hol' yuh petzel." She reached down.

"No!" His flesh was crawling.

"Den take me 'round again."

"No! No! Lemme oud!" he pushed her away.

"Waid. Yussie'll t'ink we're hidin'."

"No! I don' wanna!" He had raised his voice to a shout.

"So go!" she gave him an angry push.

But David had already opened the door and was out. She grabbed him as he crossed the bedroom. "If you tell!" she whispered venomously. "W'ea yuh goin'?"

"I'm goin tuh my mamma!"

"Stay hea! I'll kill yuh, yuh go inside!" She shook him. He wanted to cry.

"An' don' cry," she warned fiercely, and then strove desperately to engage him, "Stay hea an' I'll tell yuh a story. I'll let yuh play fiuhman. Yuh c'n have a hat. Yuh c'n climb on de foinichuh. Stay hea!"

He stood still, watching her rigidly, half hypnotized by her fierce, frightened eyes. The outer door was opened. Yussie's voice in the kitchen.

A moment later, he came in, breathlessly stripping off his coat.

"I god a penny," he crowed.

"Yuh c'n play fiuhman, if yuh wan'," she said severely.

"No foolin'? Yeh? H'ray! C'mon, Davy!"

But David held back. "I don' wanna play."

"C'mon," Yussie grabbed a sheet of newspaper and thrust it into his hands. "We mus' make a hat."

"G'wan make a hat," commanded Annie.

Cowed and almost sniffling, David began folding the paper into a hat.

He played listlessly, one eye always on Annie who watched his every move. Yussie was disgusted with him.

"David!" his mother's voice calling him.

Deliverance at last! With a cry of relief, he tore off the fireman's hat, ran down the frontroom stairs into the kitchen. His mother was standing; she seemed about to leave. He pressed close to her side.

"We must go now," she said smiling down at him. "Say good night to your friends."

"Good night," he mumbled.

"Please don't hurry off," said Mrs. Mink. "It's been such a pleasure to have you here."

"I really must go. It's past his bed time."

David was in the van stealthily tugging his mother toward the door.

"This hour I have been in heaven," said Mrs. Mink. "You must come often! I am never busy."

"Many thanks."

They hurried down the drafty stairs.

"I heard you playing in the frontroom," she said. "You must have enjoyed your visit."

She unlocked the door, lit the gas lamp.

"Dear God! The room has grown cold." And picking up the poker, she crouched before the stove, shook down the dull embers behind the grate. "I'm glad you enjoyed yourself. At least one of us has skimmed a little pleasure out of this evening! What folly! And that Mrs. Mink. If I had known she talked so much, drays could not have dragged me up there!" She lifted the coal scuttle, shook some coal vehemently into the stove. "Her tongue spun like a bobbin on a sewing machine—and she sewed nothing. It's unbelievable! I began to see motes before my eyes." She shook her head impatiently and put down the coal scuttle. "My son, do you know your mother's a fool? But you're tired, aren't you? Let me put you to bed."

Kneeling down before him, she began unbuttoning his shoes. When she had pulled his stockings off, she lifted his legs, examined them a moment, then kissed each one. "Praise God, your body is sound! How I pity that poor child upstairs!"

But she didn't know as he knew how the whole world could break into a thousand little pieces, all buzzing, all whining, and no one hearing them and no one seeing them except himself.

VIII

WHEN David awoke the next morning, it seemed to him that he had been lying in bed a long while with eyes open but without knowing who or where he was. Memory had never been so tardy in returning. He could almost feel his brain fill up like a bottle under a slow tap. Reluctant antennae groped feebly into the past. Where? What? One by one the shuttles stirred, awoke, knit morning to night, night to evening. Annie! Oh! Desperately he shook his head, but could not shake the memory out.

The window. . . . Snow still falling through the dull light of the alley, banked whitely against the sill, encroaching on the pane. David stared a while at the sinking patterns of the flakes. They fell with slow simplicity if you watched them, swiftly and devious if you looked beyond. Their monotonous descent gave him an odd feeling of being lifted higher and higher; he went floating until he was giddy. He shut his eyes.

From the street somewhere, came the frosty ring of a shovel scraping the stony sidewalk, a remote and drowsy sound.

All this stir when the world seemed trying to sleep, saddened him. Why did anyone have to clear away the snow; why did anyone disturb it? He would rather the snow were on the ground all year. The thin sound of the shovel gave him a feeling of sluggish resentment. He drew his legs up and bent his head toward his knees. Warm bed-clothes, the odor of sleep.

He would have dozed again, but the door opened. His mother came in and sat down at the edge of the bed.

"Asleep?" she asked, then bent down and kissed him. "It's time to get up for school." And sighing, she threw back the bed-clothes, and pivoted him to a sitting posture on the bed. He whimpered drowsily, then rose, shivering when his feet touched the cold floor and followed her.

The kitchen was warm. She slipped his night gown from over his head and helped him dress. When he was washed and combed, he sat down to breakfast. He ate listlessly and without relish.

"You don't seem to be very hungry?" she inquired. "You've hardly touched the oatmeal. Would you like more milk?"

"No. I'm not hungry."

"An egg?"

He shook his head.

"I shouldn't have kept you up so late. You look weary. Do you remember the strange dream you had last night?"

"Yes."

"How did such a strange dream come to you?" she mused. "A woman with a child who turned loathsome, a crowd of people following a black-bird. I don't understand it. But my, how you screamed!"

Why did she have to remind him of it again. The vigil afterwards waiting for sleep. Annie!

"Why did you kick the table so?"

"I don't know."

"Is it a growing pain?" she laughed. "But they say those happen only in sleep. Are you awake?" She looked at the clock. "Just a little more milk?"

"No."

"You'll have more at lunch then," she warned. "But it's time now you were going." She fetched his leggings and kneeling down buttoned them on. "Shall I go with you?"

"I can go by myself."

"Perhaps you ought to wait for Yussie or his sister."

The very thought made him shudder inwardly. He knew he would run from them if he met them. He shook his head.

"Will you go right into the school and not stay too long in the snow?"

"Yes." He let down the furry ear-laps of his cap as he put it on. His books were on the wash-tub.

"Good-bye, then," she stooped to kiss him. "Such an indifferent kiss! I don't think you love me this morning."

But David offered no other. He took one step through the door, started with fear, remembering. He turned.

"Mama, will you leave the door open till—till I'm gone—till you hear me down-stairs?"

"Child! What's wrong with you? Very well, I will. Does that dream still hover in your mind?"

"Yes," he felt relieved that she had given him an excuse.

"You had better go now. I'll wait in the door-way."

Feeling ashamed of himself and yet not a little supported by her presence in the doorway, David hurried out. At the bottom of the stairs the cellar door was still shut. He eyed it with horror, his heart quickening in his bosom.

"Mama?" he called.

"Yes."

He sprang from the steps, three at a time, more than he had ever tried before, stumbled to his knees, dropping his strap of books, but the next moment shot to his feet again, and sped like a hunted thing to the pale light of the doorway.

The silent white street waited for him, snow-drifts where the curb was. Footfalls silent. Before the houses, the newly swept areas of the sidewalks, black, were greying again. Flakes cold on cheek, quickening. Narrow-eyed, he peered up. Black overhead the flakes were, black till they sank below a housetop. Then suddenly white. Why? A flake settled on his eye-lash; he blinked, tearing with the wet chill, lowered his head. Snow trodden down by passing feet into crude, slippery scales. The railings before basements gliding back beside him, white pipes of snow upon them. He scooped one up as he went. Icy, setting the blood tingling, it gathered before the plow of his palm. He pressed it into a ball, threw it from one hand to the other until he dropped it.

He turned the first corner at the end of the street, turned the second. Would it be there again? He quickened his pace. It was still hanging there beside the doorway. This was the third day he had seen it, and each time he had forgotten to ask what it meant. What could it mean? The green leaves were half concealed in snow; even the purple ribbon was covered. The poor white flowers looked frozen. He stared at them thoughtfully and passed on.

He turned the last corner. Voices of children. School a little ways off, on the other side of the street.

If he saw Annie there, what would he do? Look away. Walk by—

Must cross. Before him at the corner, children were crossing a beaten path in the snow. Beside him, the untrodden white of the gutter. He stopped. Here was a place to cross. Not a single footprint, only a wagon rut. Better not. The ridge of snow near the curb was almost as tall as himself. But none had crossed before. It would be his own, all his own path. Yes. He took a running jump, only partly cleared the first ridge, landed in snow almost as high as his knees. Behind him several voices called out, jeering, but he plunged forward, plunged forward to the lower level. Shouldn't have done it! He would be all covered with it now, wet. But how miraculously clean it was, all about him, whiter than anything he knew, whiter than anything, whiter. The second ridge was packed harder than the first; he climbed up, almost sank, jumped for safety to the other side, hastily brushed himself off. Sidewalk snow, riddled with salt, tramped down by the feet of children, reddened with ashes, growing dirtier as it neared the school.

At the sound of laughter, he looked up. In front of him, straddled two boys, vying with each other, each squirting urine as far ahead as he could. The water sank in a ragged channel, steaming in the snow, yellowing at the margins.

Sidewalk snow never stayed white. The school door. He entered.

Walk by if he saw her, hurry by. . . .

IX

THE three o'clock bell sounded at last. Dismissed, he hurried through the milling crowd of noisy children. He had seen neither Yussie nor Annie, and now, as at lunch time, he darted ahead of the other children for fear of being overtaken by either.

It had stopped snowing, and although clouds still dulled

the light, the air was warmer than it had been in the morning. Beside the curb, snow-forts squatted, half built during the lunch recess, waiting completion. A long sliding-pond stretched like a black ribbon in the gutter. Where the snow had been swept from the sidewalks, treacherous grey patches of ice tenaciously clung.

He went as swiftly as he could, picking his way. From time to time, he glanced hastily over his shoulder. No, they weren't there. He had outstripped them. He turned a corner, stopped in midstride, staring at the strange sight before him; cautiously he drew near.

A line of black carriages listed away from the snow-banked curb. He had seen such carriages before. But what was that in front of the house, that curious one, square and black with windows in its sides? Black plumes on the horses. Why those small groups of people beside the doorway whispering so quietly and craning their necks to look inside the hallway? Above the street, in all the nearby houses, windows were open, men and women were leaning out. In one of these a woman gesticulated to some one behind her. A man came forward, furtively grinning, patted her jutting hips and wedged into the space beside her. What were they all staring at? What was coming out of that house? Suddenly he remembered. The flowers had been there! Yes he knew the doorway. White, flattened pillars. Flowers! What? He looked about for someone to ask, but he could see no one his own age. Near one of the carriages, stood a small group of men, all dressed alike in long black coats and tall hats. The drivers. They alone seemed unperturbed, yet even they spoke quietly. Perhaps he could hear what they said. He sidled over, straining his ears.

"An' wattayuh t'ink he had de crust to tell me?" A man with a raw, weathered face was speaking, smoke from his cigarette unwreathing his words. "He siz, wadjuh stop fer? Now wouldn't dat give yuh de shits?"

He stared at the others for affirmation. They nodded agreement with their eyes.

Vindicated, the man continued, but more slowly and with greater emphasis. "His pole smacks into my hack, and he squawks wadjuh stop fer? I coulda spit in his mug, de donkey!"

"At's twiset now, ain' it?" asked another.

"Twiset, my pudd'n," retorted the first in wrathful contempt. "It's de toid time. Wuzn't Jeff de foist one he rammed, an' wuzn't Toiner de secon'? An' yestiddy me!"

"Hey!" Another man nudged his neighbor abruptly. "Dere goes de row-boat!"

Hastily throwing their cigarettes away, they scattered, and each one swung himself up to his box on the carriage.

More confused now than before, David drew near the doorway. A man in a tall black hat had just come out and was standing on the step looking solicitously into the hallway. A hush fell on the crowd; they huddled together as if for protection. Terror seemed to emanate from the hallway. At a sign from the man in the tall hat, the doors in back of the strange carriage were thrown open. Inside the gloomy interior metal glimmered, tasseled curtains shut out the light. Suddenly out of the hallway a scraping sound and slow shuffling of feet. A soft moan came from the crowd.

"He's coming!" someone whispered, craning her neck.

A sense of desolation. A fear.

Two men came out, laboring under the front-end of a huge black box, then two more at the other end. Red-faced, they trod carefully down the steps, advanced toward the carriage, rested one end of the box on the carriage floor.

That was—! Yes! That was! He suddenly understood. Mama said—Inside! Yes! Man! Inside! His flesh went cold with terror.

"Easy," cautioned the man in the black hat.

They shoved the box in, lunging after it. It squealed softly, sliding in without effort as if on ways or wheels. The man who had opened the doors, shot a large silvered pin into a hole behind the box, then in one skilful motion shut the doors. At a nod from the man in the black hat, the carriage rolled on a little distance, then stopped. Another carriage drew up before the house.

Supported by a man on either side of her, a woman in black, all bowed and veiled, came sobbing out of the house. The crowd murmured, a woman whimpered. David had never seen a handkerchief with a black border. Hers seemed white as snow.

Voices of children. He looked around.

Annie and Yussie were there, staring at the woman as she entered the carriage. He shuddered, contracting, crept behind the crowd and broke into a run.

At the doorway of his house he stopped, peered in, stepped back. What was he going to do now? At lunch time, as he neared the house, he had seen Mrs. Nerrick, the landlady, climb up the stoop. By running frantically, he had caught up to her, had raced past the cellar, before she shut her door. But now there was no one in sight. At any moment Annie and Yussie might come round the corner. He must—before they saw—but the darkness, the door, the darkness. The man in the box in the carriage. Alone. He must.

Make a noise. Noise . . . He advanced. What? Noise. Any.

"Aaaaah! Ooooh!" he quavered, "My country 'tis of dee!" He began running. The cellar door. Louder. "Sweet land of liberty," he shrilled, and whirled toward the stairs. "Of dee I sing." His voice rose in a shriek. His feet pounded on the stair. At his back, the monstrous horde of fear. "Land where our fodders died!" The landing; he dove for the door, flinging himself upon it—Threw it open, slammed it shut, and stood there panting in terror.

His mother was standing, staring at him in wide-eyed amazement. "Was that you?"

Close to tears, he lowered his head.

"What is it?"

"I don't know," he whimpered.

She laughed hopelessly and sat down. "Come here, you strange child. Come here. You're white!"

David went over and sank against her breast.

"You're trembling," she stroked his hair.

"I'm afraid," he murmured against her throat.

"Still afraid?" she said soothingly. "Still the dream pursuing you?"

"Yes," a dry sob shook him. "And something else."

"What else?" She pressed him toward her with an encircling arm. In the other hand, she took both of his. "What?" she murmured. Her lips' soft pressure against his temples seemed to sink inward, downward, radiating a calm and a sweetness that only his body could grasp. "What else?"

"I saw a—a man who was in a box. You told me once."

"What? Oh!" her puzzled face cleared. "A funeral. God grant us life. Where was it?"

"Around the corner."

"And that frightened you?"

"Yes. And the hall was dark."

"I understand."

"Will you wait in the hall if I call you next time?"

"Yes. I'll wait as often as you like."

David heaved a quivering sigh of relief and kissed her cheek in gratitude.

"If I didn't," she laughed, "Mrs. Nerrick, the land-lady, would dispossess us. I never heard such a thunder of feet!" When she had unbuttoned his leggings she rose and set him in a chair. "Sit there, darling. It's Friday, I have so much to do."

For a while, David sat still and watched her, feeling his heart grow quiet again, then turned and looked out of the window. A fine rain had begun to fall, serrying the windows with aimless ranks. In the yard the snow under the rain was beginning to turn from white to grey. Blue smoke beat down, strove upward, was gone. Now and then, the old house creaked when the wind elbowed in and out the alley. Borne through mist and rain from some remote river, a boat horn boomed, set up strange reverberations in the heart . . .

Friday. Rain. The end of school. He could stay home now, stay home and do nothing, stay near his mother the whole afternoon. He turned from the window and regarded her. She was seated before the table paring beets. The first cut into a beet was like lifting a lid from a tiny stove. Sudden purple under the peel; her hands were stained with it. Above her blue and white checkered apron her face bent down, intent upon her work, her lips pressed gravely together. He loved her. He was happy again.

His eyes roamed about the kitchen: the confusion of Friday afternoons. Pots on the stove, parings in the sink, flour smeared on the rolling pin, the board. The air was warm, twined with many odors. His mother rose, washed the beets, drained them, set them aside.

"There!" she said. "I can begin cleaning again."

She cleared the table, washed what dishes were soiled, emptied out the peelings that cluttered the sink into the garbage can. Then she got down on all fours and began to mop the floor. With knees drawn up, David watched her wipe the linoleum beneath his chair. The shadow between her breasts, how deep! How far it—No! No! Luter! When he looked! That night! Mustn't! Mustn't! Look away! Quick! Look at—look at the linoleum there, how it glistened under a thin film of water.

"Now you'll have to sit there till it dries," she cautioned him, straightening up and brushing back the few wisps of hair that had fallen over her cheek. "It will only be a few minutes." She stooped, walked backward to the steps, trailing the mop over her footprints, then went into the frontroom.

Left alone, he became despondent again. His thoughts returned to Luter. He would come again this evening. Why? Why didn't he go away. Would they have to run away every Thursday? Go to Yussie's house? Would he have to play with Annie again? He didn't want to. He never wanted to see her again. And he would have to. The way he did this afternoon beside the carriages. The black carriage with the window. Scared. The long box. Scared. The cellar. No! No!

"Mama!" he called out.

"What is it, my son?"

"Are you going to—to sleep inside?"

"Oh, no. Of course not! I'm just straightening my hair a little."

"Are you coming in here soon?"

"Why yes. Is there anything you want?"

"Yes."

"In just a moment."

He waited impatiently for her to appear. In a little while she came out. She had changed her dress and combed her hair. She spread a frayed clean towel out on the parlor steps and sat down.

"I can't come over unless I have to," she smiled. "You're on an island. What is it you want?"

"I forgot," he said lamely.

"Oh, you're a goose!"

"It has to dry," he explained. "And I have to watch it."

"And so I do too, is that it? My, what a tyrant you'll make when you're married!"

David really didn't care what she thought of him just as long as she sat there. Besides, he did have something to ask her, only he couldn't make up his mind to venture it. It might be too unpleasant. Still no matter what her answer would be, no matter what he found out, he was always safe near her.

"Mama, did you ever see anyone dead?"

"You're very cheerful to-day!"

"Then tell me." Now that he had launched himself on this perilous sea, he was resolved to cross it. "Tell me," he insisted.

"Well," she said thoughtfully, "The twins who died when I was a little girl I don't remember. My grandmother though, she was the first I really saw and remember. I was sixteen then."

"Why did she die?"

"I don't know. No one seemed to know."

"Then why did she die?"

"What a dogged questioner you are! I'm sure she had a reason. But do you want to know what I think?"

"Yes!" eagerly.

His mother took a deep breath, lifted a finger to arouse an already fervent attention. "She was very small, my grandmother, very frail and delicate. The light came through her hands like the light through a fan. What has that to do with it? Nothing. But while my grandfather was very pious, she only pretended to be—just as I pretend, may God forgive us both. Now long ago, she had a little garden before her house. It was full of sweet flowers in the summertime, and she tended it all by herself. My grandfather, stately Jew, could never understand why she should spend a whole spring morning watering the flowers and plucking off the dead leaves, and snipping here and patting there, when she had so many servants to do it for her. You would hardly believe how cheap servants were in those days—my grandfather had five of them. Yes, he would fret when he saw her working in the garden and say it was almost irreligious for a Jewess of her rank— she was rich then remember—the forests hadn't been cut"—

"What forests?"

"I've told you about them—the great forests and the lumber camps. We were rich while the forests were there. But after they were cut and the lumber camps moved away, we grew poor. Do you understand? And so my grandfather would fret when he saw her go dirtying her hands in the soil like any peasant's wife. But my grandmother would only smile at him—I can still see her bent over and smiling up at him—and say that since she had no beautiful beard like his to stroke, what harm could there be in getting a little dirt on her hands. My grandfather had a beard that turned white early; he was very proud of it. And once she told him that she was sure the good Lord would not be angry at her if she did steal a little from Esau's heritage—the earth and the fields are Esau's heritage—since Esau himself, she said, was stealing from Isaac on every side—she meant all the new stores that were being opened by the other gentiles in our town. What could my grandfather do? He would laugh and call her a serpent. Now wait! Wait! I'm coming to it." She smiled at his impatience.

"As she grew older, she grew very strange. Shall I tell you what she used do? When autumn came and everything had died—"

"Died? Everything?" David interrupted her.

"Not everything, little goose. The flowers. When they died she didn't want to leave the house. Wasn't that strange? She stayed for days and days in her large living room—it had crystal chandeliers. You wouldn't believe how quietly she would sit—not seeing the servants, hardly hearing what was said—and her hands folded in her lap —So. Nor could my grandfather, though he begged her to come out, ever make her. He even went to ask a great Rabbi about it—it was no use. Not till the first snow fall, did she willingly leave the house again."

"Why?"

"Here is the answer. See if you can find it. When I came to visit her once on a day in late autumn, I found her sitting very quietly, as usual, in her large arm-chair. But when I was about to take my coat off, she said, keep it on, Genya, darling, there is mine on the chair in the corner. Will you get it for me, child?

"Well, I stood still staring at her in surprise. Her coat? I thought. Was she really of her own accord going out

and in Autumn? And then for the first time I noticed
that she was dressed in her prettiest Sabbath clothes—a
dark, shimmering satin—very costly. I can see her yet.
And on her head—she had never let them cut her hair—
she had set a broad round comb with rows of pearls in it
—the first present my grandfather had ever given her. It
was like a pale crown. And so I fetched her coat and
helped her put it on. Where are you going, grandmother?
I asked. I was puzzled. In the garden, she said, in the
garden. Well, an old woman must have her way, and into
the garden we went. The day was very grey and full of
winds, whirling, strong winds that could hold the trees
down like a hand. Even us it almost blew about and it
was cold. And I said to her, Grandmother, isn't it too
cold out here? Isn't the wind too strong? No, her coat
was warm, so she said. And then she said a very strange
thing. Do you remember Petrush Kolonov? I wasn't
sure. A goy, she said, a clod. He worked for your grandfather many years. He had a neck like a tree once, but
he grew old and crooked at last. And when he grew so
old he couldn't lift a faggot, he would sit on a stone and
look at the mountains. This was my grandmother talking,
you understand?"

David couldn't quite follow these threads within threads,
but nodded. "Why did he sit?" he asked, afraid that she
might stop talking.

She laughed lightly. "That same question has been asked
by three generations. You. Myself. My grandmother. He
had been a good drudge this Petrush, a good ox. And when
my grandmother asked him, Petrush, why do you sit like
a keg and stare at the mountains, his only answer was,
my teeth are all gone. And that's the story my grandmother told me while we walked. You look puzzled," she
laughed again.

He was indeed, but she didn't explain.

"And so we walked and the leaves were blowing.
Shew-w-w! How they lifted, and one blew against her
coat, and while the wind held it there, you know, like a
finger, she lifted it off and crumbled it. And then she
said suddenly, come let us turn back. And just as we
were about to go in she sighed so that she shivered—
deep—the way one sighs just before sleep—and she
dropped the bits of leaves she was holding and she said,

it is wrong being the way I am. Even a leaf grows dull and old together! Together! You understand? Oh, she was wise! And we went inside."

His mother stopped, touched the floor to see if it was dry. Then she rose and went to the stove to push the seething beet soup from where it had been over the heat of the coals to the cooler end of the stove.

"And now the floor is dry," she smiled, "I'm liberated."

But David felt cheated, even resentful. "You—you haven't told me anything!" he protested. "You haven't even told me what happened?"

"Haven't I?" She laughed. "There's hardly anything more to tell. She died the winter of that same year, before the snow fell." She stared at the rain beating against the window. Her face sobered. The last wink of her eyelids before she spoke was the slowest. "She looked so frail in death, in her shroud—how shall I tell you, my son? Like early winter snow. And I thought to myself even then, let me look deeply into her face for surely she will melt before my eyes." She smiled again. "Have I told you enough now?"

He nodded. Without knowing why, her last words stirred him. What he had failed to grasp as thought, her last gesture, the last supple huskiness of her voice conveyed. Was it in his heart this dreamlike fugitive sadness dwelled, or did it steep the feathery air of the kitchen? He could not tell. But if only the air were always this way, and he always here alone with his mother. He was near her now. He was part of her. The rain outside the window set continual seals upon their isolation, upon their intimacy, their identity. When she lifted the stove lid, the rosy glow that stained her wide brow warmed his own body as well. He was near her. He was part of her. Oh, it was good being here. He watched her every movement hungrily.

She threw a new white table cloth over the table. It hovered like a cloud in air and settled slowly. Then she took down from the shelf three brass candlesticks and placed them in the center of whiteness, then planted candles into each brass cup.

"Mama."

"Yes?"

"What do they do when they die?"

"What?" she repeated. "They are cold; they are still. They shut their eyes in sleep eternal years."

Eternal years. The words echoed in his mind. Raptly, he turned them over and over as though they had a lustre and shape of their own. *Eternal years.*

His mother set the table. Knives ringing faintly, forks, spoons, side by side. The salt shaker, secret little vessel of dull silver, the pepper, greyish-brown eye in the shallow glass, the enameled sugar bowl, headless shoulders of silver tongs leaning above the rim.

"Mama, what are eternal years?"

His mother sighed somewhat desperately, lifted her eyes a moment then dropped them to the table, her gaze wandered thoughtfully over the dishes and silverware. Then her eyes brightened. Reaching toward the sugar bowl she lifted out the tongs, carefully pinched a cube of sugar, and held it up before his eyes.

"This is how wide my brain can stretch," she said banteringly. "You see? No wider. Would you ask me to pick up a frozen sea with these narrow things? Not even the ice-man could do it." She dropped the tongs back into the bowl. "The sea to this—"

"But—" David interrupted, horrified and bewildered. "But when do they wake up, mama?"

She opened her two palms in a gesture of emptiness. "There is nothing left to waken."

"But sometime, mama," he urged.

She shook her head.

"But sometime."

"Not here, if anywhere. They say there is a heaven and in heaven they waken. But I myself do not believe it. May God forgive me for telling you this. But it's all I know. I know only that they are buried in the dark earth and their names last a few more lifetimes on their gravestones."

The dark. In the dark earth. Eternal years. It was a terrible revelation. He stared at her fixedly. Picking up a cloth that lay on the washtub, she went to the oven, flipped the door open, drew out a pan. The warmth and odor of new bread entered his being as through a rigid haze of vision. She spread out a napkin near the candlesticks, lifted the bread out of the pan and placed it on the square of linen.

"I still have the candles to light," she murmured sitting down, "and my work is done. I don't know why they made Friday so difficult a day for women."

—Dark. In the grave. Eternal years . . .

Rain in brief gusts seething at the window . . . The clock ticked too briskly. No, never. It wasn't sometime . . . In the dark.

Slowly the last belated light raveled into dusk. Across the short space of the kitchen, his mother's face trembled as if under sea, grew blurred. Flecks, intricate as foam, swirled in the churning dark—

—Like popcorn blowing in that big window in that big candystore. Blowing and settling. That day. Long ago.

His gaze followed the aimless flux of light that whirled and flickered in the room, troubling the outline of door and table.

—Snow it was, grey snow. Tiny bits of paper, floating from the window, that day. Confetti, a boy said. Confetti, he said. They threw it down on those two who were going to be married. The man in the tall, black shiny hat, hurrying. The lady in white laughing, leaning against him, dodging the confetti, winking it out of her eyes. Carriages waiting. Confetti on the step, on the horses. Funny. Then they got inside, both laughing. Confetti. Carriages.

—Carriages!

—The same!

—This afternoon! When the box came out! Carriages.

—Same!

—Carriages—!

"Dear God!" exclaimed his mother. "You startled me! What makes you leap that way in your chair? This is the second time today!"

"They were the same," he said in a voice of awe. It was solved now. He saw it clearly. Everything belonged to the same dark. Confetti and coffins.

"What were the same?"

"The carriages!"

"Oh, child!" she cried with amused desperation. "God alone knows what you're dreaming about now!" She rose from her chair, went over to the wall where the matchbox hung, "I had better light these candles before you see an angel."

The match rasped on the sandpaper, flared up, making David aware of how dark it had become.

One by one she lit the candles. The flame crept tipsily up the wick, steadied, mellowed the steadfast brass below, glowed on each knot of the crisp golden braid of the bread on the napkin. Twilight vanished, the kitchen gleamed. Day that had begun in labor and disquiet, blossomed now in candlelight and sabbath.

With a little, deprecating laugh, his mother stood before the candles, and bowing her head before them, murmured through the hands she spread before her face the ancient prayer for the Sabbath . . .

The hushed hour, the hour of tawny beatitude . . .

X

HIS mother rose, lit the gas lamp. Sudden, blue light condensed the candle flames to irrelevant kernels of yellow. He eyed them sadly, wishing that she hadn't lit the lamp.

"They will be coming soon," she said.

They! He started in dismay. They were coming! Luter. His father. They! Oh! The lull of peace was over. He could feel dread rising within him like a cloud—as though his mother's words had been a stone flung on dusty ground. The hush and the joy were leaving him! Why did Luter have to come? David would be ashamed to look at him, could not look at him. Even thinking of Luter made him feel as he felt that day in school when the boy in the next seat picked his nose and rolled the snot between his fingers, then peered round with a vacant grin and wiped it off under the seat. It made his toes curl in disgust. He shouldn't have seen him, shouldn't have known.

"Is Mr. Luter going to come here too?"

"Of course." She turned to look at him. "Why do you ask?"

"I don't know. I just thought—I—I thought maybe he didn't like the way you cooked."

"The way I—? Oh! I see!" She reddened faintly. "I didn't know you could remember so well." She looked about as though she had forgotten something and then went up the stairs into the frontroom.

He stared out of the window into the dark. Rain still beat down. They must be hurrying toward him now in the rain, hurrying because it was raining. If only he could get away before they came, hide till Luter was gone, never come back till Luter had gone away forever. How could he go? He caught his breath. If he ran away now before his mother came back—stole out through the door silently. Like that! Opened the door, crept down the stairs. The cellar! Run by and run away, leaving upstairs an empty kitchen. She would look about, under the table, in the hall; she would call—David! David! Where are you? David! He'd be gone—

In the frontroom, the sound of a window opening, shutting again. His mother came in, bearing a grey covered pot between her hands. Rain drops on its sides, water in the hollow of the lid.

"A fearful night." She emptied the overflowing lid into the sink. "The fish is frozen."

Too late now.

He must stay here now, till the end, till Luter had come and gone. But perhaps his mother was wrong and perhaps Luter wouldn't come, if only he never came again. Why should he come here again? He was here yesterday and there was nobody home. Don't come here, his mind whispered to itself again and again. Please, Mr. Luter, don't come here! Don't come here any more.

The minutes passed, and just at that moment when it seemed to David that he had forgotten about Luter, the familiar tread of feet scraped through the hallway below. Voices on the stair! Luter had come. With one look at his mother's pursed, attentive face, he sidled toward the frontroom, sneaked up the stairs and into the dark. He stood at the window, listening to the sounds behind him. The door was opened. He heard their greetings, Luter's voice and slow speech. They must be taking their coats off now. If only they would forget about him. If only it were possible. But—

"Where's the prayer?" he heard his father ask.

A pause and his mother's voice. "He's in the frontroom I think. David!"

"Yes, mama." A wave of anger and frustration shook him.

"He's there."

Satisfied that he was there, they seemed to forget him for a little while, but again his father and this time with the dangerous accent of annoyance.

"Well, why doesn't he come in? David!"

There could be no more delay. He must go in. Eyes fixed before his feet, he came out of the frontroom, shuffled to his seat and sat down, conscious all the time that the others were gazing at him curiously.

"What's the matter with him?" asked his father sharply.

"I don't quite know. Perhaps his stomach. He has eaten very little today."

"Well, he'll eat now," said his father warningly. "You feed him too many trifles."

"A doubtful stomach is a sad thing," said Luter condoningly, and David hated him for his sympathy.

"Ach," exclaimed his father, "it isn't his stomach, Joe, it's his palate—jaded with delicacies."

His mother set the soup before him. "This will taste good," she coaxed.

He dared not refuse, though the very thought of eating sickened him. Steeling himself against the first mouthful, he dipped the spoon into the shimmering red liquid, lifted it to his lips. Instead of reaching his mouth, the spoon reached only his chin, struck against the hollow under his lower lip, scalded it, fell from his nerveless fingers into the plate. A red fountain splashed out in all directions, staining his blouse, staining the white table cloth. With a feeling of terror David watched the crimson splotches on the cloth widen till they met each other.

His father lowered his spoon angrily into his plate. "Lame as a Turk!" he snapped, rapping the table with his knuckles. "Will you lift your head, or do you want that in the plate too?"

He raised frightened eyes. Luter glanced at him sidewise, sucking his teeth in wary disapproval.

"It's nothing!" exclaimed his mother comfortingly. "That's what table cloths were made for."

"To splash soup on, eh?" retorted her husband sarcastically. "And that's what shirts were made for too! Very fine. Why not the whole plate while he's at it."

Luter chuckled.

Without answering, his mother reached over and stroked his brow with her palm. "Go on and eat, child."

"What are you doing now," demanded his father, "sounding his brow for fever? Child! There's absolutely nothing wrong with the brat, except your pampering him!" He shook his finger at David ominously. "Now you swill your soup like a man, or I'll ladle you out something else instead."

David whimpered, eyed his plate in cowed rebellion.

"Take heed!"

"Perhaps he had better not eat," interposed his mother.

"Don't interfere." And to David, "Are you going to eat?"

Trembling, and almost on the verge of nausea, David picked up the spoon and forcing himself, ate. The sickening spasm passed.

Impatiently, his father turned to Luter. "What were you saying, Joe?"

"I was saying," said Luter in his slow voice, "that you would have to lock up the place after you left—only one door, you see. The rest I will close before I go." He reached into his coat pocket and drawing out a ring of keys, detached one. "This one closes it. And I'll tell you," he handed the key to David's father. "I'm putting it down as four hours. The whole job won't take you more than two—three at most."

"I see."

"You won't get the extra this week though. The bookkeeper—"

"Next week then."

Luter cleared his throat. "You're having one diner less tomorrow evening," he said to David's mother.

"Yes?" she asked in constrained surprise, and turning to David's father, "Will you be so late, Albert?"

"Not I."

"No, not Albert," chuckled Luter, "I."

David's heart leaped in secret joy.

"Then I shan't prepare dinner for you tomorrow night?"

"No, I have something to do tomorrow night," he said vaguely. "Sunday perhaps. No, I'll tell you. If I'm not here by seven o'clock Sunday, don't keep the dinner waiting for me."

"Very well."

"I'll pay for the week in full anyhow."

"If you're not coming—" she objected.

"Oh, that doesn't matter," said Luter, "that's settled." He nodded and picked up his spoon.

During the rest of the meal, David ate cautiously peering up furtively from time to time to see whether anything he did was displeasing his father. At Luter, he never ventured a glance for fear the very sight of the man would confuse him into further blunders. By the time his mother set the dessert before him, he was already casting about for some way to retréat, some place where he could hide and yet be thought present, or at least, be accounted for. He might feign drowsiness and his mother would put him to bed, but he could not do that now. It was too early. What would he do till then? Where could he escape for a little while? The rooms of the house passed before his mind. The frontroom? His father would say, "What is he doing in there in the dark?" The bedroom? No. His father would say the same thing. Where? The bathroom. Yes! He would sit on the toilet seat. Stay there till he heard some one call, then come out.

He had eaten the last prune, and was just about to slip from his chair when out of the corner of his eye, he saw Luter's hand move toward his vest-pocket and draw out his watch.

"I must go!" He smacked his lips.

He was going! David could have danced for joy. It was too good to be true!

"So soon?" asked his mother.

To David's surprise, his father laughed, and a moment later Luter joined him as if they shared some secret joke.

"I'm somewhat late as it is." Luter pushed his chair back and rose. "But first I must pay you."

David stared at his plate, listening. He could think of only one thing—Luter was going, would be gone in another minute. He glanced up. His father had just gone into the bedroom and in the moment of his absence Luter darted quick eyes at his mother. David shivered with revulsion and hastily looked down. Taking the coat which David's father had just brought out, Luter got into it, and David with all the forces of his mind, tried to hasten the feet that were moving toward the door.

"Well," Luter finally said, "a good week to you all. May the prayer," his hat pointed at David, "recover soon."

"Thank you," said his mother. "Good week."

"Lift your head," snapped his father. David hastily looked up. "Goodnight, Joe, I'll see you to-morrow. Good luck." Both men laughed.

"Good night." Luter went out.

With a quiet sigh of relief David uncurled from the tense, inner crouch his body seemed to have assumed, and looking about saw his father gazing at the door. His face had relaxed into a bare smile.

"He's looking for trouble," he said dryly.

"What do you mean?"

His father uttered an amused snort. "Didn't you notice how peculiarly he behaved tonight?"

"I did—" she hesitated, watching his face inquiringly— "at least—Why?"

He turned to her; her eyes swerved back to the dishes.

"Didn't you notice how embarrassed he was?"

"No. Well. Perhaps."

"Then you don't notice very much," he chuckled shortly. "He's off to a marriage-broker."

"Oh!" Her brow cleared.

"Yes. It's a secret. You understand? You know nothing about it."

"I understand," she smiled faintly.

"He's free as air, and he's looking for a stone around his neck."

"Perhaps he does need a wife," she reminded him. "I mean I have often heard him say he wanted a home and children."

"Ach, children! Fresh grief! It isn't children he's looking for, it's a little money. He wants to open a shop of his own. At least that's what he says."

"I thought you said he was looking for troubles?" she laughed.

"Certainly! He's hurrying things too much. If he waited a few more years he'd have enough money of his own to set up a shop—without a wife. Wait! I said to him.

Wait! No, he said. I need a thousand. I want a big place four or five presses. But he'll find out what a Yiddish thousand is. If it melts no further than five hundred the morning after he ducked under the canopy, let none call him unfortunate." He belched quietly, the adam's apple on his neck jogging, and then looked around with knit brows as though seeking something.

"I heard him ask you to close up the shop," she inquired.

"Yes, he's giving me a little overtime. I won't be home till four or five—perhaps later. Bah!" he burst out impatiently, "The man makes eighteen dollars a week—six more than I do—and he itches to pawn himself to a wife." He paused, looked about again—"Where's The Tageblatt?"

His wife looked up startled. "The Tageblatt", she repeated in dismay, "Oh, where are my wits, I've forgotten to buy it. The rain! I put it off."

He scowled.

Noisily setting the dishes down in the sink, she wiped her hands on a towel. "I'll be only a minute."

"Where are you going?"

"My shawl."

"What's the matter with him, hasn't he feet?"

"But I can do it so much more quickly."

"That's the whole trouble with you," he said curtly. "You do everything for him. Let him go down."

"But it's wet out, Albert."

His face darkened, "Let him go down," he repeated. "Is it any wonder he won't eat. He moulders in the house all day! Get your coat on." His head jerked sharply. "Shudder when I speak to you."

David sprang from his seat, gazed apprehensively at his mother.

"Oh," she protested, "why do you—"

"Be still! Well?"

"Very well," she said, annoyed yet resigned, "I'll get him his coat."

She brought his coat out of the bedroom and helped him into it, his father meanwhile standing above them and muttering, as he always did, that he was big enough to fetch and get into his clothes by himself. Uneasily he tried to take his rubbers from her, but she insisted on helping him.

"It's two cents," she gave him a dime. "Here is ten. Ask for The Tageblatt and wait till they give you change."

"Eight cents change," his father admonished. "And don't forget The Tageblatt."

As David went out, his mother trailed behind him into the hall.

"Are you going down with him too?" his father inquired.

But without making a reply, she leaned over David and whispered. "Hurry down! I'll wait!" And aloud as if giving him the last instruction. "The candy store on the corner."

David went down as quickly as he could. The cellar door was brown in the gaslight. The raw night air met him at the end of the doorway. He went out. Rain, seen only where it blurred the distant lamps, still fell, seeking his face and the nape of his neck with icy fingers. The candy store window glimmered near the corner. His breath an evanescent plume, he hurried toward it, splashing in hidden puddles, his toes curling down against the rising chill. The streets were frightening, seen in loneliness this way, rain-swept, dark and deserted.

He didn't like his father. He never would like him. He hated him.

The candy store at last. He opened the door, hearing overhead the familiar tinny jangle of the bell. Gnawing a frayed chicken bone the half-grown son of the storekeeper came out of the back.

"Waddayuh want?"

"De Tageblatt."

The boy lifted a newspaper out of a small pile on the counter, handed it to David, who having taken it, turned to go.

"Where's your money?" demanded the boy impatiently.

"Oh, hea." David reached up and handed over the dime that he had been clutching in his hand all this time.

Clamping the bone between his teeth the boy made change and returned it, greasy fingers greasing the coins.

He went out, hurried toward the house. Walking was too slow; his mother would be waiting. He began to run. He had only taken a few strides forward when his

foot suddenly landed on something that was not pavement. The sound of hollow iron warned him too late—
A coal-chute cover. He slipped. With a gasp, he teetered in air, striving, clawing for a moment at a void, and then pitched forward, sprawling in the icy slush. Money and newspaper flew from his hands and now lay scattered in the dark. Frightened, knees and stockings soaked, he pushed himself to his feet, and began wildly looking about for what he had dropped.

He found the newspaper—sopping. Then a penny. More, there was more. He peered frantically in the dark. Another penny. Two cents now. But he had eight before. He plunged his hand here, there into the numbing snow, felt along the rough pavement, retraced, groped. Further ahead! Back! Nothing. Beside the curb maybe! Nothing. He would never find it. Never! He burst into tears, ran toward the house, careless now whether he fell or not. It would be better for him if he fell now, if he were hurt. Sobbing, he entered the hallway. He heard a door open upstairs, and his mother's voice at the top of the stairs.

"Child, I'm here."

He climbed up.

"What is it? What is it? Why, you're soaked through!" She led him in.

"I lost the money." He wailed. "I only have two— two cents."

His father was staring at him angrily, "You've lost it, have you? I had a feeling you would. Paid yourself for your errand, have you?"

"I fell in the snow," he sobbed.

"It's all right," said his mother gently, taking the newspaper and the money away from him. "It's all right."

"All right? Will everything he does be all right always? How long will you tell him that?" His father snatched the paper from her. "Why, it's wringing wet. A handy young man, my son!"

His mother took his coat off. "Come sit near the stove."

"Indulge him! Indulge him!" her husband muttered wrathfully and flung himself into a chair. "Look at that paper!" He slapped it open on the table. "My way would be a few sound cuffs."

"He couldn't help it," she interposed placatingly. "It's very slippery and he fell."

"Bah! He couldn't help it! That's all I ever hear from you! He has a downright gift for stumbling into every black moment of the year. At night he breaks one's sleep with a squalling about dreams. A little while ago he flings his spoon into his soup. Now—six cents thrown away." He slapped his hand on the paper. "Two cents ruined. Who can read it! Beware!" he shook a menacing finger at David who cowered against his mother's side. "There's a good beating in store for you! I warn you! It's been gathering for years."

"Albert," said his wife reddening, "you are a man without a heart."

"I?" His father drew back, his nostrils curving out in anger. "A plague on you both—I have no heart? And have you any understanding, any knowledge of how to bring up a child?" He thrust his jaw forward.

A moment of silence followed and then "I'm sorry," she said, "I didn't mean it. I meant only—these things happen sometimes—I'm sorry!"

"Oh, you're sorry," he said bitterly. "I have no heart! Woe me, to labor as I labor, for food for the two of you and for a roof over your heads. To labor and to work overtime! In vain! I have no heart! As if I gorged myself upon my earnings, as if I drank them, wallowed in the streets. Have you ever gone without anything? Tell me!"

"No! No!"

"Well?"

"I meant only that you didn't see the child all day as I did—naturally you don't know when anything is wrong with him."

"I see enough of him when I see him. And I know better than you what medicine he needs most."

His mother was silent.

"You'll be saying he needs a doctor next."

"Perhaps he—"

But someone was knocking at the door. She stopped speaking, went over and opened it—Yussie came in; he held a wooden clothes-hanger in his hand.

"My mother wants you to go upstairs," he said in Yiddish.

David's mother shook her head impatiently.

"Have you taken to gadding about?" asked her husband disgustedly. "Only a few days ago, you had no neighbors at all."

"I've only been there once," she said apologetically. And to Yussie, "Tell your mother I can't come up just now."

"She's waiting for you," he answered without stirring. "She's got a new dress to show you."

"Not now."

"I ain' goin' op," Yussie switched into English as if to avoid any further discussion. "I'm gonna stay hea." And apparently satisfied that his mission had been performed, he approached the uneasy David who was still seated beside the stove. "See wot I got—a bow 'n' arrer." He brandished the clothes hanger.

"I'll have to go for just a minute," she said hesitantly. "This child—she'll be wondering—"

"Go! Go!" said her husband sullenly. "Am I stopping you?" He picked up the newspaper, plucked a match from the match-box and then stalked up into the frontroom and slammed the door behind him. David heard him fling himself down upon the couch.

"I'll be back in a minute," said his mother wearily, and casting a hopeless glance after her husband, went out.

"Aintcha gonna play?" asked Yussie after a pause.

"I don' wanna," he answered morosely.

"W'yncha wanna?"

"Cause I don' wanna." He eyed the clothes hanger with disgust. It had been upstairs in a closet; it was tainted.

"Aaa, c'mon!" And when David refused to be persuaded, "Den I'm gonna shootchuh!" he threatened. "Yuh wanna see me?" He lifted the clothes hanger, pulled back an imaginary string. "Bing! I'm an Innian. If you don' have a bow 'n' arrer, I c'n kill yuh. Bang!" Another shaft flew. "Right innee eye. W'yntcha wanna play?"

"I don' wanna."

"W'yntcha get a bow 'n' arrer?"

"Lemme alone!"

"I'm gonna shootchuh again den," he dropped to the floor. "Bing! Dot one went right inside. Yuh dead!"

"Go 'way!"

"I don' wanna go 'way," he had become cross. "I'm gonna shootcha all I wan'. Yuh a cowid."

David was silent. He was beginning to tremble.

"I c'n even hitcha wit my hatchet," continued Yussie. "Yuh a cowid." He crawled up defiantly. "Wanna see me hitcha wit my hatchet?" He had grasped the clothes hanger at one end, "Yuh dare me?"

"Get otta here!" hissed David frantically. "Go in yuh own house!"

"I don' wanna," said Yussie truculently. "I c'n fightchoo. Wanna see me?" He drew back his arm, "Bing!" The point of the clothes hanger struck David in the knee, sending a flash of pain through his whole leg. He cried out. The next moment, he had kicked at Yussie's face with all the force in his leg.

Yussie fell forward on his hands. He opened his mouth, but uttered no sound. Instead his eyes bulged as if he were strangling, and to David's horror the blood began to trickle from under his pinched white nostrils. For moments that seemed years of agony the blood slowly branched above his lip. He stood that way tranced and rigid. Suddenly he sucked in his breath, the sound was flat, sudden, like the sound of a stone falling into water. With terrified care, he reached up his hand to touch the scarlet bead hanging from his lips, and when he beheld the red smear on his finger tips, his face knitted with fright, and he threw back his head, and uttered the most piercing scream that David had ever heard. So piercing was it that David could feel his own throat contract as though the scream were splitting from his own body and he were trying to stifle it. With the awful realization that his father was in the next room, he sprang to his feet.

"Here, Yussie," he cried frenziedly, trying to force the clothes hanger into his hands. "Here, hit me Yussie. G'wan hit me Yussie!" And striking himself a sharp blow on the brow, "Look, Yussie, you hoited me. Ow!"

But to no avail. Once more Yussie screamed. And now David knew he was lost.

"Mama!" he moaned in terror. "Mama!" And turned toward the frontroom door as if toward doom.

It opened. His father glared at them in angry surprise.

Then his features grew taut when his eyes fixed on Yussie. His nostrils broadened and grew pale.

"What have you done?" His voice was deliberate and incredulous.

"I—I—" David stammered, shrunken with fear.

"He kicked me right in duh nose!" Yussie howled.

Never taking his blazing eyes from David, his father came down the parlor stairs. "What?" he ground, towering above him. "Speak!" Slowly his arm swung toward the sobbing Yussie; it was like a dial measuring his gathering wrath. "Tell me did you do this?" With every word he uttered his lips became thinner and more rigid. His face to David seemed slowly to recede, but recede without diminishing, growing more livid with distance, a white flame bodiless. In the molten features, only the vein upon his brow was clear, pulsing like a dark levin.

Who could bear the white heat of those features? Terror numbed his throat. He gagged. His head waited for his eyes to lower, his eyes for his head. He quivered, and in quivering wrenched free of that awful gaze.

"Answer me!"

Answer me, his words rang out. Answer me, but they meant, Despair! Who could answer his father? In that dread summons the judgement was already sealed. Like a cornered thing, he shrank within himself, deadened his mind because the body would not deaden and waited. Nothing existed any longer except his father's right hand —the hand that hung down into the electric circle of his vision. Terrific clarity was given him. Terrific leisure. Transfixed, timeless, he studied the curling fingers that twitched spasmodically, studied the printer's ink ingrained upon the finger tips, pondered, as if all there were in the world, the nail of the smallest finger, nipped by a press, that climbed in a jagged little stair to the hangnail. Terrific absorption.

The hammer in that hand when he stood! The hammer!

Suddenly he cringed. His eyelids blotted out the light like a shutter. The open hand struck him full against the cheek and temple, splintering the brain into fragments of light. Spheres, mercuric, splattered, condensed and roared. He fell to the floor. The next moment his father had snatched up the clothes hanger, and in that awful pause before it descended upon his shoulders, he saw with that accelerated vision of agony, how mute and open mouthed Yussie stood now, with what useless silence.

"You won't answer!" The voice that snarled was the voice of the clothes hanger biting like flame into his flesh. "A curse on your vicious heart! Wild beast! Here, then! Here! Here! Now I'll tame you! I've a free hand now! I warned you! I warned you! Would you heed!"

The chopping strokes of the clothes hanger flayed his wrists, his hands, his back, his breast. There was always a place for it to land no matter where he ducked or writhed or groveled. He screamed, screamed, and still the blows fell.

"Please papa! Please! No more! No more! Darling papa! Darling papa!" He knew that in another moment he would thrust his head beneath that rain of blows. Anguish! Anguish! He must escape!

"Now bawl!" the voice raged. "Now scream! But I pleaded with you! Pleaded as I would with death! You were stubborn were you! Silent were you! Secret—"

The door was thrown open. With a wild cry, his mother rushed in, flung herself between them.

"Mama!" he screamed, clutching at her dress. "Mama!"

"Oh, God!" she cried in terror and swooped him into her arms. "Stop! Stop! Albert! What have you done to him!"

"Let him go!" he snarled. "Let him go I tell you!"

"Mama!" David clung to her frenziedly. "Don't let him! Don't let him!"

"With that!" she screamed hoarsely, trying to snatch the clothes hanger from him. "With that to strike a child. Woe to you! Heart of stone! how could you!"

"I haven't struck him before!" The voice was strangled. "What I did he deserved! You've been protecting him from me long enough! It's been coming to him for a long time!"

"Your only son!" she wailed, pressing David convulsively to her. "Your only son!"

"Don't tell me that! I don't want to hear it! He's no son of mine! Would he were dead at my feet!"

"Oh, David, David beloved!" In her anguish over her child, she seemed to forget everyone else, even her husband. "What has he done to you! Hush! Hush!" She brushed his tears away with frantic hand, sat down and rocked him back and forth. "Hush, my beloved! My beautiful! Oh, look at his hand!"

"I'm harboring a fiend!" the implacable voice raged. "A butcher! And you're protecting him! Those hands of his will beat me yet! I know! My blood warns me of this son! This son! Look at this child! Look what he's done! He'll shed human blood like water!"

"You're stark, raving mad!" She turned upon him angrily. "The butcher is yourself! I'll tell you that to your face! Where he's in danger I won't yield, do you understand? With everything else have your way, but not with him!"

"Hanh! you have your reasons! But I'll beat him while I can."

"You won't touch him!"

"No? We'll see about that!"

"You won't touch him, do you hear?" Her voice had become as quiet and as menacing as a trigger that, locked and at rest, held back by a hair incredible will, incredible passion. "Never!"

"You tell me that?" His voice seemed amazed. "Do you know to whom you speak?"

"It doesn't matter! And now leave us!"

"I?" Again that immense surprise. As though one had dared to question a volcanic and incalculable force, and by questioning made it question itself. "To me? You speak to me?"

"To you. Indeed to you. Go out. Or I shall go."

"You?"

"Yes, both of us."

With terrified, tear-blurred eyes, David watched his father's body shake as if some awful strife were going on within him, saw his head lunge forward, his mouth open to speak, once, again, then grow pale and twitch, and finally he turned without a word and stumbled up the parlor steps.

His mother sat for a moment without moving, then quivered and burst into tears, but brushed them off.

Yussie was still standing there, mute and frightened, his blood smeared over his chin.

"Sit there a moment." She rose and set David on a chair. "Come here you poor child," she said to Yussie.

"He kicked me righd on de nose!"

"Hush!" She led Yussie to the sink, and wiped his face with the end of a wet towel. "There, now you feel better." And wetting the towel again, came over to David and set him on her lap.

"He hit me first."

"Now hush! We won't say anything more about it." She patted the lacerated wrist with the cold towel. "Oh! my child!" she moaned biting her lips.

"I wanna go opstai's," blubbered Yussie. "I'm gonna tell my modder on you." He snatched up the clothes hanger from the floor. "Waid'll I tell my modder on you, yuh gonna gid it!" He flung the door open and ran out bawling.

His mother, sighing painfully, shut the door after him, and began undoing David's shirt. There were angry red marks on his breast and shoulders. She touched them. He whimpered with pain.

"Hush!" she murmured again and again. "I know. I know, beloved."

She undressed him, fetched his nightgown and slipped it over him. The cold air on his bruises had stiffened his shoulders and hands. He moved stiffly, whimpering.

"It really hurts now, doesn't it?" she asked.

"Yes." He felt himself wanting to sniffle.

"Poor darling, let me put you to bed." She set him on his feet.

"I have to go now. Numbuh one."

"Yes."

She led him into the bathroom, lifted the toilet-seat. Urination was painful, affording relief only as a mournful sigh affords relief. His whole body shuddered as his bladder relaxed. A new sense of shyness invaded him; he crept furtively around to stand with his back to her, contracted when she pulled the chain above his head. He went out into the bright kitchen again, into the dark bedroom, and got into bed. There was a lingering, weary sadness in the first chill of the covers.

"And now sleep," she urged, bending down and kissing him. "And a better day."

"Stay here."

"Yes. Of course." She sat down and gave him her hand.

He curled his fingers around her thumb and lay staring up at her, his eyes drawing her features out of deep shadow. From time to time a sudden gasp would shake him, as though the waves of grief and pain had run his being's length and were returning now from some remote shore.

XI

DECEMBER sunlight, porous and cloudy, molten on upper window panes. Though it was still early in the afternoon, the tide of cold shade had risen high on wooden houses and brick. Grey clots of snow still clung under the lee of the battered curb. The air was cold yet windless. Winter. To the left of the doorway a sewer steamed.

Noises to the right. He peered out. Before the tailor shop near the corner, a cluster of boys had gathered. Did he dare go over? What if Yussie were among them? He tried to find him. No, he wasn't there. Then he could go over for a little while. He'd come back before Yussie came. Yes.

He drew near, warily. That was Sidney, Yonk. He knew them. The others? They lived around the corner maybe.

Sidney was in front; the rest followed him. David stood watching them.

"Wanna play?" Sidney asked.

"Yea."

"So git back of de line. Foller de leader. Boom! Boom! Boom!" He set the pace.

David fell into step behind the last boy. They marched cross the street in single file and stopped before a tall hydrant.

"Jump on Johnny Pump!" commanded Sidney leaping up on the two stumpy arms of the fire-plug. "One two t'ree! Yee!" He jumped off.

In their turn, the rest leaped up, and then ran after him, shouting. Sidney zig-zagged back and forth across the street, lurching against ash-cans, leaping up and down stoops, stepping only on lines in the pavement, and obeying every stray whim that drifted through his head. David liked the game.

Arrived at the barber-pole, Sidney waited for his breathless cohorts to draw up.

"Follow de blue one," he ordered, and beginning at the bottom of the blue spiral, wound around and round the pole until he stood tiptoe and the band he traced was beyond his reach. When the others had accomplished this feat, he crouched down, crept under the corbel of the barber-shop window, and when he reached the end, poked his head into the doorway and chanted in a croaking voice: "Chickee de cop, behin, de rock. De monkey's in de ba'ba shop!" And he fled.

The rest squealed the words as he had done, but with increasing haste and diminishing lustiness and sped after him. By the time David's turn had come, the barber was already at the threshold fuming with irritation. David mutely skirted the doorway and scurried on.

"He didn' say it!" they jeered.

"Sca'cat w'yntcha say it?" Sidney rebuked him.

"I couldn't," he grinned apologetically. "He wuz stannin' dere awreddy."

"Foller de leader nex' time!" Sidney warned him.

Chagrined, David resolved to do better, and thereafter followed faithfully all his leader's antics, not even balking at running up and down the wooden stairs that led into the ice-man's cellar.

The game had reached a high peak of excitement. The boy immediately preceding David had just rolled over the lower of two railings before the tailor's shop, and now it was David's turn. He grasped the bar, leaned against it, as the rest had done, and began a slow and cautious spin about it. In that strange moment of chaos when house-top and sky hung upside down and the others seemed standing on their heads in air, the inverted face of a man passed through and revolved with the revolving space. A glimpse of black pits, his nostrils, fat cheeks under the rim of his derby, all moving below legs. "Funny," he thought as the soles of his feet landed on the pavement again. "Upside down like that. Funny."

He glanced casually after the retreating figure.

Right side up now like everybody else. But—Wide shoulders, grey coat. That derby. That was—he struggled

against the ineluctable recognition. No! No! Not him! But
he walked like . . . His hands in his pockets. It was!
It was!—

"Hey, c'mon!" Sidney called out impatiently.

But never budging, David stared straight forward. Now
the man turned to cross the street, his face in profile.

It was! It was Luter! He was going to his house.

"Waddayuh lookin' at?" Sidney was provoked. "Doncha
wanna play?"

David wrenched himself from his trace. "Yea! Yea!
Sure I wanna play."

He ran into his place in the rank, but a moment later
forgot where he was and gazed toward his house in terror. Luter had reached the doorway now, was going in,
was gone.

That game now. Oh! That game now! No! No! Foller
de leader! Play!

"Hurry up!" said Sidney, "It's your chanst."

David looked at him blankly. "W'a wuz yuh doin',
I didn' see."

"Aaa!" Disgustedly. "Jump down 'em two steps."

David climbed up, jumped down, landed with a jarring
thud, and followed after.

He knew it! He knew it! That's why he had come.
That game! He was going to make her play now. Like
Annie. In the closet! . . .

"Hey, you ain' gonna play, dat's all!"

David started guiltily to see the rest waiting for him
again.

"Don' led 'im play, Sid." They turned on him.

"He ain' even follerin'."

"Yuh big dope, yuh can' even do nuttin'."

"Gid odda hea."

A sudden shout and then the patter of running feet
distracted them. They looked to see who it was.

"Hey give us a game!"

It was Yussie, heading toward them. At the sight of
him, David began edging away, but Yussie had already
spied him.

"Yee!" he squealed delightedly, "Wadda lickin' you
god!"

"Who god?" Sidney asked.

"He god!" He pointed to David. "Hey, Sidney, you

shoulda see! Bing! his fodder wend. Bang! An' he laid down, an' he wen' Yow!"

The others began to laugh.

"Ow!" Yussie capered about for their further benefit. "Please, papa, lemme go! Ooh lemme go! Bang! Annudder smack he gabe 'im. Right inne ass!"

"Wad 'e hitcha fuh?" They circled about him.

"He hid 'im becuz he kicked me righd inna nose," crowed Yussie. "Right over hea, an' made blood."

"Yuh led 'im gid away wid it?"

"I ain' gonna," growled Yussie waiting for further encouragement.

"Gib'm a fighd, Yussie!" They raised an eager cry.

"G'wan Yussie, bust'm one!"

"Righd inna puss!"

At the sight of David backing away, Yussie doubled his fists and screwed up his face pugnaciously. "C'mon, I'll fightcha."

"G'wan, yuh big cowid!" they taunted.

"I don' wanna fighd," he whimpered, looking about for a way of retreat. There was none. They had completely encircled him.

"Don' led 'im ged away, Yussie! Give 'im two, four, six, nine!"

Egged on, Yussie began hammering his shoulders. "Two, four, six, nine, I c'n beatchoo any old time!"

His fists struck the separate cores of yesterday's bruises. The places where the clothes-hanger had landed rayed out in pain. Tears sprang to his eyes. He cowered.

"He's cryin'!" they jeered.

"Look ad 'im cryin'."

"Waaa!"

"Cry baby, cry baby suck yer mudder's tiddy!" one of them began. "Cry baby, cry baby, suck yer mudder's tiddy." The rest took up the burden.

The tears streaming down his face, David groped his way blindly through them. They opened a gap to let him pass and then followed him still chanting.

"Cry baby, cry baby, suck yer mudder's tiddy!"

He began running. With a loud whoop of glee, they pursued. In a moment, someone had clutched his coat-belt and was yanking him to a halt. The pack closed in. "Ho, hussy!" they hooted, prancing about him. "Ho op!"

And suddenly a blind, shattering fury convulsed him. Why were they chasing him? Why? When he couldn't turn anywhere—not even upstairs to his mother. ▪He wouldn't let them! He hated them! He bared his teeth and screamed, tore lose from the boy who was dragging at his belt and lunged at him. Every quivering cell was martialed in that thrust. Before his savage impact, the other reeled back, tripped over his own feet and fell, arching to the ground. His head struck first, a muffled distant jar like a blast deep underground. His arms flopped down beside him, his eyes snapped shut, he lay motionless. With a grunt of terror, the rest stared down at him, their faces blank, their eyes bulging. David gasped with horror and fled toward his house.

At his doorway, he threw a last agonized glance over his shoulders. Attracted by the cries of the children, the tailor had come running out of his shop and was now bending over the boy. The rest were dancing up and down and yelling:

"Dere he is! In dat house! He done it!"

The tailor waved his fist threatening. "Bestit!" he shouted. "I'll give you! Vait! A polizman I'll get!"

David flew into the hallway. A policeman! He grew faint with terror. What had he done! What had he done! A policeman was coming. Hide! Hide! Upstairs. No! No! He was there. That game. He would tell. Where? Any place. He dove behind the bannister and under the stairs. No! They would look for him there. He darted out. Where? Up. No! Trapped, frenzied, he stared wildly about him . . . The door. . . . No! No! Not there! No! . . . Must . . . No! No! . . . Policeman . . . Run out . . . No, they'd catch . . . Thought, fear and flight, rebellion and submission, alternated through his head in sharp, feverish pulses. Must! Must! Must! His mind screamed down opposition, and he sprang to the cellar door and pulled it open—Darkness like a cataract, inexhaustible, monstrous.

"Mama!" he moaned, peering down, "Mama!"

He dipped his foot into night, feeling for the stair, found it, pulled the door shut behind him. Another step. He clung to the wall. A third. The unseen strands of a spider's web yielded against his lip. He recoiled in loathing, spat out the withered taste. No further. No! No further. He was trembling so, he could barely stand. Another step and he would fall. Weakly, he sat down.

Darkness all about him now, entire and fathomless night. No single ray threaded it, no flake of light drifted through. From the impenetrable depths below, the dull marshy stench of surreptitious decay uncurled against his nostrils. There was no silence here, but if he dared to listen, he could hear tappings and creakings, patterings and whispers, all furtive, all malign. It was horrible, the dark. The rats lived there, the hordes of nightmare, the wobbly faces, the crawling and misshapen things.

XII

HE GRITTED his teeth with the strain. Minutes had passed while he willed in a rigid pounding trance—willed that Luter would come down, willed that Luter would leave his mother. But on the stairs outside the cellar door all was still as before. Not a voice, not a footstep could he conjure out of the silence. Exhausted, he slumped back against the edge of the stair. But his ears had sharpened. He could hear sounds that he couldn't hear before. But not above him now—below him. Against his will he sifted the nether dark. It was moving—moving everywhere on a thousand feet. The stealthy horrible dark was climbing the cellar stairs, climbing toward him. He could feel its ghastly emanation wreathing about him in ragged tentacles. Nearer. The foul warmth of its breath. Nearer. The bloated grisly faces. His jaws began to chatter. Icy horror swept up and down his spine like a finger scratching a comb. His flesh flowed with terror.

—Run! Run!

He clawed his way up the gritty stairs, fumbled screaming for the doorknob. He found it, burst out with a sob of deliverance and flung himself at the light of the doorway.

—Out! Out! Before any body comes.

Down the stoop and running.

—No! That way, school! That house! Other way!

At the corner, he swerved toward the right toward less familiar streets.

—Light! Light in the streets! Could see now. Could look . . . Man there . . . No policeman . . . No one chasing . . . Could walk now.

The keen, cold-scented air revived him, filtered through his coat, quickening the flesh beneath. The swift and brittle light on corners and upper stories comforted him. Things were again steadfast and plain. With each quick breath he took, a hoop of terror snapped from his chest. He stopped running, dropped into a panting walk.

—Could stay here now . . . No one chasing . . . Could stay, could go . . . Next block, what?

He turned a corner and entered a street much like his own—brick houses and wooden houses—but no stores.

—Want different one . . . Could go next. . . .

At the next corner he stopped with a cry of delight and gazed about him. Telegraph poles! Why hadn't he come here before? On each side of the street, they stretched away, the wires on their crosses swinging into the sky. The street was wide, divided by a seamed and frozen mudgutter. At one end, the houses thinned out, faltering into open fields. The weathered poles crowded up the hill of distance into a sheen of frayed cloud. He laughed, filling his eyes with dappled reach, his lungs with heady openness.

—They go way and away . . . Way, way, way. . . . Could follow.

He patted the stout wooden pillar near his hand, examined the knots, darker than the grey, thrust at its patient bulk and laughed again.

—Next one. . . . Race him! . . . Hello Mr. High Wood. . . . Good-bye, Mr. High Wood. I can go faster. . . . Hello, Second Mr. High Wood. . . . Good-bye Second Mr. High Wood . . . Can beat you . . .

They dropped behind him. Three. . . . Four. . . . Five . . . Six. . . . drew near, floated by in silence like tall masts. Seven. . . . Eight. . . . Nine . . . Ten. . . . He stopped counting them. And with them, dwindling in the past, all he feared, all he loathed and fled from: Luter, Annie, the cellar, the boy on the ground. He remembered them still, yes, but they were tiny now, little pictures in his head that no longer writhed into his thoughts and stung him, but stood remote and harmless—something heard about someone else. He felt as if they would vanish from his mind altogether, could he only reach the top of that hill up which all the poles were, striding. He hurried on, skipping sometimes out of sheer deliverance, sometimes waving at a laggard pole, gurgling to himself, giggling at himself, absurdly weary.

And now the houses straggled, giving way to long stretches of empty lots. On either side of the street, splotches of yeasty snow still plastered the matted fields. On ledges above the rocks, the black talons of crooked trees clawed at the slippery ground. At the doorway of a chicken coop, behind a weathered, ramshackle house, a rooster clucked and gawked and strutted in. The level sidewalks had ended long ago; the grey slabs underfoot were cracked and rugged, and even these were petering out. A sharp wind was rising across the open lots, catching up cloaks of dust, golden in the slanting sun. It was growing colder and lonelier, the wintry bleakness of the hour before sunset, the earth contracting, waiting for night—

—Time to look back.

—No.

—Time to look back.

—Only to the end of that hill. There where the clouds fell.

—Time to look back.

He glanced over his shoulder and suddenly halted in surprise. Behind him as well as before, the tall spars were climbing into the sky.

—Funny. Both ways.

He turned about, gazing now behind him, now before.

—Like it was a swing. Didn't know.

His mood was buckling.

—Same. Didn't know.

His legs were growing tired.

—It's far away on the other side.

Between coat-pocket and sleeve one wrist was cold, the other was throbbing.

—And it's far away on the other side.

The tubers of pain under the skin of his shoulders were groping into consciousness now.

—And it's just the same.

Slowly, he began retracing his steps.

—Can go back.

Despite growing weariness, he quickened his pace.

They were all gone now, Luter was gone; they had finished that game. He and his mother. Could go back now. And the policeman was gone, couldn't find him. Could go back. And his mother would be there, yes, waiting for him. Didn't hate her now. Where were you? she would ask. No place. You frightened me; I couldn't find you. Wouldn't say. Why don't you tell me where you were? Because. Why? Because—But must get back before his father came. Better hurry.

Houses were gathering together again.

And I looked out of the window, and I called, David, David, and I couldn't find you. Wouldn't tell her. Maybe she even went down stairs into the street. But if the policeman told her. She wouldn't tell his father. No. When he got into his street, he'd call her. She'd look out of the window. What? Wait in the hall, I'm coming up-stairs. She'd wait and he'd run past the cellar. Hate it! Wish there were houses without cellars.

The sky was narrowing; houses had closed their ranks. Overhead, a small flock of sparrows, beading the wires between two telegraph poles, tweaked the single dry string of their voices. On the railing of a porch, a grey cat stopped licking a paw and studied them gravely, then eyed David as he passed.

Milk-supper, maybe, when he came upstairs. Sour cream, yum! Break pieces of bread into it. Sour cream with farmer-cheese. Mmm! Sour cream with eggs. Sour cream with what else? Borscht . . . Strawberries. . . . Radishes . . . Bananas . . . Borscht, strawberries, radishes, bananas. Borscht, strawberries, apples and strudel. No. They didn't eat with sour cream. Sour. Cream. Sour. Cream. Like it, like it, like it. I—like—it. I like cake but I don't like herring. I like cake, but I don't like what? I like cake, but I don't like, like, like, herring. I don't don't—How far was it still?

The sidewalks were level again.

Luter liked herring, don't like Luter. Luter likes herring,

don't like Luter. Luter likes—would he be there to-night? He said maybe. Maybe he wasn't coming. Wish he never comes. Never comes, never comes. Wishee, wishee, never comes, all on a Monday morning—How far was it still?

Eagerly, he scanned the streets ahead of him. Which one was it. Which? Which one was—Long street. Long street, lot of wooden houses. On this side. Yes. Go through the other side. Then other corner . . . Right away, right away. Be home right away . . . This one? . . . Didn't look like . . . Next one bet . . . Giddyap, giddyap, giddyap. . . . One little house . . . two little house . . . three little house . . . Corner coming, corner coming, corner—Here?

—Here? This one? Yes. Looked different. No. Same one. Wooden houses. Yes.

He turned the corner, hastened toward the opposite one.

—Same one. But looked a little teenchy weenchy bit different. Same one though.

But at the end of the block, uncertainty would not be dispelled. Though he conned every house on either side of the crossing, no single landmark stirred his memory. They were all alike—wooden houses and narrow side-walks to his right and left. A shiver of dismay ran through him.

—Thought this—? No. Maybe went two. Then, when he ran. Wasn't looking and went two. Next one. That would be it. Find it now. Mama is waiting. Next one. Quick. And then turn. That was. He'd see. Has to be.

He broke into a tired jog.

—Yes, the next one. That big yellow house on the corner. He'd see it. He'd see it. Yea! How he'd holler when he saw it. There it is! There's my street! But if— if it wasn't there. Must be! Must be!

He ran faster, sensing beside him the soft pad of easy-loping fear. That next corner would be haven or bay, and as he neared it, he burst into the anguished spring of a flagging quarry—

—Where? Where was it?

His eyes, veering in every direction, implored the stub-born street for an answer it would not yield. And sud-denly terror pounced.

"Mama!" The desolate wail split from his lips. "Mama!"

The aloof houses rebuffed his woe. "Mama!" his voice trailed off in anguished abandonment. And as if they had been waiting for a signal, the streets through his tear-blurred sight began stealthily to wheel. He could feel them turning under his feet, though never a house changed place—backward to forward, side to side—a sly, inexorable carousel.

"Mama! Mama!" he whimpered, running blindly through a street now bleak and vast as nightmare.

A man turned the corner ahead of him and walked briskly away on clicking heels. For a tense, delirious instant, he seemed no other than his own father; he was as tall. But then the film snapped open. It was someone else. His coat was greyer, he swung his arms and he walked erect. His father always hunched forward, arms bound to his side.

But with the last of his waning strength, he spurted after him. Maybe he would know. Maybe he could tell him.

"Mister!" he gasped for breath, "Mister!"

The man slackened his pace and glanced over his shoulder. At the sight of the pursuing David, he stopped and turned about in quizzical surprise. Under a long, heavy nose, he had a pointed mustache, the waxed blonde of horn.

"What's the matter, sonny," he asked in loud good humor. "What're you up to?"

"I'm losted." David sobbed.

"Oh!" He chuckled sympathetically. "Losted, eh? And where do you live?"

"On a hunnder 'n' twenny six Boddeh Stritt," he answered tremulously.

"Where?" he bent his ear down, puzzled. "What Street?"

"On Boddeh Stritt."

"Bodder Street?" He screwed a tip of his mustache to a tighter pitch and regarded David with an oblique, critical eye. "Bodder Street. Can't say that I've ever— Oh! Heh! Heh!" He exploded good-natured again. "You mean Potter Street. Heh! Heh! Bodder Street!"

"Boddeh Stritt," David reiterated weakly.

"Yea!" he said decisively. "Now listen to me." He took David's shoulder. "See that street there?" He pointed to the way David had come. "That one. Now see the street

after it—a little further away? That's two. Now you go one
street, two streets, but—" and his finger threatened—
"don't stop there. Go another one. See? Another one."

David nodded dubiously.

"Yea!" he said reassuringly. "And as soon as you're
there, ask anybody where one twenty six is. They'll tell
you. All right?" he asked heartily, giving David a slight
nudge in the desired direction.

Not too reassured but braced with a little more hope
than before, David set out, urging rebellious legs into a
plodding trot. He was a big man, that man, he must
know. Maybe it was Poddeh Street, like he said. Didn't
sound the same, but maybe it was. Everybody said it
different anyhow. His mother said Boddeh Stritt, like
that. But she couldn't talk English. So his father told her
Boddeh Street, like that. And now the man said Poddeh
Street. Puh. Puh. Poddeh. Buh. Buh. Boddeh. Corner is
coming . . . One corner. Gutter is coming . . . One gutter.

Next and next, he said. Ooh, if he could only see that
yellow house on the corner! Ooh, how he'd run! There
was a dog in it with long white hair and he ran after a
rubber ball. Here, Jack! Here, Jack! Grrrrrh! In his mouth.
Everybody knew him. Everybody knew Boddeh Stritt.
There was a grocery store in it and a candy store in it
and a barber shop. The barber had a big mustache like
that man's, only black. And a big awning on the store.
He wasn't Jewish. In the window, he had another barber,
only he wasn't real and he had a bottle in his hand and
his other fingers were like that—round. And he looked at
you with the bottle in his hand wherever you went. Walk
this way, that way, and he watched—Corner already. Gutter already.

Next and ask. Next and ask. Ooh, if he saw it. Ooh!
"Ooh, mama!" he prayed aloud. "I'm ascared to look,
ooh mama, make it on de nex' one!"

But look he did. The moment he had reached it—
up and- down, as far as the eye could see: Again a street
as alien as any he had ever passed, and like the others,
with squat, monotonous flanks receding into vacancy,
slack with risen shadow. He didn't cry out; he didn't sob.
A moment longer he stared. All hope collapsed within
him, fell, jarring in his heart. With stiff, tranced body, he
groped blindly toward the vague outline of a railing be-

fore a basement, and leaning his brow against the cold iron wept in anguish too great to bear. Only the sharp rush of his breath sheared the silence.

Minutes passed. He felt he would soon lose his grip of the iron uprights. At length, he heard behind him slow footsteps that drawing near, scuffed shortly to a halt. What good was looking up? What good was doing anything. He was locked in nightmare, and no one would ever wake him again.

"Here! Here!" A woman's crisp, almost piqued voice sounded above him, followed the next moment by prim tap on the shoulder. "Young man!"

David paid no heed.

"Do you hear me?" the voice gathered severity. "What is it?" And now the hand began forcing him away from the railing.

He turned about, head rolling in misery.

"Gracious me!" She raised a fending hand. "Whatever in the world has happened?"

Quivering, he looked at her, unable to answer. She was old, dwarfish, yet curiously compact. She wore green. A dark green hat skimmed high over a crest of white hair. From her hand hung a small black shopping bag, only vaguely bulging.

"Gracious!" she repeated, startled into scolding, "Won't you answer?"

"I—I'm losted," he sobbed, finding his breath at last. "Aaa! I'm losted."

"There! There! There! You poor thing!" and with a quick bird-like tug at a pince-nez hanging from a little reel under her coat, she fixed him in magnified grey eyes. "Tt! Tt! Tt! Don't you know where you live?"

"Yea, I know," he wept.

"Well, tell me."

"A hunner 'n' twenny six Boddeh Stritt."

"Potter Street? Why you silly child, this is Potter Street. Now, stop your crying!" A little grey finger went up.

"Id ain'd!" he moaned.

"What isn't?" The eyes behind the lenses contracted authoritatively.

"Id ain'd Boddeh Stritt!" He wept doggedly.

"Please don't rub your eyes that way! Do you mean this isn't Potter Street?"

"Id ain'd Boddeh Stritt!"

"Bodder! Bodder! Are you sure?"

"Yeah!" his voice trailed off.

"Bodder, Bother, Botter, try and think!"

"It's Boddeh Stritt!"

"And this isn't it?" she asked hopefully.

"Naaaah!"

"Oh, dear! Oh, dear! What shall we do?"

"Waa!" he wailed, "W'eas mine mama! I wan' mine mama!"

"Now you must stop crying," she scolded again. "You simply must! Where's your handkerchief?"

"Waaa!"

"Oh, dear! How trying you are!" she exclaimed and then as if struck with a new thought, "Wait!" She brightened and began hastily rummaging in her little black bag. "I have something for you!" She brought out a large, yellow banana. "Here!" And when he refused. "Now take it!" She thrust it into his fingers. "You like bananas, don't you?"

"Aaa! I wan' my mama!"

"I'll have to take you to—" she broke off. "I'm going to take you to your mother."

"You ain'd," he wailed. "You ain'd!"

"Yes, I am," she said with a positive nod. "This very moment."

He stared at her incredulously.

"We're going now. Hold your banana tightly!"

XIII

"AND so you live by dis way and dat way and straight from the school?" Mimicking him, the policeman's hand glided about.

The old woman had tricked him. She had led him to a police-station and left him. He had tried to run, but they had caught him. And now he stood weeping before a bare-headed policeman with a gold badge. A helmeted one stood behind him.

"And Boddeh Street is the name and you can't spell it?"

"N-no!"

"Mmm! Boddeh? Body Street, eh? Better look at the map." He pushed himself back from the railing. "Know it?" he inquired of the helmeted one. "Body Street—sounds like the morgue."

"Near the school on Winston Place? Boddeh? Pother? Say, I know where he lives! Barhdee Street! Sure, Barhdee! That's near Parker and Oriol—Alex's beat. Ain't that it?"

"Y-yes." Hope stirred faintly. The other names sounded familiar. "Boddeh Stritt."

"Barhdee Street!" The helmeted one barked good-naturedly. "Be-gob, he'll be havin' me talk like a Jew. Sure!"

"Well!" The bareheaded one sighed. "You were just kiddin' us, weren't ye? But look, we ain't mad. We'll get your mama in a jiffy." He nodded to the helmeted one. "See if he wants to do number one or somethin'? The mess that—last—one made—" His voice trailed off as he moved to the telephone.

"Yep!" The helmeted one patted David on the shoulder. "We could use a matron." And heartily. "C'mon, me boy, yer all roit." And led him under a low archway, past a flight of stairs and into a bleak, bare, high-ceilinged room. Chairs lined the walls. Bars ribbed the tall windows. They stopped before a white door, went into a tiled-floor toilet that reeked with nostril-searing cleanliness. Beside the doorless alcoves, stretched a drab grey slab, corrugated by a dark trickle of water that splashed into the trough below.

"Step up close an' do yer dooty, sonny me boy." He propelled the reluctant David toward the urinal. "C'mon, now. It's recess time. Sure, I've a lad of me own in school." He turned on the faucet in the wash bowl. "And ye do it with yer mittens on! Say, yer all roit! That's the way! Git a good one out o' ye. What would yer mama be sayin, if she found ye were after wetthin yer drawz? This is a divil of a joint, she'd say. What kind of cops are yiz at all? Sure!" He shut off the faucet. "No more'n three shakes, mind ye!"

And David was led out again into the bleak room.

"Any seat in the house, me lad—the winder there—tha-a-ts it. Yer a quiet kid. And we'll page ye the minute yer mother comes. Ther-r-r!" He turned and went out.

Drearily, David gazed about him. The loneliness of the huge room, made ten-fold lonelier by the bare, steep walls, the long rows of vacant chairs sunken in shadow, the barred windows barring in vacancy, oppressed him with a despair so heavy, so final, it numbed him like a drug or a drowsiness. His listless eyes turned toward the window, looked out. Back yards . . . grey scabs of ice . . . on the dead grass . . . ended in a wall of low frame houses, all built of clapboards, all painted a mud-brown, all sawing the sky with a rip-tooth slant of gabled roofs. Shades were half drawn. From all their chimneys smoke unwreathed into the wintry blue.

Time was despair, despair beyond tears. . . . He understood it now, understood it all, irrevocably, indelibly. Desolation had fused into a touchstone, a crystalline, bitter, burred reagent that would never be blunted, never dissolved. Trust nothing. Trust nothing. Trust nothing. Wherever you look, never believe. Whatever anything was or did or said, it pretended. Never believe. If you played hide'n'-go-seek, it wasn't hide'n'-go-seek, it was something else, something sinister. If you played follow the leader, the world turned upside down and an evil face passed through it. Don't play; never believe. The man who had directed him; the old woman who had left him here; the policeman; all had tricked him. They would never call his mother, never. He knew. They would keep him there. That rat cellar underneath. That rat cellar! That boy he had pushed was still. Coffin-box still. They knew it. And they knew about Annie. They made believe they didn't, but they knew. Never believe. Never play. Never believe. Not anything. Everything shifted. Everything changed. Even words. Words, you said. Wanna, you said. I wanna. Yea. I wanna. What? You know what. They were something else, something horrible! Trust nothing. Even sidewalks, even streets, houses, you looked at them. You knew where you were and they turned. You watched them and they turned. That way. Slow, cunning. Trust noth—

On the stairs outside, heavy feet tramped down, accompanied by a rhythmic clacking as if some hollow metal were bouncing against the uprights under the bannister rail—

"C'mon, Steve!" A loud voice dwindled into the room beyond. "Kick in fer a change!"

And a blurred reply met blurred rejoinders and laughter. Then the stalwart rap of dense heels approached. The helmeted one switched on the lights, revealing another beside him, a man in plain clothes, thick-set, lipless and impassive, who swung in his hand a large tin dinner-pail. The new-comer turned quizzically to the helmeted one.

"He did?"

"He did so."

"Well!" ominously.

"A banana that size! And if I hadn't winked me oiyes quicker than a flash, he'd have poked it in like a spoon into a stew!"

"A cop-fighter, hunh?"

"And a bad one, I'm tellin' ye! Me peepers are still watherin'! And he's afther kickin' me in the brisket till I'm blue as me own coat!"

"Hmm! Maybe we better not git 'im any o' dat chawklit cake."

"Well, now!" The helmeted one levered up his helmet to scratch his smoky red hair. "What d' ye think? He's been a good boy, since."

"Iz zat so?"

"Mmm! Quiet as a mouse!"

"Well, 'at makes it different. D'ye like chawklit cake? W'at's 'is name?"

"David. David—er— David himself."

"D'ye like chawklit cake, I ast ye?"

"N-no," fearfully.

"W-a-a-t?" He growled, his eyes narrowing incredulously. "Yuh—don'—like chawklit—cake? Owoo! We gotta keep ye hea den! Dere's no two ways about it!" He uttered a series of terrifying hissing noises by pinching his air-puffed nostrils.

David cringed.

"He don' like chawk—"

"Whisht!" The helmeted one kicked the other's heel. "Sure he does! It's nothin' but a bit o' shoiness that's kaipin' him from—"

"I wan' my mama!" David had begun to whimper. "I wan' my mama! Mama!"

"Arrh!" The helmeted one exploded. "Now look what yev started, ye divil of a flat-foot! Torturin' 'im for nothin' at all. Froitinin' him out of his wits the way he'll never know his own mother when he see's 'er!"

"Who me?" Faint amusement puffed his lip out. "W'y I hardly looked at 'im cock-eyed. Wat're yuh talkin' about!"

"It's yer ugly mug that does it! Go on with ye! None o' yer guff!" He pushed the other man out of the room. "Don't mind him me lad! He's nothin but a harmless bull bellowin' t' hear himself bellow! God mend 'im! We'll get ye yer mother an' yer chawklit cake too! Never fear! Now you be quiet like a good lad!" He grinned, followed the other man out.

"Mama!" He moaned. "Mama! Mama!"

It was true! All that he feared was true. They would keep him there—Keep him there always! They would never call his mother! And now that he knew, it was too late. He had learned never to trust too late. He lowered his head and sobbed.

We-e-e-e-e-e!

From somewhere a whistle began blowing—a remote, thin blast that suddenly opened into a swooping screech and as suddenly died away.

Whistles? He raised his head. Factory whistles! The others? None! Too far! So far she was. So far away! —But she heard them—she heard the other whistles that he couldn't hear. The whistles he heard in the summer time. She heard them now. Maybe she looked out of the window—now—this moment! Looked down into the street, up and down the street, searched, called. There he was— outside—on the curb. Be two Davids, be two! One here, one outside on the curb. Now watch! Wait till she looks out! Now watch! See? There she is behind the curtain. Yes, that thick lace curtain—only in the winter it was there. Now she parts them—two hands like that—stoops. See? Her face close to the pane. Cold. And, wrrrr! Up! Bet a shawl is on her. David! David! Come up! Why do you wait? Because! Why? She would have forgotten. That—

that door, mama. Oh, she'd laugh. Silly one! Come up!
I'll wait! And then he'd stand on the stoop. One-two-three.
Till she crossed the frontroom. One. Two. Three and the
kitchen. And then go in. Mama? Yes, I'm here, she'd call
down, Yes, come on! Run past the door. Bing! No. Not
run if she's there. Be there too quick. One step and one
step. Two steps and two steps. Three steps and—

"Hurhmm!"

Chuckling the helmeted one butted through the mist
of dreaming. "Is it the mounted pollies y'are with that
leg up?"

David gaped at him without answering. About him
vision tumbled into chaos.

"Or a fly-cop on his wheel?" He continued, manipulating imaginary handle-bars. "What were ye chasin'? One
o' thim noo Stootzes? But look what oiv got fer ye." He
uncurled beefy red paws—a square of brown chocolate
cake in one and a red apple in the other. "How does that
suit ye?"

He began crying again.

"Hey—! Arrrh, yer a quair one! Here I've gone an' got
ye chawklit cake—in a beer saloon of all the damn
places—an' gotten ye apples, and there y'are cryin' all
over the precinct! What's the matter?"

"W-w-w'istles!" he wailed. "W-wistles!"

"Whistles?

"Yeaa-a-aow!"

"Is it a whistle yer after?" He made a motion toward
his pocket.

"N-n-o-o-o! B-blowin'!"

"Me?"

"No-o-o! My—my mama! Ow!"

"Orrch! Fergit it. Here's a foin bit o' cake fer ye.
C'mon! Take it! And the apple. That's the way! Forst ye
eat one and then the other! Anhann! And I'll git ye a sup
o' wawther and ye'll be as snug as—No!" He bawled.

David had dropped both the cake and the apple. A
voice! A voice he never hoped to hear again. A voice!
He stared at the doorway rigid with hope.

"Now look what yev—" He stopped, turned round.

A light tread hurried toward them. Out of the slow
blur of a myriad meaningless faces, one condensed into
all meaning.

"David! David!"

"Mama!" He screamed leaping toward her. "Mama! Mama! Mama!"

She caught him up in her arms, moaning, pressed his cheek against her cold one. "David, beloved! David!"

"Mama! Mama!" The screaming of her name was itself sheer, stark ecstasy, but all bliss was outplumbed in the clasping of her neck.

"Well yer safe now be the looks of it," came the voice at his back.

Still pressing him to her, she carried him into the outer room where the bareheaded one leaned against the rail watching them.

"Hmm, I see he knows his mama."

"T-tanks so—so viel!" she stammered.

"Oh, that's all right, lady. Glad to have a visitor once in a while. It's pretty quiet here."

"And lady," the helmeted one came up, "I'm thinkin' ye'd best put a tag on him, fer he sure had us up a tree with his Pother an' Body an' Powther! Now ye spell it bee—ay—"

"T'anks so viel!" she repeated.

"Oh!" He smiled crookedly, nodded. "Yer acquainted with it."

The other man rested the corner of a grin on his finger nail.

"Now oi'll tell ye an odd thing, Lieutenant," said the helmeted one. "He's after plaguin' me about a whistle. Now it's an odd thing I tell ye—would make a man be thinkin'. He said to me, he said. I'm after hearin' me own mother's whistle. Now would ye believe it? And she still a good ways off!"

"Did he?" The bareheaded man snorted with amusement. "The only whistle I heard was the four-ten over at Chandler crossing, and that was about—"

"Er—" his mother began timidly. "Herr—Mister. Ve—er—ve go?"

"Oh certainly, lady! Just walk right out any time." He opened his arms in a flowing gesture. "He's all yours."

"T-tanks." She said gratefully and turned to go.

"Hey, hold on a minute!" The helmeted one pursued them. "Would ye be leavin' us without yer cake?" He

pried it into David's hand. "And yer apple? No? Too
much? Well, I'll kaip it fer ye till ye drop around
again. Good-bye! And don't ye go runnin' after telegraph
poles!"

XIV

THE doorway out! Freedom! The cold air of the street.
The sky tightening with dusk. And she, carrying him, her
face close to his! Things he never hoped to see again,
bliss he never hoped to feel! Deliverance too enormous
even to grasp!

"How did you—?" She stopped. "Do you want me to
carry you, darling?"

"No, I can walk, Mama! I can walk, Mama! Mama!
Mama!" The magic in the word seemed inexhaustible, gave
him new strength. He laughed at the sheer joy of the
sound.

She set him down. And hand in hand they walked as
rapidly as his pace permitted.

"We're not very far," she informed him, "though far
enough for a weary child. Now tell me, how did you ever
stray into that place? How did you get there?"

"Somebody was chasing me, Mama, and I ran and I ran
and I ran." Claws of sudden fear grazed him. "Is he still?"

"Still? Who? Who was chasing you?"

"Yussie. And—and the other boys. They called me cry-
baby—crybaby because—Papa—hit—hit me. Yussie—he
told."

"He didn't tell me that."

"Is he—is he still, Mama?"

"What do you mean?"

"I only—only pushed because he was running after me.
Mama, I didn't want to make him still."

"Oh! That boy? There's nothing wrong with him."

"No?" He bounded before her electrified with relief.
"No? I didn't? Mama-a-a!"

"Did you think you hurt him, you silly one?"

"I didn't! I didn't! I didn't!" he cheered, "Oooh, I didn't do anything!"

"No. Except to frighten me to death! But why didn't you run upstairs if they were chasing you? Hymie said you ran inside. Where did you go?"

"Is this where we live?" They had turned a corner and he scanned the darkening street. "Doesn't look like—?"

"No. Several blocks yet. Are you tired?"

"No mama!"

"We must hurry then or Albert will be there before us. He won't know what's happened to us when he comes into an empty house."

"Who told you?"

"What?"

"Where I was."

"A policeman."

"Were you scared?"

"I was frantic!"

"Because the policeman?"

"No, because of you, silly child! I had just rushed weeping into the street when I met him."

"A real policeman? For me? Did he tell you how—how to come?"

"He wrote it down for me. And people on the way directed me. He has it, that master in there."

"Oh."

"Yes! Now you tell me! First where did you go? Did you hide somewhere and run out again? What kept you from coming up?"

"I—I went—down—I went down in the cellar." Buoyancy seeped out of him. His voice ended dully.

"The cellar?" She stopped in mid-stride to look down at him. "Of all the strange places! Why did you go there?"

"I don't know—I don't know. I wanted to—to hide from the—the policeman. Mama!" He suddenly whimpered in terror. "Mama!"

"What? What is it, sweet." She gripped his hand. "Do you feel ill?"

"N-no." He was wrestling feebly with himself. "N-no."

"Frightened again? That cellar? I can't understand why you'd want to go down—Oh, but let's wait! Later, darling? You'll tell me?" They walked rapidly awhile in silence. "Are you warm?"

"Yes."

"What did you do there? In that—in that—Ach! I can't say it! With the police?"

"They made me sit down. And first—first they took me to the toilet. And then the big policeman gave me the apple. And then the cake."

"That's a handsome cake!" She smiled down at him. "An American one. I couldn't bake it myself. Do you know where you are now?"

He looked around at the twilit street. "We went a lot of blocks," he said tentatively.

"Yes. But that street, that next one?"

He shook his head. In the thickening gloom, the street ahead looked as alien as any he had passed.

"That's Boddeh Street," she informed him. "Your school is that way, further off. But it's too dark to see. Now two—three blocks that way—" She pointed to the left— "is where we live."

"That way, Mama?" He stared incredulously. "This way!" He pointed to the right. "This way is my school."

"That's why you were lost! It's the other way."

"O-o-h!" A new wonder dragged him to a halt. "It—it's turning, Mama! It's turning round—back."

"What?" Her tone was amused. "The street?"

"Yes! They stopped! Just now! The school—The school is over there now!"

"So it is. The streets turn, but you—not you! Little God!" Chuckling, she stooped, kissed him. "We must hurry, though! I left no word and it's dark. If he gets there before we do, he'll—" She broke off nervously. "Come!"

They crossed the street, turned their backs against the twilight and hurried into darkness. Lamps were already lit, street lamps, windows. They had met almost no one during their entire journey, and now against the wintry vacancy and the dark, David listened with immense gratitude to the click of his mother's heels that measured the quicker shuffle-tripping of his own. Suppose he were alone? Heard only his own slight footsteps wrenched from the grip of quiet? Suppose his father—? No! He shivered, added the middle finger of his mother's hand to the two he already held.

They neared the open lot. He knew where he was now, certain of every step. There was a wind that prowled over that area of rock and dead grass, that would spring at them when they passed it. And the wind did. He squinted into it. Beyond the patch of rock and dead grass, a bright rind of moon barely cleared the roof tops. He watched it till the next house over-took it and then looked away. A vague apprehension came over him. An hour ago, had he been by some miracle transplanted to this spot, he would have rushed home screaming for joy. But now, each familiar house that he passed—here was the one with the leaning palings; this was yellow long-boards in daylight and had a railed-in porch, this was brick and had an odd veined transom over the door—each was nearer home. And home—His fears reared up again. And suddenly he wished himself—but with his mother beside him —twice as far away as when they had left the police station.

"After next block, Mama?" He knew perfectly well how far his own house lay.

"Yes." She was staring ahead eagerly.

"You know where the next street is, Mama?" He motioned to the side. "Over this way?"

"Yes."

"I saw the—that box and those carriages."

"Did you?"

"Yes. Are they going to—to move out now—You think?"

"I don't know, darling. Perhaps they own the house. Why do you ask?"

He was silent a moment and then, "Is Papa home?"

"I hope not."

"You—you—are you going to say—tell him?"

"What? Where you've been? Why of course!"

"Aaaaa!" His head dropped resentfully.

"What's the matter?" She tugged his arm gently. "Don't you want me to?"

"I— I thought you wouldn't tell if—if we came home first—just before."

"Why no, I was worried about Albert, that's all. Are you afraid about having him know?"

"I— I was in a- a p'lice station—that's why."

"Well, what if you were? You've done nothing. Oh, you silly child! Being lost is no crime. Though I could blame others if I chose!"

There was a tight sound of restrained anger in her voice though David knew it was not directed against him.

"You wont let him h-hit me?"

"Tt! Darling, I'll never let him strike you again—neither he nor anyone if I can help it. There, are you satisfied? Now don't be afraid any longer!"

David walked in silence awhile, mind reassured, heart not yet free from doubt.

"Mr. Luter— Mr. Luter isn't going to come?"

"To-night? No." Her pace slackened slightly. "What makes you think of that?"

"Will he come here, Mama? Come here anymore?"

"Why —Well— I don't—" From confusion her voice condensed into suddenness. "Why do you ask?"

"I—I don't like him. That's why."

"Oh, is that it?" She was silent a moment. And though they had entered their own block, her pace instead of quickening, slackened even more. When she spoke again, her voice was strangely cautious. "Did—did anyone else frighten you, beloved? Anyone else beside those bad boys?"

"N-no." He felt his mind sharpen now, watchful. "No. Nobody else."

"You're sure? You—you saw nobody? Nothing that would frighten you?"

"I—I only saw the boys. And Yussie told them, and then they all began to—to chase me."

"Of course. I'm glad there was nothing else. God knows that was enough!"

Her pace quickened again. Without eagerness, David singled out his own house among the dark ones. It struck him as odd that he should only have noticed now and at night that his house had a flat and not a gabled roof. They lived under the roof then, Hymie and Annie. Suppose Annie had looked out of the window when he made his mother look out in the police station. Suppose she was there now watching him! He shuddered, looked away.

"In our block, the first stores, Mama—the first stores begin."

"Yes . . . And tell me, will I still have to stand in the hallway when you go down? Or have you seen how little there is to fear in cellars?"

"No!" Fear lunged within him. "No, Mama! You'll have to wait—always!"

"How desperate you sound!"

"And I'm not going to play with—with anybody! Any more!"

"You're not?"

"No! Never!"

He could feel his lips pouting despite himself, stretching out as if to loosen the tears. Another moment and he would have wept, but the hallway door was before him now, and now his mother pressed it open. Imperious terror dispersed his tears. He entered—thrust of warmth of the gaslit hallway, stagnant air suffused with the dusty, torpid odor of carpets. The cellar door was brown—closed again. For an instant he wondered whether he or another had shut it, but could not recall. Fear printed on his back and breast the cold, metallic squares of a wiry net. He shrank against his mother, clung to her till they mounted the carpeted stairs. She seemed not to have noticed.

"If he's in," she murmured aloud, "he'll be distraught! After what I said to him last night! Hurry! He'll think I've— But why not?" She appeared suddenly to remember. "Why won't you play?"

"I don't—" He faltered dully, evasively. "I don't want to." It no longer mattered.

She hurried up the stairs, tarried a moment at the landing till he reached her and then tried the door. Unlocked, it yielded—gave upon darkness. Alarm tightened her features. She entered.

"Albert!"

There was no answer . . . Only the soft shifting of embers in the stove. For a weird, spinning instant, David, lingering on the threshold, visualized his father gone, miraculously, forever gone.

"Albert!" She was groping toward the wall where the match-safe hung. "Albert!"

"Unh!" His startled groan came from the bedroom. "You? Genya!" For once his voice was stripped of harshness, stripped of pride, power, was nothing but a cry such as David might have uttered, alone in the dark, despairing. "Genya!"

"Oh! Thank God, you're here!"

"Yes . . ." And the harshness returned and the inflexible

pride, and the voice was again his father's, awakened, surly. "Hmph! Where else would I be?"

She had struck a match and now she lit the mantle-light.

"I tried so hard to get back before you arrived! Were you worried?"

"I?" Deliberate, again, sardonic. "No . . . And so you decided to return did you? Even the fixed word wavers, eh? In the cold? In the empty streets at ni—"

"Return? Albert, what are you saying! I never went!" She hurried up the front room stairs. "Shut the door, David, darling! Take off your coat! Sit down!" She went inside. "I feared you'd think—!" And her voice was suddenly lowered.

David shed his coat, found a chair and listened morosely to the sounds in the bed-room. From the drift of the occasional words, snatches of phrases, exclamations that rose like crests above their low tones, he knew their conversation was not only about him, but about the night before. His mother was explaining, he guessed, where she had been, why she had gone. Of Luter, he could hear no mention made. He divined that no mention would be made. Finally, his father exclaimed in an impatient voice:

"Well, you've said enough! I take your word for it! That son of yours has to be watched day and night!"

"But it wasn't his fault, Albert!"

"Mine then? Is that what you mean. Are you hinting that I'm to blame?"

"No! No! No! It's the fault of no one! You're right, there's no more to say! Are you hungry?"

"Naturally."

"I've made that veal the way you like it. And those shredded carrots. Do you want them to-night?"

"Hmm."

David could hear her moving toward the frontroom, open the window. A few seconds later, she appeared, carrying two covered pots.

"To bed early to-night." She came down, smiling solicitously. "To forget early."

Silently, on stockinged feet, his father loomed into the threshold. His vest was unbuttoned, the neck-band of his shirt open on the pit of the strong, corded neck. Gripping the doorpost with lank, ink-spotted fingers, he blinked at the light, and then regarded David gloomily.

"And so you're acquainted with the police now?"

David dropped his gaze. He hadn't seen his father since last night when he was beaten. The face was still the face of a foe.

"Yes!" His mother laughed, looking round from the stove. "But in friendship only! Wait till I show you the cake they gave him. It's in my pocket-book."

"They gave him cake, eh?"

To David there was something peculiarly significant in the way his father uttered the words.

"Yes," she continued cheerfully. "And how they must have laughed at my English!"

"How did you ever let him get so far? You're always watching after him."

"I don't know. He was gone before I thought to look."

"Hmm!" He glanced at David, reached for the newspaper on the table, became engrossed.

His mother lifted a bunch of carrots from a bag, dropped them into a dishpan and while she pared them, eyed David, fondly.

He was silent, met her gaze a moment and then vacantly tightened the table cloth against the table's edge.

—*Don't believe Don't believe. Don't believe. Never!*

XV

ON SUNDAY, David stayed in bed the whole morning, and then, dressed, spent the rest of the day in-doors. He had sneezed several times last night and again this morning, and what with his back aching—which David was sure ached for other reasons—his mother maintained that he might have caught a cold as a result of wandering through the streets. His father scoffed at the idea, but refrained from interfering. Although it meant having to be near his father all day, David was grateful not to have to face Yussie or Annie or the boy he pushed or anyone in fact. He clung to his mother or retreated to his bedroom, avoided the room his father was in, and in general, made himself as inconspicuous as possible. Toward evening, however, the dark forced him into the kitchen together with his father. Whereupon he fetched out his box of trinkets, found a corner least in the way, and sitting down on the linoleum floor, began constructing with the odds and ends that filled the box a zig-zag and precarious tower which his father's or mother's tread invariably sent toppling down.

During the late afternoon and even until supper-time, his father had several times confidently remarked that Luter would come to his senses, forego this folly of hunting for a wife and eventually appear at the table in time for the meal . . . However, though they waited almost an hour past the usual time, he never came. It was only when David's mother began to complain mildly that half her cooking was over-done and the other half cold, that he gave up waiting, and shrugging his shoulders in brusque irritation, permitted her to serve the meal.

"In Tysmenicz," he scowled sourly as he settled into a chair, "the peasant who tended my—" (There was always that hitch in his speech before the word) "my father's cattle used to say that a man had to be born a fool to be one. My friend Luter should come on his second childhood early in years—God's given him a new soul." He pulled the plate toward him with abrupt impatience. "All I hope is he doesn't blame my married happiness for his marriage!" He uttered the last words with a peculiar challenging emphasis.

David who was watching his mother as she stood above her husband serving him, saw her bosom swell up slowly as though responding to minute increments of pain, and then without response, exhaled tautly her muted breath and look off blankly and resigned. David himself knew only one thing—that the relief Luter's absence afforded him was as sharp and fervent as a prayer, and that every wordless nerve begged never to see the man again.

At bed-time, his mind seemed strangely calm, reposed without being resolved, inert after long discord. Beneath the film of apathy, the events of yesterday ruffled the surface only rarely, like the tardy infrequent wreckage of a ship long sunken. They would never be answered these questions of why his mother had let Luter do what Annie had tried to do; why she hadn't run away the second time as she had the first; why she hadn't told his father; or had she; or didn't he care. Nor would there ever be the equilibrium again between his knowing what she had done and her unawareness that he knew; her unawareness of what he had done with Annie, of why he had run away; his father's unawareness of every thing. They would never be solved, never be answered. No one would say anything, no one dared, no one could. Just don't believe, don't believe, never. But when would that queer weight, that odd something lodged in his bosom, that was so spiny, ramified, reminding, when would that vanish? Tomorrow, maybe? Maybe tomorrow.

Tomorrow came. Monday. The cold of the day before had either been imaginary or been thrown off. David was sent to school. Once out of the house, he walked guardedly, even taking a new route to avoid meeting Annie or Yussie. In the morning, he succeeded and again at noon, but when school was out for the day, they ran into him as he came out into the open of the crossing. David, himself, shrank away when they hailed him, but they on the other hand seemed to have forgotten all hostilities. Instead they were merely curious.

"W'od id 'ey do t'yuh in de polliss station?" Yussie engaged his arm to keep him in step with the slower limping Annie.

"Nutt'n'!" He shook him off sullenly. "Lemme go!"

"Hey, yuh mad?" Yussie looked surprised.

"Yea, I'm mad! I'll never get glad!"

"He's mad, Annie!"

"Nisht gefiddled!" she said spitefully. "Pooh! Who wants yuh!"

"Cry baby!" said Yussie disdainfully.

But David was already hurrying off.

At home, he could not help but observe in his mother's actions a concealed nervousness, an irresolution as if under the strain of waiting. Unlike the fluent, methodical way in which she habitually moved about the kitchen, her manner now was disjointed, uncertain. In the midst of doing something or of saying something, she would suddenly utter a curious, suppressed exclamation like a sudden groan of dismay, or lift her hand in an obscure and hopeless gesture, or open her eyes as though staring at perplexity and brush back her hair. Everything she did seemed insecure and unfinished. She went from the sink to the window and left the water running and then remembering it was an odd overhastiness, turned, missed the handkerchief she was pegging to the clothesline and let it fall into the yard. A few minutes later, separating the yolks from the whites of the eggs to make the thick yellow pancakes that were to go with the soup, she cut the film of the yolk with eggshell, lost it in the whites. She stamped her foot, chirped with annoyance and brushed back her hair.

"I'm like my father," she exclaimed suddenly. "Vexation makes my scalp itch! Today you can learn what kind of a woman not to marry."

Several times during the afternoon, David had been on the point of asking her whether Luter were coming for supper. But something always checked him and he never formed the question.

To avoid the strange emotion, that his mother's behavior aroused in him, he would have gone downstairs again, even at the risk of encountering Annie or Yussie, but there again, he divined how impatient she would be if he asked her to wait in the hallway. She had seemed cross when he called to her frantically after his meeting with them at three. As she offered no objections he remained indoors and occupied himself in a score of ways—now frightening himself by making faces at the pier glass, now staring out of the window, now fingering the haze of breath upon it, now crawling under beds, now scribbling. He spent an hour tying himself to the bed post with a bit of washline and attempting to escape, and another constructing strange devices with his trinkets. He tried to play the four-handed game of manipulating patterns out of a double string with two hands and the leg of a chair. It was difficult, the old patterns slipped before they were clinched, ended in a snarl. The mind too was tangled, apprehensive, pent-up.

Meanwhile he had observed that his mother's nervousness was increasing. She seemed neither able to divert her mind nor complete any task other than was absolutely necessary. She had begun to sew the new linen she had bought to make pillow-cases with and had ended by ripping out the thread and throwing the cloth back into the drawer with a harassed cry. "God knows why I can't make these stitches any shorter! Six to a yard almost! They'd have parted with a shroud's wear!" And then later, gave up the attempt to thread a cupful of large red beads and dropped them into the cup again and shut her eyes. The newspaper received only a worried glance and was folded up again and dropped in her lap. After which, she sat for such a long time staring at him, that David's uneasiness grew intolerable. His eyes fluttered hurriedly about the room, searching for something that might distract the fixity of that stare. And grazing the coal sack beside the stove, the seams of the ceiling, the passover dishes on top of the china closet, sink legs, garbage pail, doorhinges, chandelier, lighted on the mantle burning with its soft, bluish flame.

"Mama!" He made no attempt to conceal the anxiety in his voice.

Her lids flickered. She who was always near him in spirit, now seemed hardly aware. "What?"

"Why does that light—that light in the mantle stay inside? In the mantle?"

She looked up, combed her upper lip with her teeth a moment. "That's because there are great brains in the world."

"But it breaks all up," he urged her attention closer. "All up if you—if you even just blow."

"Yes."

"It doesn't burn even when you light it?"

"No." The dull remote tone never left her voice—as if speech were mechanical, forced.

"Why?" He demanded desperately. "Why doesn't it?"

"Doesn't what? I don't know." She rose, shivered suddenly. "As though it pierced the marrow! Is it cold in here? Or where I sit? Chill?" And stared at the stove, then followed her gaze after a long pause as if her very thought were delayed, and picked up the poker.

"I don't feel cold." David reminded her sullenly.

But she hadn't heard him. Instead her eyes had swerved from his face to the wall and she stood as if listening beyond him, as if she had heard a sound in the hallway outside. No one. She shook her head. And still with the poker in one hand, lifted the other to adjust the gas-cock under the mantle-light—

"Ach!" Exasperatedly she flung her hand down to her side. "Where are my senses? What am I doing?" She crouched down before the stove, buried the poker into the ashes with a provoked stab. "Have you ever seen your mother so mixed? So lost? God have mercy, my wits are milling! Ach! I go here and I'm there! I go there and I'm here. And of a sudden I'm nowhere." She lifted the stove lid, threw a shovel-ful of coal into the red pit. "David darling, you were saying—?" Her voice had become solicitous, penitent. She smiled. "You were saying what? Light? Why what?"

Heartened by her new interest, he began again eagerly. "What makes it burn?"

"The gas? Gas of course?"

"Why?"

"One lights it—with a match. And then—Er. And then—" As abruptly as her mood had changed a moment ago, it reverted again. That odd look of strain spindled the corners of her eyes, her face resumed that hunted, alert look. "And then one turns—the—the—". She broke off. "Only a moment, darling! I'm going into the front room."

That was the end! He wasn't going to talk to her any more! He wasn't going to ask her anything. No, even if she talked to him, he wouldn't answer. Sullenly, he slumped down into his chair and sullenly watched her hurry up the steps into darkness . . . heard the window slide open, softly, cautiously . . . and then close again . . . She came down.

"Not even the cold air can rouse me." Her fingers drummed nervously on the ridge of a chair. "Nothing does any good. My head is—Oh, I'm sorry, David, beloved! I'm sorry! I didn't mean to run off in the middle of answering you." She came over, bent down and kissed him. "Do you forgive me?"

Unappeased, he regarded her in steady silence.

"Offended? I shan't do it again! I promise!" Where the broad waxen plane of her cheeks curved into the chin, small dents of contrition appeared—the very furthest away a smile could get from the distracted brown eyes, the creased brow. She shook herself. "Er . . . Burns, you said. Burns! Everything burns! Yes! Or almost. Kerosene, coal, wood, candles, paper, almost everything. And so gas—at least I think so. Er . . . And so gas, you see?

They keep it in great vats, you know. Some tall—like the ash-cans out in the street, some short, like drums, only bigger. I don't understand them."

"But mama!" He wasn't going to permit her to pause; she would fade back into her old mood if he did. "Mama! Water doesn't burn when you throw a match in a puddle."

"Puttle?" she repeated. "What is puttle? Your Yiddish is more than one-half English now. I'm being left behind."

"Puddle. It's water—in the street—when it rains sometimes."

"Oh! Water. No, tears sometimes—No! You're right. Water doesn't burn."

"Is there always a—something burning—when it's light —like that!"

"Yes I think so. When I was a girl, the goyim built an 'altar' near a town some distance from Veljish because two peasants saw a light among the trees—yet nothing burning."

"What's a—what you said? Altar?" It was his turn to be puzzled. "Means old man?"

"No!" She laughed shortly. "An altar is a broad stone —about so high." Her downturned palms impatiently leveled the air at bosom's height. "They have a flat top. So. And because the ground was holy, they fenced it in."

"Because why? They saw a light and—and nothing burned? So that was holy?"

"Yes. So it pleased them to say. I suppose that was because Moses too saw a tree on fire that didn't burn. And there the gound was also holy."

"Oh."

"Yes. And when you begin going to cheder you'll know more about these things than I do." She stopped pacing, moved abruptly toward the china-closet. "I think I'll set the table—do something."

"Was it holy?" He drew her on.

"What? The light the peasants saw? Ach, nonsense! My father said that the truth was an old Jewess had been walking along the road through the woods. Where she was coming from I don't know—"

She paused again. Three plates had been taken from the china closet and set on the table. The fourth, still in her hand, kept fluttering back and forth as though it were impossible for her to decide whether to set it on the table or to replace it on the stack she had taken it from. Finally, with a throat exclamation, she set it on the table—before the chair on which Luter usually sat.

"Yes! So! Oh!" Her head went back as if returning thought were an impact. "Yes. Coming home, she was. Without doubt. And on the way, dusk overtook her. Yes. It was Friday. Now it chanced that she had candles with her—or so my father said, though he never said why. Perhaps she foresaw that she would be delayed. There's no telling what women will do when they're pious." Her lips pressed together and she reddened ever so faintly setting the clinking silverware beside Luter's plate. "She foresaw. Let us say, she foresaw. And with night coming on, she stopped beside the road and lit the candles and prayed over them as you've seen me pray. And having prayed, went on, leaving them lit—a Jew may not tamper with the candles once they're burning and the prayer said. Then these peasants came along at night. And devout as she or more perhaps—" With a slight, spattering sound from the end of her lip, one cheek eddied in; she set the cup and saucer above Luter's plate. "And perhaps drunk or surely dull-witted, saw the light in the woods—so my father said—and ran back and roused the village. They saw it and saw it vanish, and approaching, found nothing, heard nothing, only the sound of the woods. What more could they want? Priests came and high priests and consecrated the place." Her eyes, momentarily meditative, kindled again, whisked to the door. She was listening again.

"Didn't the candles leave another candle?" David strove to force her attention back again. "Like our candles? It's water and candles."

She shrugged impatiently. "Who bothered to look? The ground was holy; people soon remembered having seen angels; and there's an end. And why hunt for candle-drippings. The altar did the village a mass of good."

"How?"

"People, benighted ones, they came from all over Austria. They brought their sick, their maimed. They asked aid, they prayed for the dead and for better fortune. And they still do. And—" She paused, almost losing the thread, but regained it with a jolt. "While they were there, they had to eat, they had to buy things, they had to sleep somewhere. Fear not, those little candles kindled the day for the storekeepers in Lagronow. You see?"

"Yes, mama."

"So much did they benefit Lagronow that Jews, merchants, in other villages also left a burning candle here or there. It never succeeded again."

"But that wasn't a real one," he reminded her. "That wasn't a real light. And—and without burning. But Moses, he—"

"Sh!" Sudden and sharp her warning.

David listened: The quick creak of the outer doorway. The slow and heavy footfall, carpet-muffled. That was his father's way, a thrust of impatience followed by deliberation.

His mother, looking very pale, had opened the door a crack and stood there with one ear pressed against it. No sound of voices drifted up, no interweaving of a second footfall. She drew back, staring, shut the door carefully, sighed, but whether out of relief or apprehension, there was no telling, then stood attentive, waiting for him to enter.

In a few seconds, he did, and David knew by the very way the door swung open that his father was irritated. He came in—alone. The muscles under the dark jaws were bumpy, distinct, like cords twisted about and bulging. His eyes held a steady glower.

"Albert." She smiled.

He made no answer, but breathing gustily, stripped off his coat—the jacket beneath always peeled with it—and removed his hat and handed them to her.

"I hope you haven't prepared too much supper," he began brusquely as he whipped his tie and collar off. "He wouldn't come. Do you hear?" She had gone into David's bedroom to hang up his coat.

"Yes." Her voice preceded her. "I can use what's left over. There's no loss—especially in the winter—nothing spoils."

"Hm!" He turned his back to her, rolled up his sleeves and bent over the sink. "And don't prepare anything extra for him to-morrow. He's not coming then either." The squeezed soap slipped clacking into the sink. His teeth ground as he picked it up.

"No?" Her eyes, resting on his bent back opened in a

worried flicker; her face sagged. But the next moment her
voice was as barely surprised as a voice dared be and yet
be non-committal. "What's the matter?"

"Would I had known as little of him as I know his reasons!" He slapped his dripping palms angrily against his
lean neck. "He wouldn't say anything! He wouldn't even
ride home with me—had to go somewhere—some lame
excuse! And that marriage-broker affair! Not a word! As
though it had never been! As though he had never spoken
about it! He took the keys from me in the morning,
checked my overtime, and that was all!" He shut the water
off with a wrathful jerk, snatched the towel. "God knows
what he's found or done or achieved! It's too much for me!
But why, tell me?" The towel paused in its swirling. "Do
you think that if he found a woman who thought he was
agreeable and had—she, I mean—a great deal of money,
do you think that that might have given him a wry neck?"

A faint, troubled groan ushered in her answer. "I
don't know, Albert."

"Now be honest!" He suddenly swung the towel into
a ball, glared and thrust his lips out. "Answer me with a
brunt!"

"What is it, Albert?" She lifted startled, fending hands.
"What is it?"

Seeing her alarm, David squirmed back into his chair
and watched them apprehensively under the rims of lowered eyes.

"I—" his father broke off, bit his lip. "Was anything
said by—by me? Did I seem to be mocking him—when
was it?—Friday night? When I told you he was going to
a marriage broker?"

"Why, no, Albert!" Her body seemed to slacken. "No!
Not at all! You said nothing that would offend any one!
I thought he was amused!"

"You're sure? You're sure he didn't leave so early because I—because of some jest I made?"

"No. You said nothing out of the way."

"Unh! I thought I hadn't! Well, what fiend is it that
eggs him on then? He was like a man with a secret
grudge. He wouldn't speak! He wouldn't look at me
straight. A man I've known for months! A man who's
been here night after night!" He pulled a chair toward
him, slumped into it. "At noon today, he ate his lunch

with that Paul Zeeman. He knows I hate the man. He did that to hurt me. I know!"

"But—don't—don't let that upset you, Albert. I mean, don't take offense at that! It's—why—" She laughed nervously—"It's too much like a school-girl's device—this—this eating with another."

"Is it?" he asked sarcastically. "Much you know about it! You haven't seen him all day. It wasn't only that! There were other things! I tell you there's something seething in that skull of his! A hatred, for some mad reason! A vengeance biding its time! Do you know?" He suddenly drew back, looked up at her with narrowed, suspicious eyes. "You don't seem dismayed—you don't seem down-cast enough!"

"Why, Albert!" She flinched before his harsh scrutiny. "I *am* dismayed! I *am* down-cast. But what can I do? My only hope is that this—this hostility—or what one may call it—is—is only temporary! What can it be? For a time perhaps! Something worrying him that he won't disclose! Why, it may be all over by to-morrow!"

"Yes. It may indeed! Something may! But my belief is that no man would become a stranger to me overnight unless he thought I had wronged him. Isn't that so? And he—he's worse than a stranger—he's a foe! Avoiding me as if the sight of my face were a stab! Looking past me darkly! Ha! It's more than something transient! It's—what's the matter?"

She was pale. With the glass pitcher in one hand, she strained vainly with the other to open the tap of the faucet. "I can't open it, Albert! You must have shut it too tightly when you washed. I want some water for the table."

"Are you weak suddenly?" He rose, strode sourly to the sink, twisted the tap open—"And as for him," He stared ominously at the gushing water. "If he doesn't change, he'd better be careful! He'll find that I can change even more!"

There was a pause, a gathering of strain. Silently his mother set the pitcher on the table, went to the stove and began ladling out the steaming yellow pea-soup into the bowls. Stray drops that fell from the brown pancakes as she transferred them from the pot to the dishes hissed over the stove lids. The odor was savory.

But David, glancing hurriedly at his father's gloomy face, resolved to eat more carefully than he had ever eaten in his life. So far these sombre eyes had scarcely rested on him; now he felt himself trying to contract within himself to vanish from their ken. And failing, concentrated on the frosted moisture of the glass pitcher and how each drop awaited ripeness before it slid.

His father reached for the bread—it seemed to ease the strain. Relieved, David glanced up. His mother came near, her face strangely sorrowful and brooding, incongruous somehow, dissociated completely from her task of carrying a platter of soup. She set it down before his father, and straightening, touched his shoulder timidly.

"Albert!"

"Hm?" He stopped chewing, twirled the spoon he had just picked up.

"Perhaps I should ask you this after supper when your mind is easier, but—"

"What?"

"You—you won't do anything rash? Please! I beg you!"

"I'll know what to do when the hour falls," he answered darkly. "Don't let that trouble you."

In spite of himself, David started. Against a sudden screen of darkness he had seen a dark roof, a hammer brandished over pale and staring cobbles.

"Pouh!" his father snorted, lowering his spoon. "Salt? Don't you use that any more?"

"Not salted? I'm sorry Albert! Everything I've done today has gone awry—even the soup!" She laughed desperately. "I'm a good cook!"

"What should trouble *you* so much?" His sharp gaze rested on David. "Has he been lost again or up to some new madness?"

"No! No! Not him—! Begin eating, child! Not him! I don't know! Nothing I did today had my eyes and my wits in the doing. Every hour brought some fresh confusion. It was one of those fateful days that make people superstitious. There's a handkerchief in the yard this very moment. Who knows what made me drop it!"

His father shrugged. "At least you were alone. There was no watching you! No one prodding you with his eyes into blunders."

"You mean—him again?"

"Yes! Him! Twice I didn't feed the sheet into the press just so. They wrinkled, crushed! The underpad was inked! I was ten minutes each time cleaning them! I tell you he gloated! I saw him!" He stopped eating, hammered the spoon on the table. "There's evil brewing inside him! He's waiting, waiting for something! I could feel his eyes on my back all day, but never there when I turned to face him! It took my mind off my work! I fed the press as though I were lame! I couldn't have done worse the first day I began! Now too soon! Now too late! Now just missing! And then the mussed paper caught in the roller —in the gummy ink. I had to take the whole thing apart! And every minute the feeling that he was watching me. Ha!" He breathed harshly. His lips writhed back and his words battered against the barred teeth. "It's more than I can bear! It's more than I'll stand! If he's waiting for something, he'll get it!"

"Albert!" She had stopped eating as well and was gazing at him panic stricken. "Don't—!" Her unsteady fingers closed her lips.

"I tell you he'll hear from me! I'm no lamb!"

"If—if it's that bad, Albert. If it doesn't change, and he's—he's that way—why don't you l-leave! There are other places!"

"Leave?" He repeated ominously. "Leave! So. But the first man I've ever trusted in this cursed land to treat me like a foe. The worst of all! Leave!" He stared at his plate bitterly, shook his head. "You're a strange one yourself. You've trembled every time I had a new job— trembled for me to keep it. I could read it in your face— you pressed me to be patient. And now you urge me to leave. Well, we'll see! We'll see! But when I leave he'll know it, never fear! And do me a favor. Take those plates away." He nodded toward Luter's place. "It's as though someone were dead."

XVI

TUESDAY afternoon, his mother's drawn, distracted face was too much for him to bear. Without asking her to wait in the hallway, he had fled into the street, and without calling to her, had come up again, alone. Neither Annie, who never hobbled past without sticking out her awl-like tongue, nor Yussie's reiterated, "Cry-baby," nor the cellar-door at the end of the vacant hallway were half as painful to endure as the stiff anguish in his mother's face or the numb silence of the hours of waiting for his father. Again and again, he could almost have wished that by some miracle Luter would return, would be there beside his father when the door was opened. But his mother set only three places around the table. There would be no miracle then. She knew. Luter would never return!

And when his father came home, he came in alone again. The sight of him this evening was terrifying. Never, not even the night he had beaten David, did he radiate, so fell, so electric a fury. It was as though his whole body were smouldering, a stark, throbbing, curdling emanation flowed from him, a dark, corrosive haze that was all the more fearful because David sensed how thin an aura it was of the terrific volcano clamped within. He refused to speak. He scarcely touched his food. His eyelids, normally narrow, seemed to have stretched beyond human roundness, revealing the whole globe of the eye in which the black pupils almost engulfed the brown. He looked at no one. His mad, burnished gaze roved constantly above their heads along the walls as if he were tracing and retracing the line of the moulding beneath the ceiling. Between the hollow of mouth and chin, his twitching lips threw a continual flicker of shadow. There was a place above the stiff sickle nostrils that looked dented—so pinched and white they were. Only once did he break his silence and then only for a brief time in a voice as harsh and labored as a croak.

"Flour? Why? Two sacks of flour? Two? Under the shelf? Under the Passover dishes?"

She stared at him mutely, too bewildered, too panic-stricken to answer.

"Hanh? Are they going to wall you in? Or is the long lean year crouching?"

Her whole body before she answered quivered forward as though shaking off layers and layers of some muffling, suffocating fabric.

"Flour!" Her voice under the strain was high-pitched and hysteric. "A sale at the grocer's. Nev-Neven's Street! There in that market!" She trembled again, swallowed, striving desperately to calm herself. "I thought since we used so much, it would be wise to—oh!" She sprang to her feet in horror. "You mean why did I leave them under the Passover dishes! I'll take them away! This moment!"

"No! No! Leave them! Leave them! Leave them!" (David thought the fierce crescendo of his voice would never end) "Sit down. The mice won't get them!"

She sat down stunned. "I'll get them later," she said dully. "I shouldn't have left them there. I can no longer think." And taking a deep breath. "One is tempted to buy more than one needs these days, things are so cheap. Is there anything you'd like me to get you? Smoked salmon? Sour cream, thick almost as butter. They say they mix flour into it! Black olives?"

"My head is splitting." His eyes were roving along the walls again. "Don't say more than you can help."

"Can't I do something for you? A cold compress?"

"No."

She shut her eyes, rocked slightly and said no more.

David would have whimpered, but dared not. The intolerable minutes unreeled from an endless spool of nightmare. . . .

By Wednesday afternoon, another and even more disturbing change had come over his mother. Yesterday afternoon and the day before, she had been impatient with him, unresponsive to his questions, distracted, disjointed in her answers. Now she listened to him with a fixity that made him increasingly uneasy. Wherever he walked about the kitchen, wherever he stood or sat, her eyes followed him, and there was something so fervent, so focused in her gaze that he found his own eyes not daring to meet hers. She did not chide him to-day for dawdling over his after-school bread and butter, or postponing the moment of having to go down. On the contrary, everything was reversed. This afternoon it was he who ate rapidly in order to be ready to go down sooner, and it was his mother who sought to delay him. "And what else?" She would ask. The moment he had completed narrating some incident in school. "And what else happened? What did you see then?" And always her tone had the same rapt, insistent note, and she hung on his every word with such a feverish hungered gaze that several times a curious shudder ran through him, a chill, as if the floor for a second had opened beneath him and he were plunging down a void.

"But on your way home," she urged. "You haven't told me. Was there nothing new?"

"No-o." He hesitated, his eyes wandering about the kitchen avoiding that over-bright, clinging gaze. When would she be satisfied, he wondered, when would she let him go? Uneasily he rummaged among his memories, found the only thing he knew he hadn't told her yet. "There was a man yesterday." He began. "On the street that's the other side of school." He paused, hoping against hope her interest had flagged.

"Yes! Yes!" Her voice was like a prod. "Yes!"

"And the man, he was making a sidewalk. Like that." He palmed the green sheet of oil cloth on the table. "With an iron with a handle. A new sidewalk."

"They're building up Brownsville!" She smiled at him with frightening intentness. "And? You unwilling, silent, beloved one! And?"

"And when the man wasn't looking . . . and the sidewalk was green—it's green when it's new."

"I have seen that also."

"And a boy came and the man wasn't looking—he was pushing the iron here. And the boy stepped on it—like that." He slipped down from the chair, toed the linoleum, "And made a hole with his shoe. Like that—"

Her face had sagged strangely, lips parting before a slow emission of breath. The taut, pale planes of her cheeks seemed to have slipped the chin-bone, overlapped it. Under the raised brows the intent brown eyes were focused on a distance so vast it returned upon her. In dismay, David stopped speaking and blinking with dismay watched her.

"I heard you! I heard you!" She shook her head breathlessly. "Yes! Yes! I heard you!" Through long corridors of brooding her gaze skimmed toward him again. "Yes!"

"Why did you look th-that way?" He wavered between alarm and curiosity.

"Nothing! Nothing at all! I did that too when I was a girl, stepping on a road, new-made. But mine was black! Nothing! Nothing at all! And then what? What did the man do!"

"The man," he continued uneasily, "the man didn't see. And yesterday he did it . . . When I went to school after lunch yesterday. And now there aren't any more boards on it. And it's hard like other sidewalks. Nearly white they powder it. And—and you can jump on it. Like that. And you can't do anything. But he made that hole. And there's a hole now. You can even see that little red iron on his shoe—in front. It made a hole too! And there's a piece of cigarette in it already."

"Naturally!"

"Why does it get so you can't make a hole any more—even with an umbrella. A broken one I saw. Only sparks when you hit it." He ducked under the hungering, round eyes. "You talk now."

"No, you!"

"Aaaaa!"

"Won't you?" she coaxed.

"I'm all finished now—with my bread," he reminded her crossly.

"Do you want some more? Some milk?" The eager intensity with which her words followed one another seemed to squeeze letters out of syllables.

He shook his head, eyed her obliquely.

"You can stay with me for a while, beloved." She opened her arms for him to come to her. "You don't have to go down."

He drooped, pouted, but finally trudged over to her and settled on her knee. All this time he had wanted very much to go down, to escape, but he had again caught a sound of pleading in her voice, an expectancy.

"I—I'll stay here."

"Oh, you do want to go down!" She unlocked her arms. "Yes you do! I've been keeping you. Come! I'll get your coat!"

"No! No! I don't! No, mama! I just—I just wanted to look out of the window. That's what I wanted."

"Is that all? Are you sure?"

"Yes. Only open. It has to be open." Some condition was necessary to justify his hesitance. "Will you open it?"

"Of course!" She suddenly pressed him to her fervently, rocked him against her breast. "What would I do without my son in bitter hours? My son! But, darling, the window with the fire-escape before it. Not the other. Good? Sweet fragment! I'll get a pillow for you to lean on. Do you want to go now?"

"Yes." He squirmed free.

"First your sweater then. It's cold out."

She fetched it. And when he had pulled it on, both went up to the front-room where she opened the window before the little fire-escape, pulled the heavy white curtains aside, cleared the sill of pots and milk bottles and placed a pillow on it.

"And this you'll want to kneel on." She drew a chair up. "It can't damage it any and you can look out much better. Your mittens?"

"No. I'm not cold."

She leaned over his shoulder, sniffed the air. "It drills the nostrils. Do you see how blue it's gotten over there, over those brown houses. How early! In the summer this would be late and Albert soon—" She stopped. The fingers on his shoulders twitched. "Ach! I threw a stone upon my own heart then!" With a slack and suddenly aimless hand she fondled his ears and the nape of his neck. "One cannot hide himself long from his fear." She groaned softly and began drumming on the window pane just as she had drummed on the table yesterday and the day before. "Will you knit another dream for me if I come up later? No?" She patted his head and walked slowly from the front room.

Moodily, he leaned further out to stare down the street.

On the right there were children near the stores at the

end of the block, girls skipping rope. Annie was turning.
He could see the brace. When he squinted tightly he
thought he could make out Yussie standing beside the
boy on a tricycle, but wasn't quite sure if that really was
Yussie. Then he could have gone down and stayed near
the house without being molested. It would have been
better than just being half in the street and half out. He
wondered why it was that one could be half in the street
and half out and yet never be able to picture the street
and the inside of the house together. He could picture
the street and the yellow wall of his house, but not the
inside. Once he had seen men tearing down the wall of
an old wooden house. You could see the inside from the
street—the wall paper and the chandelier, the black thick-
ness between floors, windows, open doors. It was strange.
Everything looked shrunken. Everything looked frightened.

There was a shout down the street. The boy on
the tricycle had begun pedaling followed by the other
who alternately propelled or jumped on the axle between
the rear wheels. It *was* Yussie. They swerved, jounced off
the curb onto the gutter, circled careening, zigzagged tipsily and bucked the curb again. With a feeling of jealousy
he strained his ears to catch what Yussie was shouting
between shrieks of laughter. He wouldn't give Yussie a
ride if he had a wheel. Never. He wouldn't even stay in
this block. No, he'd go far away. Where, far? He'd get
lost again. The thought sent a shiver through him. Not
this time though. His mother would write the address
down for him and he'd carry it with him always, in his
pocket. They wouldn't fool him again. He'd ride away.
Maybe after those telegraph poles, if you went way, way
on, there was a place like a picture in the candy store.
That lady who stood on a big box of cigarettes and wore a
handkerchief under her eyes and funny fat pants without a dress and carried a round sword. A place where
those houses were that she lived in, that all ended in sharp
points. He had seen a man in a hat once like that,
with a sharp point. He had a mustache and was in the
Jewish paper his mother bought. The Tageblatt! When he
went that night and—No! Lost the money—No! No!
And—and! No! . . . Houses, he was saying. Points.
Points they had, yes, not corners on top like those across
the street. Yellow and old wood corner. Brown and green

corner. And the grey one with the little window in it that looked like the roof was going to be a star—went down and then didn't go so down. Why?

He couldn't answer it, and stared again at the two on the tricycle. Yussie had gotten off, and the owner, his feet removed from the whirling pedals was letting the other push him as fast as he could. The peaks of their caps were turned backwards. Tooting breathlessly they bounced swiftly over the pitted gutter toward David's house. They were racing. He could tell by their caps. And as they drew near, the driver's shrill, spurring, "We're beatin'! We're beatin'! Horry op!" sent the blood tingling through his own veins. They were almost in front of the house now. In another moment, they would pass beneath his window—when suddenly with a sharp scrape of sliding shoes, Yussie braked the flying wheels to a stop and gaped over the other's shoulder. Wonderingly, David turned his head to the left to follow his gaze.

Only a few yards off, a tall, lean stranger approached, stooping slightly and bearing close to his dark coat, a white parcel, high, as though he meant to proffer it to the two boys before him. An instant David stared, and suddenly in the space of one stride, it was neither stranger nor parcel he saw, but his own father, and the right hand against his coat was hanging from a sling and swathed in bandages. He screamed.

"Papa! Papa!"

The slow head lifted, grim jaws, beaked nose and steady-glaring eyeballs. The two boys astride and beside the wheel sidled out of his way. David flung himself back from the window, fled screaming into the kitchen. His mother was already on the stair, frightened—

"David! What is it!"

"Papa's coming! His hand! His hand! It's all in"— He circled his own. "All in white! He's coming!"

"Dear God! Hurt! He's hurt?" She shook him. The starting brown eyes seemed to waken the pallor of her skin, the clutching hand among her hair its bronze. "Albert!" She flew to the door. "Albert!" Her voice in the hallway was hoarse. "Albert! Albert!"

To David, crouched back against the frontroom stairs, his father's harsh, suppressed words snapped through the open doorway.

"Hush! Hush, I say! An end to your wailing! Get back!"

"Blood! Blood!"

Moaning, clawing at her cheek, his mother came in—backwards held at arm's-thrust by his father. His face was grey, so grey the bluish stubble on his hard and bulging jaws stood out in separate dots. On the thick white bandage around his hand, a red spot glowered where the thumb should be.

"Yes! Blood!" He rapped out, slamming the door. "Have you never seen it? First that idiot barks from the window at my approach! Now you! Lament! Lament! Bring all your neighbors in here cackling!"

"Oh, Albert! Albert!" She swayed back and forth. "What is it? What's happened?" The tears braided on her cheek-bones.

"You always were a fool!" he growled. "You see me alive! Will you stop it!"

"Tell me! Tell me!" Her voice dwindled with anguish. "Tell me—! What have you—done? I—alas! before I—"

"Done? Me?"

"What! Tell me!" She was breathing thickly "Hurry!"

"You're not far from wrong!" he snarled. "You've almost guessed it! Yes! I would have done, but that cursed press ground me first! Anh! That press saved him! He doesn't know it! I would have—What!"

With a whispered groan her head sank. She stumbled toward a chair, dropped into it, slumped, her limp arms hanging beside her. At the sight of her awful pallor David burst into tears.

"Bah!" his father scoffed angrily. "In God's name I thought you had more wisdom." He strode to the sink, filled up a glass of water, pried it between her lips. The water runneled her chin, spattered on her dress. "And you're the one to faint!" he snorted bitterly.

"I'm all right!" she said weakly, lifting her head. "I'm all right, Albert. But—but you didn't strike him!"

"No!" savagely. "I told you I didn't! He escaped. Are you more worried about him than about me? Is that it?"

"No! No!"

"Then what are you fainting for? It's only my thumb. The jaws of the press! I wasn't quick enough! It jammed, that's all. You didn't take on this way when I caught the nail of that finger, did you?"

She hissed, wincing.

"I've still got it with me—my thumb—if that's what's troubling you. If you hadn't deafened me with your clamor I could have told you sooner! Now help me off with my coat—or are you still too weak?"

She rose unsteadily, took hold of his coat-collar.

"Curse him!" he muttered squirming free slowly. "The treacherous dog! God's flame make a candle of him! You don't have any more privileges than any one else! That's what he said to me before this—Unh!" He groaned between his teeth as the sleeve slid over his injured hand. "I shouldn't have let—the jacket—go with it."

"Is it so bad, Albert!" She put out her hand. "I didn't mean to—"

"Stop coming at me that way, will you! I don't need support!"

He stared at the bandage which now that his coat was off seemed to David's tear-blurred eyes to have swollen to twice its bulk.

"He didn't have to cover the fingers too, the fool!" He dropped into a chair, masked his eyes with his bony hand. It was heavily ink-blacked, unwashed. "Doctors! They'd rather use the whole ribbon than bother cutting it. And why not? They won't have to carry it around." His head dropped back.

"Can I give you anything? Coffee? We still have some wine left."

"No," wearily. "I'll be drowsy soon without wine. I'll sleep well." He hooked the heel of his dull black shoe on the lowest rung of the chair, grunted as he stooped down.

"Let me!" She started forward.

He waved her back. "One hand is enough!" And pulling the buttons open. "The angel of Fate strikes always on the side you never guard. I thought that before that dog saw the last of me, I'd make him writhe. And I would have!" His teeth grated. "There was enough venom in me to finish a score of Luters. But they led me out like a sheep." He kicked his shoe off, watched it roll over on its side, dully. "But you can't think too much when you're feeding a press. You can't dwell too much on the one you hate. That's the foreman's privilege. His hands are free!"

He shook his foot loose from the other shoe. "Anh! But he was pale when they led me into the bosses' office. He must have seen what was in my eyes. He must have known who was to blame. And I had one good hand left. Or maybe it was the blood he couldn't bear. I left it on their carpets."

She had been watching him rigidly. And when he stopped speaking a tremor ran through her. "Did—did the doctor say anything? Will it heal soon?"

He shrugged. "It won't have anything else to do. I can't use it for weeks—at least, that's what he said. It's well munched."

She groaned.

"They spoke of paying me something for the time I was out. Of their own free will they offered it. I don't know why. But much they'll give me. Tomorrow I see them again and the doct—tomorrow!" He caught his breath loudly. "Tomorrow is Thursday!"

His lips swelled out in hatred, his eyes burned savagely. Both David and his mother stared at him in fascinated terror.

"Curse him and his gifts!" he suddenly snarled. "May he burn with them! God bray him into bits!"

His right elbow moved downward, but the sling checked his hand. With writhing lips, he reached his left hand behind his back, fumbled in the right rear pocket and drew out his black leather pocket-book.

"Curse him!"

He drew out a small slip of white paper, the theatre-pass, crumpled it in grinding fingers to a crackling wad and threw it down on the table.

"Nothing fulfills itself with me! It's all doomed! But what made him give me this? And what made him change? If I only knew! If I only knew!" His left hand drummed on the table.

There was a horrible silence while they stared at the wad of paper on the table. Then his father slipped the bandaged hand free from the sling and began slowly stretching it back and forth to flex the cramped and clicking elbow. His face wore an expression of grim aloofness as though it were not his own hand he was experimenting with but someone else's. On his mother's feature horror and pity were written. David gazed from one to the other and finally like theirs his eyes came to rest on the hand that had just settled softly on the table, glimmering and peninsular on the green oilcloth. Minutes seemed to pass in a dull dragging vacancy in which no word was spoken. David looked up. His mother's face was unchanged as though that anguished look were caught in stone. But his father's face had become flushed, relaxed; the deep breath hissed softly at his nostrils. His eyelids had begun to linger at their shutting, opening not in one but in two stages. He spoke. Faint ratchets of effort against drowsiness and fatigue ticked and caught in his voice, thickening it. And as though to himself—

"I'll never go back to work there again. I'll never go back to printing at all. I'm through. Whatever work I do hereafter, it's going to be out doors—alone if I can. But out doors always . . . I'll not let myself be hemmed in by ink and iron any more. I don't want any foremen for my friends. I don't want anybody. I—I have no fortune with men."

He sighed harshly, rose and yawned as if he were groaning. The bandaged hand stretched ceilingward, and when he brought it down into the sling again, one eye shut in pain—

"It's as though it were hollow." He turned toward the front room, eyed David a moment and went up.

"I'll get you a quilt," she trailed him.

He made no answer and both climbed up the front room stairs.

Sitting in numb silence beside the window, David stared after them, watched them disappear, listened. The bed creaked. In a few moments, he heard his mother's quick tread and then the slither of something dragged from the couch—the quilt. And then the bedroom was closed and he heard only the ticking of the clock. The strange start of dread he had felt when his father's eyes had rested on him still lingered with him. He had seen it before—that look, that flicker of veiled suspicion more frightening than wrath—had seen it almost always the day his father had thrown up a job. Why? What had he done? He didn't know. He didn't even want to know. It frightened him too much. Everything he knew frightened him. Why did he have to be here when his father came home? Why had his mother kept him? Why did he have to know? You had to know everything and suddenly what you knew became something else. You forgot why, but it was something else just the same. Scaring you—

There was a noise in the hallway—the door below. Hurrying feet mounted the stairs, climbed; but as they passed his floor, stopped, descended, approached his door uncertainly. He slid from his chair, listened, opened the door a crack. It was Yussie. His cap, still turned backward, gave his red face an even pudgier look.

"Hey, Davy!" he whispered hesitantly, spying through the partly open door.

"Waddayuh wan'?" Somehow he felt less grieved at Yussie now, even relieved at seeing him. It suddenly occurred to him that it was not Yussie but his sister he disliked so much. Still he wasn't going to appear too friendly. "Wadjuh comm hea fuh?" he inquired morosely.

"Yuh mad on me yed, Davy?" He looked at him with innocent resignation.

"I don' know," he muttered tentatively. "Yea."

"So I'll take beck de cry-baby," he offered placatingly. "I'll never call yuh again, I shuh live so! It wuz all Ennie's fault—she made me."

"You don' like her?" suspiciously.

"No! I'm mad on her! She's a lousy mut!"

"So comm in."

Yussie sidled in eagerly, looked around. "Aw!" His lips fell in disappointment. "He ain' hea! Did he go 'way awreddy?"

"My fodder yuh wan'?" He suddenly saw through Yussie's ruse. "So dat's w'y yuh comm hea? Don' make no noise! He's sleepin'."

"Oh!" And then inquisitively. "Wadda big bendige he had on. I seen it. So wad'd he get id fuh?"

"He god hoided in a printin' press. Dot's w'y. His fingeh. So dey put id on."

"Yeh? I t'ought maybe—I know sommbody wod he hoided his hand on de Futt f'om Jillai—wid a fiyuh crecker. He had id in his house so he lighded id. Den he wanned t' t'row id oud f'om de windeh. So de windeh woz cluz. So he didn' know w'ea he sh't'row id. So bang—!"

"Sh!"

They turned. She had tip-toed so quietly from his father's bedroom that neither of them had heard her.

While they watched her silently, she shut the front room door, came down the steps with a slow uncertainty.

"Don't be offended with me, Yussele." In the blank immobility of her face, a bare mechanical smile stirred her lips. "Go on. Speak further if you like."

"Yea." Impatiently Yussie summarized his narrative, nor bothered to switch tongue. "I wuz tellin' him about a yuh crecker wod a boy wuz holdin' an' id wen' bang! So ftuh id w'en bang, id hoided him de hand so he had t' ud a bendige on like Misteh Schoil."

The name seemed to waken her momentarily. She shook her head wearily.

"An' aftuh, so his ear woz makin' Kling! Kling! Kling! s' like dat! Kling! Kling! Kling! Cauze de fiyuh crecker en' bang by his ears! Den he wannid me I sh' hea' by im de ears, bod I couldn' hea' nottin'. Bot he said id oz! So I—" He stopped, regarded her in perplexity, and then uneasily to David. "Don' she wan' I sh' talk t' huh Engklish?"

"I don' know." He answered sullenly. His mother's xed, unseeing stare, her trembling lips, trembling as if an inner speech, was anguish enough for him to bear ithout the added humiliation of having Yussie notice it. Yuh goin'?" he invited.

"Yeh, opstehs! Yuh wonna comm?"

"No!" Inflexibly.

"Bod I'm on'y gonna ged my noo bow'n' arrer." He rged. "Den I'm commin' donn. My modder t'rew huh ussit away, so dere's big, long w'ite iyons in id. So I wen' n pulled 'em oud. An' I'm gonna tie 'em all t'gedder. An' ool is id gonna be strong! Way strong! Yuh wanna waid h me till I comm down? I'll call yuh."

He hesitated, looked up at his mother. Her breast was eaving slowly, deeply, making a slight moaning creak in er throat. Her eyes, unwinking, round and liquid, swam the lustre of unshed tears. For a shattering instant a rong of impulses, diverse, fierce, maddening, hurtled gainst the very core of his being. He wanted to shrink way, to run, to hide, anywhere, under the table, in a orner, in his bedroom, to burst into tears, to scream at er. So many they paralyzed him. He stood quivering, aping at her, waiting for her to weep. Then suddenly he membered! Yussie was looking at her! He would know!

He would see! He mustn't! He whirled on him. "You go
op, Yussie! G'wan! Horry op! I'll waid f'yuh in mine
house. Den you come down and den I'll go! Horry op!"

"Yuh wan' me t'call ye?" Yussie cast a confused
glance over his shoulder at David's mother.

"Yeh! Yeh! So go!" His shame at the other's knowing
was agonizing. "G'wan!" He opened the door.

His mother sniffed sharply. "Are you driving him out,
child?" The flat twang of tears thickened her voice. "You
mustn't do that!"

"No! No!" David reverted desperately to Yiddish. "He's
going by himself! I'm not pushing him!"

"Yeh! I'm goin'!" Yussie seconded him hastily. "I'll call
yuh." He went out.

"What made you part so abruptly?" She sniffed again,
pressed her eyelids down, followed the dark margins with
thumb and forefinger, and regarded her humid fingertips.

David hung his head, not daring to look at her for fear
of weeping. "He's coming down to call me. And then
we're both going into the street."

"Oh, are you friends again?" She lifted weary tear-
stained eyes to the window. "It's growing dark. You won't
stay out too long, will you? Nor go too far?"

"No." It was becoming difficult for him to talk against
the choking in his throat. "I'll get my coat."

He retreated suddenly into his bedroom. In the brief
solitude of finding his coat, his whole body began to
quiver. But he tensed it, jammed his lips together to keep
them still. The spasm passed. He dragged his hat and coat
from the bed and returned.

"I must light the gas," she said without stirring. "Do
you want to come here and sit beside me?"

"No! I—I have to put my coat on." He struggled into
it. He mustn't, he mustn't go near her.

She shrugged, not at him, but at herself. "This is the
way of the years, my son. Each new one shows you both
hands this way—" She held out her two closed hands before her. "Here, choose!" And opening them. "And
they're both empty. We do what we can. But the bitter
thing is to strive—and save none but yourself." She rose,
went to the stove, lifted the lid and peered down into the
glow that stained the wide brow, the flat cheek. "Eat we
must though."

"I'm going, mama." He had heard the door slam upstairs.

"You won't be late for supper, beloved?" She replaced the eclipsing lid, half-turned, "Will you?"

"No, mama." He went out. His whole being felt crushed, worn-out, defeated.

Yussie came tripping down out of the upper shadow, and seeing him below, rattled the dim, slender corset-stays.

"Hey, yuh see watta a bow'n'arrer I'll hev? I got cawd in mine pocket too, so I'll tie id." He joined David at the landing, took his arm. "C'mon! So I'll show yuh how I'll tie id over hea an' over hea in de middle. Den I'll tie id over hea."

Descending, they neared the cellar door at which when he glanced, David felt a wave not so much of fear as of anger run through him—as though he defied it, as though he had slammed the door within him and locked it.

"An' we'll go maybe by de bobber shop, becuz by de bobber shop now is lighd. He a'ways lighds foist. So we c'n see how t' do it. Yuh commin?"

"Yeh."

They came out into the frosty blue of early dusk, turned toward the stores, some of which were lit; there were several children before the tailor shop and the barber's. They trudged toward it, Yussie flexing the sheaf of corset stays.

"Didja ask yuh modder fuh a nickel fuh de Xmas poddy in school?"

"No. I fuhgod."

"My ticher calls id Xmas, bod de kids call id Chrizmas. Id's a goyish holiday anyways. Wunst I hanged op a stockin' in Brooklyn. Bod mine fodder pud in a eggshells wid terlit paper an' a piece f'om a ol' kendle. So he leffed w'en he seen me. Id ain' no Sendy Klaws, didja know?"

"Yeh."

"How does a prindin' press look wot hoitshuh fodder?"

"Id's like a big mechine."

"Id don' go boof?"

"No. Id makes like dat calenduh I woz saving."

"Oh . . ."

They neared the group. Annie was still among them. David no longer cared.

"Hey!" Yussie seized his arm eagerly. "Dey's Jujjy de

one wod fell w'en yuh pushed him. Yuh wan' me t' make yuh glad on him?"

"Yeh."

"So tell him f'om de p'lice station. He'll be glad! Tell me too! So yeh?"

"Yeh."

"Hey Jujjy!" Yussie hailed them. "Hea's Davy! He wandsuh be glad on yuh. He's gonna tell yuh aboud de p'lice station! Aintcha, Davy?"

"Yeh."

BOOK II
The Picture

I

IN FEBRUARY David's father found the job he wanted
—he was to be a milkman. And in order that he might be
nearer the stables, they moved a few days later to 9th
Street and Avenue D on the lower East Side. For David it
was a new and violent world, as different from Brownsville as quiet from turmoil. Here in 9th Street it wasn't the
sun that swamped one as one left the doorway, it was
sound—an avalanche of sound. There were countless children, there were countless baby carriages, there were
countless mothers. And to the screams, rebukes and bick-
erings of these, a seemingly endless file of hucksters joined
their bawling cries. On Avenue D horse-cars clattered and
banged. Avenue D was thronged with beer wagons, garbage carts and coal trucks. There were many automobiles,
some blunt and rangey, some with high straw poops,
honking. Beyond Avenue D, at the end of a stunted, ruined
block that began with shacks and smithies and seltzer
bottling works and ended in a junk heap, was the East
River on which many boat horns sounded. On 10th Street,
the 8th Street Crosstown car ground its way toward the
switch.

His own home was different too. They lived on the
fourth floor now, the top floor of the house. There was no
cellar door, though a door did lead to the yard. The stairs
were of stone and one could hear himself climb. The
toilets were in the hall. Sometimes the people in them

rattled newspapers, sometimes they hummed, sometimes they groaned. That was cheering.

He became very fond of his own floor. There was a frosted skylight over the roofstair housing that diffused a cloudy yellow glow at morning and a soft grey haze at afternoon. After one climbed from the tumult of the street, climbed the lower, shadowier stairs, a little tense, listening to toilets, entering this light was like reaching a haven. There was a mild, relaxing hush about it, a luminous silence, static and embalmed. He would have liked to explore it, or at least to see whether the roof door was locked, but the thought of that height, that mysterious vacancy and isolation dissuaded him. There was something else besides. The stairs that led up were not like the stairs that led down, although both were of stone. Common stairs were beveled to an edge, hollowed to an aching trough by the tread of many feet, blackened beyond washing by the ground-in dirt of streets. But these that led up to the roof still had a pearliness mingled with their grey. Each slab was still square and clean. No palms of sliding hands had buffed the wrinkled paint from off their bannisters. No palms had oiled them tusk-smooth and green as an ax-helve. They were inviolable those stairs, guarding the light and the silence.

There were four rooms in the flat they lived in. There were eight windows. Some faced 9th Street, some faced Avenue D, and one looked out upon the dizzying pit of an airshaft. There was no bathtub. The partition separating the two adjacent washtubs had been knocked down, and they bathed in that. The bottom felt like sandpaper. One had to be careful not to draw too much water or one might float.

At home the routine of life had changed. His father no longer left for work early in the morning to return at night. Instead he left at night, in the incredible depths of night, and returned early in the morning. During the first few nights, his father's arising from bed had wakened him also, and he had lain perfectly quiet, listening to the slow heavy tread in the kitchen that was followed soon by the alternate sounds of a bare foot and a shod foot, and then the running water and the scuffing chairs; had lain there listening till his father had left, and then in drowsy thought had followed him down the stone stairs, had imagined in snugness the graduate cold, the night wind on the stoop, the silence, and sunk again through cloudy desolation into sleep.

Brownsville was fading from his mind, becoming soon a troubled nebulous land, alien and diverging. He was glad they had moved away . . .

II

AT THE beginning of April, David began hearing rumors of an aunt, Bertha, a younger sister of his mother, who was coming to this country. When at first, his mother had suggested that Bertha be permitted to live with them awhile, his father refused to hear of it. Had he not thrown himself at his wife's feet and begged her to permit Luter to live with them? May fire consume Luter now, but hadn't he? She had refused then; well he would repay her now. Bertha wouldn't be allowed in the house.

But David's mother persisted. "Where could the poor creature go alone in a strange land?"

"Poor creature!" His father had scoffed. As far as he was concerned, let her find a home under earth. He would have nothing to do with her. Did she think he had forgotten her, that gross, ill-favored wench with her red hair and green teeth. And heaven preserve him—her mouth!

But she was only a girl then, forward and flighty. She would have changed by now.

"For the worse!" he had answered. "But I know what you want her here for. You want her here so you can spend the entire day clacking your tongue with an endless he-said-and-I-said."

No, there would be very little of that. Bertha was handy with the needle. She would soon be working and not at home at all. And hadn't he himself come to this land alone and a stranger? Had he no pity on another in the same plight? And a woman at that! Could he be so inhuman as to expect her to turn away someone of her own blood in this wilderness?

At last, he had been won over and finally growled his consent. "Talking won't help me," he said bitterly, "But don't blame me if anything goes wrong. Remember!"

It was some time in May that Aunt Bertha arrived, and the first thing that David thought when he saw her was that his father's sarcastic description had not been exaggerated. Aunt Bertha was distressingly homely. She had a mass of rebellious, coarse red hair, that was darker than a carrot and lighter than a violin. And the color of her teeth, if one had to decide upon it, *was* green. She used salt, she said—when she remembered. The first thing David's mother did was to buy her a tooth brush.

She had no figure and no vanity about her appearance. "Alas!" she said. "I look like one butter firkin on another."

A single crease divided fat fore-arm from pudgy hand. Her legs landed into her shoes without benefit of ankles. No matter what she wore, no matter how new or clean, she always managed to look untidy. "Pearl and cloth of gold would stink on me," she confessed.

Her ruddy skin always looked as if it were about to flake with sunburn. She perspired more than any woman David had ever seen. Compared to his mother, whose pale skin always had a glossy look that no heat seemed able to flush, his aunt's red face was like a steaming cauldron. As the weather grew warmer, she began using the largest men's handkerchiefs, and at home she always tied a napkin around her short throat. "The sweat tickles me at the bend," she explained.

On those infrequent occasions when his mother bought herself a dress, she sometimes frankly preferred to stand rather than sit down and wrinkle it. His aunt, on the contrary, made hers look like a limp rag so quickly that she would take her Sunday afternoon nap in a new dress to get over the feeling that she had to be solicitous about it.

Apart from their complete difference in appearance, David soon observed that his mother and Aunt were worlds apart in temperament. His mother was grave, attentive, mild in her speech: his aunt was merry, tart and ready-tongued. His mother was infinitely patient, careful about everything she did; his aunt was rebellious and scatter-brained.

"Sister," she would tease, "do you remember that Salt Sea that grandfather used to speak of—by Judah or by

Jordan, where-ever it was—no storms and it bore everything? That's how you are. You use all your salt for tears. Now a wise woman uses some of it for sharpness." Aunt Bertha used all of it.

III

ON a clear Sunday afternoon in July, David and his aunt set out together toward the Third Avenue Elevated. They were going to the Metropolitan Museum. Sweat runneled his aunt's cheeks, hung down from her chin, fell sometimes, spotting the bosom of her green dress. With her handkerchief, she slapped at the beads viciously as though they were flies and cursed the heat. When they reached the elevated, David was compelled to ask innumerable people what the right train was, and during the whole trip, she sent him forward to plague the conductor.

At 86th Street, they got off and after further inquiry walked west toward Fifth Avenue. The further they got from Third Avenue, the more aloof grew the houses, the more silent the streets. David began to feel uneasy at his aunt's loud voice and Yiddish speech both of which seemed out of place here.

"Hmm!" she marveled in resounding accents. "Not a single child on the street. Children, I see, are not in style in this portion of America." And after gaping about her. "Bah! It is quiet as a forest here. Who would want to live in these houses? You see that house?" She pointed at a red brick structure. "Just such a house did Baron Kobelien have, with just such shades. He was an old monster, the Baron, may he rot away! His eyes were rheumy, and his lips munched as though he were chewing a cud. He had a back as crooked as his soul." And in the role of the Baron, she tottered onto Fifth Avenue.

Before them, stood a stately white-stone edifice set in the midst of the green park.

"That must be it," she said. "So they described it to me at the shop."

But before they crossed the street, she decided to take her bearings and cautioned David to remember a certain brown-stone house with gabled roofs and iron railings before it. Thus assured of a certain return, they hurried across the avenue and stopped again at the foot of a flight of broad stairs that led up to a door. A number of people were going in.

"Whom shall we ask to make sure we are right?"

A short distance from the building stood a peanut-vender with his cart and whistling box. They walked over to him. He was a lean, swarthy fellow with black mustaches and bright eyes.

"Ask him!" she ordered.

"Is dat a museum?"

"Dotsa duh musee," he flickered his eyebrows at her while he spoke. "You go inna straight," he pushed out his chest and hips, "you come out all tire."

David felt his arm clutched; his aunt hurried him away.

"Kiss my arse," she flung over her shoulder in Yiddish; "What did that black worm say?"

"He said it was a museum."

"Then let's go in. The worst we can get is a kick in the rear."

His aunt's audacity scared him quite a bit, but there was nothing to do except follow her up the stairs. Ahead of them, a man and woman were on the point of entering the door. His aunt pressed his arm and whispered hastily.

"Those two people! They seem knowing. We'll follow them till they come out again, else we'll surely be lost in this stupendous castle!"

The couple before them passed through a turn-stile. David and his aunt did likewise. The others turned to the right and entered a room full of grotesque granite figures seated bolt upright upon granite thrones. They followed in their wake.

"We must look at things with only one eye," she cautioned him, "the other must always be on them."

And keeping to this plan, wherever their two unwitting guides strolled, his aunt and he tagged along behind. Now and then, however, when she was particularly struck by some piece of sculpture, they allowed their leaders to draw so far ahead that they almost lost them. This hap-

pened once when she stood gawking at the spectacle of a
stone wolf suckling two infants.

"Woe is me!" Her tone was loud enough for the guard
to knit his brows at her. "Who would believe it—a dog
with babies! No! It could not have been!"

David had to pluck her dress several times and remind
her that their companions had disappeared before she
could tear herself away.

Again, when they arrived before an enormous marble
figure seated on an equally huge horse, his aunt was so
overcome that her tongue hung out in awe. "This is how
they looked in the old days," she breathed reverently.
"Gigantic they were, Moses and Abraham and Jacob, and
the others in the earth's youth. Ai!" Her eyes bulged.

"They're going, Aunt Bertha," he warned. "Hurry,
They're going away!"

"Who? Oh, may they burst! Won't they ever stop a moment! But come! We must cleave to them like mire on a
pig!"

In this fashion, hours seemed to go by. David was growing weary. Their quarry had led them past miles and
miles of armor, tapestries, coins, furniture and mummies
under glass, and still they showed no sign of flagging. His
aunt's interest in the passing splendors had long since
worn off and she was beginning to curse her guides
heartily.

"A plague on you," she muttered every time those
walking ahead stopped to glance into a show case.
"Haven't you crammed your eyes full yet! Enough!" She
waved her sopping handkerchief. "May your heart burn
the way my feet are burning!"

At last the man ahead of them stopped to tell one of
the uniformed guards something. Aunt Bertha halted
abruptly. "Hoorrah! He's complaining about our following him! God be praised! Let them kick us out now.
That's all I ask!"

But alas, such was not the case; the guards paid no
attention to them, but seemed instead to be giving the
others directions of some kind.

"They're leaving now," she said with a great sigh of
relief. "I'm sure he's telling them how to get out. What
a fool I was not to have had you ask him myself. But

who would have known! Come, we may as well follow them out, since we've followed them in."

Instead of leaving, however, the man and woman, after walking a short distance, separated, one going into one door and one into another.

"Bah!" Her rage knew no bounds. "Why they're only going to pee. Ach! I follow no longer. Ask that blockhead in uniform, how one escapes this jungle of stone and fabric."

The guard directed them, but his directions were so involved that in a short space they were lost again. They had to ask another and still another. It was only by a long series of inquiries that they finally managed to get out at all.

"Pheh!" she spat on the stairs as they went down. "May a bolt shatter you to bits! If I ever walk up these stairs again, I hope I give birth to a pair of pewter twins!" And she yanked David toward their landmark.

His mother and father were home when they entered. His aunt sprawled into a chair with a moan of fatigue.

"You look as though you've stumbled into every corner of the world!" His mother seated him on her knee. "Where have you led the poor child, Bertha?"

"Led?" she groaned. "Where was I led you mean? We were fastened to a he and a she-devil with a black power in their legs. And they dragged us through a wilderness of man's work. A wilderness I tell you! And now I'm so weary, my breast seems empty of its heart!"

"Why didn't you leave when you had seen enough?"

She laughed weakly. "That place wasn't made for leaving. Ach, green rump that I am, the dirt of Austria is still under my toe-nails and I plunge into museums." She buried her nose under her arm-pit. "Phew, I reek!"

As always, when she indulged herself in some coarse expression or gesture, his father grimaced and tapped his foot.

"It serves you right," he said abruptly.

"Humph!" she tossed her head sarcastically.

"Yes!"

"And why?" Irritation and weariness were getting the better of her.

"A raw jade like yourself ought learn a little more before she butts into America."

"My cultivated American!" she drawled, drawing down the corners of her under lip in imitation of the grim curve on the face of her brother-in-law. "How long is it since you shit on the ocean?"

"Chops like those," he glowered warningly, "deserve to drop off."

"That's what I say, but they're not mine."

The ominous purple vein began to throb on his temple. "To me you can't talk that way," his eyelids grew heavy. "Save that fishwives' lip for your father, the old glutton!"

"And you, what have you——"

"Bertha!" his mother broke in warningly. "Don't!"

Aunt Bertha's lips quivered rebelliously a moment and she reddened as though she had throttled a powerful impulse to blurt out something.

"Come, you're all worn out," continued his mother gently. "Why don't you lie down for a little space while I make you some dinner."

"Very well," she answered and flounced out of the room.

IV

"HERE is a man," Aunt Bertha said vehemently to her sister, "who drives a milk wagon and mingles with peddlars and truckmen, who sits at a horse's tail all morning long, and yet when I say—what! When I say nothing! Nothing at all!—he begins to tap his feet or rustle his newspaper as though an ague were upon him! Did anyone ever hear of the like? He's as squeamish as a newly-minted nun. One is not even permitted to fart when he's around!"

"You're making the most of Albert's absence, aren't you?" his mother asked.

"And why not? I don't have much opportunity to speak my mind when he's around. And what's more, it won't

hurt your son to know what I think of all fathers. His
father he knows. A sour spirit. Gloomy. The world slapped
him on both chins and so everyone he meets must suffer.
But my father, the good Reb Benjamin Krollman, was this
way." And she began to shake and mumble rapidly and
look furtively around and draw closer to herself a figment
praying shawl. "His praying was an excuse for his lazi-
ness. As long as he prayed he didn't have to do anything
else. Let Genya or his wife take care of the store, he had
to take care of God. A pious Jew with a beard—who dared
ask more of him? Work? God spare him! He played the
lotteries!"

"Why do you say that?" his mother objected. "No one
can blame father because he was pious. Well, he lacked
business sense, but he tried to do his best."

"Tried? Don't defend him. I've just left him and I
know. If I remember grandfather he worked till the
cancer stretched him out—after grandmother died. And
he was seventy then. But father—God keep him from
cancer—he was old at forty—Ai! Ai!" She switched with
characteristic suddenness into mimicry. "Ai! Unhappy!
Ai! My back, my bones! Slivers of death have lodged in
me! Ai! There are dots before my eyes! Is that you,
Bertha? I can't see. Ai! Groaning about the house as though
he already stank for earth—God forbid! And not a grey
hair in his head. But let one of us get in his road—Ho!
Ho! He was suddenly spry as a colt! And could he
shower blows? Tireless! Like a bandmaster's his stick
would wave."

His mother sighed and then laughed acknowledging
defeat.

"It was mother's fault too," Aunt Bertha added warningly as if giving her an object lesson. "A wife should
have driven a man like that, not coddled him, not pam-
pered him to ruin. Soft and meek, she was." Aunt Bertha
became soft and meek. "She let herself be trampled on.
Nine children she bore him beside the twins that died between your birth and mine. She's grey now. You'd weep to
see her. Bloodless as a rag in the weather. You wouldn't
know her. Still trailing after him. Still saving him the
dainties—the breast and giblets of the hen, the middle of
herrings, the crispest rolls! Do you remember how he
would stretch out over the table, pawing each roll, pump-

ing it in his glutton's haste to feel how soft it was? And then hide away the new-baked cake from the rest of us? His nose was in every pot. But whenever you saw him—" she broke off, stretched out her hands in a gesture of injured innocence—"What have I eaten today? What? An age-old crust, a glass of coffee. I tremble with hunger. Bah!"

"I sometimes don't think he could help it. There were so many mouths to feed. It must have frightened him."

"Well, whose fault was it? Not mother's certainly. Why even when she was ailing he—" And at this point she did what she often did in her speech—finish her sentence in Polish, a language David had come to hate because he couldn't understand it.

"Tell me, would you go back to Austria if you had the money?"

"Never!"

"No?"

"Money I'd send them," Aunt Bertha asserted flatly. "But go home—never! I'm too glad I escaped. And why should I go home? To quarrel?"

"Not even to see mother?"

"God pity her more than any. But what good would my seeing her do her? Or me? It would only give me grief. No! Neither her, nor father, nor Yetta, nor Adolf, nor Herman, nor even Saul, the baby, though God knows I was fond of him. You see I'm one who doesn't yearn for the home land."

"You haven't been here long enough," said his mother. "One grapples this land at first closer to one's self than it's worth."

"Closer than it's worth? Why? True I work like a horse and I stink like one with my own sweat. But there's life here, isn't there? There's a stir here always. Listen! The street! The cars! High laughter! Ha, good! Veljish was still as a fart in company. Who could endure it? Trees! Fields! Again trees! Who can talk to trees? Here at least I can find other pastimes than sliding down the gable on a roof!"

"I suppose you're right," his mother laughed at her vehemence. "It appears to me that you'll grow from green to yellow in this land years before I do. Yes, there are other pastimes here than—" She broke off, flinched even though she laughed. "That sliver of wood in your flesh! Dear God you were rash!"

"It was nothing! Nothing!" Aunt Bertha chuckled lightly. "My rump has forgotten it long ago! But that should prove to you that I'm better off here than I was there. Anyone is! That quiet was enough to spring the brain!"

His mother shook her head non-committally.

"What? No?" Aunt Bertha mistook her gesture. "Can you say no?" She began counting on her fingers. "Ha-a-d A-Adolf come here as a boy, would he have to run away to the lumber camps and gotten a rupture that big? Ha? A-And Yetta-a. She could have found a better husband than that idiot tailor she's married to. He finds diamonds in the road, I tell you, and loses them before he gets home. He sees children falling into the frozen river and not a child in the village is missing. Awful! Awful! And Herman and that peasant wench. And the peasant looking for him with an ax. You don't see that in this land! Fortunate for him anyway that he fled to Strij in time, and fortunate too that it wasn't Russia. There might have been a pogrom! There was nothing to do and so they went mad, and because they were mad they did whatever came into their heads. That's how I was, and if you want to know, my dear, close-mouthed sister, as quiet and gentle as you were," her tone became sly— "there was still, well a rumor of some sort. Someone, something-er-done. But only a rumor!" she added hastily. "A lie of course!"

His mother turned abruptly toward the window, and her own irrelevant words crossed her sister's before the other and finished—"Look, Bertha! That new automobile. What a pretty blue! Wouldn't you like to be rich enough to own one?"

Aunt Bertha made a face, but came over and looked down. "Yes. What a grinder it has in front of it. Like a hand-organ, no? Do you remember when we saw our first one on the new road in Veljish—the black one?" The least bit of resentment crept into her voice. "You eternal, close-mouth, when will that secret be weaned?"

Something about their tones and expressions, so curiously guarded in both stirred David's curiosity. But since their conversation on that score went no further, he could only wonder in a vague and transient way what his mother had done, and hope that another time would reveal the meaning.

V

HOSTILITIES between Aunt Bertha and David's father were rapidly reaching the breaking point. David was sure that something would happen soon if Aunt Bertha did not curb her over-ready tongue. He marveled at her rashness.

On that Saturday night Aunt Bertha had arrived home bearing a large cardboard box. She was later tonight than usual and had delayed the supper almost an hour. The fast had not helped to put David's father in an amiable frame of mind. He had been grumbling before she came, and now, though she was washing her face and hands with as great dispatch as possible, he could not restrain a testy—

"Hurry up. You'll never wash that stench off!"

To which Aunt Bertha made no other reply than to bob her ample buttocks in his general direction. Glaring furiously at her back, he said nothing, but savagely toyed with the table knife in his hands.

Aunt Bertha at length straightened up, and apparently unconscious of the rage she had put him in, began drying herself.

"I suppose you've been shopping," said her sister amiably, setting the food on the table.

"Indeed I have," she seated herself. "I'm coming up in the world."

"What did you buy?"

"Bargains of course!" his father broke in contemptuously. He seemed to have been waiting for just this opportunity. "The storekeeper who couldn't lift the head from her shoulders without her knowing it might as well close up shop!"

"Is that so?" she retorted sarcastically. "Speak for

yourself! I don't spend my life hunting for rusty horse-shoes. That gramophone you bought in the summer—Ha! Ha! Mute and motionless as the day before creation."

"Hold your tongue!"

"Your noodles and cheese are growing cold," said David's mother. "Both of you!"

There was a pause while everyone ate. From time to time, Aunt Bertha cast her eyes happily at the cardboard box resting on the chair.

"Apparel?" asked his mother discreetly.

"What else? Half the country's goods!"

His mother smiled at his aunt's fervor.

"Blessed is this golden land," she let herself be carried away by enthusiasm. "Such beautiful things to wear!"

"Much good that does you," said his father over a forkful of noodles.

"Albert!" his wife protested.

Aunt Bertha abruptly stopped eating. "Who was speaking to you? Go snarl up your own wits! You're one person I don't have to please."

"To please me, the Lord need grant you a new soul."

"To spite you, I'd stay just as I am!" She tossed her head scornfully, "I'd sooner have a pig admire me."

"No doubt he would."

"Tell me, dear Bertha," said her sister desperately. "What did you buy?"

"Oh, a parcel of rags! With what I earn what else can I buy?" Then brightening a little. "I'll show them to you."

Casting a hasty glance at her husband, David's mother put up a restraining hand, but too late. Aunt Bertha had seized a table knife and was already cutting the strings off the box.

"Are we having dinner or going to a fair?" he asked.

"Perhaps a little later—" suggested his mother.

"Not at all," Aunt Bertha said with vindictive cheerfulness. "Let him gorge himself if he wants to. My appetite can wait." And she whipped open the box.

Lifting out first one article of woman's wear and then another—a corset cover, a petticoat, stockings—she commented blithely on each and quoted its price. Finally, she brought into view a pair of large white drawers and turned them over admiringly in her hands. David's father abruptly shoved his chair around to cut them from his field of vision.

"Aren't they beautiful?" she chattered on. "See the lace at the bottom. And so cheap. Only twenty cents. I saw such small ones in the store. Some poor women have no buttocks at all!" Then she giggled, "when I hold them at a distance upside down this way they look like peaks in Austria."

"Yes, yes," said his mother apprehensively.

"Ha! Ha!" She went on entirely enchanted by the charm of her purchase. "But what can I do? I *am* fat below. But isn't it a miracle? Twenty cents, and I can wear what only a baroness in Austria could wear. And so convenient and so neatly cut—these buttons here. See how this drops down! The newest style, he told me. Do you remember the drawers we wore in Austria—into the stockings? Winter and Summer my legs looked like a gypsy's accordion."

But David's father could restrain himself no longer. "Put those things away!" he rapped out.

Aunt Bertha drew back startled. Then narrowed her eyes and thrust out stubborn lips. "Don't shout at me!"

"Put those away!" He banged his fist on the table so that the dishes danced and the yellow noodles cast their long necks over the rim of the platters.

"Please, Bertha!" her sister implored, "You know how—"

"Do you side with him too?" She interrupted her. "I'll put them away when I please! I'm not his slave!"

"Are you going to do what I say?"

Aunt Bertha clapped one hand to her hip, "When I please! It's time you knew what women wore on their bottoms."

"I'll ask you once more, you vile slut," he shoved his chair back and rose in slow wrath.

David began to cry.

"Let me go!" Aunt Bertha pushed back her sister who had interposed herself. "Is he so pious, he can't bear to look at a pair of drawers? Does he piss water as mortals do, or only the purest of vegetable oil?"

His father advanced on her. "I'm pleading with you as with Death!" He always said that at moments of intense anger. His voice had taken on that thin terrific hardness that meant he was about to strike. "Will you put them away?"

"Make me!" she screamed and waved the drawers like a goad in his very eyes.

Before she could recoil, his long arm had swept out, and with a bark of rage, he plucked the drawers from her. A moment later, he had ripped them in two. "Here, you slut!" he roared. "Here are your peaks!" And he flung them in her face.

Raging with fury, Aunt Bertha leapt at him with clawing fingers. The flat thrust of his palm against her bosom sent her reeling to the wall. He turned on his heel, and his eyeballs glaring in demonic rage, he tore his hat and coat from a peg near the door and stalked out.

Aunt Bertha dropped into a chair and began weeping loudly and hysterically. Her sister, her own eyes filling with tears, tried to comfort her.

"Madman! Mad!" came his aunt's stifled words. "Savage beast!" She picked up the drawers at her feet and wrung them in the frenzy of her anguish. "My new drawers! What did he have against them? May his head be cloven as they are! Oh!" The tears streamed down her cheeks. Stray strands of her red hair parted on her clammy brow and nose.

David's mother stroked her shoulders soothingly. "Hush, dear sister! Don't weep so, child! You'll break your heart!"

Aunt Bertha only lamented the more, "Why did I ever set foot on this stinking land? Why did I ever come here? Ten hours a day in a smothering shop—paper flowers! Rag flowers! Ten long hours, afraid to pee too often because the foreman might think I was shirking. And now when I've bought with the sweat of my brow a little of what my heart desires, that butcher rends it. Ai!"

"I tried to save you, sister. You must know what he's like by now. Listen to me, I have some money. I'll buy you a new pair."

"Oh! Woe is me!"

"And even the ones you have there may be mended."

"May his heart be broken as mine is, they'll never be mended."

"Look, they're torn exactly at the seam."

"What?" Aunt Bertha opened grief stricken eyes. She

stared at the drawers a moment and then jumped frenziedly from her chair. "He threw them at me too, dashed them
in my face. He flung me to the wall! I'm not going to stay
here another minute! I'll not endure it another minute.
I'm going to pack my things! I'm going!" She made for
the door.

David's mother hastened after her. "Wait," she
pleaded, "where will you run at this time of night?
Please, I beg you!"

"I'll go anywhere! What did I leave Europe for if not
to escape that tyrant of a father. And this is what I
came to—a madman! May a trolley-car crack his bones!
Slaughter him, Almighty God!" And she ran weeping
loudly into her bedroom.

David's mother followed her sadly. . . .

Although Aunt Bertha did not move out of their house
as she had threatened to do, the next day and the next,
there was no exchange of communication between her
and David's father. Dinners at night were eaten in silence, and if either of them required anything of the
other, David or his mother were impressed as inter-
mediaries. However after several nights of this embarras-
sing constraint, Aunt Bertha's self-imposed shackles
grew too much for her. Quite suddenly one evening, she
broke them.

"Pass me the herring jar," she muttered—this time directly at her brother-in-law.

His face darkened when she spoke, but sullenly though
he did it, he nevertheless did push the herring jar toward
her.

Thus an armistice was signed and relations, if not cor-
dial, were at least established. And thereafter, as much as
it was possible for her, Aunt Bertha kept her peace.

"He's a mad dog," she told her sister. "He has to run.
There's nothing to do but keep out of his way."

And she did for many months.

VI

"A HEART full of pity!" said Aunt Bertha derisively. "Yes! Yes, indeed! For plucking a tooth out, he asks only fifty cents. You understand what that means? What will hurt me most is only fifty cents. After my teeth are gone, and I look like my grandmother, God rest her where she lies, then his price stiffens. I can see through these bandits, never fear!"

Aunt Bertha had been indulging herself in enormous quantities of sugary, vanilla "bum bonnies" as she called them, "pinnit brettlich" and "turra frurra" ice-cream. Severe toothaches had followed. Aunt Bertha had claimed that during the last few nights she had felt her mouth expand to the size of half a watermelon. Whether it had actually grown that large, David didn't know, but looking at her green teeth and red mouth he could see a certain resemblance. After much urging, her sister had finally succeeded in getting her to go to the dentist. Tomorrow night he would draw several of her teeth.

"In Veljish," she continued, "they say that 'kockin' will clear the brow of pain. But here in America—didn't he call it that? 'Kockin'?—will clear the mouth of pain."

His father's newspaper rustled warningly.

"Cocaine?" said her sister hastily.

"Oh, is that how you say it?"

'Kockin,' as David had learned long ago, was a Yiddish word meaning to sit on the toilet.

"And another thing," his aunt indulged in a sly laugh. "I am going to lose six teeth. And of the six teeth, three he called 'mollehs'. Now isn't this a miracle? He's going to take away a 'molleh' and then he's going to make me 'molleh'."

David didn't know what 'molleh' might mean in English. He did know that 'molleh' in Yiddish had something to do with circumcision. Aunt Bertha was being reckless to-night . . .

But if his father had suffered because of Aunt Bertha's puns, the next night it was Aunt Bertha who was suffering. His mother related what had happened. She had sat down very meekly and very quietly in the dentist's chair, she had shut her eyes when the needle was put in her mouth, she had behaved very bravely. But when the first tooth was drawn and Doctor Goldberg had told her to spit, she had spat—not in the cuspidor beside the chair, but at Doctor Goldberg.

"Very worthy of praise!" his father snorted. "An example for sages!"

"So!" Aunt Bertha forgot her dolor. "May they pull all your teeth out soon. We'll see how brave and how clever you are then! At least, it gives me satisfaction to think I spat at him, not at myself. And you!" she turned petulantly on her sister. "You're very clever too! You saw I was stunned with fright! You saw my eyes were shut because my head was whirling so hard I didn't know where I was. He said open your mouth, I opened it—wide as a sack! Shut it. I shut it. Spit—! Go look for a spittoon when you're ready to faint! It serves him right for standing in the way."

His mother's lips trembled in laughter, but she pressed them soberly together. "I didn't mean to hurt you, sister. I know how much you've suffered already. I'm sorry! But come! You're three teeth nearer to those golden kernels you admire so much."

"Nearer?" She touched the bare red gums gingerly. "Emptier you mean. You're sure he won't plant the new ones in the holes he's made?"

"No! No!" His mother reassured her. "He told you, didn't he? They hang like a gate."

"Britches, he called them, no?" Aunt Bertha cheered up ruefully. "Pritchig, he ought to call them, a hearth in other words, there's such a fire in my mouth. But I will look handsomer soon, won't I?"

"What else!" Her brother-in-law's cheek scrolled into a sour smile. . . .

After Aunt Bertha's gums had healed, she began visiting the dentist's twice a week, and at first complained bitterly and went there only with the greatest reluctance. In the space of a fortnight, however, her attitude under-

went a remarkable change. She now began to go there
eagerly, expectantly, and to stay sometimes twice as long.
There were no longer any complaints, no longer any de-
tailed descriptions of the various types of pain different
dental instruments could inflict. All that seemed to have
been forgotten. A new excitement had seized her, a guilty
excitement that made her run to a mirror and regard herself closely and then look about to see if she was being
watched. She began to fuss with her hair and blouse, arch
her short neck, smile in a way that would reveal her temporary gold crown, dowse herself with densely redolent
perfume. Something was wrong. At least twice a week
David was excluded from the kitchen while she bathed
in the washtubs. And here it was Autumn. And she bought
face powder which caked and flaked on her cheeks and
looked very queer and white flecking her reddish eye-
brows. Something was very wrong. Presently her visits to
the dentist's increased from two to three times a week
and shortly to four.

This unwonted frequency, unwonted eagerness and
strange behavior in general had aroused not only the curiosity of David and his mother, but his father's silent,
impassive questioning as well. To his mother's circum-
spect inquiries, Aunt Bertha had at first explained that
there was much work being done on her teeth, work of a
subtle and occult nature, a delicate prying and adjusting
that could only be felt but hardly demonstrated. Of course,
she confessed with a cryptic giggle, were she to insist, she
could probably get the same amount of work done in two
visits as easily as in four, but she really preferred going
there as many times as possible. It was so pleasant being
there now, she explained. There was hardly any pain, or
at least so little it wasn't worth mentioning. One grows accustomed to sorrows, she elucidated. And beside, the waiting room where all the patients gathered was so homelike, and the people so fluent in English that it was both
pleasant and instructive to be among them. Also, it was
disclosed, Doctor Goldberg's wife frequently came into
the waiting room to chat with them in really "fency Eng-
alish." And what especially put everyone at their ease was
that while Mrs. Goldberg conversed in this very superior
English, she also carried on some homely domestic duty
such as chipping noodles or mixing the batter of a sponge-

cake. Aunt Bertha would show his mother some day how to make a sponge-cake. And so it was all homely and refined. And of course, one had to look decent! And she, Mrs. Goldberg, had introduced Aunt Bertha to a very fine man, albeit a Russian, who was a children's legging's cutter and who was having the identical type of work done to his mouth that was being done to Aunt Bertha's. His name, by the way, was Nathan Sternowitz, and was he jolly! And so, all over again, it was all very homelike, very jolly and very refined.

Nothing more was said about the matter for a short time—at least nothing while David was within earshot. But on Friday night, a few days later, Aunt Bertha decided to take her sister completely into her confidence. On that night, the dentist's office was regularly closed and Aunt Bertha remained at home. She had been silent until David's father had gone to bed, which was at about eight-thirty, and only began speaking when the regular hiss of his breathing could be heard behind the bedroom door. Fortunately for David, it had become his privilege to defer his bed-time till nine o'clock and even later on Fridays and Saturdays, there being no school the following mornings. He heard it all. As it chanced, his mother was at that moment tracing for him the crooked boundary of a pink Austria on the map of a geography book not yet begun in school. And she had just informed him laughingly that Veljish was too much of a dot in reality to be seen even by the combined lights of candle and gas, when Aunt Bertha cleared her throat suddenly and spoke:

"Well, Genya, your man is asleep."

The cautious, subdued nervousness of her tone made both David and his mother look up. Aunt Bertha was frowning warily and fingering her gold crown. His mother glanced first at her and then at the bedroom door.

"So he is. What is it?"

"I'm not going to the dentist's tomorrow," she said bluntly. "I haven't been going there for weeks—at least not every time I left here. I'm going 'kippin' companyih'!"

"Going what?" His mother knit her brow. "What are you doing?"

"Kippin' companyih! It's time you learned a little more of this tongue. It means I have a suitor."

"Then blessed is God!" his mother laughed. "Who is he— But I know! This Sternowitz!"

"Yes. I've hinted his name to you. But I don't want *him* to know." She nodded warningly toward the bedroom. "He'd gloat if it went all to smash. That's why I've said nothing."

"You're too harsh with him, Bertha," her sister smiled placatingly. "He doesn't wish you any harm. Really he doesn't. It's his nature. It will be that way always."

"A bitter nature." Aunt Bertha rejoined spitefully. "And always is the time one spends under earth. That's where he ought—"

"Ach, Bertha! Hush!"

"Yes, let's not talk too much. He may hear me. And after all he is your husband. But you won't tell him, will you? Not till all is certain. You promise? Remember," she pointed her remark. "I've kept your secrets well."

Her words sent a sudden wave of curiosity through David. Secrets! His mother's! Looking up, he saw a deep rose in his mother's throat and fainter petals dappling the waxen sheen of her flat cheek. Their eyes met. She was silent, touched the water in the candlestick cups that would ultimately quench the flame.

"Forgive me!" Aunt Bertha said hastily. "Really I didn't mean—I didn't mean to be so—so thick! May my tongue fall out if I meant to offend you!"

His mother glanced at the bedroom door and then smiled suddenly. "Don't be embarrassed! I'm not offended."

"Are you sure?" Aunt Bertha asked hesitantly.

"Why, of course!"

"But you grew so red, I thought I had angered you. Or—" Her voice dropped to a whisper. "Is it Albert?"

"No." She answered calmly. "None of those things. The son was staring in my eyes."

"Oh!" Aunt Bertha was relieved. "I thought that—" and she fixed on David accusingly. "Are you listening, you rogue?"

"What?" His eyes wandered vacantly from the open book on the table to Aunt Bertha, and dropped to the book again.

"Ach!" Aunt Bertha brushed away her sister's objections. "He's dreaming of Veljish, the little oaf."

"I'm not so sure." His mother laughed. "But what were you saying? The man is what? A legging's cutter?"

"Yes. A children's legging's cutter. He has a very good job and he makes good money. But—" She scratched her head vehemently and left her sentence hanging in air.

"Well, what's troubling you? Is he so homely? What?"

"Ach! Pt! Do you believe in love?"

"I?" His mother smiled. "No."

"No! Tell that to your grandmother there in her grave. You've read every German Romance in Austria. Do you know?" She looked at her sister as if a new thought had struck her. "I've never seen you read a book since I've been here."

"Who has time even to read a paper?"

"They were bad for you." Aunt Bertha continued after a moment of reflection. "They made you odd and made your thoughts odd. They gave you strange notions you shouldn't have had."

"So you've told me. And so did father—scores of times."

"Well, it would have been better if you had listened to him. They spoiled you—understand? You weren't—not what shall I say?—good. You were good enough, the gentlest of us all. But you weren't truly Jewish. You were strange. You didn't have a Jew's nature."

"And what kind of a nature is that?"

"Ach!" Aunt Bertha said impatiently. "You see? You smile! You're too calm, too generous. That's wrong! That's bad! Don't be offended with me, but perhaps you've forgotten what a mopish, calf-eyed creature you were. You looked so—" Aunt Bertha's jaw dropped. Her red tongue hung out. "And so—" Her eyes climbed up into some cranny under the lids. "Always a cloudy look! Not a suitor they brought you would you accept. And there were some among them at whose feet I would have fallen!" She perched her head back further on her shoulders to stress her own worth and the consequent immensity of that gesture. "German Romances! They did that! And then you married Albert—of all the choices to make."

His mother regarded her with a mixture of perplexity and despair. "What are you talking about? Is it me, yourself or German Romances?"

"Nothing!" Aunt Bertha shrugged her shoulders huffily. "I was talking about love. Lupka—"

There was that Polish again. David felt a twinge of resentment.

"Oh now, I know," said his mother lightly in Yiddish. "Go on."

"How can I, when you mock everything I say."

"I? How?"

"I know you've been in love, but when I ask you whether you believe in it, you answer, no."

"Very well, I do. Listening to you convinces me. But what has that to do with it?"

"You see? Now you do! You're exactly what father said you were! You were gentle of heart, but only the devil understood you. I'm your sister. You've never told me about yourself. You don't even care to hear what vexes me."

"Sh!" his mother raised a warning finger. "Now just what is vexing you? Tell me."

"First tell me why you married Albert." Her voice suddenly dropped. "After you knew what he had—what kind of a man he—"

"Ach! Hush!" his mother shook her head impatiently. "Bertha, sister, you're the silliest woman I've ever known. What is there to tell? I was the oldest. There were three daughters younger than I—you, Yetta, Sadie—pushing me toward the canopy. What else could I do?"

"Tell that to your grandmother also." Aunt Bertha continued peevishly. "Father wouldn't say anything. Mother wouldn't speak. And yet there was a rumor among us—a saying. But who? Why won't you—"

"Come! No more!" His mother's voice was curt, strangely severe for her. "Not here!"

David had just enough time to duck his head toward his geography book before her glance flashed his way. In the pause that followed, he kept his eyes there, intently, rigidly, turning the book now this way, now that, feigning the greatest abstraction. Much that he had heard, he hadn't quite understood, it was all so vague, flurried, mysterious. Aunt Bertha had a suitor. His name was Nathan something or other. He made leggings. What was love? But he didn't care about that. He didn't care if Aunt Bertha had a dozen suitors. What fascinated him, stirred him to the depths, were the two threads he had unearthed, the two threads he clung to. His father had done something.

What? No one would say. His mother? Even Aunt Bertha didn't know. What? What? He was so excited, he didn't dare look up, didn't dare move his eyes on his tracing finger. He prayed his mother would go on, would answer, would reveal what Aunt Bertha had been hinting at. But she didn't. To his great disappointment, she veered suddenly. When she spoke again, her voice had regained its calm.

"Tell me, sister, why are you so irritable?"

Aunt Bertha twisted stubby fingers together, scratched her head frantically, sending the hair pins shooting up out of her red hair. "Because I'm frightened."

"But why? What have you done in God's name?"

"Nothing. Do you think I'm a fool! Let that man dare—! But why is it that since you married, everyone in our family has married as I would wish my enemies?"

"I don't know." His mother sat back hopelessly. "Are you going to begin that all over again?"

"Haven't I right to be frightened?" She rubbed her palms against her thighs, thumbed them to see if they were dry and then dried them on her disheveled hair. "Who wouldn't be if he felt like a calf being led to the shambles?"

"Don't be foolish, Bertha."

"There's a curse on this tribe, I tell you. It's a bruised seed."

"Ach!" Impatiently. "Who is he? Tell me about him."

"I'm ashamed to."

"Shall we stop talking about it then?" His mother's look had an air of finality about it.

"No." Aunt Bertha frowned sullenly. "Even though you wouldn't tell me about yourself I'll tell you. Nathan Sternowitz is a—a widower. There you have it! Now you're satisfied, aren't you?"

"Well, in God's name!" his mother relaxed, relieved. "Is that all? Is that why you've been plaguing yourself and me? A widower. I thought he was—I don't know what— without legs or arms!"

"God forbid!" And then eagerly, "So you don't think it's a shame, a scandal that I should marry a widower —I'm not really an old maid."

"Nonsense!"

"But he's thirteen years older than I am. Thirty-eight,

mind you. And ai! he has two children already. It is a scandal!" she moaned dismally. "It is a scandal!"

"It's scandalous how silly you are!" her sister laughed shortly. "Do you love him?"

"Woe is me, no! And he doesn't love me either, so don't ask me."

"Well?"

"Oh, we're fond of each other. We laugh a great deal when we're together. We talk a great deal. But anybody can be fond of anybody who's fond of—Ai!" she exclaimed desperately. "I'm fond of him! But he doesn't believe in love! He says that love is a pinch here," she indicated her ample busts and then her thighs, "and a pinch there and nothing more. And if that's all it is, then I don't believe in it myself. But I'm not sure."

"It really isn't much more," his mother's upper lips creased into a smile. "If you want to look at it that way."

"But will they laugh at me? The girls in the shop? Or the folks in Veljish? When they hear I've married a widower with two daughters? They're half-grown, you know, ten and eleven."

"Veljish is too far away to worry about, sister. And even if it were only as far away as that Brownsville we lived in, why should you care? And you of all people worrying about what others think! For shame! I thought you were bold!"

"But to be a stepmother at twenty-five! Or even at twenty-six! What will it be like? To take the place of a woman in her grave? Ai!" She gnawed her thumb. "And they say they always forget and call you sometimes by their wife's name. Rachel! And she lies in her shroud! It makes me shudder!"

"So that's what you're really afraid of? You're superstitious! Well, if that's not the silliest thing I've ever heard!"

"I don't know," she answered spiritlessly. "I hate quiet and I hate death."

"Then don't fear! You probably won't meet either for a long time. I see you're just a child after all. But listen to me. Women in their shrouds aren't a bit jealous. It's the dead within yourself who won't sleep. That would be the least of my troubles. Still, if you can't get over it, if the very thought makes you so frightened, why do you want to marry him at all?"

Aunt Bertha's customary verve and impudence had vanished, and with it her boisterous manner that was part of her even when she spoke quietly. But though her lips drooped and she seemed to address her words to the floor, dully, falteringly, there was still a remnant of stubborn, blunt defiance in her tone and the way she jerked her head. "I'm not handsome—that you know—not even with that new powder on my face—or this bit of gold." She lifted her lip. "Don't cheer me! At me no one ever looks—not even on Sunday and you know I've stopped sleeping in my new dresses. Money for marriage brokers—may they choke—I haven't. So what else? He's the first one to ask me—well really the first—and he may be all. I don't want to wear my buttocks to the bone sitting in a shop," her calloused thumb and forefinger began rubbing together, "and weave paper flowers and rag flowers all my life."

"That's foolish, Bertha," her sister remonstrated gently. "You speak as though you had not one good quality, as though you were hopeless. Come, if one has asked, others will."

"The longer I wait, the more money I'll have to save. And out of my three dollars a week, if I save anything, it will be a long wait."

"No, it won't! Don't worry so much about saving. Just give the men a chance! You haven't been in the country long enough. Why, Bertha, New York is full of all kinds of men who would want you!"

"Yes!" was her gloomy answer. "It's also full of all kinds of glib, limber Jewesses who can play the piano. Go! Go!" she tossed her head petulantly. "By the time I learn to speak this tongue I'll be what? Thirty! Old and dry! Others have money, others can dance, can sing with their hands so—Tuh-Tuh-ruh! All I can do is laugh and eat—my only talents! If I don't get a man now—" She waved her hand as if throwing something away. "Maybe I won't even be able to do that."

"Ach! You won't lose your gusto so quickly." And after a short pause. "What is he like?"

She thrust her lips out deprecatingly. "A Jew, like others."

"Yes. Well?"

"In appearance, nothing, short as I am and as homely. He's slender though, and here and here," she pointed to the peaks of her brows, "his hair is creeping out. What he has is brown, curly. Two small eyes," she sighed gustily, "a long nose like a hinge. He's neat. He doesn't smoke—he's like Albert!" She snickered significantly. "But he has one habit I'm going to break him of—he cuts his bread into little boxes when he eats. He takes his own knife out and cuts it up. Pheh! But he's very pliant and he never grows angry. He's jolly. He tells long yarns. You see I could rule."

"I see."

"And I'll tell you more!" A swell of eagerness washed away her gloom. "He's not dull! He has schemes for making money. We could get ahead! This week he asked me whether I would like to run a candy store if we were married. He would buy it and I would run it. You know what that means? He could earn money cutting leggings. I would earn money in the store—"

"And the house?"

"To the devil with it! I hate housekeeping! Anyway, his two wenches are big enough to take care of that! A candy store! Life would be lusty that way! Heh! It would be like living at a fair all the time."

"And you could have your candy that way!" his mother laughed slyly. "You'll like that."

"So I would!" Aunt Bertha continued unaware. "Isn't it queer how it turns out—from candy to teeth to candy?"

"Yes. And may it all be with good fortune!"

"God willing! Then I can bring him here sometimes to have supper?"

"Why, of course!"

"And you won't say anything to Albert—at least till I tell you, till I'm sure? An engagement ring soon with God's blessing!"

"No."

"Ai!" Aunt Bertha put her palms together and prayed, "May he forget Rachel soon, that's my only wish! And if he doesn't," she suddenly screwed her mouth together shrewishly. "I'll take two stones and pound it out of his head!"

"With you for a wife, I think he'll forget her soon enough." His mother smiled . . .

VII

ABOUT a week had passed. On coming around the corner of Avenue D that afternoon, David spied his mother walking on the other side of the street. She was hurrying toward the house and carried several parcels in her hand. Catching sight of her accidentally this way always gave him an intense thrill of pleasure. It was as though the street's shifting intricacy had flowered into the simple steadiness of her presence, as though days not hours had passed since he had seen her before, because days not hours had passed since he had last seen her in the street. He bounded across the gutter and after her.

"Mama!"

She stopped, smiled down at him. "Is it you?"

"Yes." He fell into step beside her. "Where are you going?"

"Home, naturally," she answered. "Are you coming up stairs with me?"

"Yes."

"Carry this then," she handed him a parcel.

Laundry. He knew it by the clean smell and the yellow paper it was wrapped in. "Did the Chinaman give you those sweet candy-nuts?"

"I didn't think of asking," she answered apologetically. "A pity!"

"Mmm." He said mournfully.

"Next time, I will though."

"What are you carrying there?" he pointed to a small, square newspaper-wrapped object she held in her hand.

"A surprise."

"For me?" he asked hopefully.

"Well," she hesitated, "for everyone."

"Oh!" he looked at it dubiously. It seemed far too small a package to surprise everyone.

They had reached the house and went in.

"Can I see?"

"Yes, as soon as we've gotten upstairs."

At their door at last, he waited impatiently for her to find the right key. They tiptoed in. They never spoke above a whisper in the afternoon when his father was asleep in the bedroom.

His mother opened the newspaper—a picture.

"Oh!" He felt mildly disappointed.

"It doesn't pass muster?" she laughed.

David examined it more closely. It was a picture of a small patch of ground full of tall green stalks, at the foot of which, tiny blue flowers grew.

"Yes, I like it," he said uncertainly.

"I bought it on a pushcart," she informed him with one of her curious, unaccountable sighs. "It reminded me of Austria and my home. Do you know what that is you're looking at?"

"Flowers?" he guessed, shaking his head at the same time.

"That's corn. That's how it grows. It grows out of the earth, you know, the sweet corn in the summer—it isn't made by pushcart pedlars."

"What are those blue flowers under it?"

"In July those little flowers come out. They're pretty, aren't they? You've seen them, yes, you have, fields and fields of them, only you've forgotten, you were so young." She looked up at the walls. "And where shall I hang it? I saw a nail, a nail. When I was a little girl," she said irrelevantly, "a fire broke out in a neighboring house, and my cousin grew so excited that all he could do was cry— A ladder, a ladder, a ladder! An ax, an ax, an ax! Foolish things people say—There! There's one." She carried a chair carefully to the wall, stood up on it.

David had hardly ever seen his mother so animated, so gay before. He felt like laughing at her.

She stepped down and gazed up at the picture she had just hung. "It's a bit lofty even for corn but it will do. It's better than a calendar, anyway."

"What did you get it for?"

She shook her finger at him in playful warning. "We're having company, don't you know? Bertha's 'kippin-company-man' is coming. Do I say it well? She taught me." And after a pause. "Are you eager to see him?"

"Aaa!" He shrugged indifferently.

"Ach! What a bad nephew you are! Not even eager to behold you aunt's new suitor! He'll be your uncle if she marries him. You'll have an American uncle then. A yellow one. Did you ever think of that? Of course not! Ach, you!"

David regarded her silently, wondering why that should excite anyone.

"I really believe," she continued in a scolding, bantering whisper, "that you think of nothing. Now honest, isn't that so? Aren't you just a pair of eyes and ears! You see, you hear, you remember, but when will you know? If you didn't bring home those handsome report cards, I'd say you were a dunce, my only son."

"I'm going down," he answered steadfastly.

"Oh, you are a dunce!" she laughed ruefully. "Bertha is right! But wait! You'll have to be back a little earlier, darling. I must wash you and comb your hair and change your shirt for our visitor's sake."

"Naaa!" He was at the door.

"And no kiss?" She caught him by the shoulders, kissed him. "There! Savory, thrifty lips! Don't be late!"

He went down—wonderingly and just a little disturbed. He didn't mind being called a dunce. After all, she was only joking. Hadn't she laughed and kissed him? And beside, if he hadn't shown any interest in his future uncle, she hadn't shown any in himself. Forgetting Chinee nuts that way! When they were free too, and she knew how fond of them he was. He wondered if the Chinaman would give him any if he went in now and told him that his mother had just gotten some laundry out—what kind? Shirts. Yes. His father was going to dress up too. Maybe stiff collars, though the parcel didn't feel that way. Will you give me some nuts, Mr.—Mr. What? She forgot to ask, my mother forgot! Mr.—Mr. Chinee-Chink! Funny. Walk past anyway and look in. Funny. But—what? What? He had been wondering about something he told himself. Yes. Something. But now he couldn't remember. Not chinee-nuts. No. Company was coming? Maybe, no.

He left the stoop, turned west. The Chinese laundry was near the corner of Tenth Street and Avenue C. He walked slowly, idly, aware but no longer overcome or even troubled by the movement of vehicles and people. He knew his world now. With a kind of meditative assurance, he singled out the elements of the ever-present din—the far voices, the near, the bells of a junk wagon, the sing-song cry of the I-Cash-clothes-man, waving his truncheon-newspaper, the sloshing jangle of the keys on the huge ring on the back of the tinker. There was more blue in the air of afternoons now; the air was brisker fixing houses in a cold, sunless, brittle light. He looked up. They were both gone—the two cages on the first floor fire-escape. A parrot and a canary. Awk! awk! the first cried. Eee—tee—tee—tweet! the other. A smooth and a rusty pulley. He wondered if they understood each other. Maybe it was like Yiddish and English, or Yiddish and Polish, the way his mother and aunt sometimes spoke. Secrets. What? Was wondering. What? Too cold now. Birds go south, teacher said. But pigeons don't. Sparrows don't. So how? Funny, birds were. In the park on Avenue C. Eat brown. Shit green. On the benches is green. On the railings. So how? Don't you? Apples is red and white. Chicken is white. Bread, watermelon, gum-drops, all different colors. But—Don't say. Is bad. But everybody says. Is bad though. . . . And he drifted on toward the corner drug-store, glanced at the red and green mysterious fluid in the glass vases and turned right.

But was wondering. He sifted the mind's trinkets, searching for one elusive. Was wondering. Birds? Not birds. Bad words? No. Before that. When? Aunt Bertha, the new man? No. Can't find. Funny. Maybe his name? Mr—Mr. What. Yes. Maybe. No—But—Approaching the laundry, he gazed up at the low sign, the dull black letters against the dull red. C-h-Chuh-Ch-ar-ley. Charley, American name. Just like Charley in school. But something else maybe, like Yussie is Joey. Gee, forgot. Yussie! L-i-ng. Ling. Ling-a-ling. Is Jewish. Can't be. Ling. Don't like. How it hangs in the butcher shop. Mister Ling.

He stopped, looked at the window and as he was about to step closer, shrill familiar voices hailed him from behind.

"Hey, Davy!"

He turned. They were Izzy and Maxie; both lived in his block and both were in his class in school.

"W'ea yuh goin'?" Izzy asked.

"No place."

"So w'y wuz yuh lookin' in de Chinkee-chinaman's windeh?"

" 'Cause my modder god hea de lundry w'en I comm from cheder, bot she didn' ged no nots."

"So yuh wanna esk?" Izzy caught hold of the idea quickly. "Comm on, we'll all go in."

"Naa, I jos' wannid t'look," David thought rapidly. "Maybe my modder'll comm hea after, so I'll go in."

With one accord, they drew near the window, peered in under the shade of cupped hands. Within, behind the high-counter, painted green, the queued and slant-eyed laundry-man blew a spray of water on a piece of laundry out of a tin atomizer. He seemed too absorbed in his work to notice them.

"Betcha yuh could ged now!" Izzy urged. "Hey, Maxie, you go in an' say yuh Davy, like dat. So he'll t'ink yuh Davy, so he'll give. So we'll ged. Yeh? Den Davy's mama'll comm so we'll ged again."

"Yaa!" Maxie declined. "Go in yuhself! Dey god long knifes!"

"Like a lady, he looks," said Izzy reflectively. "Wod a big tail he's god on his head. Led's knock on de windeh. Maybe he'll look op."

"Maybe he'll run afteh yuh too." Maxie objected.

Izzy pressed his nose against the glass. "I knew a Chinky," he declared. "Wot he didn' hev no hen's. So he wrote wit' de mout' wit' dot stick all de funny like dat"—he squirmed and contracted into ideographs—"on de tickets."

"So how did he irun, wise guy?" Maxie sneered almost wearily. "How did he hol' de bigl-irun?"

"He didn' hol' id. Sommbody else holded id."

"Yuh see w'ea de Chinee nots is?" Maxie peered obliquely into the window. "In dot box? Yee! yum! yum! Dey break foist easy. Den dere's inside soft an' good. Yum! Den dere's inside black wood. So id's hod an' slippery. So yuh hol' id in yuh mout', so it gives wawdeh."

"I know sommbody," Izzy contributed, "wod he bruck de hod pod wid a hemmeh. An' inside wuz annuder liddle suft an' good. An' inside wuz anudder liddle black one. So he bruck dat. An' inside wuz anudder liddle suft an' good one an' inside wuz unudder liddle hod one. So—"

"So wot?" Maxie demanded belligerently.

"So he lost id."

"Pfuy!"

They were silent a moment, and then Izzy wistfully. "Bet I could eat a million!"

"Me too!" Maxie concurred eagerly. "W'en's yuh modder commin'?"

David was startled. He hadn't thought they would take him seriously. "I don' know," he answered evasively and began backing away from the window.

"But yuh said she wuz commin'," they insisted, following him.

"Maybe she ain'. I don' know."

"So w'ea yuh goin'?" They turned south toward Ninth, he north toward Tenth.

"No place." He looked blank.

"Wadda boob!" said Izzy vehemently. "He neveh hengs oud wid nobody."

And so they parted.

VIII

WHEN he came home, his father had already risen. Naked above the waist, the upper half of his heavy underwear hanging below his knees, he stood before the sink, drying the gleaming razor between the pinched ends of a towel. Under the blue mantle-light, his shaven face was stone-grey, harsher yet handsomer. The broad spindles and mounds of muscles along his arm and shoulders knotted powerfully as he moved. The muscles on his breast and smooth belly were square and flat. A few dark hairs curled over the white skin of his chest. He was powerful, his father, much more powerful than he looked fully dressed. It seemed to David, standing there before the door that he had never seen him before. And he stood there almost in awe until the single cursory glance his father cast at him, pricked him into motion and he walked waveringly toward his mother. She smiled.

"And now my second man," she said lightly. "Come! To your labors."

Looking round while he shed his coat and sweater, he saw that the kitchen was immaculate. The stove had been polished. The linoleum, newly mopped, glistened warmly. The windows were stainless against the blue twilight. The table, already set, had been covered with his favorite cloth, white, with narrow gold lines crossing in broad squares. He unbuttoned his shirt, removed it, slid out of his under-wear just as his father was wrestling into his, and glancing at his own slender, puny arms, glanced up in time to see the last flicker of long sinews before the naked arm was sheathed. How long would it be, he wondered, before those knots appeared above his own elbow and those tough, taut braids on his own forearm. He wished it were soon, wished it were today, this minute. Strong, how strong his father was, stronger than he'd ever be. A twinge of envy and despair ran through him. He'd never have those tendons, those muscles that even beneath the thick undershirt, bulged and flattened between shoulder and armpit, No, he'd never be that strong, and yet he had to be, he had to be. He didn't know why, but he had to be!

"Good warm water," said his mother filling a basin in the sink. "Now that we've a fire in the stove."

She pulled up a chair before the sink. David climbed up and began washing. Behind him, they were silent a few seconds and then he heard above the water he splashed about his ears, a crackling sound that reminded him of frozen wash bending. And his father's growl.

"One needs a wedge to get into these sleeves. Do they starch them with plaster?"

"Apparently! I don't know why they do it." She paused. "But only this once! And if we suit him, only once more!"

"Hmph!" he grunted while the crackling continued. "Let it come soon! If she thinks I of all people would throw obstacles in her way, she's out of her head. I wouldn't wear this plaster shirt if I didn't hope to get rid of her. You can tell her that for me if that's why she's been so secretive."

"It wasn't because of that, Albert. She wasn't afraid you would interfere. But after all, these things happen—well—not very often in a woman's life, and she wasn't sure. Besides, she was a little frightened—a widower, a wife in her grave—a little ashamed, you see."

"Pph! I'd call her fortunate if she were his sixth wife! And as far as he's concerned, a Russian doesn't know better and doesn't deserve better. But these underhanded wiles—Dentists four nights a week, gold-teeth, powder, mirrors! That fidgeting! Only God knew what she was up to!"

"They weren't so underhanded, Albert!" While she spoke, she pointed out to David, who had turned with dripping face, the towel beside the clean white shirt on the washtub. "Love, marriage, whatever one calls it, does that to one, makes one uncertain, wary. One wants to appear better than one is."

"It did that to you I suppose."

"Yes." She seemed hesitant. "Of course!"

"Bah!"

"Of course!" she reiterated, and then laughing. "You know how the old song goes: In this way and that, one beguiles the groom."

"Beguiles!" The lean, grey features sharpened. "Beguiles!" And then looking away absently, "Much to beguile—a Russian and a widower."

"But Albert!" she smiled slyly. "A Russian-Jew is also a man."

"I grant you."

"And she'll make him a good wife. Bertha is shrewd and what counts more she isn't shy. Clothes, she has no use for. And with a candy store of her own," she laughed, "there will be nothing for her to spend money on. From what she's told me, that's the kind of wife this Nathan wants."

"If she ever owns a candy-store and if she runs it the way she keeps her room there, then God help her customers. Here when she leaves hair-pins on the floor as thick as a stubble, all one can do is tread on them; there, they'll eat them, mark me. They'll be in every tray. And that red fox-tail she wears in her hair, they'll find it in the ice-cream. Has she ever put anything back where it belonged? Does she ever do anything with care? And the meals she'll cook him, Almighty God! With that rash, blind haste of hers, his stomach will be like mine the years before you came."

"Oh, she'll learn, Albert! She'll learn! She'll have to! I couldn't cook either before I married! After all we had servants when I was a girl—they did all the house-keeping, house-cleaning, cooking."

"Bah!" he interrupted her contemptuously. "I don't believe it. She'll never learn anything! And what does she know about children? Nothing! What a life they'll lead her! And she them. Two half-grown wenches on her hands the day she marries! Strangers to her. Hi! What a bedlam! A fate to befall one's enemies! Well!" He shrugged impatiently. "All I ask is to have it over with soon!"

David who had gotten on his clean shirt and tie by this time, maneuvered about to catch his mother's eye. She opened them wide in pleasure.

"Look how he gleams, your son!"

Impassively, his father's eyes rested on him, a moment, and away. "Why doesn't he comb his hair?"

"I'll do it!" She went quickly to the sink, wet the comb and passed it caressingly through his hair. "It was browner when you were very young, my son. My handsome son!"

His father reached out for the grey milk-route book that lay on the ice-box, opened it impassively, let the page ruffle under his fingers, (David remembered the ink stains once engraved upon them) and scowled.

"This belongs in my coat." He said abruptly, and was silent.

About half an hour later, Aunt Bertha and the new-comer arrived. Being present when a stranger was introduced to his father was always an ordeal for David, and this time it seemed more trying than ever. Aunt Bertha was flustered and red with embarrassment, which made her speech and her movements all the more hectic; so that her clipped, flighty, whirlwind of words and gestures caused his father to grow as stiff and aloof as if he were carved from stone. When the two men shook hands, his father merely grunted in reply to the greeting, and never meeting the other's eyes, glared grimly over his shoulders. Mr. Sternowitz, disconcerted, cast a quick, bewildered glance at Aunt Bertha who stabbed her brother-in-law first with a frown of pucker-nosed hate, and then replied with a reassuring, I-told-you-so smile. That dread moment over, at the suggestion of David's mother, they sat down, and seated, relaxed guardedly.

While conversation, in which David's father took no part, circulated about the room in short nervous spurts, concerned chiefly with dentists and with the difference between Aunt Bertha's "absah" and Mr. Sternowitz's "ulster," David examined the newcomer. He was, as Aunt Bertha had said, a little man, very long-nosed, blue-eyed, and sallow. A pale, narrow mustache, the tips of which he kept trying to draw down and bite, followed the margin of thin lips. His ears were overly large, soft-looking and fuzzy almost as red plush. In his small mouth as he spoke, gold teeth gleamed, and his sallow brow that knitted easily into long wrinkles, crept up in quick perspectives into the brownish kinky hair. Above his mustache, his face appeared good-natured, meek yet shrewd, below it, despite the small mouth and receding chin, he gave one the impression of peevish stubbornness. Altogether he looked rather insignificant and even a little absurd. And David scrutinizing him felt increasingly disappointed not so much for himself but for his aunt's sake.

After lauding the dentist—both he and Aunt Bertha had been present the evening an old woman had come to the office to test out her newly-made plates, and after eating a pear and a heavily poppy-seeded roll, had gone away satisfied—Mr. Sternowitz drifted to the leggings business and prophesied that it would soon disappear under earth. Children were wearing far less leggings than before. And it was because of the uncertainty of his future earnings, he informed them hesitantly, that he thought a man's wife ought to have an independent income—with which Aunt Bertha emphatically concurred. Uncertain at first, but continually spurred on and encouraged by Aunt Bertha and David's mother, Mr. Sternowitz gradually lost some of his apprehension at the other man's chill taciturnity and began to speak more freely. However, whenever his eyes met David's father's, the expression on his face tended to freeze into one of ingratiating self-effacement. David sympathized with him. He guessed that like himself, Mr. Sternowitz felt the necessity of continually humbling himself before the relentless, unwinking scrutiny of those eyes, the grey unrelaxing visage. Everyone had to bow down before his father, except Aunt Bertha, and as Mr. Sterno- witz's humility and self-deprecation increased, she became more chagrined and defiant.

David's mother had begun serving supper when Mr. Sternowitz, taking a preliminary nip at his mustache said, "My father was a servant!"

Up till now Aunt Bertha had given vent to her impatience by merely clicking her tongue against the roof of the mouth. But now apparently deciding on more strenuous measures, she inquired in a barbed tone, "And in rainy weather he carried two children on his back to the cheder. Didn't he, Nathan?"

"Yes." Mr. Sternowitz lifted hurt eyes from his plate. "So he did. I think I told you."

"Well, do you have to blare it out to everyone the first time you meet them? Won't it keep? Isn't it dry enough? Why don't you tell us about your mother's cousin who was a doctor? That's something to brag about!"

Above his mustache, Mr. Sternowitz looked crushed. "I didn't think of it," he said apologetically. But below it, as if some belated impulse thrust it out, his small chin worked its way forward. And he looked confidentially at David's father. "But he *was* a servant!" he maintained.

"Yes! Tell them everything!" Aunt Bertha tossed her head resentfully. "And your mother was blind when she bore you and purblind during your infancy. And she fed you vinegar instead of sugar-water. That's why you're so homely!"

"One has to speak about something," he maintained persistently. "Especially if everyone else is quiet."

"Ach! There's a forest of somethings!" Aunt Bertha countered fretfully. "I suppose when I go to see your relatives, you'll expect me to tell them in the first gasp that the only suitor I ever had——" Here she began to gesticulate and grimace violently——"Was a man who s-s-stammered. And when the marriage-broker said to him, Speak! Ox! What does he say, but, D-d-did y-your g-g-grand-m-mother l-like ch-ch-ch-cheese. Bah! Well I won't!" she concluded breathlessly.

"Have mercy, Bertha!" Her sister said. "What difference will it make whether he tells it sooner or later. We're bound to know one another."

"Perhaps!" was her significant retort.

Dejected, Mr. Sternowitz peeped up furtively from his plate first at David's father, still unsmiling and aloof, and then at Aunt Bertha, petulant. Then he blinked embarrassedly, tried to laugh, but without success, and uncertainly, "What did you say? I mean you—to—to the suitor?"

"I said, you'll have to ask my grandmother." She screwed her lips together tartly. "She's dead."

"Ai!" Mr. Sternowitz gnawed his mustache and looked around half-rueful, half-pleased. "She's going to lead me a fearful life, no? And even if I am a father of children, nothing will help me. Now, my first wife was older than I. But she had no tongue and she submitted. It may be that I'll have a younger one this time and—"

"And there won't be any third!" Aunt Bertha grinned maliciously.

"No," he acquiesced obediently. And then as if to reassure himself, "We're not married yet, no?"

"Pooh!"

"What was the matter with your mother?" David's mother asked after a pause.

Mr. Sternowitz, slice of bread in one hand had begun slowly and aimlessly to fish in his vest pockets with the other. "No one knew. The doctors" he shrugged, drew out a pearl-handled pen-knife, "they didn't know." His eyes met Aunt Bertha's. Her severe scowl swept down from his face to the knife. With an oddly remote movement, his neck bent stiffly and he stared at the knife also, turning it round and round as though he had never seen it before. "Er! They didn't know!" And sighing, "Woe me! A fearful life!" He dropped the knife back into his pocket and bit off too large a mouthful so that speech was engulfed in an oozy palatal smacking.

Aunt Bertha suddenly smiled, fondly, benevolently. "Champ it down, Nathan, my star, then you can tell what happened—or shall I?"

His temples bulging, Mr. Sternowitz chewed faster and shook his head hurriedly. He meant to speak.

"It was this way," Aunt Bertha ignored him. "He'll make a yarn of it as long as an ant climbing a mountain. His mother was going blind and so when the doctors couldn't cure her, his father took her to a rabbi and he cured her. No, Nathan?"

"Yes." Mr. Sternowitz swallowed glumly.

"Who was the rabbi they took her to?" asked David's mother.

Mr. Sternowitz cheered up. "Not one of those polite, wellbred rabbis, have no fear. Is it right," he turned to David's father for approval, "that a rabbi should allow Russian officers to visit his daughters? Or that they should be 'fency pipple' and not wear white socks and high shoes and trim their beards and their ringlets. Ha? No!" He seemed to interpret the other man's steady gaze. "That's what I believe. The more 'fency' they become, the less of God's power do they have. Reb Leibish, this rabbi, was so pious that he made his wife turn over the whole day's receipts to charity. He would keep no money over-night— not even a kopek. Not Reb Leibish! He hated the joys of life. He never accepted the Thursday invitation for the sabbath. He fasted twice a week. That's what I call a rabbi! And when my father brought her to him, he didn't say, Go home, I'll pray to God for a remedy. No. He had God by his side. He said to my father, Let her go! Take your hands away! And then he said, Come here, my daughter! And she said, Where? I can't see! And he cried out. Look at me! Open your eyes! The Almighty gives you light! And she opened her eyes and she saw! That's a rabbi!"

"How well she must have seen," Aunt Bertha patted her mouth vigorously—the sign of expiation for mockery, "if she gave you vinegar instead of sugar-water."

"Not all at once," Mr. Sternowitz protested. "But little by little, she saw. When I left Pskov she could see fairly well, but she squinted and—Look!" he laughed and pointed at David. "Look how he's staring at me. Isn't that wonderful?"

David ducked his head in intense embarrassment. It was true. Without knowing why he had been strangely stirred by Mr. Sternowitz's short narrative. He had been staring at him, hoping he would go on. But now he suddenly felt ashamed, feeling all eyes upon him and especially his father's. He stared down at his plate.

"Do you want to ask me something?" Mr. Sternowitz inquired indulgently.

"No."

"Sweet Golem with the big eyes!" his aunt teased. "You'll have to get him a pair of leggins, Nathan. Winter is coming."

"Indeed, yes! I'll steal a pair and finish them at home.

We must get his size. Such a quiet, quiet child!" he nodded approvingly. "Like—" His glance veered for a moment to David's father and then retreated hastily to Aunt Bertha again. "Like my daughters," he said jocularly. "No, Bertha?"

"To the dot!" was her derisive answer. "But they'll mind me, don't forget that."

"What else!" he grinned. "Just as they mind me? How old is he, did you say?"

"This one?" His mother patted his head. "Seven and a few months."

"He's well grown, no evil eye!" he dropped his fork and knocked on the table. "Mine are ten and eleven and they're no taller. Perhaps we'll match him with one of mine yet."

"Speaking of matches," Aunt Bertha suddenly placed a warning finger across her lips. "Nothing must be said to the 'dentistka', do you hear, Nathan? Else she'll sniff around for a marriage-broker's bounty. A turd I'll give her!"

"Have you reached that stage already?" her sister laughed. "May joy go with you then."

"I?" Mr. Sternowitz put out his palms. "I haven't reached it. She's reached it—headlong!"

"Is that so?" Aunt Bertha bridled. "Didn't you tell me last night you were already looking for a candy-store— in a good location—at a corner maybe—and at a reasonable price—and for me! Didn't you? If you think I'm yanking you too hard toward the canopy, then don't have Rachel's engagement ring reset. Pooh I can wait!" The scattering motion of her hand scattered Mr. Sternowitz away. "He's like all men. He thinks first of how he can use you, then in good time when he's going to marry you. You can't have the one without the other with me."

"Wait! Wait!" Mr. Sternowitz halted her. "What have I said that you burn so! I said that we didn't hold the yard-stick at a marriage yet. I meant we weren't engaged yet, that's all. I was thinking that if I gave you a ring—"

"If you give me the ring!" Aunt Bertha wagged her head mockingly.

"When I give you the ring then! When I give you the ring it will be better that you take it off before going to the dentist's, you understand? There won't be any trouble and nobody'll speak through the nose and we'll save fifty dollars."

"Now you're talking like a sage!" said Aunt Bertha approvingly. "Why didn't you say that in the first place?"

"Well," said Mr. Sternowitz uncomfortably. "Only give me room to breathe!"

"Have you found a candy-store that suits you?" asked David's mother. "I mean have you any in mind?"

"No, not yet." Mr. Sternowitz replied. "I really haven't begun to look for them seriously—naturally. But now I will. I know something about them. My cousin had one and I spent whole nights there. There's only one trouble. Most candy-stores have only two rooms in the back. That's all right for two people. But we—I mean I—have two children. They're with my sister now. So when I take them to live with me we'll need at least three rooms."

"It's going to be a hard life," David's mother shook her head, "living in the back of a store that way. The hurry and the noise! Wouldn't it be better to get rooms somewhere else? In the same house, perhaps?"

"If we live somewhere else," said Mr. Sternowitz, "there go half of the profits. Why throw away money on rent when you can get it free? A place to sleep in is all we need—and a place to eat a breakfast and a supper."

"I don't care where we live," said Aunt Bertha, "as long as we make money. Money, cursed money! What if it is a little uncomfortable. I never refused pot-roast because it got between my teeth. Now is the time to save. Later when we've sold the store and made a little money, we'll talk again."

"That's what I think also," Mr. Sternowitz rubbed his hands.

"Well, hurry to the jeweler then!" She rocked back and forth dreamily. "A little while we'll struggle; we'll pee in the dark. And then we'll have a home. And when we'll have a home we'll have a decent home. Thick furniture with red legs such as I see in the store windows. Everything covered with glass. Handsome chandeliers! A phonograph! We'll work our way up! 'Stimm hitt' like bosses! What bliss to wake up in the morning without chilling the marrow! A white sink! A toilet inside! A bath-tub! A genuine bath-tub for my suffering hide in July! A bath-tub! Not that radish grate there," she pointed to the washtubs. "Everytime I take a bath, it stamps a cluster of cherries on my rump!"

Heavy lidded, David's father frowned, nostrils twitching. David's toes crawled back and forth upon a small space on the soles of his shoe.

"You hear, Nathan?" As usual, whenever his father's wrath was kindling, Aunt Bertha never seemed to realize it. And now as before, she launched out unheeding upon a sea of extravagant vision. And almost intoned. "We'll have a white bath-tub! Hot water! A white bath-tub! Let it be the smoothest in the land! Let it be the slipperiest in the land! Like snot let it be slippery—"

"As you were wont to have in your old home." David's father broke his silence with deliberate words.

"So we did!" retorted Aunt Bertha, and with all the resentment of one jarred while drowsy. "Even though it did look like a coffin, it was made of tin and smoother than *that* sidewalk there! I thought when I came to this golden land, there would be something better to bathe in than a box full of stony burrs that scuff your—"

"Yes, I know! I know!" he interrupted harshly. "You're very delicately made!"

"And I'll get a better one!" she added vindictively. "I'll not be content with a cold water flat. I'll not live on a top-floor that was meant for goyim and paupers! This is a land where a Jew can make his fortune if he's got it in him—not to sit piously at a horse's tail all his life!"

"Bertha!" her sister exclaimed. "Bertha! Have you lost your senses! Don't make this event fatal!"

By some extraordinary act of will, David's father controlled himself. He spoke through his teeth—"The sooner you're on the road to your fortune, the better I'll like it. And don't think," he added with biting significance, "that if I don't go to your wedding I won't dance!"

Mr. Sternowitz was looking from one to the other with diffident, half-frightened eyes. "Ai, Bertha!" he attempted lightness. "Are you awful! Over—over a bath-tub to get so enraged! Come, what is a bath-tub!"

"A bath-tub is a bath-tub." She pouted sullenly. "What a bright suitor I've got!"

Mr. Sternowitz squirmed, blinked, dared not look at anyone. The hard-won relaxation of a few moments ago was destroyed entirely and everyone was on guard again.

Nor was there any hope of the tension ever easing, since dinner was almost over, and there would be nothing more to divert one. David's mother assayed a few vague remarks. They went unanswered. In the strained silence, Aunt Bertha, who looked close to tears, kept muttering under her breath—"Begrudges me everything. . . . His spite, his sour silence . . . God blacken his destiny." David looked around fearfully, hardly daring to think of what might happen. Finally, Mr. Sternowitz, after several preliminary coughs, thrust out his chin and smiled with forced and wavering heartiness.

"I'll tell you Bertha," he said. "Let us go for a walk. After such a fine dinner, nothing could be better, what? And we can step into one or two stores on the way."

"Anything!" she answered defiantly. "So long as we get away from here!"

Both rose, rather precipitately, and with a toss of her head, Aunt Bertha hurried into the front room to get their coats, leaving Mr. Sternowitz stranded in the kitchen. He looked about as though trapped, mumbled something about the dinner and watched the front-room door anxiously. In a few seconds, Aunt Bertha returned and both got into their coats. As she fitted her wide hat on over her red hair, Aunt Bertha raised her eyes to the overhanging brim and then stared beyond it at the wall—where the new picture hung.

David started. *That was it!* Now he remembered! The thing he was searching for! That he forgot down stairs! Funny—

She approached, scrutinized it. "Look, Nathan," she beckoned him, "what fine corn grows in my sister's garden. I didn't see it before." She turned questioningly to David's mother.

"I was wondering when someone would notice it," she laughed. "Perhaps in my haste I hung it too high."

"Quite pretty," Aunt Bertha looked at herself in her pocket-book mirror. "Are you starting a museum?"

"No. It was just a whim. And I found the ten cents to gratify it. Wasted money, I suppose." She looked up at the picture.

"Well, we must go," said Aunt Bertha resolutely. "I'll be back later, sister."

Good-nights were exchanged. Aunt Bertha and David's

father, the former fervid, the latter stony, crossed snubbing glances. Invited by David's mother to pay them many visits, Mr. Sternowitz accepted without too much zest, and after a bare smile from David's father, crowded out of the door in Aunt Bertha's lee. Silence followed. His father tilted his chair back against the wall with a violent thump and stared morosely at the ceiling. His mother cleared the dishes carefully, impinging on a look of anxiety, a look of abstraction. David wished they would talk. Silence only made his father more ominous. But the silence continued, and David feeling himself caught as if in talons of stress dared not move—at least not until his father spoke and eased the strain—and for escape meanwhile, could only stare at the new picture his mother had bought.

He began to wonder vaguely why it had followed him all afternoon, why it had tugged at the mind from the ambush of the mind. It was strange. Like someone trailing you behind a wall. And never know what it was until a few minutes ago. Funny. And then find out it isn't anything—only a picture of long green corn and blue flowers under it. Maybe it was because she had been so happy when she looked for the nail. She laughed when she hung it up. Maybe that was it. He didn't know why she was laughing. And she had said he had seen it too, real ones, long ago in Europe. But she said he couldn't remember. So maybe he was trying to remember the real ones instead of the picture ones. But how? If— No. Funny. Getting mixed and mixed and—

His father straightened suddenly, shoes and chair legs rapping the oil cloth smartly. His anger would break now! David stared at him half-welcoming the easing of the strain, half-terrified of the consequences.

"The vulgar jade!" he snapped. "The slut! How could you both have come from one mother! She and her dirty mouth and her bath-tubs and her manners. A million bath-tubs couldn't clean her. She and her bath-tubs! Who asked her to come here anyway! I've controlled myself long enough. I'll throw her out of this house yet!"

His mother had hung up the dish-rag and had turned slowly as though loath to undertake the task of appeasing him and stood silent, placing no obstacles in the path of his anger.

"Stabbing me in the back about my earnings. Boasting of the fortune she'll make and the palaces she'll live in! Making a fool of me before a stranger. As though I loafed, as though I didn't sweat for my bread as honestly and as much as any man! But I'll repay her, don't fret! No one can treat me that way. I've a notion to get up this moment and throw all her belongings out into the hall!"

"They'll be gone soon enough, Albert. Just be patient a little longer."

"Be patient with that wasp!"

"You see, she was frightened. She thought perhaps you had maimed her chances of marriage."

"I? I maim her chances? I'd rather maim her! And that filthy, clapping tongue of hers. She never moves it but my flesh begins to crawl—as though she were scattering vermin on me. Maim her chances! I want to get rid of her!"

"She doesn't want to stay here any longer than necessary either."

"She'd better not. And him! He's harmless. I might have pitied him. I might have thought, the poor idiot, he doesn't know what he's getting. Perhaps she's hidden her true self from him. But now I despise him! A weakling! After what he's seen and heard to want to marry that— that vile mouth! It would shame the water-carrier in a Russian bath! To give his children into the keeping of such a one. He deserves nothing but scorn!"

"Let him look out for that. Surely he's old enough and has seen enough and experienced enough to know what he wants. Perhaps he can even learn to handle her, one can never tell."

"Handle her! That button-hole maker. It takes a whip hand! I say he'd best begin digging his grave. But what do I care?" He shook his head savagely as though enraged at himself for showing any concern about Aunt Bertha's future. "Let her marry anyone, and anyone her. Let her listen to that fool's drivel about blindness and vinegar all her life. But if she thinks she can make light with me because she has a man with her, she'd better be careful. She's jesting with the angel of death!"

"Just don't mind her, Albert! Please! Let her go her own way. She'll let you go yours. I know! She'll probably not bring him here any more than she can help. They're already talking about rings."

"Well, as long as she stays here, she'd better be careful or I'll shorten her stay." He snuffed grimly through his nostrils, stared darkly before him at the opposite wall. His eyes lit on the picture. He frowned. "On what heap did you find that?"

"That?" Her eyes traveled upward. "On a pushcart on Avenue C. I thought I couldn't make more than a ten-cent mistake, so I bought it. You don't like it?"

He shrugged. "Perhaps I would if you had gotten it for some other occasion. But now—" He scowled. "Why did you get a picture of corn anyway?"

"Green," she said mildly. "Austrian lands. What would you have chosen?"

"Something alive." He reached for the newspaper. "A herd of cattle drinking such as I've seen in the stores. Or a prize bull with a shine to his flanks and the black fire in his eyes."

"That ought not to be difficult. I'm sure I could find you one of those as well."

"You'd better let me get it," he said curtly. And flapping the newspaper open, leaned over it. "I'm apt to be a better judge."

She lifted her brow resignedly and then glanced at David with a faint, significant smile as though letting him share with her the knowledge that his father had been mollified and danger was over. She turned back to the sink.

IX

ON SUNDAY—a bright Sunday just before Election day —David's father had gotten up from the table after lunch, and with some curt remark about going to listen to a campaign speech, had left. After he was gone however, Aunt Bertha scoffed at his sudden interest in political candidates and resentfully put her finger on what she declared was the real reason for his departure: Nathan (They all called Mr. Sternowitz by his first name now) was coming to call on her later this afternoon, and so David's father had gone away merely to avoid him. Which act, Aunt Bertha added venomously, was a very gracious one, albeit unwitting, and one for which she was very thankful, since she saw no reason to inflict that man's rude and surly presence on poor Nathan Sternowitz. Thus instead of insulting her, she concluded with spiteful triumph, David's father had really done her a good turn—but now that he had done it, she devoutly hoped he would break a leg on the way to wherever he was going. And when David's mother objected, Aunt Bertha charitably informed her that had her husband not been the sole support of his family, she would have prayed he had broken both legs. There! Wasn't that solicitude? And then followed her usual, disgusted query of why her sister had married such a lunatic.

David's mother had just folded the table cloth and now she waved it warningly at Aunt Bertha. "He'll overhear you some day, sister, and you'll pay for it dearly."

"Even with my head!" she retorted defiantly. "Just so he knows what I think of him."

His mother shook her head impatiently. "He does know! Don't you think he's had enough time to find out? And honestly I'm so weary of keeping you two from flying at each other. Albert must go his own way, but you—you might think of me sometimes and not make it so difficult. Let there be peace for a while. You're going to get married. You won't be here very much longer. Are you seeking to make your last months here end in a catastrophe?"

"Not for me!" her sister tossed her red head wilfully. "He won't throw me against the wall again. I'll gouge his eyes out."

His mother shrugged. "Why tempt him?"

"Ach, you make me sick—you and your mildness! Put poison in his coffee, that's what I'd do."

And David who was staring at her partly in wonder at her rashness, partly in guilty elation, caught his mother's apprehensive look directed at himself. And his aunt, detecting it also, added vociferously,

"I would! I would poison him! Let him hear me! I'm not afraid."

"But Bertha! I *am* afraid! You mustn't say those things before—ach!" she broke off. "That's enough Bertha." And turning to David. "Are you going downstairs, beloved?"

"Right away, Mama," he answered. But inwardly, he was too fascinated by his aunt's bold vituperations to want to leave just yet.

Rebuked by his mother, Aunt Bertha shrugged discontentedly, clucked her lips, wagged her head, but the next moment rebounded in her usual mad-cap fashion, and with head tilted upward bayed some Polish phrases at the ceiling. To David's mystification, the unknown words seemed to sting his mother, for she stiffened and suddenly exclaimed with uncommon sharpness—

"That's nonsense, Bertha!"

"Are you angry this time?" Her sister shook down several strands of coarse red hair before a provocatively wrinkled nose.

"Yes! I wish you'd stop!"

"Beloved and holy Name, give ear! She really can get angry! But listen to me! I have a right to be angry as well. I've been living with you for six months. For six months I've told you every thing, and what have you told me? Nothing! I'm no longer a child! I'm not the fourteen year old I was when you were a grown young lady. I'm about to be married. Can't you trust me? Won't I understand? Aaaah!" she sighed vehemently. "Would God, those twins had lived instead of died. They'd have been old enough to have seen, to have known. Then I'd have known too—Well?" She demanded challengingly.

"I don't want to go into it." His mother was curt. "I've told you before. It's too long ago. It's too painful. And further I haven't time."

"Bah!" she flopped suddenly into a chair. "Now you haven't time. It's just as I said. First—" She lapsed suddenly into Polish. "Very well. You might be forgiven. Then—" Again meaning disappeared. "Then—It's just as I said! Keep it for yourself! I'll get married without knowing." And she was silent, staring morosely out of the window.

At the opposite side of the room, his mother was also silent, also before a window, head lifted, gazing meditatively up at the brown, glazed brim of the rooftop and the red brick chimneys overhead. To David, they looked very odd suddenly, each woman back to back, each gazing out of different windows, one down out of the curtained, noisy, street-window, the other up out of the curtainless, quiet one; one seated, fidgeting and ineffectually trying to cross thick knees, the other standing motionless and abstracted. Despite powder his aunt was ruddy in the sunlight, short-necked and squat beside the open sky; in the thin shadow where she stood, his mother was tall, brown-haired and pale against the cramping air-shaft wall.

And what was it about, he wondered. What did those Polish words mean that made his mother straighten out so. Intuition prompted him. He divined vaguely that what he had just heard must be linked to the sparse hints of meaning he had heard before, that had stirred him at first so strangely and afterwards scared him. Now perhaps he might learn what it was about, but if he did, something might change again, be the something else that had been lurking all the time beneath the thing that was. He didn't want that to happen. Perhaps he had better avoid it, better go down. Now was the time, before anybody spoke. But what? His breath quickened before a danger that was also a fascination. What was it? Why wouldn't she speak? He would stay here only until—until— No! Better go down—

"Look David!" Without getting up from her chair, Aunt Bertha was craning her neck to stare out into the street. "Come here. Look how they're hauling that box."

David drew near the window, looked down. In the dull street below, their shouts muffled by the window, a swarm of boys of various heights and ages now dragged, now tumbled a bulky packing-box along the gutter, and in their eagerness to lend a hand, impeded one another, shoved one another out of the way, shook fists and forgot about it promptly and grappled with the box again.

"What are they yelping about?" his aunt inquired. "Whose wood is it?"

"It's nobody's," he enlightened her. "It's 'Lection' wood."

"What do you mean 'Lection' wood?"

"They're going to burn it on 'Lection' day. They always make a big, big fire on 'Lection' day. That's where

Papa went. There's pictures on the barrels and all the beer saloons."

His mother turned from the air-shaft window. "I've seen it in Brownsville too, in the open lots. Such is the custom here. To make a fire on the day they vote—it falls on Tuesday. Is Nathan a citizen, Bertha?" she asked placatingly.

"Yes, of course!" Aunt Bertha's tone was still sulky, the movement of her shoulders as she turned brusquely toward the window again, still offended. "What else!"

Seeing the queer hopeless lift of his mother's brow, David again resolved to go down. Whatever it was that caused this tension, and it was the most determined he had ever seen between his aunt and his mother, it was not only baffling but disagreeable. Yes. He would go down.

"Well, why are they dragging it now?" Aunt Bertha turned to him peevishly. "Are they going to burn it for a taste of what's to come?"

"No. They hide it," he said self-defensively. "In a cellar. It's in 732 cellar and 712 cellar near where the rabbi is. But yesterday, big men came and a street cleaning wagon, a brown one, and took it all away."

"And now they're getting more! Bah! American idiots! Pull their bowels out for a fire in the street they'll never make. But when it comes to dragging wood for their mothers, they're too lame, ha? And you!" she demanded accusingly. "Do you haul wood?"

"N-no," he lied. It was true though that he hadn't helped get election wood more than once or twice.

"Hum-m-m!" Aunt Bertha sighed with boredom and glanced at the clock. "An hour and a half before my nosey one comes. I feel lonely."

"Listen to me, Bertha," his mother said in a suddenly strained voice as though she had resolved upon a step but prayed it wasn't necessary. "Do you really want to hear?"

David's heart tripped with excitement. Better go down, his mind warned almost dizzily. Better go down. But instead, he dropped to his knees and crawled vacantly toward the stove.

As if jabbed with a pin, Aunt Bertha had wheeled around half-leaping from her chair. "Do I want to hear?" she exploded. "A question! After these months of asking?

Do I want to hear!" She stopped suddenly. Her look of
avid interest gave place to one of apology and self-
reproach. "No, no, sister! If it's difficult for you, then say
nothing. Don't even begin! Really I'm ashamed of myself
for plaguing you."

"There's nothing to be ashamed of," his mother's smile
was at once bitter and forgiving. "One has to speak of
these things sometimes. I don't know what possesses me
to want to keep them sealed up so tight."

"And as I've said to you a thousand times," Aunt
Bertha urged reasonably, persuasively, bridling her eagerness. "It was all so long ago, it should be a jest to you
by now. And whatever it is, can it frighten *me?* I know
you, sister, how good of heart you are. Too great a wrong
you couldn't have done."

"It was great enough. Enough for one life-time."

"Yes?" Aunt Bertha scratched her back against the back
of her chair. "Yes?" She settled down receptively.

"There are only three people who know," she began
with an effort. "Mother, father, myself of course, and—
and another—in part. I shouldn't want—"

"Oh! No! No! No! Trust me, Genya."

David squirmed, shivered with anticipation, fear.

"You remember," she began and then stopped, her
eyes meeting his from where he gazed up at her. "Let
it be so."

The oblique nod of her head seemed to beckon her
sister to join her in the realm of another speech. For
when she spoke again her words had fused into that alien,
aggravating tongue that David could never fathom.
Chagrined, he looked at Aunt Bertha. She was leaning
forward eagerly the better to devour all that was said,
her mobile features sometimes aping his mother's, sometimes contradicting. Her eagerness tantalized him,
goaded him into sharper listening. It was no use. He
scrutinized his mother. The color had risen in her throat.
Now her eyes stared and were dark and she spoke rapidly. Now they narrowed and the wide brows knit crookedly. Pain. What hurt her? Now she sighed and dropped
her hand and her face grew slack and mournful and her
slow lids heavy. What? But though he pried here, there,
everywhere among the gutturals and surds striving with

all his power to split the stubborn scales of speech, he could not. The mind could get no purchase.

Sullen, resentful almost to tears, he rolled over on his back, stared at the ceiling. He didn't care, that's all. He wouldn't tell her anything either. There! He was going down, that's what he would do. Never tell her anything —But—Listen! That was a yiddish word! A whole phrase! "After the old organist, dead" . . . Another! "Alone in the store" . . . A word! "Handsome" . . . Like mica-glints in the sidewalk, another phrase! "A box of matches" . . . He turned stealthily to watch her.

"And he seized my hand." A whole sentence emerged.

Aunt Bertha, who with hand on cheek had been shaking her head in a shocked manner, now beat the air angrily with her fists. "Even if he was educated," she exclaimed heatedly, "and even if he was an organist, he was a goy! And right then and there you should have sent him looking for his teeth!"

"Hush!" she said warningly and again blotted out import under a screen of Polish.

A little ashamed of himself, but secretly gratified nevertheless, David looked vacantly away. Here at last was something to brood on, perhaps even to worry a meaning out of, certainly to remember. A goy, Aunt Bertha had said, an 'orghaneest'. What was an 'orghaneest'? He was educated, that was clear. And what else, what did he do? He might find out later if he listened. So he was a goy. A Christian. They didn't sound the same. Christian. Downstairs, the janitor was a Hungarian. Christian too. Chrize. Jesus Chrize they said down stairs. Chrize. Christmas. School-parties. Then long ago, remember? Yussie. See him on the stairs, white-iron arrows white-iron, Annie, leg. Christmas. Then no school. Gee! Yea! And new calendars, remember? Lots of pages. Christmas. Jesus Crotzmich, the grocery man said and he always laughed. Crotzmich means scratch me. Jesus scratch me. Funny. And why did Aunt Bertha say hit him? Because he was a goy? She didn't like goyim. But mama? She did. Wonder? Who was he?

He turned to regard his mother. When would another phrase break from that alien thicket? He waited impatiently, mind beating the coverts . . . Nothing . . . Like a fabric the unknown speech flowed on riftless, opaque, until—

"Bah!" Aunt Bertha sheared it with contempt. "All these rogues have tongues on castors!"

"My fault as well!" protested his mother, reverting to Yiddish in forgetful haste. "Toward May I grew so, I spent the whole day waiting for a half hour at twilight. How many times a day did I wish it were winter, mid-winter when the moon is yellow before five. Long before sunset, I was already at the store, and it was all I could do to keep from reminding father to hurry off to the synagogue."

"Ach! You were mad."

"But that was only a taste. You don't know how mad I was—" Her voice took on a throbbing richness now that David had never heard in it before. The very sound seemed to reverberate in his flesh sending pulse after pulse of a nameless, tingling excitement through his body. "Day grew worse than darkness. I welcomed the light only when some Polish townsman died—You recall the priest and the banners and the funeral procession that went through the town? Ludwig was always in the train, chanting the services. I could watch him then as he went by, follow with the others a little ways, stare at him unafraid, Love—"

With the same suddenness as before, meaning scaled the horizon to another idiom, leaving David stranded on a sounding but empty shore. Words here and there, phrases shimmering like distant sails tantalized him, but never drew near.

He writhed inwardly at his own impotence.

It seemed to him, lying there almost paralyzed with the strain, that his mind would fly apart if he brought no order into this confusion. Each phrase he heard, each exclamation, each word only made the tension within him worse. Not knowing became almost unbearable. He felt as if nothing he had ever known were as important as knowing this. Who was Ludwig? Was that he, the goy! Why was he at funerals? What did she mean when she let a word drop about wicker baskets? Attics? Letters? Mere curiosity had petrified into obsession. But still the phrases flickered on as ephemeral and capricious as before, as thwart-

ing—the abrupt and fragmentary glimpses of a figure passing behind the brief notches of parapets.

"And the welcome over . . . And mother also down-
cast . . . But too deep in joy to notice . . . These things,"
she tapped her brow, "they wait their time inside one's
head . . . Stone under water till the eddies rest . . . And I
sought him . . . Nowhere . . . And I remembered it
. . . one glance would comfort me . . . The attic stairs
. . . And on my nails across the loose boards . . . The wicker
basket lay . . . Safe I thought . . . Carefully!" Her clenched
hands went up as though she were lifting a heavy lid.
"You know how wicker creaks—"

Her sudden, involuntary gasp was like a steep, sheer
drop in the level-flowing matrix of her speech. Her hand
went to her lips. The horror that came into her face was
such that it seemed to David not something thought or remembered, but something she beheld this moment, something present in this very room. A shudder ran through
him, watching her, "The light before my eyes grew black!
Dear God! There on the very top of the pile of coats lay
the portrait. Gazing up at me, there on top!"

"They knew," Aunt Bertha exclaimed.

"They knew," his mother repeated.

"But how?"

"I found out later. I had forgotten that mother went
through the trunk every summer with camphor."

"While you were away?"

"No. Before. They sent me away because they knew."

"Ah!"

"My despair then! My shame! You wouldn't know unless you had felt it. There are no words. I thought I should
faint. I picked up the portrait—They had read the back
no doubt. They knew all. Had I—"

And again his mother's eyes met his and again her
speech changed abruptly. David rose to his feet. He
couldn't bear it any longer, this suspense, this waiting for
significance to cut the surface like momentary fins of sunk-
en shapes. He was going down, that's what he was going
to do. He wouldn't listen a moment longer. And if the
time came when he knew something they didn't know, he'd
pay them back in the same coin. He'd learn to talk the way
the girls talked in the street—alligay walligay. Look at
them! They weren't even noticing him they were so en-

grossed. Even when he stood up and stared at them, no one paid any attention to him. They wouldn't even know he had gone into the front room to get his coat. They wouldn't even know he had gone. No! Then he wouldn't say goodbye. That's what. He'd just go down without a word.

He went petulantly into the front room and found his coat. But as he put it on, frustration forced a cunning thought into his brain. He would sit here and wait. He'd give them their last chance. If they didn't know where he was, perhaps they'd speak in Yiddish again. With the door open between them, he could hear in the front room as well as he could in the kitchen. He sat down stealthily beside the doorway and listened. But even though he was out of her sight, his mother seemed not to realize it. The significance of what she said still continued to be fragmentary.

"Must see him . . ." The words and phrases pulsed out as before. "Comfort . . . On the church step . . . She held both . . . Fluttered her parasol . . . Ogled him like a lamp . . . Lace, elegant ribbons . . But old, as I say . . . Gave her no thought . . . Finally . . . And parted . . . Crossed his path . . . He followed . . . Waited among the trees . . ."

Trembling with silent fury and despair he was about to give up. She would never speak. There was no use waiting, no use hiding. He would hear nothing. But as he pushed himself to his feet, Aunt Bertha's impatient voice interrupted his mother's—

"Who was this woman? Speak. Do you know? I'm curious."

"She? I was coming to that." This time his mother's words were entirely in Yiddish and completely intelligible. "When I told him what had happened, that they knew, that I was willing to follow him to the corners of the world, he answered—What folly! Don't you ever think beyond the morrow? How can I marry you? Where will we go? With what? And he was right. Of course he was right!"

"He may have been right," Aunt Bertha spat out vehemently. "But cholera choke him anyway!"

He had sat down and now was secretly hugging himself in guilty elation. They had forgotten about him. They had! He pressed closer to the wall and prayed his mother would go on speaking in Yiddish. She did.

"Anywhere, I said. I'm ashamed to tell you, Bertha, but it's true. I said I'd go with him just as he saw me."

"What a fool you were!"

"Yes. That's what he said also. A love affair is one thing, marriage another. Didn't I understand? I didn't. I'm already engaged, he said."

"She!" Aunt Bertha exclaimed. "That older woman you spoke of?"

"Yes."

"Did you spit in his face?"

"No. I stood like one frozen. You love her, I asked? Bah! he said. Could I? You saw her! I may as well tell you. She's rich; she has a dowry. Her brother is a road-engineer, the best-known in Austria. He'll provide the rest. As for me, I'm poor as the dark. All I could ever hope to be is a threadbare organist in a village church. And I refuse. Do you understand? Surely you yourself wouldn't wish that fate on me! But listen, he said and tried to seize me in his arms. We can go on again. In a little while, after this cursed marriage is over, we can go on again, just as we are. Be just what we've always been to each other. No one need know! I pushed him away. Does this make so much difference to you? he asked. Because I must marry? Will you now tear out all the love you held for me?

"I don't know why? I can't tell. But suddenly I began to feel like laughing. It was as though everything inside of me were lifting up with laughter. By the mad smile on my face, he must have thought I was yielding, for he seized my arm and said: Look at me Genya! Forgive me! See how poor I am! I haven't even the clothes decent enough to marry in. Genya, I'll repay you. Get me the cloth as you love me! Your father's store! A little while and we'll be together always!

"How shall I put it into words—the fullest cup of death! It seemed to me that heaven and air were filled with laughter, but strange, black laughter. God forgive me! And words I heard, gnashing in it like teeth. Strange words about roses! I came running, I came running with flowers! Like a child! Good-bye and good-bye! Madness, I tell you Bertha, sheer madness!

"Well, he left me standing there. I came home at last.

Mother was already in the doorway, waiting for me. Father wants to see you in the store, she said.

"I knew why and turned without a word and walked toward the store. She was behind me; we both went in together; she shut the door. None of you were there. It was kept secret from you. Father was standing before the counter. Well, my gentle Genya, he said—you know how bitingly he could sneer—Is gall a spicy drink? How does it taste? Does one smack the lips after it? I didn't answer. All I could do was weep. Weep! So! He was like a mother gone insane. Weep! Ah! He rubbed his paunch as though he were eating a delicacy. Ah! It does my heart great good! Don't torment me, father, I said. I've suffered enough! Ha! he said as if he were shocked. Are you suffering? Miserable, pitiful little child! I kept quiet then and let him have his way. You call that suffering, he cried, Why? Because he held you under him like dung in the privy and drops you now? That was father's way!" A deep sigh interrupted her.

"I know," said Aunt Bertha vindictively. "May his tongue also fall out."

"He kept on. Like screws into my breast his words. Torment more than I could bear. I tried to run past him to the door. He seized me and slapped me across both cheeks."

Her voice had become strangely throaty now, dull, labored.

"Then nothing mattered. Suddenly nothing mattered. I can't tell you how, but all pain seemed to end. I shrank. I felt smaller suddenly than the meanest creature crawling on earth. Oh, humble, empty! His words fell on me now as on the empty air. And where will you go? he screamed. Esau's filth. He has a new one! He has a new one! A rich one! Kicked you out, has he not? You false slut! And meanwhile mother kept crying out, They'll hear you outdoors Benjamin, they'll hear you! And he would answer, let them hear me, shall I not howl with a heart on fire. I'm bursting I tell you! I'm strangling! And then he plucked off his black skull-cap and threw it in my face and stamped with his feet like a child in convulsions. Ach! It was frightful!

"Finally mother began weeping. I beg you, Benjamin, she cried, You will overtax your strength. You'll have a stroke, Stop! Stop in the name of God!

"And father did stop. Suddenly, he fell into a chair and covered his face with his hands and began rocking back and forth. Alas! Alas! he moaned. Somewhere, in some way I have sinned. Somehow, somewhere, Him I have offended. Him! Else why does He visit me with anguish great as this?—You know him!"

"I know him!" said Aunt Bertha significantly.

"Now you may see what you have wrought my daughter, said mother, Was your heart of iron? Had you no pity on a Yiddish heart? No pity on your father? I wept —What else was there to do. Not only is she herself ruined, said father, Let her be! Let her die! But me! Me! And my poor, young daughters and the daughters to come. How shall I marry them? Who will marry them if this is known? And he was right. You would all of you have been on his hands forever. Well, he wished himself dead. Hush, said mother, none will speak; none will ever know. They will! They will, I say! Foulness like hers can never be hidden! And who knows, who knows, tomorrow another goy will find favor in her eyes. She's begun with goyim. Why should she stop? And he began shouting again. I tell you she'll bring me a 'Benkart' yet, shame me to the dust. How do you know there isn't one in that lewd belly already—That's a father for you!" Her words were bitter as she paused.

—Benkart! (Beside the doorway David fastened on the word) What? Know it. No, don't. Heard it. In her belly. Listen!

"And you defended him before!" Aunt Bertha reproached her.

"Well, I wasn't entirely innocent."

"Go on!"

"If you drive her away, mother said, all will know it. You've cursed your other daughters as well. I? I cursed them? She! That shameless one! And he spat at me. But you must forgive her mother begged. Never! Never! She is foul! And so it went on until mother took me by the arm, and said, she will kneel before you Benjamin, she will weep at your feet, only forgive her—Shrunk, I say, less than nothing." His mother's voice became curiously flat and monotonous as though she were enumerating a list of items all of equal unimportance. "Mother led me over to him. From her apron pocket, she drew out Ludwig's picture. I must have left it on the bed when I took it out of the wicker basket. She thrust it between my fingers and she said, lift your eyes, Benjamin. See, she tears it to bits. She will never sin again. Only look at her. He lifted his eyes, and I tore it—once and again and threw myself at his feet and wept on his hand.

"You can't imagine how awful I felt. I can hardly talk about it even yet, it afflicts me so. But fortunately no shadow ever broke a rock, and one can ask himself why he lives a thousand times and yet never die."

"Did he finally forgive you?" Aunt Bertha asked.

"Oh, yes! In his fashion. He said, may God forgive you. If you ever marry a Jew I'll take it as a sign. You see I married one. It was about six months later I met Albert."

"I see," Aunt Bertha said. "That's how it played itself out?" And then eagerly. "And him Esau, swine, did he ever come near you again?"

"No. Of course, I saw him often from afar. And once near—a few days before they left for Vienna. To get married."

"All the way to Vienna? Hmph! And the town church, may it burn to the ground, didn't that suit the new aristocrat?"

"No, I don't think that was the reason. Her brother had some business there, at least so his servants told me who came into the store."

"Did he speak to you?"

"When?"

"You say you saw him near at hand."

"Oh. No, we didn't speak. He didn't see me. I was standing in the road one afternoon when I saw a yellow cart coming toward me. It had two yellow wheels—The kind the rich drove in those days. And I knew even before I could see who was driving, that it was the brother of his betrothed. He drove in it often to where the men were working on the new road. I hid in the corn field nearby. It wasn't the brother-in-law this time, but Ludwig himself and the grand lady beside him. They passed. I felt empty as a bell till I looked at the blue cornflowers at my feet. They cheered me. That was the last I saw of him I think."

—Blue corn flowers? Likes them! Corn! That was—!

Inside on the wall! Gee! Look at it later! Listen! Listen now!

"And such was the ugly plague the new road brought with it." Aunt Bertha mused sourly. "But taking it all in all, you were fortunate, sister, fortunate that someone came to take that enemy of Israel away. If not, if, God forbid, you had married him—Pheh! How frightful! Where would you have hidden your head when the day came and he called you scabby Jew! Oy! You were better dead! So you see," she suggested cheerfully, "the road didn't bring evil after all. But just the same," she concluded with meticulous piety, "may it be God's will that the maker of the road and his sister and his brother-in-law meet with years as black and as long as that road! No?"

—Road. Black! Black! Where did I hear it before? Black? Not now.

His mother had paused. Now she clucked her lips in a slight sound of distaste. "Well, I've told you. And now that I have I don't know whether I'm glad I did or not."

"Pooh!" Aunt Bertha scoffed, belligerently. "Why? I promised you I wouldn't say anything about it. Besides, whom is there to tell? The shop-girls in the flower factory? Well, Nathan perhaps. But he wouldn't—What are you so afraid of?" she interrupted herself. "Would Albert be jealous if he knew?"

"I don't know. I've never tested him. Besides, he doesn't seem to want to know these things, and so I'm just a little afraid of your—well—rashness! But come!" she said abruptly. "Let's talk of the living."

"Yes!" There was alacrity in Aunt Bertha's voice. "My Nathan will be here soon. Has any of the powder come off my nose?"

His mother laughed. "No. It will take longer than that."

"I can always smear it down from my nose to my cheeks. That's the advantage of having plenty there. You know, Nathan is very fond of your baking?"

"I'm happy to hear it. We'll get some kupfel out."

"Too bad we haven't any schnapps."

"Schnapps? Why schnapps? A Russian wants tea."

"Yes," Aunt Bertha laughed. "And thank God he's a good pliant man and a Jew. I'll never have a heartbreak such as yours. But one never knows. And tell me," she switched in her sudden giddy fashion. "Your husband says I do everything with my left hand now that I have an engagement ring. Is that true?"

"Oh, no! Not at all!"

David started. They had begun stirring about the kitchen, and here he was still squatting beside the doorway. They would see him. They would know he knew. They mustn't. He got softly to his feet, sneaked to the furthest window and peered out intently. Pretend he had just been looking out all this time, that he hadn't heard. Yes. But now he knew. What? Had anything changed? No. Everything was the same. Sure. Didn't have to get scared. What had happened? She liked somebody. Who? Lud—Ludwig, she said. A goy. An organeest. Father didn't like him, her father. And his too, maybe. Didn't want him to know. Gee! He knew more than his father. So she married a Jew. What did she say before? Benkart, yes, benkart in belly, her father said. What did that mean? He almost knew. Somebody said—who? Where? Gee! Stop asking! Look outside before they come in.

Realizing intuitively the necessity of having to explain his presence in the front room, his eyes swept the outdoors hastily, seeking some object prodigious enough immediately to distract curiosity from himself the moment he called his mother's attention to it. Beyond the straggly roof-tops was the thin band of grey-green river and the smoke stacks on the further shore. Against the dusty-blue sky above the horizon, the cold, white smoke of an unseen tugboat frayed out and drifted. No. That wouldn't do. Couldn't ask anything about those. What then? He pressed his brow against the cold window pane and peered down into the avenue. Passersby walked more briskly now that November was here; they leaned a little in the wind, head sunken in coat-collars, hands in pockets. The breath of horse-car teams and hurrying pushcart peddlars had become visible. Getting colder . . . Sewers did that too . . . Saw them when? Could ask why. No. A Negro passed. Was his? Yes. White too. He could ask that. Why does he breathe white if he's black? No! Dumb-ox! They'll laugh! But something, something he had to ask, to pretend to be fascinated by or they'd guess—

Two small boys crossed the car tracks on Avenue D and squatted down on the curb. One of them had been carrying a round, tawny-colored object that not until it was set in the gutter against the curb did David recognize it. It was a headless, stove-in celluloid doll with an egg-shaped bottom, the kind that when they were pushed, bounced upright again. He had seen them before in the candy-stores. But what were they going to do? They looked so engrossed, so expectant. He squinted to see better. Exultantly he told himself that here was his excuse, here was the fascinating thing that had kept him there all this time. If only they would hurry up. One of them, apparently the owner, took something out of his pocket, struck it against the sidewalk—a match. Cupping it carefully, he touched it to a cracked edge of the doll—It flared up with a burst of yellow flame. They recoiled. He could hear their muffled shouts. And then one pointed to the spot where the doll had been and where now nothing remained except the char against the curbstone. The other bent down and picked up something. It glittered like a bit of metal. Both stared at it—and David did too from his height.

Behind him he heard his mother mention his name. He turned to listen.

"I lost him somewhere," she said casually. "Did he go down, Bertha?"

"That's queer," was the reply. "I thought I saw him go into—Why I think he must have gone down."

"Without a good-bye?" His mother's voice preceded her through the doorway. "Oh!" She looked at him keenly. "Are you still here? I thought—What makes you stay in this cold room?"

"In the street," he answered, pointing gravely to the window. "Come here, mama, I'll show you a trick."

"Oh, then he is here." Aunt Bertha came in also. "He's been something too quiet even for him."

"He's going to show me a 'drick'," his mother laughed. She understood 'drick' to mean kick, which in Yiddish had the same sound.

"A 'drick'," Aunt Bertha asked grinning. "Where? In the pants?"

"You see downstairs?" he continued soberly. "That boy? He has a green stocking-hat. He burned a doll and he made 'mejick'. And now he's got a piece of iron. You see it? In his hands? Look!"

"Do you know what the simpleton's jabbering about?" Aunt Bertha inquired.

"Not yet." Smiling, his mother peered down at the two boys below. "Yes. I do see a bit of iron. What do you mean 'mejick'?"

"There's a little piece of iron," he explained. "In that kind of doll. That's what makes it stand up when you push it over. And the doll burned. And only the iron is left."

"Aha!" Still smiling, she shrugged. "Well, come into the kitchen anyway. You'll get a chill here. Do you know it's growing cold, Bertha?"

David followed them out of the front-room. Easy, he thought in hazy satisfaction. Easy fool them. But they didn't fool him. Didn't scare him either. Didn't change . . . Gee! The picture! Not now, though. Look at it later, when nobody's here . . . Green and blue it's—Sh!

BOOK III
The Coal

I

TOWARD the end of February, a few weeks after Aunt Bertha had married, David's father came home from work a little later than usual. David was already at home. The morning had been snapping cold, surprising for that time of the year; the afternoon had turned dull and sleety. With his customary brusqueness, his father flung his dripping, blue milkman's cap on the washtub and began peeling off his rain-soaked mackinaw; then the vest beneath and the grey sweater. That sense of drowsy desolation that David had felt a long time ago when his father's arising had wakened him, he felt again, watching him, reminded of the bitter cold and the long darkness. Puffing, his father worked his heavy rubbers loose and kicked them under a chair. They left a slimy trail on the linoleum.

"You're a little late this afternoon," his wife ventured.

"Yes." He dropped wearily into a chair. "That nag of mine fell on the way to the stables."

"The poor beast! Was she hurt?"

"No. But I had to unharness her and fetch ashes and then harness her again. And all the while a crowd of numbskulls gawking. It took time. I shall curse tomorrow's dawn if it freezes again." He stretched, his jaw-muscles quivering. "It's about time they gave me a sounder animal anyway."

After a year of working as a milkman, that was the only thing his father consistently grumbled about—the horse he drove. And David, who saw the grey angular beast almost every day, had to admit that his father's complaint was just. Tilly, she was called, and she had one eye the cloudy color of singed celluloid, or a drop of oil on a sunless puddle. She would stand patiently, even when children were pulling the hairs out of her tail to plait rings with. And yet she seemed no weaker and no worse than most of the horses who passed through Ninth Street. It was just one of his father's fixations, David had concluded, to want tremendous power in the beast he handled just as he himself seemed possessed of tremendous power. Though he pitied poor Tilly immensely, David hoped that for his father's sake, the milk company would soon replace her with a livelier beast.

"Will you get out that old blanket," his father resumed, "so if it does freeze tomorrow, I'll have something to wrap my knees in. This sudden cold seems to crack one's bones open to the marrow."

"Yes, of course," solicitously. "Don't you want to take your shoes off?"

"No."

It was curious to David what a subtle difference there was between his father's brusqueness as a milkman and his brusqueness as a printer. The former seemed to be merely the result of weariness on a naturally high-strung temperament; the latter, the result of strain, of inner maladjustment. His brusqueness now was infinitely less dangerous to those about him.

"This corn-meal is ready," said his mother. "And after that some tea?"

He grunted, threw his arms back over the shoulder of his chair and watched her ladle out the boiled corn-meal into a bowl.

"Some jam."

"I'm bringing it." She set a jar of home-made strawberry preserves on the table.

"This is what I ate," he smeared the deep, red jam on the corn-meal, "when I was a boy."

David was waiting to hear his father say just that. He always said it when he ate corn-meal mush, and that was one of the few facts that David had ever learnt of his father's boyhood.

"I was thinking," he continued between cooling gusts

at the smoking spoon. "It came to me while I was cross-ing a roof."

"I wish you didn't have to cross them!"

"Don't fret about what you know nothing of," he waved his hand at her curtly. "I don't pretend to be a mountain-goat. I merely climb over walls, I don't leap alleyways. Besides, it isn't the roofs that trouble me, it's who may be on them. And now that I've told you this for the tenth time, where was I?" He put down his spoon and looked at her perplexed. "There's nothing like good, womanly worry to beat the thought out of your head— Yes! I remember now." He stared at David. "The prayer. I was thinking should anything happen to me— Now I don't mean the roofs— Anything! It would be a comfort to me to know that whatever else he becomes— and God only knows what he may become—at least he shan't be an utter pagan because I didn't try."

"You mean?"

"I mean I'm little enough a Jew myself. But I want to make sure he'll become at least something of a Jew also. I want you to find a cheder for him and a rabbi who isn't too exorbitant. I would have entered him long ago if that red-headed sister of yours hadn't thought it her place to advise me."

David remembered the incident. His father had told her to mind her own business.

His mother shook her head doubtfully. "A cheder? Couldn't he start a little later. Children in America often do."

"Do they? I'm not so sure. Anyway, it will keep him busy and out of the house. And it won't hurt him to learn what it means to be a Jew."

"He really isn't home as often as he used to be." She smiled at David. "He leaves me quite forlorn. And as for learning what it means to be a Jew, I think he knows how hard that is already."

His father nodded curtly—in token that his decree had been passed. "You would do well to seek out a stern one —a rabbi I mean. He needs a little curbing since I don't do it. It might redeem him. A lout of eight and all he's ever known is pampering."

David was still only seven. But that foible his father

had of increasing his age to magnify his guilt had long ago become familiar to him. He had even stopped wondering about it.

"Where's the tea?" he concluded.

II

ONE edge shining in the vanishing sunlight, the little white-washed house of the cheder lay before them. It was only one story high, the windows quite close to the ground. Its bulkier neighbors, the tall tenements that surrounded it, seemed to puff out their littered fire-escapes in scorn. Smoke curled from a little, black chimney in the middle of its roof, and overhead myriads of wash-lines criss-crossed intricately, snaring the sky in a dark net. Most of the lines were bare, but here and there was one sagging with white and colored wash, from which now and again a flurry of rinsings splashed into the yard or drummed on the cheder roof.

"I hope," said his mother, as they went down the wooden stairs that led into the yard, "that you'll prove more gifted in the ancient tongue than I was. When I went to cheder, my rabbi was always wagging his head at me and swearing I had a calf's brain." And she laughed. "But I think the reason I was such a dunce was that I could never wrench my nose far enough away to escape his breath. Pray this one is not so fond of onions!"

They crossed the short space of the yard and his mother opened the cheder door. A billow of drowsy air rolled out at them. It seemed dark inside. On their entrance, the hum of voices ceased.

The rabbi, a man in a skull cap, who had been sitting near the window beside one of his pupils, looked up when he saw them and rose. Against the window, he looked short and bulbous, oddly round beneath the square outline of the skull cap.

"Good day," he ambled toward them. "I'm Reb Yidel Pankower. You wish—?" He ran large, hairy fingers through a glossy, crinkled beard.

David's mother introduced herself and then went on to explain her mission.

"And this is he?"

"Yes. The only one I have."

"Only one such pretty star?" He chuckled and reaching out, caught David's cheek in a tobacco-reeking pinch. David shied slightly.

While his mother and the rabbi were discussing the hours and the price and the manner of David's tuition, David scanned his future teacher more closely. He was not at all like the teachers at school, but David had seen rabbis before and knew he wouldn't be. He appeared old and was certainly untidy. He wore soft leather shoes like house-slippers, that had no place for either laces or buttons. His trousers were baggy and stained, a great area of striped and crumpled shirt intervened between his belt and his bulging vest. The knot of his tie, which was nearer one ear than the other, hung away from his soiled collar. What features were visible were large and had an oily gleam. Beneath his skull cap, his black hair was closely cropped. Though full of misgivings about his future relations with the rabbi, David felt that he must accept his fate. Was it not his father's decree that he attend a cheder?

From the rabbi his eyes wandered about the room. Bare walls, the brown paint on it full of long wavering cracks. Against one wall, stood a round-bellied stove whose shape reminded him of his rabbi, except that it was heated a dull red and his rabbi's apparel was black. Against the other wall a long line of benches ran to the rabbi's table. Boys of varying ages were seated upon them, jabbering, disputing, gambling for various things, scuffling over what looked to David like a few sticks. Seated upon the bench before the rabbi's table were several others obviously waiting their turn at the book lying open in front of the rabbi's cushioned chair.

What had been, when he and his mother had entered, a low hum of voices, had now swollen to a roar. It looked as though half of the boys in the room had engaged the other half in some verbal or physical conflict. The rabbi, excusing himself to David's mother, turned toward them, and with a thunderous rap of his fist against the door, uttered a ferocious, "Shah!" The noise subsided some-what. He swept the room with angry, glittering eyes, then softening into a smile again returned to David's mother.

At last it was arranged and the rabbi wrote down his new pupil's name and address. David gathered that he was to receive his instruction somewhere between the hours of three and six, that he was to come to the cheder shortly after three, and that the fee for his education would be twenty-five cents a week. Moreover he was to begin that afternoon. This was something of an unpleas-ant surprise and at first he protested, but when his mother urged him and the rabbi assured him that his first lesson would not take long, he consented, and mourn-fully received his mother's parting kiss.

"Sit down over there," said the rabbi curtly as soon as his mother had left. "And don't forget," he brought a crooked knuckle to his lips. "In a cheder one must be quiet."

David sat down, and the rabbi walked back to his seat beside the window. Instead of sitting down however, he reached under his chair, and bringing out a short-thonged cat-o'-nine-tails, struck the table loudly with the butt-end and pronounced in a menacing voice: "Let there be a hush among you!" And a scared silence instantly lock-ing all mouths, he seated himself. He then picked up a lit-tle stick lying on the table and pointed to the book, whereupon a boy sitting next to him began droning out sounds in a strange and secret tongue.

For awhile, David listened intently to the sound of the words. It was Hebrew, he knew, the same mysterious lan-guage his mother used before the candles, the same his father used when he read from a book during the holi-days—and that time before dinking wine. Not Yiddish, Hebrew. God's tongue, the rabbi had said. If you knew it, then you could talk to God. Who was He? He would learn about Him now—

The boy sitting nearest David, slid along the bench to his side. "Yuh jost stottin' cheder?"

"Yea."

"Uhh!" he groaned, indicating the rabbi with his eyes. "He's a louser! He hits!"

David regarded the rabbi with panicky eyes. He had seen boys slapped by teachers in school for disobedience,

although he himself had never been struck. The thought
of being flogged with that vicious scourge he had seen
the rabbi produce sealed his lips. He even refused to answer when next the boy asked him whether he had any
match-pictures to match, and hastily shook his head. With
a shrug, the boy slid back along the bench to the place he
had come from.

Presently, with the arrival of several late-comers, older
boys, tongues once more began to wag and a hum of
voices filled the room. When David saw that the rabbi
brandished his scourge several times without wielding it,
his fear abated somewhat. However, he did not venture
to join in the conversation, but cautiously watched the
rabbi.

The boy who had been reading when David had come
in had finished, and his place was taken by a second
who seemed less able to maintain the rapid drone of his
predecessor. At first, when he faltered, the rabbi corrected him by uttering what was apparently the right
sound, for the boy always repeated it. But gradually, as
his pupil continued in his error, a harsh note of warning crept into the rabbi's voice. After awhile he began to
yank the boy by the arm whenever he corrected him, then
to slap him smartly on the thigh, and finally, just before
the boy had finished, the rabbi cuffed him on the ear.

As time went by, David saw this procedure repeated
in part or whole in the case of almost every other boy
who read. There were several exceptions, and these, as
far as David could observe, gained their exemption from
punishment because the drone that issued from their lips
was as breathless and uninterrupted as the roll of a drum.
He also noticed that whenever the rabbi administered one
of these manual corrections, he first dropped from his
hand the little stick with which he seemed to set the pace
on the page, and an instant later reached out or struck
out, as the case might demand. So that, whenever he
dropped the stick, whether to scratch his beard or adjust
his skull-cap or fish out a half-burned cigarette from a
box, the pupil before him invariably jerked up an arm or
ducked his head defensively. The dropping of that little
stick, seemed to have become a warning to his pupils that
a blow was on the way.

The light in the windows was waning to a blank pallor.

The room was warm; the stagnant air had lulled even the most restive. Drowsily, David wondered when his turn would come.

"Aha!" he heard the rabbi sarcastically exclaim. "Is it you, Hershele, scholar from the land of scholars?"

This was addressed to the boy who had just slid into the vacant place before the book. David had observed him before, a fat boy with a dull face and an open mouth. By the cowed, sullen stoop of his shoulders, it was clear that he was not one in good standing with the rabbi.

"Herry is gonna loin," giggled one of the boys at David's side.

"Perhaps, today, you can glitter a little," suggested the rabbi with a freezing smile. "Who knows, a puppet may yet be made who can fart. Come!" He picked up the stick and pointed to the page.

The boy began to read. Though a big boy, as big as any that preceded him, he read more slowly and faltered more often than any of the others. It was evident that the rabbi was restraining his impatience, for instead of actually striking his pupil, he grimaced violently when he corrected him, groaned frequently, stamped his foot under the table and gnawed his under-lip. The other students had grown quiet and were listening. From their strained silence—their faces were by now half obscured in shadow—David was sure they were expecting some catastrophe any instant. The boy fumbled on. As far as David could tell, he seemed to be making the same error over and over again, for the rabbi kept repeating the same sound. At last, the rabbi's patience gave out. He dropped the pointer; the boy ducked, but not soon enough. The speeding plane of the rabbi's palm rang against his ear like a clapper on a gong.

"You plaster dunce!" he roared, "when will you learn a byse is a byse and not a vyse. Head of filth, where are your eyes?" He shook a menacing hand at the cringing boy and picked up the pointer.

But a few moments later, again the same error and again the same correction.

"May a demon fly off with your father's father! Won't blows help you? A byse, Esau, pig! A byse! Remember, a byse, even though you die of convulsions!"

The boy whimpered and went on. He had not uttered more than a few sounds, when again he paused on the awful brink, and as if out of sheer malice, again repeated his error. The last stroke of the bastinado! The effect on the rabbi was terrific. A frightful bellow clove his beard. In a moment he had fastened the pincers of his fingers on the cheeks of his howling pupil, and wrenching the boy's head from side to side roared out.—

"A byse! A byse! A byse! All buttocks have only one eye. A byse! May your brains boil over! A byse! Creator of earth and firmament, ten thousand cheders are in this land and me you single out for torment! A byse! Most abject of God's fools! A byse!"

While he raved and dragged the boy's head from side to side with one hand, with the other he hammered the pointer with such fury against the table that David expected at any moment to see the slender stick buried in the wood. It snapped instead!

"He busted it!" gleefully announced the boy sitting near.

"He busted it!" the suppressed giggle went round. Horrified himself by what he saw, David wondered what the rest could possibly be so amused about.

"I couldn't see," the boy at the table was blubbering. "I couldn't see! It's dark in here!"

"May your skull be dark!" the rabbi intoned in short frenzied yelps, "and your eyes be dark and your fate be of such dearth and darkness that you will call a poppy-seed the sun and a carroway the moon. Get up! Away! Or I'll empty my bitter heart upon you!"

Tears streaming down his cheeks, and wailing loudly, the boy slid off the bench and slunk away.

"Stay here till I give you leave to go," the rabbi called after him. "Wipe your muddy nose. Hurry, I say! If you could read as easily as your eyes can piss, you were a fine scholar indeed!"

The boy sat down, wiped his nose and eyes with his coat-sleeve and quieted to a suppressed snuffling.

Glancing at the window, the rabbi fished in his pockets, drew out a match and lit the low gas jet sticking out from the wall over head. While he watched the visibility of the open book on the table, he frugally shaved down the light to a haggard leaf. Then he seated himself again, unlocked a drawer in the table and drew out a fresh stick which looked exactly like the one he had just broken. David wondered whether the rabbi whittled a large supply of sticks for himself, knowing what would happen to them.

"Move back!" He waved the boy away who had reluctantly slipped into the place just vacated before the table. "David Schearl!" he called out, tempering the harshness of his voice. "Come here, my gold."

Qualing with fright, David drew near.

"Sit down, my child," he was still breathing hard with exertion. "Don't be alarmed." He drew out of his pocket a package of cigarette-papers and a tobacco pouch, carefully rolled a cigarette, took a few puffs, then snuffed it out and put it into an empty cigarette box. David's heart pounded with fear. "Now then," he turned the leaves of a book beside him to the last page. "Show me how blessed is your understanding." He drew David's tense shoulder down toward the table, and picking up the new stick, pointed to a large hieroglyph at the top of the page. "This is called Komitz. You see? Komitz. And this is an Aleph. Now, whenever one sees a Komitz under an Aleph, one says, Aw." His hot tobacco-laden breath swirled about David's face.

His mother's words about her rabbi flashed through his mind. He thrust them aside and riveted his gaze to the indicated letter as if he would seal it on his eyes.

"Say after me," continued the rabbi, "Komitz-Aleph—Aw!"

David repeated the sounds.

"So!" commanded the rabbi. "Once more! Komitz-Aleph-Aw!"

And after David had repeated it several times. "And this" continued the rabbi pointing to the next character "is called Bais, and a Komitz under a Bais—Baw! Say it! Komitz-Bais-Baw!"

"Komitz-Bais—Baw!" said David.

"Well done! Again."

And so the lesson progressed with repetition upon repetition. Whether out of fear or aptitude, David went through these first steps with hardly a single error. And when he was dismissed, the rabbi pinched his cheek in praise and said:

"Go home. You have an iron head!"

III

"ODDS!" said Izzy.

"Evens!" said Solly.

"Skinner!" said Izzy. "Don' hold back yuh finergs till yuh see wad I'm puttin' oud."

They were gambling for pointers as usual, and David stood by watching the turns of fortune. In other corners of the yard were others engrossed in the same game. There were a great many pointers in circulation to-day —someone had rifled the rabbi's drawer. Nothing else had been taken, neither his phylacteries, nor his clock, nor his stationery, nothing except his pointers. He had been furious, but since everyone else had looked blank, he hadn't been able to convict anyone. Yet here they were, all gambling for them. David was amused. In fact everything that had to do with pointers amused him. They were one of the few things that relieved the dullness of the cheder. He had thought when he first saw them that the rabbi whittled them out himself, but he soon found out he was wrong: the rabbi broke so many that that would have taken all day. No, the pointers were just ordinary lollipop sticks. And even that had been amusing. An incongruous picture had risen in his mind: He saw his severe, black-bearded rabbi wearing away an all-day sucker. But his fellow-pupils soon enlightened him. It was they who brought the rabbi the lollipop sticks. A gift of pointers meant a certain amount of leniency on the rabbi's part, a certain amount of preference. But the gift had to be substantial, else the rabbi forgot about it, and since few of his pupils could afford more than one lollipop a day, they gambled for them. Izzy's luck to-day was running high.

"Yuh god any more?" he asked.

"Yeah," said Solly. "Make or break! Odds!"

"Waid a secon'. I'm all wet." He bent sideways and wrung his knee-pants and coattails. They had been arguing so violently a little while ago that someone in an adjacent house had thrown a bagful of water into their midst. Izzy had caught the brunt of it.

"Yowooee!" From a distance a long-drawn cat-call. They looked around. "Who is it?"

"I'll see." Yonk who was standing near the fence shinnied up a wash-pole. "It's Moish," he announced. "He's t'ree fences."

"Only t'ree fences?" Contemptuously they resumed their game.

There was an approaching scuff and clatter. Moish climbed over the fence. "Any janitors?" he asked.

"No janitors," said Yonk patronizingly and slid down the wash-pole. "Yuh don' make enough noise, dat's why. Yuh oughta hea' Wildy."

"Who don' make enough noise? I hollered loud like anyt'ing. Who beats?"

"Who'djuh t'ink? Wildy beats. He god faw fences an' one janitor. Mrs. Lechtenstein on seven-sixty-eight house. She went smack wit' de broom, but Wildy ducked."

Fence-climbing was one of the ways by which the rabbi's pupils entered the cheder. The doorway that led into the cheder yard was too prosaic for most of them; they preferred to carve their own routes. And the champion of this, as of everything else, was Wildy. Wildy was nearing his thirteenth birthday and consequently his 'bar mitzvah', which made him one of the oldest boys in the cheder. He was the idol of everyone and had even threatened to punch the rabbi in the nose.

"W'ea's Wildy now?" someone asked.

"He's waitin' fuh Shaih an' Toik t' comm down," Yonk looked significantly up at one of the houses. "He's gonna show em dey ain't de highest ones wad comms into de cheder."

"I god t'ree poinders," said Moish. "Who'll match me?"

"I'll play yuh." Izzy had just cleaned out his opponent. "W'ea didja ged 'em? From de swipe?"

"Naa. Dey's two goils in my class, an' anudder kid— a goy. So dey all bought lollipops, an' de goy too. So I follered dem aroun' an' aroun' an' den w'en dey finished, dey trowed away de sticks. So I picked 'em up. Goys is dumb."

"Lucky guy," they said enviously.

It took more than luck though, as David very well

knew. It took a great deal of patience. He had tried that method of collecting lollipop sticks himself, but it had proved too tedious. Anyway he didn't really have to do it. He happened to be bright enough to avoid punishment, and could read Hebrew as fast as anyone, although he still didn't know what he read. Translation, which was called Chumish, would come later.

"Yowooee!" The cry came from overhead this time. They looked up. Shaih and Toik, the two brothers who lived on the third floor back had climbed out on their fire-escapes. They were the only ones in the cheder privileged to enter the yard via the fire-escape ladders—and they made the most of it. The rest watched enviously. But they had climbed down only a few steps, when again the cry, and now from a great height—

"Yowooee!"

Everyone gasped. It was Wildy and he was on the roof!

"I tol' yuh I wuz gonna comm down higher den dem!" With a triumphant shout he mounted the ladder and with many a flourish climbed down.

"Gee, Wildy!" they breathed reverently—all except the two brothers and they eyed him sullenly.

"We'll tell de janitor on you."

"I'll smack yuh one," he answered easily, and turning to the rest. "Yuh know wad I c'n do if one o' youz is game. I betcha I c'n go up on de fawt' flaw an' I betcha I c'n grab hol' from dat wash-line an' I betcha I c'n hol' id till sommbody pulls me across t' de wash-pole an I betcha I c'n comm down!"

"Gee, Wildy!"

"An' somm day I'm gonna stott way over on Avenyuh C an' jump all de fences in de whole two blocks!"

"Gee!"

"Hey, guys, I'm goin' in." Izzy had won the last of the pointers. "C'mon, I'm gonna give 'im."

"How many yuh god?" They trooped after him.

"Look!" There was a fat sheaf of them in his hand. They approached the reading table. The rabbi looked up.

"I've got pointers for you, rabbi," said Izzy in Yiddish.

"Let me see them," was the suspicious answer. "Quite a contribution you're making."

Izzy was silent.

"Do you know my pointers were stolen yesterday?"

"Yes, I know."

"Well, where did you get these?"

"I won them."

"From whom?"

"From everybody."

"Thieves!" he shook his hand at them ominously. "Fortunately for you I don't recognize any of them."

IV

TWO months had passed since David entered the cheder. Spring had come and with the milder weather, a sense of wary contentment, a curious pause in himself as though he were waiting for some sign, some seal that would forever relieve him of watchfulness and forever insure his well-being. Sometimes he thought he had already beheld the sign—he went to cheder; he often went to the synagogue on Saturdays; he could utter God's syllables glibly. But he wasn't quite sure. Perhaps the sign would be revealed when he finally learned to translate Hebrew. At any rate, ever since he had begun attending cheder, life had leveled out miraculously, and this he attributed to his increasing nearness to God. He never thought about his father's job any longer. There was no more of that old dread of waiting for the cycle to fulfill itself. There no longer seemed to be any cycle. Nor did his mother ever appear to worry about his father's job; she too seemed reassured and at peace. And those curious secrets he had gleaned long ago from his mother's story seemed submerged within him and were met only at reminiscent street-corners among houses or in the brain. Everything unpleasant and past was like that, David decided, lost within one. All one had to do was to imagine that it wasn't there, just as the cellar in one's house could be conjured away if there were a bright yard between the hallway and the cellar-stairs. One needed only a bright yard. At times David almost believed he had found that brightness.

It was a few days before Passover. The morning had
been so gay, warmer and brighter than any in the sheaf
of Easter just past. Noon had been so full of promise—
a leaf of Summer in the book of Spring. And all that
afternoon he had waited, restless and inattentive, for
the three o'clock gong to release him from school. Instead
of blackboards, he had studied the sharp grids of sunlight
that brindled the red wall under the fire-escapes; and behind his tall geography book, had built a sail of a blotter
and pencil to catch the mild breeze that curled in
through the open window. Miss Steigman had caught him,
had tightly puckered her lips (the heavy fuzz about them
always darkened when she did that) and screamed:

"Get out of that seat, you little loafer! This minute!
This very minute! And take that seat near the door and
stay there! The audacity!" She always used that word, and
David always wondered what it meant. Then she had
begun to belch, which was what she always did after she
had been made angry.

And even in his new seat, David had been unable to
sit still, had fidgeted and waited, fingered the grain of
his desk, stealthily rolled the sole of his shoe over a round
lead pencil, attempted to tie a hair that had fallen on his
book into little knots. He had waited and waited, but
now that he was free, what good was it? The air was
darkening, the naked wind was spinning itself a grey
conch of the dust and rubbish scooped from the gutter.
The street-cleaner was pulling on his black rain-coat. The
weather had cheated him, that's all! He couldn't go anywhere now. He'd get wet. He might as well be the first
one in the cheder. Disconsolately, he crossed the street.

But how did his mother know this morning it was
going to rain? She had gone to the window and looked
out, and then she said, the sun is up too early. Well what
if it—Whee!

Before his feet a flat sheet of newspaper, driven by a
gust of damp wind, whipped into the air and dipped and
fluttered languidly, melting into sky. He watched it a moment and then quickened his step. Above store windows,
awnings were heaving and bellying upward, rattling. Yelling, a boy raced across the gutter, his cap flying before
him.

"Wow! Look!" The shout made him turn around.

"Shame! Shame! Everybody knows your name." A chorus of boys and girls chanted emphatically. "Shame! Shame! Everybody knows your name."

Red and giggling a big girl was thrusting down the billow of her dress. Above plump, knock-kneed legs, a glimpse of scalloped, white drawers. The wind relenting, the dress finally sank. David turned round again, feeling a faint disgust, a wisp of the old horror. With what prompt spasms the mummified images in the brain started from their niches, aped former antics and lapsed. It recalled that time, way long ago. Knish and closet. Puh! And that time when two dogs were stuck together. Puh! Threw water that man. Shame! Shame!

"Sophe-e!" Above him the cry. "Sophe-e!"

"Ye-es mama-a!" from a girl across the street.

"Comm opstehs! Balt!"

"Awaa!"

"Balt or I'll give you! Nooo!"

With a rebellious shudder, the girl began crossing the street. The window slammed down.

Pushing a milk-stained, rancid baby carriage before them, squat buttocks waddled past, one arm from somewhere dragging two reeling children, each hooked by its hand to the other, each bouncing against the other and against their mother like tops, flagging and whipped. A boy ran in front of the carriage. It rammed him.

"Ow! Kencha see wea yuh goin?" He rubbed his ankle.

"Snott nuzz! Oll—balt a frosk, Oll—give!"

"Aaa! Buzjwa!"

A drop of rain spattered on his chin.

—It's gonna—

He flung his strap of books over his shoulder and broke into a quick trot.

—Before I get all wet.

Ahead of him, flying toward the shore beyond the East River, shaggy clouds trooped after their van. And across the river the white smoke of nearer stacks were flattened out and stormy as though the stacks were the funnels of a flying ship. In the gutter, wagon wheels trailed black ribbons. Curtains overhead paddled out of open windows. The air had shivered into a thousand shrill, splintered cries, wedged here and there by the sudden whoop of a boy or the impatient squawk of a mother. At the doorway to the cheder corridor, he stopped and cast one lingering glance up and down the street. The black sidewalks had cleared. Rain shook out wan tresses in the gathering dark. Against the piebald press of cloud in the craggy furrow of the west, a lone flag on top of a school-steeple blew out stiff as a key. In the shelter of a doorway, across the gutter, a cluster of children shouted in monotone up at the sky:

"Rain, rain, go away, come again some oddeh day. Rain, rain, go away, come again some oddeh day. Rain, rain—"

He'd better go in before the rest of the rabbi's pupils came. They'd get ahead of him otherwise. He turned and trudged through the dim battered corridor. The yard was gloomy. Wash-poles creaked and swayed, pulleys jangled. In a window overhead, a bulky, bare-armed woman shrilled curses at someone behind her and hastily hauled in the bedding that straddled the sills like bulging sacks.

"And your guts be plucked!" her words rang out over the yard. "Couldn't you tell me it was raining?"

He dove through the rain, skidded over the broken flagstones and fell against the cheder door. As he stumbled in, the rabbi, who was lighting the gas-jet, looked around.

"A black year befall you!" he growled. "Why don't you come in like a man?"

Without answering, he sidled meekly over to the bench beside the wall and sat down. What did he yell at him for? He hadn't meant to burst in that way. Gee! The growing gas-light revealed another pupil in the room whom he hadn't noticed before. It was Mendel. His neck swathed in white bandages, sickly white under the bleary yellow flicker of gas, he sat before the reading table, head propped by elbows. Mendel was nearing his bar-mitzvah but had never learned to read chumish because he had entered the cheder at a rather late age. He was lucky, so every one said, because he had a carbuncle on the back of his neck which prevented him from attending school. And so all week long, he had arrived first at the cheder. David wondered if he dared sit down beside him. The rabbi looked angry. However, he decided to venture it and crawled quietly over the bench beside Mendel. The pungent reek of medicine pried his nostrils.

—Peeuh! It stinks!

He edged away. Dull-eyed, droopy-lipped, Mendel glanced down at him and then turned to watch the rabbi. The latter drew a large blue book from a heap on the shelf and then settled himself on his pillowed chair.

"Strange darkness," he said, squinting at the rain-chipped window. "A stormy Friday."

David shivered. Beguiled by the mildness of noon, he had left the house wearing only his thin blue jersey. Now, without a fire in the round-bellied stove and without other bodies to lend their warmth to the damp room, he felt cold.

"Now," said the rabbi stroking his beard, "this is the 'Haftorah' to Jethro—something you will read at your bar mitzvah, if you live that long." He wet his thumb and forefinger and began pinching the top of each page in such a way that the whole leaf seemed to wince from his hand and flip over as if fleeing of its own accord. David noted with surprise that unlike the rabbi's other books this one had as yet none of its corners lopped off. "It's the 'Sedrah' for that week," he continued, "and since you don't know any chumish, I'll tell you what it means after you've read it." He picked up the pointer, but instead of pointing to the page suddenly lifted his hand.

In spite of himself, Mendel contracted.

"Ach!" came the rabbi's impatient grunt. "Why do you spring like a goat? Can I hit *you?*" And with the blunt end of the pointer, he probed his ear, his swarthy face painfully rippling about his bulbous nose into the margins of his beard and skull-cap. He scraped the brown clot of wax against the table leg and pointed to the page. "Begin, Beshnos mos."

"Beshnos mos hamelech Uziyahu vaereh es adonoi," Medel swung into the drone.

For want of anything better to do, David looked on, vying silently with Mendel. But the pace soon proved too fast for him—Mendel's swift sputter of gibberish tripped his own laggard lipping. He gave up the chase and gazed vacantly at the rain-chipped window. In a house across the darkened yard, lights had been lit and blurry figures moved before them. Rain strummed on the roof, and once or twice through the steady patter, a muffled rumble filtered down, as if a heavy object were being dragged across the floor above.

—Bed on wheels. Upstairs. (His thoughts rambled absently between the confines of the drone of the voice and the drone of the rain.) Gee how it's raining. It won't stop. Even if he finishes, I can't go. If he read chumish, could race him, could beat him I bet. But that's because he has to stop . . . Why do you have to read chumish? No fun . . . First you read, Adonoi elahenoo abababa, and then you say, And Moses said you mustn't, and then you read some more abababa and then you say, mustn't eat in the traife butcher store. Don't like it any way. Big brown bags hang down from the hooks. Ham. And all kinds of grey wurst with like marbles in 'em. Peeuh! And chickens without feathers in boxes, and little bunnies in that store on First Avenue by the elevated. In a wooden cage with lettuce, and rocks, they eat too, on those stands. Rocks all colors. They bust 'em open with a knife and shake out ketchup on the snot inside. Yich! and long, black, skinny snakes. Peeuh! Goyim eat everything . . .

"Veeshma es kol adonoi omair es mi eshlach." Mendel was reading swiftly this afternoon. The rabbi turned the page. Overhead that distant rumbling sound.

—Bed on wheels again . . . But how did Moses know? Who told him? God told him. Only eat kosher meat, that's how. Mustn't eat meat and then drink milk. Mama don't care except when Bertha was looking! How she used to holler on her because she mixed up the meat-knives with the milk-knives. It's a sin. . . . So God told him eat in your own meat markets . . . That time with mama in the chicken market when we went. Where all the chicken ran around —cuckacucka—when did I say? Cucka. Gee! Funny. Some place I said. And then the man with a knife went zing! Eee! Blood and wings. And threw him down. Even kosher meat when you see, you don't want to eat—

"Enough!" The rabbi tapped his pointer on the table.

Mendel stopped reading and slumped back with a puff of relief.

"Now I'll tell you a little of what you read, then what it means. Listen to me well that you may remember it. Beshnas mos hamelech." The two nails of his thumb and forefinger met. "In the year that King Uzziah died, Isaiah saw God. And God was sitting on his throne, high in heaven and in his temple—Understand?" He pointed upward.

Mendel nodded, grimacing as he eased the bandage round his neck.

—Gee! And he saw Him. Wonder where? (David, his interest aroused, was listening intently. This was something new.)

"Now!" resumed the rabbi. "Around Him stood the angels, God's blessed angels. How beautiful they were you yourself may imagine. And they cried: Kadosh! Kadosh! Kadosh—Holy! Holy! Holy! And the temple rang and quivered with the sound of their voices. So!" He paused, peering into Mendel's face. "Understand?"

"Yeh," said Mendel understandingly.

—And angels there were and he saw 'em. Wonder if—

"But when Isaiah saw the Almighty in His majesty and His terrible light—Woe me! he cried, What shall I do! I am lost!" The rabbi seized his skull-cap and crumpled it. "I, common man, have seen the Almighty, I, unclean one have seen him! Behold, my lips are unclean and I live in a land unclean—for the Jews at that time were sinful—"

—Clean? Light? Wonder if—? Wish I could ask him why the Jews were dirty. What did they do? Better not! Get mad. Where? (Furtively, while the rabbi still spoke David leaned over and stole a glance at the number of the page.) On sixty-eight. After, maybe, can ask. On page sixty-eight. That blue book—Gee! it's God.

"But just when Isaiah let out this cry—I am unclean —one of the angels flew to the altar and with tongs drew out a fiery coal. Understand? With tongs. And with that coal, down he flew to Isaiah and with that coal touched his lips—Here!" The rabbi's fingers stabbed the air. You are clean! And the instant that coal touched Isaiah's lips, then he heard God's own voice say, Whom shall I send? Who will go for us? And Isaiah spoke and—"

But a sudden blast of voices out doors interrupted him. Running feet stamped across the yard. The door burst open. A squabbling tussling band stormed the doorway, jamming it. Scuffling, laughing boisterously, they shoved each other in, yanked each other out—

"Leggo!"

"Leggo me!"

"Yuh pushed me in id, yuh lousy stinkuh!"

"Next after Davy," one flew toward the reading table.

"Moishe flopped inna puddle!"

"Hey! Don' led 'im in!"

"Next after Sammy!" Another bolted after the first.

"I come—!"

"Shah!" grated the rabbi. "Be butchered, all of you! You hear me! Not one be spared!"

The babel sank to an undertone.

"And you there be maimed forever, shut that door."

The milling about the doorway dissolved.

"Quick! May your life be closed with it."

Someone pulled the door after him.

"And now, sweet Sammy," his voice took on a venomous wheedling tone. "*Nex* are you? I'll give you *nex*. In your belly it will *nex*. Out of there! Wriggle!"

Sammy hastily scrambled back over the bench.

"And you too," he waved David away. "Go sit down over there." And when David hung back, "Quick! Or—!"

David sprang from the bench.

"And quiet!" he rasped. "As if your tongues had rotted." And when complete silence had been established. "Now," he said, rising. "I'll give you something to do— Yitzchuck!"

"Waauh! I didn' do nottin'!" Yitzchuck raised a terrified whine.

"Who asked you to speak? Come here!"

"Wadda yuh wan' f'om me?" Yitzchuck prepared to blubber.

"Sit here." He beckoned to the end of the bench which was nearest the reading table. "And don't speak to me in goyish. Out of there, you! And you, David, sit where you are— Simke!"

"Yea."

"Beside him. Srool! Moishe! Avrum! Yankel! Schulim!" He was gathering all the younger students into a group. "Schmiel! And you Meyer, sit here." With a warning glance he went over to the closet behind his chair and drew out a number of small books.

"Aaa! Phuh!" Yitzchuck spat out in a whisper. "De lousy Hagaddah again!"

They sat silent until the rabbi returned and distributed the books. Moishe, seated a short distance away from

David dropped his, but then pounced upon it hastily, and for the rabbi's benefit, kissed it and looked about with an expression of idiotic piety.

"First, louse-heads," began the rabbi when he had done distributing the books, "the Four Questions of the Passover. Read them again and again. But this time let them flow from your lips like a torrent. And woe to that plaster dunce who still cannot say them in Yiddish! Blows will he scoop like sand! And when you have done that, turn the leaves to the 'Chad Godya'. Read it over. But remember, quiet as death— Well?" Shmaike had raised his hand as though he were in school. "What do you want?"

"Can't we hear each other?"

"Mouldered brains! Do you still need to hear each other? Do then. But take care I don't hear a goyish word out of you." He went back to his chair and sat down. For a few seconds longer his fierce gaze raked the long bench, then his eyes dropped momentarily to the book before him. "I was telling you," he addressed Mendel, "how Isaiah came to see God and what happened after—"

But as if his own words had unleashed theirs, a seething of whispers began to chafe the room.

"You hea' me say it. You hea' me! Shid on you. C'mon Solly, you hea' me. Yuh did push! Mendy's god a bendige yet on—"

"Said whom shall I send?" The rabbi's words were baffling on thickening briers of sound. "Who will go for us?"

"Izzy Pissy! Cock-eye Mulligan! Mah nishtanah halilaw hazeh— Wanna play me Yonk?"

—Couldn't ask him though (David's eyes merely rested on the page). Get mad. Maybe later when I have to read. Where was it? Yea. Page sixty-eight. I'll say, on page sixty-eight in that blue book that's new, where Mendel read, you were saying that man saw God. And a light—

"How many? I god more den you. Shebchol haleylos onu ochlim-. I had a mockee on mine head too. Wuz you unner de awningh? Us all wuz. In de rain."

"And tell this people, this fallen people—"

"Yea, and I'll kickyuh innee ass! Odds! Halaylaw hazeh kulo mazo— So from t'rowin' sand on my head I god a big mockee. I seen a blitz just w'en I commed in."

—Where did he go to see Him? God? Didn't say. Wonder if the rabbi knows? Wish I could ask. Page sixty-

eight. Way, way, way, maybe. Where? Gee! Some place,
me too . . . When I— When I—in the street far away . . .
Hello, Mr. Highwood, goodbye Mr. Highwood. Heee!
Funny!

"C'mere Joey, here's room. De rebbeh wants—Fences is
all slippery. Now wadda yuh cry?"

"Nor ever be healed, nor even clean."

"A blitz, yuh dope! Hey Solly, he says— Shebchol
haleylos onu ochlim— Yea, my fadder'll beat chaw big
brudder. Evens!"

—Some place Isaiah saw Him, just like that. I bet! He
was sitting on a chair. So he's got chairs, so he can sit.
Gee! Sit Shit! Sh! Please God, I didn't mean it! Please
God, somebody else said it! Please—

"So hoddy you say blitz wise guy? Moishee loozed his
bean shooduh! And den after de sand I pud wawduh on
duh head, so— Lousy bestia! Miss Ryan tooked it!"

"How long? I asked. Lord, how long-"

—And why did the angel do it? Why did he want to
burn Isaiah's mouth with coal? He said, You're clean.
But coal makes smoke and ashes. So how clean? Couldn't
he just say, Your mouth is clean? Couldn't he? Why wasn't
it clean, anyway? He didn't wash it, I bet. So that . . .

"A lighten', yuh dope. A blitz! Kent'cha tuck Englitch?
Ha! Ha! Sheor yerokos halaylo hazeh—Dat's two on dot!
I wuz shootin chalk wid it. Somm bean shooduh! My fod-
der'll give your fodder soch a kick—"

—With a zwank, he said it was. Zwank. Where did I
see? Zwank some place. Mama? No. Like in blacksmith
shop by the river. Pincers and horseshoe. Yes must be.
With pincers, zwank means pincers. So why with pincers?
Coal was hot. That's why. But he was a angel. Is angels
afraid? Afraid to get burned? Gee! Must have been hot,
real hot. How I jumped when the rabbi pushed out with
his fingers when he said coal. Nearly thought it was me.
Wonder if Isaiah hollered when the coal touched him.
Maybe angel-coal don't burn live people. Wonder—

"Dere! Chinky shows! Id's mine! How many fences
didja go? I tore it f'om a tree in duh pock, mine beanshooduh! T'ree fences. So a lighten den, wise guy!"

"And the whole land waste and empty."

"T'ree is a lie, mine fodder says. Yea? Matbilim afilu

pa'am echos halaylo hazeh—Always wear yuh hat when a lighten' gives—"

—He said dirty words, I bet. Shit, pee, fuckenbestit—Stop! You're sayin' it yourself. It's a sin again! That's why he—Gee! I didn't mean it. But your mouth don't get dirty. I don't feel no dirt. (He rolled his tongue about) Maybe inside. Way, way in, where you can't taste it. What did Isaiah say that made his mouth dirty? Real dirty, so he'd know it was? Maybe—

"Shebchol haleylos onu ochlim—. De rain wedded my cockamamy! Ow! Leggo! Yuh can't cover books wit' newspaper. My teacher don' let. An aftuh she took mine beanshooduh, she pinched me by duh teet! Lousey bestia! Bein yoshvim uvein mesubim. So wad's de nex' woid? Mine hen'ball wend down duh sewuh! Now, I god six poinduhs!

—You couldn't do it with a regular coal. You'd burn all up. Even hot tea if you drink—ooh! But where could you get angel-coal? Mr. Ice-man, give me a pail of angel-coal. Hee! Hee! In a cellar is coal. But other kind, black coal, not angel coal. Only God had angel-coal. Where is God's cellar I wonder? How light it must be there. Wouldn't be scared like I once was in Brownsville. Remember?

"C'mon chick! Hey Louie! Yuh last! Wed mine feed! Look! Me! Yea! Hea! Two!"

—Angel-coal. In God's cellar is—

All the belated ones had straggled in. A hail of jabbering now rocked the cheder.

"And-not-a-tree—" As the rabbi stooped lower and lower, his voice shot up a steep ladder of menace. "Shall-be-upright in the land!" He straightened, scaling crescendo with a roar. "Noo!" His final shattering bellow mowed down the last shrill reeds of voices. "Now it's my turn!" Smiling fiercely he rose, cat-o-nine in hand, and advanced toward the silent, cowering row. "Here!" the scourge whistled down, whacked against a thigh. "Here's for you!"

"Wow!"

"And you!"

"Ouch! Waddid I—do?"

"And you for your squirming tongue!"

"Leggo! Ooh!"

"And you that your rump is on fire! Now sit still!"

"Umph! Ow!"

"And you for your grin! And you for your nickering, and you for your bickering. Catch! Catch! Hold! Dance!"

The straps flew, legs plunged. Shrill squibs of pain popped up and down the bench. No one escaped, not even David. Wearied at length, and snorting for breath, the rabbi stopped and glared at them. Suppressed curses, whimpers, sniffles soughed from one end of the bench to the other.

"Shah!"

Even these died out.

"Now! To your books! Dig your eyes into them. The four Questions. Noo! Begin! Ma nishtanaw."

"Mah nishtanaw halilaw hazeh," they bellowed, "mikawl halaylos. Sheb chol halaylos onu ochlim chametz umazoh."

"Schulim!" The rabbi's chin went down, his voice diving past it to an ominous bass. "Dumb are you?"

"Haliylaw hazeh." A new voice vigorously swelled the already lusty chorus, "kulo mazoh!"

When they had finished the four questions, repeated them and rendered them thrice into Yiddish—

"Now the chad gadyaw," commanded the rabbi. "And with one voice. Hurry!"

Hastily, they turned the pages.

"Chad godyaw, chad godyaw," they bayed raggedly, "disabin abaw bis rai zuzaw, chad godyaw, chad godyaw—"

"Your teeth fall out, Simkeh." snarled the rabbi, grinning venomously, "what are you laughing at?"

"Nuttin!" protested Simkeh in an abused voice. "I wasn't laughing!" He was though—some one had been chanting "fot God Yaw" instead of Chad-Godyaw.

"So!" said the rabbi sourly when they had finished. "And now where is the blessed understanding that remembers yesterday? Who can render this into Yiddish? Ha? Where?"

A few faltering ones raised their hands.

"But all of it!" he warned. "Not piece-meal, all of it without stuttering. Or—" He snapped the cat-o-nine. "The noodles!"

Scared, the volunteers lowered their hands.

"What? None? Not a single one." His eyes swept back and forth. "Oh, you!" With a sarcastic wave of the hand, he flung back the offers of the older, chumish students.

"It's time you mastered this feat! No one!" He wagged his head at them bitterly. "May you never know where your teeth are! Hi! Hi! none strives to be a Jew any more. Woe unto you! Even a goy knows more about his filth than you know of holiness. Woe! Woe!" He glared at David accusingly. "You too? Is your head full of turds like the rest of them? Speak!"

"I know it," he confessed, but the same time feigned sullenness lest he stir the hatred of the others.

"Well! Have you ribs in your tongue? Begin! I'm waiting!"

"One kid, one only kid," cautiously he picked up the thread, "one kid that my father bought for two zuzim. One kids, one only kid. And a cat came and ate the kid that my father had bought for two zuzim. One kid, one only kid. And a dog came and bit the cat that ate the kid that my father bought for two zuzim. One kid, one only kid." He felt more and more as he went on as if the others were crouching to pounce upon him should he miss one rung in the long ladder of guilt and requital. Carefully, he climbed past the cow and the butcher and the angel of death. "And then the Almighty, blessed be He— (*Gee! Last. Nobody after. Didn't know before. But sometime, mama, Gee!*) Unbidden, the alien thoughts crowded into the gap. For an instant he faltered. (*No! No! Don't stop!*) "Blessed be He," he repeated hurriedly, "killed the angel of death, who killed the butcher, who killed the ox, who drank the water, that quenched the fire, that burned the stick, that beat the dog, that bit the cat, that ate the kid, that my father bought for two zuzim. One kid, one only kid!" Breathlessly he came to an end, wondering if the rabbi were angry with him for having halted in the middle.

But the rabbi was smiling. "So!" he patted his big palms together. "This one I call my child. This is memory. This is intellect. You may be a great rabbi yet—who knows!" He stroked his black beard with a satisfied air and regarded David a moment, then suddenly he reached his hand into his pocket and drew out a battered black purse.

A murmur of incredulous astonishment rose from the bench.

Snapping open the pronged, metal catch, the rabbi jingled the coins inside and pinched out a copper. "Here!

Because you have a true Yiddish head. Take it!"

Automatically, David lifted his hand and closed it round the penny. The rest gaped silently.

"Now come and read," he was peremptory again. "And the rest of you dullards, take care! Let me hear you wink and I'll tear you not into shreds, but into shreds of shreds!"

A little dazed by the windfall, David followed him to the reading bench and sat down. While the rabbi carefully rolled himself a cigarette, David gazed out of the window. The rain had stopped, though the yard was still dark. He could sense a strange quietness holding the outdoors in its grip. Behind him, the first whisper flickered up somewhere along the bench. The rabbi lit his cigarette, shut the book from which Mendel had been reading and pushed it to one side.

—Could ask him now, I bet. He gave me a penny. About Isaiah and the coal. Where? Yes. Page sixty-eight. I could ask—

Chaa! Wuuh! Thin smoke glanced off the table. The rabbi reached over for the battered book and picked up the pointer.

"Rabbi?"

"Noo?" He pinched over the leaves.

"When Mendel was reading about that—that man who you said, who——" He never finished. Twice through the yard, as though a lantern had been swung back and forth above the roof-tops, violet light rocked the opposite walls —and darkness for a moment and a clap of thunder and a rumbling like a barrel rolling down cellar stairs.

"Shma yisroel!" the rabbi ducked his head and clutched David's arm. "Woe is me!"

"Ow!" David squealed. And the pressure on his arm relaxing, giggled.

Behind him the sharp, excited voices. "Yuh see it! Bang! Bang wot a bust it gave! I tol' yuh I see a blitz before!"

"Shah!" The rabbi regained his composure. "Lightning before the Passover! A warm summer." And to David as if remembering, "Why did you cry out and why did you laugh?"

"You pinched me," he explained cautiously, "and then—"

"Well?"

"And then you bent down—like us when you drop the pointer, and then I thought—"

"Before God," the rabbi interrupted, "none may stand upright."

—Before God.

"But what did you think?"

"I thought it was a bed before. Upstairs. But it wasn't."

"A bed! It wasn't!" He stared at David. "Don't play the fool with me because I gave you a penny." He thrust the book before him. "Come then!" he said brusquely. "It grows late."

—Can't ask now.

"Begin! Shohain ad mawrom—"

"Shohain ad mawrom vekawdosh shmo vakawsuv ronnu zadekim ladonoi." Thought lapsed into monotone.

After a short reading, the rabbi excused him, and David slid off the bench and went over to where the rest were sitting to get his strap of books. Schloime, who held them in his lap, had risen with alacrity as he approached and proffered them to him.

"Dey wanted t' take dem, but I was holdin' 'em." He informed him. "Watcha gonna buy?"

"Nuttin."

"Aa!" And eagerly. "I know w'ea dere's orange-balls—eight fuh a cent."

"I ain' gonna ged nuttin."

"Yuh stingy louse!"

The others had swarmed about. "I told yuh, yuh wouldn' get nuttin for holdin' his books. Yaah, yuh see! Aaa, let's see duh penny. We'll go witchah. Who couldn'a said dat!"

"Shah!"

They scattered back to the bench. David eased his way through the door.

V

THE air had freshened, the dark became lighter. The wind, cooler now, wrinkled the dark puddles between the flagstones, lifted the wash-lines. From somewhere, large drops of water still spattered down, though walls and fences showed broad dry patches. His fingers still closed around the penny in his pocket, David climbed up the brown, water-stained stairs, passed through the warm corridor and out into the street. Sidewalks and gutter were drying to grey again, dark rills thinning under curbs. In the west clearing toward sunset, clouds were a silver havoc, their light in the rugged stone frame of the street, sombre and silver.

—Show her the penny when I get upstairs. And she'll tell Papa. What would he say? Bet he wouldn't believe. He'd say I found it. But I could say it for him—all over again. One kid, one only kid, and then he'd have to— That candy store.

He stopped, stared thoughtfully at the clutter of toys and tin horns, masks, soda bottles and cigarette posters.

—No. Have to show her first. See what I got. Then could buy. What? Candy? No. Like to get those little balls in the hoople-cage. You blow and catch. Only can't catch so good. When will I catch good? Maybe better wait till to-morrow when I get another penny. And then—Gee! Go to Aunt Bertha's candy store. When was I? Long time ago, that time with mama! Too far. And girls, Esther and Polly. Hate them. How they fight, gee! How they eat soup! Poppa'd murder me if I did. But Uncle Nathan only hollers, and Aunt Bertha hollers on him. Remember Uncle Nathan and his mama? Vinegar and light when he told. Light! Gee! And Isaiah and that angel-coal. On his mouth. But remember. Blue book—so big. On page sixty-eight. Maybe ask next time. Maybe mama knows. Penny? Where? Oh! Here! Nearly didn't get it. When that funny

jumped into the middle of the chad godyuh. Wonder
what! I was saying. Yes. I was saying—

"Little boy." The words were in Yiddish.

He started and looked up. He had almost run into her
—a shriveled old woman with a face so lined with short,
thin wrinkles, they slanted down the sere skin like a rain.
She was stooped. A striped blue and white apron covered
the front of her rusty black satin dress. The whites of her
eyes were cloudy as an old tusk and caught in a net of
red veins. Her nostrils were wet. Between her brow and
the white kerchief on her head a stiff brown wig pro-
truded like a ledge.

"Little boy." She repeated in a quavering treble, head
rocking infirmly from side to side. "Are you a Jew?"

For a fleeting instant, David wondered how he could
have understood her if he hadn't been a Jew.

"Yes."

"Well, it won't harm you anyway," she mumbled.
"You're not old enough to sin. Come with me and I'll
give you a penny."

He stared at her. There was something terrifying and
dreamlike about it all. The gingerbread boys the old witch
baked. In two A one.

"You'll light the gas stove for me, yes?"

That's what they did too—only it wasn't gas. Gee! He
felt half-impelled to take to his heels.

"I lit the candles", she explained, "and it's too late
now."

"Oh!" He understood now. It was Friday. Still why had
she lit them so early? It wasn't night yet.

"Are you coming?" she asked and turned to go. "I'll
give you a penny."

After all, this was his street. There was his house only
two houses away. And he would have another penny. He
followed her. She shuffled toward a nearby house and
labored slowly up the stoop. Her panting breath on the
second step turned to groaning on the fifth. Above him
the slow, wrinkled, cracked shoes stopped at the threshold.
He drew up beside her.

"We haven't any more steps to climb," she muttered,
waiting for her loud breathing to quiet. "A curse on the
black sleep that took me. When I awoke it was dark, and
I, sodden with sleep, lit the candles. Too fuddled to look

at the clock first, too dull to light the gas-stove. Woe me."
She wavered into motion again. A few steps through the
hallway and she stopped before a door, opened it and
went in. The kitchen, swept and drear, glaze worn from
the linoleum; four candles glimmering above the heavy,
red-and-white table-cloth. Odor of fish. Stagnancy.

"First pull over a chair," she said, "and light the gas
up there. Can you reach the matches?"

David pulled open the drawer she pointed to and found
the box of matches; then he dragged a chair under the
gas lamp and climbed up.

"Do you know how?" she asked.

"Yea." He struck a match, turned on the gas and lit it.

"Good! And now under the pots."

He lit those too.

"Smaller," she said. "Smaller. As small as small is."

When he had done this, she pointed to her purse on
the table. "Take it," she said and began nodding and
nodded as if she couldn't stop, "and take out a penny."

"I don't want it—" he hung back.

"Go! Go!"

While she watched him, he fished out a penny.

"Now close it." And when he did. "You're a good
child," she said. "May God bless you," and she opened
the door.

VI

NO, HE thought as he went out, she wasn't a witch—
just a 9th street old woman, that's all. But even so, an unaccountable sadness thickened the joy he should have felt
at getting another penny. Even if he hadn't been turned
into gingerbread, something had turned the heart heavy.
Why? A sin, maybe? Yes, bet that's why. But too young,
she said. No. Bet nobody was too young. So which is the
sin penny? He looked at them. Indian this. Lincoln this.
Lincoln just got. But the cool air of the outdoors as he
entered the street whipped away remorse as it whipped

the nostrils clear of kitchen odors. He turned toward his
house and quickened his step. Dusk was resuming the
alley of the east. Smokestacks across the dark river had
begun their pilgrimage into night. On the corner of Avenue D, the shadowy lamplighter with the pale, uplifted
face was thrusting his long, glow-tipped lance into the
hazy globe of the street lamp. David stopped a moment
to see whether the gas inside and the mantle would catch.
A faint puff and the globe filled with a yellow bloom.
He climbed up the stairs of the stoop, wondering whether
lamp-lighters were ever disturbed by their own sacrilege
or whether they were all goyim. As he mounted the hallway stairs, the voices of boys drifted down.

"So yuh have tuh."

"Yuh don'!" another answered.

"Id ain' Shabis yet."

"Id is so. Id's dock."

'Id's dock in hea, but id ain' Shabis."

Before the half-open doorway of a water closet, inside
of which a boy was squatting, stood two of his companions.

"I am gonna tear it," came the rebellious voice inside.
"Dere ain' nutt'n else."

And as David walked by the doorway, he saw the boy
who was squatting on the seat inside tear a long swath
out of one of the newspapers that littered the floor.

"Now yuh god it!" said one of the onlookers vindictively.

"An' ids a double sin too," added the other.

"So w'y is id a double sin?" the squatter's provoked
voice demanded.

"Cause it's Shabis." The righteous voice below meted
out. "An' dat's one sin. Yuh can't tear on Shabis. An'
because id's a Jewish noospaper wid Jewish on id, dat's
two sins. Dere!"

"Yea!" the other chimed in. "You'd a only god one
sin if you tord a Englitch noospaper."

"Well, w'yntcha gimme a Englitch noospaper?" demanded the first voice disgustedly. "I ain' goin' haffee
witchoo no more."

"So don'."

Their bickering voices faded below.

—Looks every place, He. Knew I shouldn't have lit

the gas. One penny is bad. Real bad. But one penny is good. So that makes it even, don't it? Maybe He won't get mad. Gee, didn't know He was so every place. How can he look in every dark, if He's light—the rabbi said—and it's real dark. How can He see in the real dark and we can't see Him. What's real dark? Real dark. Gee! That time—Annie—closet. Cellar—Luter. Sh! Don't! Gee! Sin it was. Hurry up! Sin it was! Every place, sin it is. Didn't know. Hurry up! Coal He touched him. Hurry up!

Eagerly he glanced up at the transom above his door. It was unlit—stained only by indigo twilight. His heart sank. Then she was out—his mother was out—and only his father was there, asleep probably. He stopped irresolutely, hedged in by two fears, the dark and his father. He would have to wake him if the door were locked, and that—there was peril in that. The rungs of the shutters of memory snapped open and closed—a fragmentary fleeting image, but clear. Better run then, wait in the street until she came home. No. He would try the knob first—just once. He turned it; the door opened. That was strange. He tiptoed into a blue room, aware of a blue washboard on a blue washtub, aware of his father's throaty breathing in the further bedroom. He sheered away from it—where was she?—and entered the frontroom. She was sitting beside the window, her dark face in outline against the frosty blue of the pane. His heart leapt.

"Mama!" he tried to keep his voice down to a whisper, but failed.

"Oh!" she started. "You frightened me!" and then stretched out her arms.

"I didn't know you were here." He entered the delicious circle of her embrace.

"My head is like an old bell," she sighed pressing him to her. "Idle and without hearing, but murmuring sometimes, a little insecure." Then she laughed and kissed his brow. "Did you get your shoes wet in the rain?"

"No I ran into the cheder just before."

"That sweater is too thin."

He had been holding the Indian penny in one hand to keep it from jingling against the other. And now he held it up. "Look what I've got."

"My!" she marveled. "How did you come by that?"

"The rabbi gave it to me."

"The rabbi?"

"Yes. I was the only one who knew the chad godyuh from last time."

She laughed and hugged him. "Solomon, Sage!"

He took a deep breath. He had asked her before, but somehow the thought was too elusive. He needed to be told again.

"Who is God, mama?"

"You keep asking exactly the right person," she smiled. "Doesn't the rabbi ever tell you?"

"You can't ask him anything."

"Well, why are you so interested?"

"I don't know. I mean you didn't tell me what he looked like."

"That was because I didn't know." She chuckled at his chagrin. "Still I'll tell you what—"

But breaking her speech, his father's painful, awakening groan reached them from the bedroom.

"Genya!"

"I'm in here, Albert."

"Hmm!" Always he seemed to need reassurance, always he seemed reassured. And was silent. David hoped she would hurry on before he came in.

"Yes," she continued. "I'll tell you what a pious old woman in Veljish told me when I was a little girl. And that's all I know. She said that He was brighter than the day is brighter than the night. You understand? But she always used to add if darkest midnight were bright enough to see whether a black hair were straight or curly. Brighter than day."

Brighter than day. That much seemed definite, seemed to conform with his own belief, that much he could grasp. It reminded him of the steps of the chad godyuh. "And He lives in the sky?"

"And in the earth and in the water and in the world."

"But what does He do?"

"He holds us in His hand, they say—us and the world."

His father had come in, hacking, clearing his sleep-clogged breath. He stood darkly in the doorway. There was room for one more question and that was all.

"Could He break it? Us? The streets? Everything?"

"Of course. He has all power. He can break and rebuild, but He holds."

His father made an impatient sound with his lips. "Why do you sit in darkness?"

"My washing," she laughed apologetically. "The little curtains for the Passover. It grew dark as I was about to hang them up. And I thought, well, Friday, best the neighbors didn't see me or they'll cluck. Do you know your son won a penny in the cheder?"

"What for? Because he asks such bright questions? Makes and breaks. A fool in a sand heap." He yawned. His stretching arms pressed against both sides of the door-frame till it creaked. "We need some light."

VII

IT WAS Monday morning, the morning of the first Passover night. One was lucky in being a Jew to-day. There was no school. David had just come down the stairs carrying the wooden spoon into which the night before his father had swept up the last crumbs of leavened bread, swept them up with a feather and bound them with a rag —chumitz—leavened bread to be burned in the fire. And now on the top step of the stoop, he paused awhile and watched the Hungarian janitor polish one of the brass bannisters in front of the house. It had a corrupt odor, brass, as of something rotting away, and yet where the sun struck the burnished metal, it splintered into brilliant yellow light. Decay. Radiance. Funny.

"You no touch!" warned the janitor, scowling while he rubbed the bannister. "No stayin' here." Then his eyes lighted on the spoon and feathers in David's hand. "Matziss, huh?" A grin dove up through the depths of the frown, hovered and plunged down again. "Dun boin frun' dis house."

David went down the stairs and walked toward the middle of the block. Someone had kindled a small fire there. Once the spoon had been dropped into the flames, his duty was done and he could do what he pleased until cheder time—it would be a little earlier to-day. And then with two cents at call upstairs—he had reserved the spending of them until after lunch when he would probably get another penny from his mother—he looked forward to an exciting afternoon.

Three boys, all bigger than himself guarded the flame, and when he drew near, "Waddaye wan'?" one of them demanded.

"I wanna t'row my chumitz on hea."

"We'ea's yuh penny?"

"Wa penny?"

"Us boin chumitz for a penny. De t'ree of us is potnes, ain' we Chink?"

"Yeah, dis is our fiuh."

"Aintchuh gonna led me boin mine? I only god one liddle one."

"No!"

"Make yuh own fiuh."

"Gwan if yuh ain' god a penny, we don't wan yuh lousy chumitz—"

A sudden scraping sound followed by a snarl of foreign words, made them all spin about.

"Mannagia chi ti battiavo!"

The broad, glitter-edged, half laden shovel of a white-garbed street-cleaner plowed toward them.

In their turn, the lords of the flame became suddenly suppliants. "Hey mister! Don' push id! Id's a sin. Look out! Dot's chumitz! An id's on duh sewer too. Wadduh yuh wan'?" They danced about him. "Id's on duh sewer! Id don' make de street soft we'en we boin on de sewer."

"Ah kicka duh assuh! Geedah duh!" The implacable shovel bit through the coals scattering them before it.

"Yuh lousy bestitt!" shrieked the guardians. "Leave our chumitz alone! We c'n boin id hea—de cop lets us!"

"Waid'll I call my fodder!" threatened the one who had first kept David at bay. "He'll make yuh stop! Hey Pop! Pop! Tateh! Comm oud!"

A man with a short beard and a blood-smeared apron looked out of the butcher-shop.

"Pop! Look. He's pushin' our chumitz wid all duh shit!"

With an outraged cry, the butcher came running out,

followed a few seconds later by his wife, aproned like himself.

"Fav'y you push dis, ha?" The butcher flung an angry hand at the choked, smouldering embers mixed now with rubbish and manure.

"Wadda you wa-an?" The street cleaner stopped angrily, black brows leaping together as stiff as carbon rods under the white helmet. "You no tella me waddaduh push! I cleanuh dis street. Dey no makuh duh fiuh hea!" His intricate gestures jig-sawed space.

"No? I ken't tell you, ha? Verstinkeneh Goy!" The butcher planted himself directly before the mound upon the shovel. "Now moof!"

"Sonnomo bitzah you! I fix!" He leaned viciously on the shovel-handle. The smouldering hummock sprang forward. The butcher leaped heavily sideways to avoid being mowed down into the variegated debris.

"You vanna push me?" he roared. "I'll zebreak you het."

"Vai a fanculo te!" The sweeper threw down the shovel. "Come on! Jew bast!"

But before either could strike a blow, the butcher's wife had seized her husband's arm.

"You ox!" she shrilled in Yiddish. "Do you oppose an Italian? Don't you know they carry knives—all of them! Quick!" She dragged him back. "Inside!"

"I don't care," stormed her husband, though he made no effort to break her hold. "And I? Have I no knives?"

"Are you mad?" she shrieked. "Let Italian cut-throats stab him to death, not you!" And redoubling her efforts, she hauled him into the store.

Left master of the field, the street cleaner still growling and gnashing his teeth snatched up the shovel and glaring at the retreating boys hacked fiercely at the piled heap before him. David, who had been watching from the curb, decided it would be better to withdraw—especially since he still had the wooden spoon in his hand.

But what to do with the spoon now? One had to burn it or one would sin. And one couldn't burn it now because the sweeper was there. One could wait of course, and then when the sweeper was gone, build a little fire. But that wasn't altogether pleasing either. He'd have to stay right here and wait till the man had left. He couldn't go anywhere—not with a big wooden spoon in your pocket. He'd lose it maybe, and that would be a sin. And anyway, its mere presence hobbled the free mind. Nor did he like starting a fire by himself—the policeman might not understand. And the street cleaner might even come back.

Where could he go? Where find another fire? Another block maybe? But maybe they wouldn't let him throw it in. They'd want a penny too. Some crust! Maybe he could sneak up to a fire if he found one, and throw it in. No, they'd throw it away— No. But he'd have to burn it or get a sin. Where go?

He had already been walking aimlessly toward Avenue D, and now at the corner, he stopped and gazed vacantly about him. Seventh Street . . . Eighth Street . . . The River . . . The River! There! Nobody was there. He wanted to go there anyhow. He could make a little fire— a tiny fire in front of the junk-yard and watch it. Yes, there! The matches? Yes, he had four. He'd get here quick and light it, and then sit down on the dock. That was it.

Elated at having found a solution, he crossed Avenue D, passed the tenements; loitered a moment beside the open door of the smithy. Inside stood the shadowy and submissive horse, the shadowy smith. Acrid odor of seared hooves lingered about the place. Now a horse-shoe glowed under the hammer—ong-jonga-ong-jong-jong-jong—ringing on the anvil as the pincers turned it.

—Zwank. Zwank. In a cellar is—

He passed the seltzer bottlery—the rattle and gurgle —passed the stable. Out of the dark manure-smell into the sunlight, the Negro stable-boy came out on patent leather shoes, holes cut for bunions. He was laughing— strong teeth and head thrown back—and his laughter, sleeve within larger sleeve of mirth, opened like a telescope, rich, warm, contagious. David grinned as he went by. Grey sparrows by puddles, pecked at the yellow oats among the cobbles, among the cobbles miraculous blades of grass. And there, just before the shore sank beneath the mossy piles of the dock (these driven through blackened rocks, past oil-barrels, stove-in, moss-green and rusty, past scummy wreckage) he squatted down beside a ledge of the open junk-heap, the salt-stink of ebbtide in his nostrils.

—Right here on the cobbles could. Nobody here, nobody watching. Get little pieces—there's a big one—paper. Catch before it flies. It cracks, big piece. Long tear. Another. That boy in the toilet. Bet he had a sin. This way tear. Little pieces. He's watchin' I bet. God. Always. Little, little sticks. Grass over here between. Who puts grass here? Won't burn. And the Italian got a sin. Like the boy said. But I bet the butcher had a bigger knife. Cardboard, good too. Wonder can He see I'm being good? It's like a tent. Now stay on top, chumitz. Now wait.

He fetched out one of his matches, scraped it against a cobble and shielding its flame touched it to the bits of paper under the kindling. A live, golden flame awoke; wood and cardboard caught, and in a few minutes the whole tindery mound was ablaze. Content yet strangely nostalgic, he crouched down beside the fire and watched the first tiny beads of flame run up the raveled threads of the rag that bound feather and spoon together. The blue, merging smoke crossed his nostrils—

—Gee, how feathers stink! No, they don't! It's holy and He's looking. Feathers don't stink! No!

The cloth burned rapidly; feathers and spoon sank into the shifting embers, separated; the half-charred crumbs spilled out and were consumed.

—No more chumitz. All burned black. See God, I was good? Now only white Matzohs are left. Can go. Don't sit on the edge of the dock, mama says. It frightens her. It don't frighten me. Just once, for a tiny little while. Was good, wasn't I?

A few steps toward the river, the cobbles gave place to the broad wooden slabs of the wharf. On one side a paint-blistered boat rotted vacantly on the water, on the other side an empty scow tugged at its yellow hawsers and grunted against the dock. On a pier, two blocks away, the black jaws of a steam-scuttle, yawning, dove into the hold of a coal-barge, and dripping, swung back to the huge bins. When he had come almost to the end of the dock, he sat down, and with his feet hanging over the water leaned against the horned and bulbous stanchion to which boats were moored. Out here the wind was fresher. The uncommon quiet excited him. Beneath him and under his palms, the dry, splintering timbers radiated warmth. And beneath them, secret, unseen, and always faintly sinister, the tireless lipping of water among the piles. Before him, the river and to the right, the long, grey bridges spanning it—

—Like that sword with the big middle on Mecca cigarettes.

That clipped the plumes of a long ship steaming beneath it. Gulls, beaked faces ugly as their flight was graceful, wheeled through the wide air on sickle wings. A tug on the other side pecked spryly at a stolid barge. Yoked at length to its sluggish mate, it puffed briskly out into the river, gathered momentum.

—Makes the fat one make a mustache when he goes.

The sunlit rhythmic spray sprouted up before the blunt bow of the barge, hung whitely, lapsed.

—Bricks on it. Bet a whole house.

A cloud sheared the sunlight from the wharf; his back felt cooler; the wind sharpened . . . Smokestacks on the other bank darkened slowly, fluting filmy distance with iron-grey shadow.

—Like forks they stick up. Like for—Fu— Sh! Was good today. Look other place.

His gaze shifted to the left. As the cloud began to pass, a long slim lathe of sunlight burned silver on the water—

—Gee, didn't see before!

Widened to a swath, a lane, widened.

—Like a ship just went.

A plain, flawless, sheer as foil to the serried margins. His eyes dazzled.

—Fire on the water. White.

His lids grew heavy.

—In the water she said. White. Brighter than day. Whiter. And He was.

Minutes passed while he stared. The brilliance was hypnotic. He could not take his eyes away. His spirit yielded, melted into light. In the molten sheen memories and objects overlapped. Smokestacks fused to palings flickering in silence by. Pale lathes grew grey, turned dusky, contracted and in the swimming dimness, he saw sparse teeth that gnawed upon a lip; and ladders on the ground turned into hasty fingers pressing on a thigh

and again smokestacks. Straight in air they stood a moment, only to fall on silvered cardboard corrugating brilliance. And he heard the rubbing on a wash-board and
the splashing suds, smelled again the acrid soap and a
voice speaking words that opened like the bands of a
burnished silver accordion—Brighter than day . . . Brighter . . . Sin melted into light . . .

Uh chug chug, ug chug!
—Cucka cucka . . . Is a chicken . . .
Uh chug ug ch ch ch—Tew weet!
—No . . . Can't be . . .
Ug chug, ug chug, ug—TEW WEET!

What! He started as if out of a dream. A tremor
shook him from head to foot so violently that his ears
whirred and rang. His eyes bulged, staring. What?
Water! Down below! He flung himself back against the
mooring post.

Directly in front of him, with only a short space of
water intervening, a black tugboat churned its way. In a
doorway amidships, his back to the bright brass engine,
stood a man in his undershirt, bare, outstretched arms
gripping the doorpost on either side. He whistled again,
shrill from mobile lips, grinned, spat, and "Wake up,
Kid!" his sudden, amused hail rolled over the water,
" 'fore you throw a belly-w'opper!" Then he poked his
dark-blond head inside as though he were speaking to
someone behind him.

Terrified, rigid, David watched the tug wallow by. Ages
seemed to pass, but in spite of himself he could not
move. Twice he sighed and with such depth as though he
had been weeping for hours. And with the suddenness
of snapping fetters the spell broke, and he stared about
him too unsteady to rise. What was it he had seen? He
couldn't tell now. It was as though he had seen it in another world, a world that once left could not be recalled.
All that he knew about it was that it had been complete and dazzling.

VIII

HE HAD sat there a long time. Steadiness slowly returned to him. The planks of the dock stiffened and grew firm. He rose.

—Funny little lights all gone. Like when you squeeze too hard on a toilet. Better go home.

He approached the end of the dock. Voices, as he neared the cobbles made him look over to the left. Three boys, coming from Eighth Street, climbed nimbly over the snarled chaos of the open junk heap. At the sight of David, they hallooed, leapt down to level ground and raced toward him. All wore caps cocked sideways and sweaters, red and green, smeared, torn at the breast and elbows. Two were taller than David, wiry, blue-eyed, up-turned noses freckled. The other, dark-skinned and runty, looked older than the rest and carried in his hand a sword made of a thin strip of metal that looked like sheet zinc and a long bolt wired across it near one end. One glance at their tough, hostile faces, smirched by the grime and rust of the junk heap and screwed up into malicious watch-fulness was enough. David's eyes darted about for an open-ing. There was none—except back to the dock. Trapped, he stood still, his frightened gaze wavering from one men-acing face to another.

"Wadda yiz doin' on 'at dock?" growled the runty one side-mouthed. The sunlight glanced along the sheet zinc sword as he pointed.

"N—Nottin. I was'n' doin' nott'n. Dey was boats dere."

"How old 're youse?"

"I'm—I'm eight already."

"Well, w'y aintchjis in school?"

"Cause id'd, cause—" But something warned him. "Cause I— cause my brudder's god measles."

"Dot's a lodda bullshit, Pedey." This from the freckled one. "He's onna hook."

"Yea. Tell 'at tuh Sweeney."

"We oughta take yiz tuh a cop," added the second ckled one.

"Betcha de cop'll tell yuh," urged David, hoping for no better fate.

"Nah! *We* know," Pedey scornfully rejected the idea. "W'ere d'yiz live?"

"Dere." He could see the very windows of his own floor. "Dat house on nint' stritt. My mudders gonna look oud righd away."

Pedey squinted in the direction David pointed.

"Dat's a sheeney block, Pedey," prompted the second freckled lieutenant with ominous eagerness.

"Yea. Yer a Jew aintchiz?"

"No I ain'!" he protested hotly. "I ain' nod a Jew!"

"Only sheenies live in dat block!" countered Pedey narrowly.

"I'm a Hungarian. My mudder 'n' fodder's Hungarian. We're de janitors."

"W'y wuz yuh lookin upstairs?"

"Cause my mudder wuz washin' de floors."

"Talk Hungarian," challenged the first lieutenant.

"Sure like dis. Abashishishabababyo tomama wawa. Like dot."

"Aa, yuh full o' shit!" sneered the second lieutenant angrily. "C'mom, Pedey, let's give 'im 'is lumps."

"Yea!" the other freckled one urged. "C'mon. He ain' w'ite. Yi! Yi! Yi!" He wagged his palms under his chin.

"Naa!" Pedey nudged his neighbor sharply. "He's awri'. Led 'im alone." And to David. "Got any dough? We'll match yiz pennies."

"No, I ain' god nodd'n. Id's all in mine house." He would have been glad to have the two pennies now if only they would let him go.

"Let's see yer pockets?"

"Hea, I'll show yuh," he hastily turned them inside out. "Nod even in duh watch pocket."

"C'mon, Pedey," urged first lieutenant, advancing.

"Lemme go!" David whimpered, shrinking back.

"Naa! Let 'im alone," ordered Pedey. "He's awright. Let's show 'im de magic. Waddayah say?"

"Yea! At's right!" The other two seconded him. "C'mon! Yuh wanna see some magic?"

"No-no. I don' wanna."

"Yuh don'!" Pedey's voice rose fiercely. The others strained at the leash.

"W—wa' kind o' magic?"

"C'mon, we'll show yiz, won' we, Weasel? Over dis way." His sword pointed across the junk-heap toward Tenth Street. "Where de car tracks is."

"So wod yuh gonna do?" he held back.

"C'mon we'll show yiz." They hemmed him in cutting off retreat. "Ah' here's my sword—G'wan take it, fore we—" He thrust it into David's hands. He took it. They moved forward.

At the foot of the junk-heap, the lieutenant named Weasel stopped. "Waid a minute," he announced, "I godda take a piss."

"Me too," said the others halting as well. They unbuttoned. David edged away.

"Lager beer," chanted Pedey as he tapped forehead, mouth, chest and navel, "comes from here—"

"Ye see," Weasel pointed triumphantly at the shrinking David. "I tol' yuh he ain' w'ite. W'y don'tchiz piss?"

"Don' wanna. I peed befaw."

"Aw, hosschit." He lifted one leg.

"Phuwee!"

With a howl of glee, the other two pounced on him.

"Eli, eli, a bundle of strawr," they thumped his back. "Farting is against de lawr—"

"Leggo!" Weasel shook them off viciously.

"Well yiz farted—Hey!" Pedey swooped down on David. "Stay here, or yuh'll get a bust on de bugle! C'mon! An' don't try to duck on us."

With one on either side of him and one behind, David climbed up the junk heap and threaded his way cautiously over the savage iron morraine. Only one hope sustained him—that was to find a man on the other side to run to. Before him the soft, impartial April sunlight spilt over a hill of shattered stoves, splintered wheels, cracked drain pipes, potsherds, marine engines split along cruel and jagged edges. Eagerly, he looked beyond—only the suddenly alien, empty street and the glittering cartracks, branching off at the end.

"Peugh! Wadda stink!" Pedey spat. "Who opened his hole?"

From somewhere in the filth and ruin, the stench of mouldering flesh fouled the nostrils. A dead cat.

"C'mon, hurry up!"

As they neared the street, a rusty wire, tough root of a brutal soil, tripped David who had quickened his pace, and he fell against the sword bending it.

"He pissed in his w'iskers," guffawed the second lieutenant.

Pedey grinned. Only Weasel kept his features immobile. He seemed to take pride in never laughing.

"Hol' it, yuh dumb bassid," he barked, "yuh bent it!"

"Waid a secon'," Pedey warned them when they had reached the edge of the junk-heap. "Lemme lay putso." He slid down, and after a furtive glance toward Avenue D, "Come on! Shake! Nobody's aroun'."

They followed him.

"Now we're gonna show yiz de magic."

"Waid'll ye sees it," Weasel chimed in significantly.

"Yea, better'n movin' pitchiz!"

"Wadda yuh wan' I shul do?" Their growing excitement added to his terror.

"Hurry up an' take dat sword an' go to dem tracks and t'row it in— See like dis. In de middle."

"I don't wanna go." He began to weep.

"G'wan yuh blubber-mout'." Weasel's fist tightened.

"G'wan!" The other lieutenant's face screwed up. " 'Fore we kick de piss ouda yiz."

"G'wan, an' we'll letchiz go," promised Pedey. "G'wan! Shake!"

"If I jost pud id in?"

"Yea. Like I showed yuh."

"An' den yuh'll led me go?"

"Sure. G'wan. Id ain' gonna hoitcha. Ye'll see all de movies in de woil! An' vawderville too! G'wan before a car comes."

"Sure, an' all de angels."

"G'wan!" Their fists were drawn back.

Imploringly, his eyes darted to the west. The people on Avenue D seemed miles away. The saloon-door in the middle of the block was closed. East. No none! Not a soul! Beyond the tarry rocks of the river-shore, the wind had scattered the silver plain into rippling scales. He was trapped.

"G'wan!" Their faces were cruel, their bodies stiff with expectancy.

He turned toward the tracks. The long dark grooves between each pair looked as harmless as they had always looked. He had stepped over them hundreds of times without a thought. What was there about them now that made the others watch him so? Just drop it, they said, and they would let him go. Just drop it. He edged closer, stood tip-toe on the cobbles. The point of the sheet-zinc sword wavered before him, clicked on the stone as he fumbled, then finding the slot at last, rasped part way down the wide grinning lips like a tongue in an iron mouth. He stepped back. From open fingers, the blade plunged into darkness.

Power!

Like a paw ripping through all the stable fibres of the earth, power, gigantic, fetterless, thudded into day! And light, unleashed, terrific light bellowed out of iron lips. The street quaked and roared, and like a tortured thing, the sheet zinc sword, leapt writhing, fell back, consumed with radiance. Blinded, stunned by the brunt of brilliance, David staggered back. A moment later, he was spurting madly toward Avenue D.

IX

WHEN he looked behind him again, the light was gone, the roaring stilled. Pedey and his mates had fled. At the crossing, several people had stopped and were staring toward the river. Eyes shifted to David as he neared Avenue D, but since no one tried to block his way, he twisted around the corner and fled toward Ninth Street. His father's milk wagon was standing beside the curb. His father was home. He might guess that something had gone wrong. He'd better not go up. He slunk past his house, cut across the street and broke into a run. At the cheder entrance he turned, scurried through the sheltering doorway, and came out into the sunlit and empty yard. The cheder door was closed. He had come far too early. Trembling in every limb, weak with fright, he looked about for a place to rest. The wide wooden doors that covered a cellar sloped gently into the sun. A new, brass padlock gleamed at their seam—too many of the rabbi's pupils had been banging them on their subterranean way into the cheder yard. He dragged himself over, dropped down on one of the wooden wings and shut his eyes. In the red sea of sun-lit eyelids his spirit sickeningly rolled and dipped. Though the planks were warm and the sun was warm, his teeth chattered and he shivered as if an icy gale were blowing. With a groan of anguish, he turned on his side hardly feeling the warm padlock under his cheek. Deep, shaking sobs caught on the snag of his throat. The hot tears crowded through his sealed eyelids, trickled unheeded across his cheek and nostril. He wept silently.

How long he lay there he did not know. But little by little the anguish lifted, his blood thawed, the sobbing calmed. Empty and nerveless, he opened his eyes; the rough-walled familiar houses, the leaning fences, the motley washing, wash-poles, sunlight, the cramped and cluttered patch of blue above him were good. A mottled, yellow cat crept carefully out upon a fire-escape, leapt down behind a fence. Realities warm and palpable. From open windows, the sound of voices, rattling of pots, rush of water in a sink, laughter shearing away loud snatches of familiar speech. It was good. In the veering of the light wind, the odors of cooking, strong and savory, hung and drifted. From somewhere up above a steady chop-chopping began. Meat or fish or perhaps the bitter herbs of the Passover. The limp, vacant body expanded, filled with certainties.

Chop. Chop. The sound was secure. His thoughts took the rhythm of the sound. Something within him chanted. Words flowed out of him of their own accord. Chop. Chop. Showed him, showed. In the river, showed him, showed. Chop. Chop. Showed him, showed. If He wants. Showed him, showed.

—In the dark, chop, chop. In the river, showed him, showed. In the dark, in the river was there. Came out if He wanted, was there. Stayed in if He wanted, was there. Came out if He wanted, stayed in if He wanted, came out if He wanted, was there . . .

—Could break it in his hands if He wanted. Could hold it in His hands if He wanted. Could break it, could hold it, could break it, could hold it, could break it, could hold it, was there.

—In the dark, in the hallways, was there. In the dark, in the cellars was there. Where cellars is locked, where cellars is coal, where cellars is coal, is

—Coal!

—Coal!

He sat bolt upright.

"Rabbi!" his startled cry rang out over the yard. "Rabbi! Is coal under! White in cellars!" He sprang to his feet in exaltation, stared about him wildly. On all the multi-colored walls that hemmed him in, one single vision was written. "Is coal under! White!" Dazedly, he lurched toward the door. "Rabbi!" He rattled it; it held. "Rabbi!" He had to get in. He had to. He raced around the corner of the cheder. The window! He clawed at it. Loose, unbolted, it squealed up easily. There was no hesitation. There could be none. An enormous hand was shoving him forward. He leapt up, abdomen landing on the sill, teetered half in, half out, sprawled into the cheder, hands forward.

That closet! Where all of them were! He ran to it. It was just out of reach. He dragged the rabbi's chair over, stood up, flung open the door. The blue one! The blue one! Feverishly he pried among them—found it. He leapt down, already turning the pages. Page sixty-eight it was—twenty-six—forty—seventy-two— sixty-nine —sixty-eight! On top! With all your might! He wriggled over the bench.

"Beshnas mos hamelech Uziyahu vawere es adonoi yoshav al kesai rum venesaw, vshulav malaiim es hahahol. Serafim omidim memal lo shash kanowfayim, sash kanow-fayim lawehhad, beshtayim yahase fanav uvishtayim yahase raglov uvishtayim yaofaif."

All his senses dissolved into the sound. The lines, unknown, dimly surmised, thundered in his heart with limitless meaning, rolled out and flooded the last shores of his being. Unmoored in space, he saw one walking on impalpable pavements that rose with the rising trees. Or were they trees or telegraph-poles, each crossed and leafy, none could say, but forms stood there with footholds in unmitigated light. And their faces shone because the light in their midst was luminous laughter. He read on.

The book returned. The table hardened . . . Behind him the sound of a key probing a keyhole screeked across infinite space. The lock snapped open—suddenly near at hand. Realization struck like an icy gust. With a start of dismay, he spun around over the bench, threw himself at the window. Too late! The rabbi, long black coat and derby, stepped into the light of the open door. He drew back with a groan of fright, but recognizing who it was, his eyes opened wrathfully and he came forward, head cocked sideways.

"How did you get in?" he demanded fiercely, "Ha?" The open window caught his eye. He stared at it, disbelief wrangling with ire. "You crawled in?"

"The book!" David stammered. "The book! I wanted it."

"You broke into my cheder!" The rabbi seemed not to have heard a single syllable. "You opened the window? You climbed in? You dared do this?"

"No! No!"

"Hush!" He paid no heed to his outcry. "I understand." And before David could budge, the rabbi's heavy hands had fallen on his neck and he was being dragged toward the cat-o-nine on the floor. "Fearful bastard!" he roared. "You crawled in to steal my pointers!"

"I didn't! I didn't touch them!"

"You it was took them before!" the rabbi drowned him out. "Sly one! You! Different I thought you were! Hi! Will you scoop!" He reached down for the scourge.

"I didn't! I came for the book! The blue book with the coal in it! The man and the coal!"

His iron grip still unrelenting, the rabbi lowered the cat-o-nine. "The man! The coal! You try to gull *me!*" But uncertainty had crept into his voice. "Stop your screeching!" And haling David after him, he yanked out the drawer of the reading table in which he kept his pointers. One glance was enough. Savagely, he thrust it back. "What man? And what coal?"

"Here in the book! The man the angel touched—Mendel read it! Isaiah!" The name suddenly returned to him. "Isaiah!"

The rabbi glared at the book as if he meant to burn it with his eyes, then his gaze rose slowly to David's face. In the silence, his clogged, apoplectic breathing was as loud as snoring. "Tell me, did you climb in only to read this book." His fingers uncurled from David's shoulder.

"Y-es! About th-that Isaiah."

"But what do you want of it?" His open palms barely sustained the weight of his question. "Can you read a word of chumish?"

"No, but I remembered, and I—I wanted to read it."

"Why?" From under his derby, pushed back by aimless fingers, his black skull-cap peeped out. "Are you mad or what? Couldn't you wait until I came? I would have let you read a belly-full."

"I didn't know when you—you were coming."

"But why did you want to read it? And why with such black haste?"

"Because I went and I saw a coal like—like Isaiah."

"What kind of a coal? Where?"

"Where the car-tracks run I saw it. On Tenth Street."

"Car tracks? You saw a coal?" He shut his eyes like one completely befuddled.

"Yes. It gave a big light in the middle, between the crack!"

"A what—! A—! Between a crack? You saw a light between a crack? A black year befall you!" Suddenly he stopped. His brow darkened. His beard rose. His head rolled back. "Chah! Chah! Chah! Chah!" Splitting salvoes of laughter suddenly burst from the cavern behind the whiskers. "Chah! Chah! Chah! Oy! Chah! Chah! Chah! This must be told." A hasty hand plugged back his slipping derby. "He saw a light! Oy! Chah! Chah! In the crack! Oy! Chah! Chah! Chah! I'll split like a herring! Yesterday, he heard a bed in the thunder! Today he sees a vision in a crack! Oy! Chah! Chah! Chah! Chah!" Minutes seemed to pass before he sobered. "Fool!" he gasped at length. "Go beat your head on a wall! God's light is not between car-tracks."

Ashamed, yet immensely relieved, David stood mute, eyes staring at the floor. The rabbi didn't know as he knew what the light was, what it meant, what it had done to him. But he would reveal no more. It was enough that the light had saved him from being whipped.

Uttering a short, hopeless snort, the rabbi moved off and hung his coat and derby on a nail. Returned, he pinched David's ear. "Come and read, simpleton," he ordered with amused contempt. "And if you ever crawl into my cheder again when I'm gone, nothing will help you. Not even a light."

David slid over the bench. The rabbi dragged out the tattered book, picked up his pointer.

"Begin!" he said. "Ma tovu".

"Ma tovu oholeha yaakov meshkanoseha Yisroel." He poured the sounds out in a breathless, chaotic stream. "Va ani berov hasdeha awvo baseha eshtahave el hahol kodshehe beyeerosehaw." They were growing funny! "Adonoi awhavti maon baseha umkom mishcan knovdhaw." It was hard for him now to keep his face straight. "Shalom alachem malachi homlac him malchai elyon, me melech malchai homlachim hakadosh boruch hu." Ripples of laughter were trembling in his belly. He read faster to escape them. "Boachem lesholom malachai ha sholom malachai elyon me melech molachai haomlachim ha kodash boruch hu." The ripples had swelled to breakers. Immense hilarity battered against his throat and sides. Faster!

"Noo!" The rabbi grabbed his arm. "Is the devil after you, or what? You fly like a felon."

By an enormous effort, David braked his speed. A short, high giggle pried its way through his lips.

"Fool! What are you laughing at, ha?" But strangely enough, behind his black beard, a faint smile stretched his lips as well. "Read," he growled, "before I give you a cuff."

David bent his head down, bit his lips till he thought the teeth would meet and read on.

The surges of laughter, plunging within him, were so overwhelming he could feel himself grow faint restraining them. Cold sweat was on his brow. He felt he would burst soon if he couldn't give outlet to his swollen mirth. Almost sickened by restraint, he finished the page, looked up imploringly.

"Go!" The rabbi pinched his ear.

The relief was so vast it was sobering.

"Play with those tracks again," he shook his spread

palm significantly. "And you'll lack only death among your woes. Your mother ought to—"

But David was already racing laughter to the door. Across the yard he sprinted, up the stairs, and barely had he reached the hallway when the fit overtook him. There, leaning against the wall, he screamed till his eyes and his drawers were wet, screamed till he could no longer stand, but screaming slumped to the floor and rolled from side to side.

—Gee! It's funny! Gee! Ow! It's funny! Ow! Ooh! Ow! I'm peeing! It's funny! Ow! Funny!

Slowly, by gasps, giggles, chuckles, giggles again, the paroxysm relented. On buckling knees he pushed himself erect, stood swaying. Sudden tears, as void of bitterness as of cause, deep as they were random, runneled his cheeks. Frightened now, he wiped them off hurriedly on his sleeve, stumbled sniffling out of the corridor, ribs aching at every step.

—Gee, what'd I laugh at? Crying now. Crazy! Wet all down. Ooh! move it away! Gee, bath too I have to take! She'll see. Pissy-pants. Gee, it was funny! Ooh! No more! No! No! Forget! Gee! Crazy! Don't know what! Walk and get dry. G'wan!

He turned west, wandered uncertainly toward Avenue C, straddling the air in mid-strides from time to time to ease the chafing of his wet drawers against his thighs. As he walked he gazed about him—avidly—as though familiar sights would more quickly still the gales within him. The stores he peered into were closing or preparing to close—even candy stores and they almost never closed. In the bakery store no bread was to be seen. Instead of a heap of rolls on the oilcloth covered base behind the window, lay a white baker's apron, crumpled and discarded. They were scraping the chopping blocks in the butcher shop, hanging large paper bags from the gleaming meat hooks in the window. Before the stand of the greengrocer's an old woman in a blue kerchief picked off the tiers of a pyramid of apples. Leaning into the mirror, the white-coated barber was shaving himself. The tinsmith, standing in the doorway was washing his grimy hands with kerosene. Hurrying faces passed, all curved into the same smiling absorption, all sharpened toward the same goal. And now by housewives shrilled, and now by ped-

dlars bellowed, and now muttered by aged Jews with blunt
or cloven beards, out of windows, out of doorways, from
sidewalks, from gutters, up, down and across, the greeting flew—

"A guten yuntif!"

Deliverance was in the air—The Passover—deliverance
from Egypt and from winter, from bondage and death!

—Still wet! Gee! Better go another block.

He crossed Avenue C and continued westward. Here
and there children, already dressed in their best, were
coming out of hallways and stoops. Gleaming in neat
braid, broad ribbon, washed face, pressed Sabbath suits,
they gathered in little groups apart from their ungroomed
fellows—or approached with the new diffidence of cleanliness. At Avenue B, the open stretch of the park lay before him and beyond in the distance, the city's towers
pried chiseled edges between spume and clarity. He entered, sat down on a bench; and while he watched the
children romp noisily over the brown and barren ground,
mechanically aired his crotch with hand in pocket. Dry at
last, rested somewhat, he rose, retraced his steps.

While seated in the park he had felt nothing but a
lethargy, a dull vacancy, hollow as it was leaden. But
now as he walked homeward his spirit uncurled again,
expanded. All laughter had gone from him and all tears
with it, and now only a deep untroubled gentleness was
left, a wordless faith, a fixity, mellow and benign. With
every step he took his body seemed to grow less his own,
his limbs so light and rare, his legs drifted over the pavement with a tranquil, feathery ease. Even the swing of
his arm by his side set up ichorous eddies along his
bosom as though a hand were caressing him. The cool,
limber April air was suddenly winy to his nostrils, teas-
ing the breast into swelling. The sunlight on his face laved
his cheeks with so soft a touch, it lifted the throat into its
bounty, lifted it, and—

E-e-e! Twee-twee-twee. Tweet! Tweet! Cheep! Cheep!
Eet! R-rawk!

Gee! Whistle. Thought it was that man. In the tugboat. In the shirt. Whistling. Only birds. Canary. That
lady's. Polly too—Polly want a cracker—is out already.
On the fire-escape. Whistle.

Reluctantly, he neared his doorway, climbed the iron

stoop, reluctantly, entered the hallway, sighed.

—Gee! Used to be darker. Funny. Gee! Look! Look! Is a light! In the corner where baby-carriages—No. Looks like though. On the stairs too. Ain't really there. Inside my head. Better is inside. Can carry it. Funny! Ain't so dark anyway. Ain't even scared. Remember how I was? Way long ago? Scared. Used to run up bing-bang-biff. Hee! Hee! Funny I was. I'm big now. Can go up alone. Can go up slow, slow, slow as I like. Can even stand here and don't even care. Even between the windows, even if nobody's in the toilet, even if nobody's in the whole house. Don't even care. I'm big now, that's why. Wonder if—Yea, all dry now. Can go in now. New underwear she'll give me like the other kids already. For Passover . . .

—Funny. Still can see it. There. And over there. And over in the corner where it's real dark. It sticks inside all the time, gee, can't never be scared. Never. Never. Never . . .

—Fo-o-urth floor. All off! Gee, happy I'm!

He sighed.

BOOK IV

The Rail

I

TRANQUILLY the months had passed. Summer had come
and the advanced grade and the glowing, incalculable and
unlimned vista of the school vacation—that had remained
unlimned. But David felt little disappointment on that
score. Let other boys boast of prolonged visits to the sea-
shore or to the mountains or to camps. For him the mere
passing of time was a joy. The body was aware of a lyric
indolence, a golden lolling within itself. He felt secure
at home and in the street—that was all the activity he
asked.

It was a day in that season when the sun bolsters a
fallen wing with a show of soaring, a day of heat and
light. Light so massive stout brick walls could scarcely
breast it when it leaned upon them; light that seemed to
shiver windows with a single beam; that crashed against
the careless eye like rivets. A day when clouds played ad-
vocates for pavements, stemming the glare on tenuous
bucklers, growing stainless with what they staunched. A
day so bright that streets would slacken when shaded momentarily, façade and wall would slump as if relaxing,
gather new strength against new kindling. It was late July.

Walking home from the free baths on 6th Street, David,
already flushed and perspiring, wished he were back again.
It had been cool under the showers. One could slide on
one's belly down the chill, slippery marble aisle for almost a block—at least it looked that long. But the moment
one came out into the hot streets, the coolness vanished.

262

Only one's hair remained damp—and that was the worst part of it—the man at the door always ran his fingers through one's hair and chased the repeaters from the line.

He trudged on, breathing through his mouth from time to time because the air had grown so hot it seemed to sear the nostrils. Although he had not yet crossed Avenue C, the street was so deserted and the sun so bright, he could see the glint on the brass bannisters before his house. He glanced at the clock in the corner drug store—it pointed to a quarter past nine. Past nine? Where was his father's milk wagon? Good! He was gone. Despite his feeling of greater security these days, that same sense of relief still cropped up. Good! He didn't have to think about him now. He could go upstairs now and have his second breakfast—his first before going to the baths had been a glass of milk. After that the day was his. He quickened his step—

What were they doing?

Near the curb, diagonally across Avenue D, squatted a circle of four or five boys, their sharp, eager cries prodding the drugged quiet of the street. One or two he recognized—they lived somewhere on 9th Street. And there was Izzy who went to his cheder. What was it they were all stooping over so intently? As he drew near his house, he saw rise from their midst a languid spiral of smoke, and a moment after, heard exultant cries. He tip-toed to catch a glimpse over their heads. A black box? Red? No. What? Their heads were packed too close. It deserved a minute's consideration. He crossed the Avenue, drew near.

"I told yuh!" their shrill voices clashed. "Look how id boins! Now pud id in! Gimme!"

Between bobbing heads, he saw a rusty toy stove and pale yellow flames creeping out of it. Smoke spouted from all the cracks. The small oven door, also full of smoke, was open. Between the feet of the boy tending the stove, lay a brown paper bag, once large, now rolled into a tight scroll. Their faces were red. They jabbered, rubbing smoke-filled eyes. One blew intently at the flame.

"Watcha doin?" David tugged Izzy's shirt.

"We all gonna ead good righd away!" the reply rushed at him.

"W'a'? Watcha gonna ead?"

"Pop-cunn! See?" He pointed to the rolled-up bag. "Nickel a bag. Id's chicken cunn, bod the wagon wuz busted, so it spilled oud on de dock."

"Oh!"

"Yuh gid somm if you waid."

"Yea?"

"Yea! See de nice stuv we god? Kushy fond id on de junk yod."

Kushy had unfurled the bag and was pouring the yellow grains into the oven.

"Shake it up!" they advised. "Give id a spread oud wid a stick. Now cluz id. Mum! Yom! Yom! I'll ead a hull beg."

"Led's gid somm sult." Kushy suggested. "Hey Toik, you live on de foist fluh! G'wan!"

"Naa! We'll ead like dis!"

"Yuh see?" Izzy concluded. "Yuh'll gid somm if yuh waid."

Fascinated by the prospect, David wedged in among the rest and squatted down. The stove smoked lustily, growing redder and redder as now one and now another stoked it. All faces sweated profusely.

"Id's hod!" they finally decided. "Betcha id's cooked. G'wan open id Kush! Gid a stick. Wooy! Pop-cunn!"

With the end of a stick, Kushy pried the oven door open. Heads drew closer. Inside, on the red-hot bottom of the oven, what had once been yellow grains were now charred and shriveled beads.

"Aaa, shit!" A groan of disgust burst from lifted throats. "Dey ain' w'ite!"

"But mebbe we can ead anyway," one of the invincibles comforted himself. "Ain' id pop-cunn?"

"Sure, betcha dey taste good! I'll try foist. Push id in my hand. Ooy! Id's hod!"

"Da-a-a-vid! Da-a-avid!"

"Me?" He gazed about, startled.

"Da-a-avid!"

Up! Oh! It was his mother, leaning from a window.

"Wa-a-at?"

"Come u-up!"

"Ye-e-es!"

Her head disappeared inside.

That was strange. She almost never called him from

the window. What did she—Gee! He stared. There, beside his house stood his father's milk wagon. That was even stranger. What was he doing home at this hour? He never came back so late in the morning. Something must be wrong. Disquieted, he crossed the street, scrutinized the black horse resting his feed-bag on the curb. Perhaps it was some other milk man. No, it was Billy sure enough, the black, powerful animal they had recently given his father. Reluctantly he went into the hall-way, climbed the stairs and hung back a moment before he opened his door —familiar blue cap and black whip on the washtub. His father, already seated before the table, glanced at him as he entered and then turned to his mother who was standing before the ice-box:

"Have you any sour cream left?"

"Without end," she answered, smiling at David as he entered. "And a few more scallions?"

"Let it be—" And to David. "Wash your hands and sit down."

Completely at a loss now, David went over to the sink. When he returned to the table, his mother had set his combination lunch and breakfast before him—things he liked: Golden-skinned, smoked white-fish, cucumbers and tomatoes, pumpernickel, milk, purple plums. His mouth watered; in the twinges of awakening hunger apprehensions were momentarily forgotten. He had just opened the white-fish—a middle-piece, it opened like a golden volume—when his father, nodding curtly, said:

"After you've finished, I want you to stay near the wagon where I can find you."

David sought his mother's eyes.

"You're going with father," she explained.

"Me?"

"Yes!" his father interposed. "Don't jump as though you saw the gloomy angel."

"It will only be for a short time," his mother reassured him. "An hour—no, Albert?"

"Perhaps longer," was his curt reply.

"He has the cheder," she reminded him. "It's early during the summer."

"I told you he'd be there in good time. Do you know, if you go on keeping him from seeing how I earn his bread, he'll begin to believe I'm one of God's playfellows."

"I didn't mean that," she answered. "I—"

"Yes! Yes! Yes! Another child would have been with me long ago—would have begged to go. But enough of this—You stay near the wagon." He scooped a dripping radish from the cream, slumped back, still chewing. There was silence for a few seconds.

"When is he coming," ventured his mother, "the other I mean."

"Tomorrow maybe. I can't tell."

"Poor man!"

"It happens . . . Lucky for me I brought an extra cake of ice along. I wouldn't have had enough with this heat— But better the summer than the winter."

"At least the ways aren't so icy."

"Yes. And you can see the stairs at four in the morning. And the handle of the tray isn't so frozen it burns through your gloves like fire."

"It's all bitter, Albert."

"Mm!" he grunted. "You hardly know. I sell my days for a little silver—a little paper—sixteen smirched leaves a week—I'll never buy them back with gold. It's enough sometimes to make one savage with man and beast."

"But other men work as well."

"You needn't tell me that!"

There was silence again, while his father ate, staring with heavy eyes at the table.

"And you'd really want your days back?" She sat down, hands in her lap.

He snorted. "What a question!"

"I wouldn't."

"You mean days such as you've had? Like these?"

"Any kind."

"Hmph!" he grunted. "Won't you be a grandmother soon enough without posting?"

"No," she smiled, her wide brown eyes lifted to the ceiling. "I want to be one tomorrow."

"You're a fool!"

"When I can say as mine did. It's over. I stepped into the sun, I took one breath and suddenly I was a grandmother—Throw clocks away!"

"She grew wise as she grew old?" he asked with dry sarcasm.

"They measure nothing, she would say. Only the

swing of cranes in the tides of their flight is worth reckoning. The rest is a rattle on Purim—deliverance from Haman long hanged."

He chuckled once, sneered. "You and your grandmother!"

She laughed with him.

He pushed his plate away, breathing heavily, ran weathered powerful fingers through his thinning black hair, pressed down the ridge in the back of his head where the cap had bitten in.

"No more?" she asked.

"No." He rose, tilted his head back, stretched. Drowsiness slowly cobwebbed the taut, impassive face. "No later than half-past ten."

"I'll wake you, Albert."

He plodded into the bedroom, shut the door behind him. The bed creaked . . .

"Mama!" David whispered.

"Yes, child?"

"What does he want?"

"Oh—! There's a milkman out. He cut his hand on a bottle—fearful thing!" she shuddered. "And they've divided his route among the rest."

"Why does he want me?"

"He's delivering to the gas houses there—the other man's route. And he wants you to sit in the wagon while he's gone."

"Aaa! I don't want to go."

"I know. I'm worried too," she confessed. "The other man always had a dog in his wagon—you'll be the dog this time." She smiled. "Just this once, won't you? You'll like it, riding on the wagon, seeing new streets. It will be cool when the horse is running."

He shook his head resentfully. Her words aroused a foreboding in him.

"Come!" she coaxed, "just this once."

Moodily, he pecked at his food. "How far are the gas houses?"

"Not at all far. Twentieth Street—I think that's what your father said."

"That *is* far!"

"Sh!" She looked uneasily at the bedroom door. "Do finish your lunch,"

"Only one side of the white fish," he said sullenly. "Don't you like it any more?"

"No."

"Why are you so frightened, child! You're not leaving me! Drink the rest of your milk."

But his appetite had vanished. It was only after a great deal of urging that she prevailed upon him to finish his lunch.

"Can I go now?" he asked, rising.

"Don't you want to wait here? It's cooler than the street."

He hesitated a moment. "No, I'll go down."

"Very well," she sighed. "I beg you stay near the wagon." She bent down, let him kiss her brow. "Come straight home after cheder."

II

HE WENT down the stairs, and reaching the street, looked eagerly toward Avenue D. He had meant to return to the pop-corn oven when he came down in order to forget his uneasiness and at the same time be near the wagon. But now they were gone. The pop-corn oven lay beside the curb, a shattered heap of iron. Evidently, they had repaid it for its recalcitrance. But where had they gone to? Eating perhaps. No, it wasn't their lunch time yet. It was only ten o'clock.

Disconsolately he sat down, stretched out athwart the uppermost step of the stoop where the shady threshold of the hallway joined the burning stairs. Just outside the doorway, and under the fierce glare, the horse, black flanks rippling like water, lashed out viciously with hoof and tail at the glinting flies. His straw bonnet with much tossing was awry. Yellow oats, flung up from his feed-bag, lay strewn on the grey-bright gutter. Muted with heat, the city droned remotely. He wished he didn't have to go.

He had been sitting there for only a few minutes,

ferreting about in his mind for some subterfuge, some
invulnerable excuse that would prevent his accompany-
ing his father, when the sound of running feet reached
him. He looked out on the street. With a shrill cry of
"Here's a wagon!" preceding them, Kushy and another
boy ran past the doorway, came to a sudden halt before the milk-wagon.

"Hea's a good w'eel, Maxey." Kushy grasped the spokes
and squatted down to examine the hub. David noticed that
from his hand dangled something that looked like a flat
piece of iron tied to a string.

"Yea, a lot!" Maxey, a short stick in his fist, hopped
down eagerly beside him.

Prompted more by curiosity than possessiveness,
David rose. "Hey, wodda yuh wan'? Dat's my fodder's
wagon."

"So wadda yuh hollerin' about?" Kushy retorted, bel-
ligerent after a single glance over his shoulder.

"We ain' takin' nott'n." Maxey explained. "Only grease
from de axle." Industriously he probed the black inside
of the hub with the stick.

"Way in deep!" Kushy directed.

"Wotcha gonna do?" David came down the steps.

"We're goin fishin'." Maxey drew out a large black gob
of grease. "On Tent' Stritt. We're potners. We seen id
foist."

"C'mon!" Kushy interrupted him. "Don' led id flop!"

And with a "No akey! No akey!" flung over their shoulders, the two partners raced toward Avenue D and disappeared around the corner.

Mystified, longing desperately to follow, David stared
after them. Half past ten, his father had said. That was
a long ways off. He could watch them awhile and be
back before his father came down. No one would know.
Involuntarily, so it seemed to him, he gravitated toward
the corner and went around it. They had said that
they would be on Tenth Street, the next block. Should
he go that far? At the last moment he decided that he
had better not. It was too risky. He would only go as
far as the new photography shop in the middle of the
block and then return. He peered into the window. It
was full of pictures, big and small, bridal pictures, the
bride and groom standing stiffly apart despite their ap-

parent closeness, their faces frozen in an impending smile; pictures of prize-fighters crouching in sash and tights; pictures of infants, the little girls seated, holding tiny muffs where the pudgy legs joined the small torso; the little boys always lay on their bellies. And horrible, enlarged pictures of old men and women, colored and acid-clear, the magnified expanse of their brown and sunken cheeks wrinkled the way the wind wrinkles sand. Pictures. Pictures. How did they stretch the big ones out of the little ones? And that bar of glass, that extended across the top of the show window, where did it get that strange green light that changed the color of everyone's face when one passed it?

He'd better return now. But there was Tenth Street just a little ways off. He would only look once and then go back. Which way?

One glance toward Avenue C sufficed: As many as had been crouching about the pop-corn oven were now clustered before a building this side of the wood-turning shop. He broke into an eager trot, drew up. Most of them were the same boys he had seen a short time ago. Breathless, silent, absorbed, they kneeled on all fours on the iron grate over the cellar. All faces pointed downwards, all eyes riveted on something beneath. Not one looked up when David crawled in among them.

Kushy was doing the fishing. David peered down. Because of the depth of the cellar, it took some time for his eyes to become accustomed to the gloom. But squinting tightly, he at last discerned a something silver glimmering on the grimy cellar floor. Little by little, the gleam settled into the round, smudged surface of a coin. And above it, like a pendulum swinging slowly to and fro, the flat piece of iron hung from Kushy's hand. His eyes at length completely accustomed to the shadows, David observed that the entire surface of the sinker was daubed with axle grease.

"Leggo now!" someone hissed between the grate. "Now! Id's righd oveh!"

"Shod op!" Kushy shot back.

As the sinker swung it descended, its area of vibration slowly decreasing. For a moment it hovered directly over the glistening coin—then dropped as if on a prey!

"Easy Kushy!" their admonitions seethed. "Easy! Easy!

'At's id! Id'll stick, g'wan! Yuh god it! Betcha million! Slow! Slow!"

"No akey! No akey!" Maxey murmured exultantly.

Pop-eyed, taut with excitement, Kushy hauled in the slack with infinite deliberation. The grease-coated sinker stirred, rose—the coin, smeared now with grease, never budged, but lay where it had lain before. Barbed cackles of derision flew from all but the two partners' lips.

"I'll punch yuh innuh nose," growled Kushy, crimson and bridling.

"Jost you waid!" Maxey spat out venomously. "Ask me fuh sompt'n youse guys. Bubbikiss you'll ged! G'wan, Kush, you'll ged it op yet! G'wan!"

The strain broken now, they jabbered turbulently. "See! I tol' yuh de stuv-iron is hod luck! Yea, yuh shoulda taken somp'n else. Aaa! I coulda god id if yuh did'n holler."

"You'll never ged id." Izzy announced smugly. "Betcha I could ged id."

"Balls you'll ged!"

"An I ain' gonna tell yuh how," he added spitefully.

"Balls you'll ged," repeated Kushy, "an' a rusky-chooy!"

"Yea?"

"Yea, an' a bust onna beezer!"

Opposition silenced, Kushy once more lowered the iron shard; once more it dropped only to rise without the coin. He tried again. As often as the grease touched the coin, the latter became a shade darker, a shade more like its surroundings, and by degrees more difficult to distinguish. The minutes passed. While Kushy fished the rest hitched their tongues in tow of their imaginations.

"If it wuz a nickel," said one broody voice between the gratings, "I could buy fuh two cends cockamamies an' pud em on mine hull arm. An' den fuh t'ree cends I'll go to duh movies."

"Yuh c'n buy fuh t'ree cends cockamamies." Izzy crisply revised the dream.

"W'y?"

"Cuz yuh c'n ged in duh movies lods o' times fuh on'y two cends. Id's two fuh a nickel ain' id, fuh kids? Make de odder guy give t'ree cends."

"Fot smeller," sneered Kushy vainly lifting the sinker for the twentieth time. The rest brayed their approval.

"Yuh c'n ged in fuh nutt'n wise guy!" another voice affirmed. "Woddayuh tink o' dat? Yuh jos' make believe yuh lookin' on duh pickchiss outside. An' w'en dat ticket-chopper ain' lookin'—zool Yuh go in—an' id's all dock inside."

"Yea!" Izzy parried. "An' zoo! If he catches yuh! Wadda roost innee ass he gives. Membuh w'en Hoish god caught? Wuz he cryin'?"

"Make believe w'at I had a nickel," another rapt voice announced, "so I'll go to Kaplan's on Evenyuh C and I'll buy a tousan' rubbuh ben's an' make a bounceh—a real high bounceh—"

"A lod ain' good." Izzy interrupted with authority. "I know somebody, he made a bounceh—bigger'n dis." His two palms slid through the gratings about a foot apart. "Mor'n' a zillion rubbuh ben's he had on id, and id wouldn't even go high like dis cellah. So he made five liddle ones, an' duh liddle ones bounced ten flaws w'en he ga'm a good shod."

"Ten flaws?"

"Yea!"

"Buzjwa!" they chorused.

"Yea?"

A short space of silence followed while eyes again glued to the coin on the cellar floor. It was practically indistinguishable now, but still Kushy fished, declining all the offers of those who suggested spitting down at the coin to clean it. Oblivious of the passing time, David peered down with the rest.

"You'll never ged id," said Izzy at length. "An' maybe id ain' even a nickel," he added waspishly.

"Maybe you ain' gonna ged mobilized," Kushy answered ominously. It was evident to all that long frustration had exhausted his patience.

"Aaa, don' mobilize so fast!" muttered Izzy.

"Yuh wan' me to show yuh?" The sinker jogged ominously across the cellar floor.

"Tough guy!"

"I'll spid in yer eye in a minute!"

"You an' who else?"

"Me an' myself!" The sinker flew up. The next moment Kushy had sprung to his feet.

(From somewhere an obscure drum of hooves)

"Wan' me to show yuh?" he blustered.

"Yea!" Izzy rose as well.

David shrank away. He hated fights. Why did they have to fight and spoil everything? But before the two pugilists had time to fly at each other, a loud, imperious rapping startled them all. They stared at the gutter. With a cry David recoiled. Poised on the side step of the milk wagon, sleeveless shirt dazzling in the light, his father was rapping the butt-end of the whip against the wagon—"Come here!" He bit off the Yiddish words.

David flung himself toward the curb. "I didn' know, papa! I didn' know! I thought you—you weren't ready."

"Get in!"

He could hear the amazed whispers of the other boys on the side-walk. With numb, aimless haste, he grasped the first thing that seemed to offer a way up, the spokes of the wagon wheel. His feet, cramped with kneeling, slipped toward the hub. His father's jarring hand hooked under his armpit, yanked him roughly aboard.

"Witless block!" he ground out, "Lucky for you I found you. If I hadn't I would have flayed you—!" He flicked the reins. "Giddap Billy!" The wagon rolled forward. "Why I don't give a blow to crack your head I don't know!"

Whimpering David cowered against the loose milk-boxes rattling behind him.

"If I had the time—!" he broke off significantly. "But disobey me again!" And with a furious sidelong glare, leaned out through the window-like opening in the front of the wagon and nipped the horse with the end of the whip. "C'mon Billy!"

The horse broke into a heavy gallop. At Avenue C, they turned and headed north. Letting the reins rest on the front bar a few seconds, his father reached behind him, pried loose an empty box and set it down beside David. "Sit down! But hold on to the side there, so you won't fall off as only *you* are able."

They drove on rapidly; Ninth Street dropped far behind—it seemed to him forever. Relieved by slight flurries in traffic from his father's smouldering eye, David stared unhappily at the houses gliding past the doorway. He felt strange—feverish almost. Whether it was that he had been staring down into the cellar too long, or whether because his fear of his father clouded and distorted all the things he saw, he could not tell. But he felt as though his mind had slackened its grip on realities. The houses, pavements, teams, people on the street no longer had that singleness and certainty about them that they had had before. Solidities baffled him now, eluded him with a veiled shifting of contour. He could not wholly identify even the rhythm and the clap of hooves; something alien and malign had fused with all the familiar sounds and sights of the world. The sunlight that had been so dazzling before was mysteriously dulled now as though filtered by an invisible film. Something of its assertion had been drained from stone, something of inflexible precision from iron. Surfaces had hollowed a little, sagged, edges had blurred. The stable lineaments of the mask of the world had overlapped, shifted configuration as secretly and minutely as clock-hands, as sudden as the wink of an eye. It was strange. It had happened before. A vague, diffuse aching filled his breast. Again and again, he sighed, uncontrollable, shivery, stealthy sighs. Suddenly, he realized that he had not known how happy he had been—only a little while ago, unaccountably free and happy—July, June, May. It was gone now. He was haunted again.

He looked from the street to his father. Too tall for the wagon, he stooped forward, black reins loose in weathered hand. Nothing about him ever changed. Let worlds heave and freeze, he remained the same—always the thin inscrutable mouth, always the harsh pride of taut nostrils, heavy lidded eyes. Under the sheer, unswerving steep of his aloofness, there was shelter sometimes, but never foothold.

They turned east, left the pavements behind. On the cobbled streets, the horse's hooves rang out now sharp now hollow. The wagon bounced and clattered. As the streets grew empty, the houses grew smaller and shoddier. There were no children to be seen, only cats sunning themselves before battered doorways. They turned a corner. Between the looming of enormous gas tanks, the river looked as if the shore beyond were only a blunt wedge sideways through the sky, so alike in azure were water and heaven. Here were no habitations. Beside the curb, a long, deep ditch through the pavement had been left uncovered. From the bottom of the trench as they neared it, rose the sweetish, festering stench of the city's iron entrails. His father swung out wide, passed the embankment of rusty soil set with red lanterns, and drawing up to the curb, reined in his horse.

"Move!" he said.

David scrambled to one side. His father reached into the back of the wagon, dragged out two steel trays and set them on the ribbed wagon floor. From three boxes, all of which were filled with bottled milk and covered with ice, he loaded both trays, and when every square in the trays had been planted, shored bottles against leaning bottles in glistening white pyramids. In the last box only four bottles sprouted from between the cracked ice. These he left behind, and shoving both trays near the door-way, he climbed out into the sunlight. One after another he swung them down, grunting as he did so, the sinews of his throat leaping like bow-strings.

"This time don't forget," he said, glancing about. "Stay where you're told, hear me?" His brief nod was full of meaning, and then he turned away and lunged forward and with stiff, jerky gait, hurried down a narrow lane between squat and dingy shacks. As he drew away, deeper and deeper shadows pitted the stretched thews of his long bare arms. Under his flat springless tread, the crushed stones on the ground slid and crunched. The path turned, curving round a gas tank. With a last clink of bottles he disappeared.

III

UNREAL quiet . . . Against the drowsy, dwindled hum of the city only the sound of the horse champing softly on his bit, pawing or rattling his traces could be heard. The arid cobbles, distinct close at hand and hemmed in by peeling bill boards, blackened hovels, vacant storage houses, contracted to scales in middle distance, slurred further on and slid up a narrow groove of houses into dusty blue sky. Rarely and even then too far for a sound to travel, a horse and wagon crossed the street. From the trench in the pavement, the rank, persistent damp mingled with the odor of rancid milk in the wagon. Time dragged.

Two men slanted past the corner. After the strange silence of the street and the strange disquiet in himself, David found the scrape of soles on sidewalk suddenly welcome. One of the men seemed about to cross the street, but his companion gave his arm a short tug, said something and both swerved from their course and shambled leisurely toward the wagon. Their coats were slung over their shoulders and as they walked they wiped their faces in the lining. A grey rope held up the pants of one, the other had safety pins in his suspenders. Both wore dirty, blurry, striped shirts, torn under the neck-bands and collarless. Their features, as they grew more distinct, were blunt and coarse, pocked and purplish as peach-stones. The leaner was the shaggier of the two, his hair, the blonde of a gunny sack, matted under his brown felt hat. The stockier, under his tilted cap, had a moon-shaped brow, good-humored, piggish eyes, and between puffy jowls a short mustache like oiled hemp, smoke-singed at the fat lips. There had been something significant about the way they had nudged each other and then changed their course, and now as they sauntered within a few feet of the wagon, David began to hope that they would pass without stopping.

"I told yuh it wuz a kid," he heard the stocky one say. And then loudly. "Hullo dere, big boy!" Opposite the doorway of the wagon, he smiled affably, widely, yellow butts of his teeth circled on top like bitten grains of corn. "Waddaye say?"

"Hot ain' id?" the other grinned beside him. "Whew!" Saliva on his protruding upper teeth glistened, gathered; leisurely he sucked it in as it fell.

Without answering, David stared at them irresolutely.

"Ol' man's wagon?" asked the first, his pudgy finger sliding from his mustache to worry a pimple on his chin. "Go in wid a big load, didn't 'e?" His bright, amiable eyes fixed on the graveled lane, "Didn't 'e?"

"Yea."

"Long ago?"

"Yea."

"Nice kid, ain' 'e?"

The other winked, curled his tongue out for the sliding drop. "Maybe he wantzuh see de gas house? Woik fast!"

"Say! I'll betcha shirt he does! Ever been in a gas house?"

"No!" apprehensively. He wished they would go away.

"No? Say, we'll show yuh de whole woiks!"

"No!"

"Layin' out?" He leaned inside the doorway.

"Yep," the other grunted. He had shifted his position so that he partly faced the graveled lane.

"C'mon!" the stocky one urged pleasantly. "We c'n show yuh all de fires—biggest fires, biggest foinisses in Noo Yawk. Show yuh yer ol' man." Suddenly he leaned forward. Blacknailed, outstretched fingers gripped David's buttocks. He wrenched free, sprang away.

"No!" Sudden fear made him cling to the opposite side of the wagon. "No! I don't wanna go—no place! Lemme alone!"

"Gettin' hot, Augie?"

The other cackled. "No go, Wally. We gotta get it an' skin out o' hea."

"Yea," drawled the other still smiling, and then briskly. "All right, kid, won't show 'em to yuh dis time— I see yer ol' man's got a liddle milk left, ain' he? Nice and cool, I bet. Well, we'll buy a couple o' bottles. He knows us, see—? Clear, Augie?"

"Shoot!"

"Jest a couple." He swept away the ice, calmly uprooted two bottles of milk. "We gid it every day. Tell 'im Hennesy took it. T'ree Star Hennesy—he'll remember." He passed a bottle to the other. "We pays him reggileh," he added, slouching off in the direction he had come. "So long, big boy! Show yuh de gas house sometime."

His lips quivering in terror and too dazed even to breathe, David watched them wrap their coats about the bottles, quicken their pace as they neared the corner, wheel round it and vanish.

He gasped. They had stolen the bottles! He knew it! He knew the moment that man reached over he was going to steal them. What would his father say? You left the

wagon! You left the wagon! And after I told you not to.
Papa, no! I never left it! I thought you knew them! They
said you did. You left the wagon! I didn't! They came—!
His mind seemed to have burst into myriads of razor-edged
shards hurtling through his skull. Ow! When he comes!
When he looks in! And two missing. Why didn't you stop
them? Why didn't you tell them to wait till I came? Why
didn't you cry out? I did, papa! I did! I mean—! they
said—! The whip—there. He'd take it. Ow!

His frantic nails dug under his cap, barrowed the scalp
beneath, which stung and prickled as though a rash had
broken out upon it. A cold sweat sprang out over his
face and throat, and his writhing body grew suddenly
hollow and agonized. Without desire or strength to still
them, he listened to the sick chattering of his teeth. Already feeling the lash on his back, he cowered down and
lifted his hands to his face.

—Ow! Ow! Papa! Papa! Ow! Don't! I didn't mean it.
They tried to grab me. Push me out . . . (He tried to
flee from himself as he had once done in the darkness
behind his palms. Where could he flee to? Where?) Like
that time then. In cellar was and ran. In up-and-out
pictures ran. In street now, where—? Mama! Make her
look. Make how she looks. Her face. Make! MAKE! I
want her face. Mama! MAMA! Make her look. (He concentrated, culling dispersion with every force of his will
—failed. Tried again, failed. The face would not fuse.
His own mother's face eluded him.) Can't! I can't! Oh,
mama! Mama! Can't! . . . (He rocked back and forth).
I'll make believe I'll go home first. Yes. Like that I'll get
it. All the streets. Rrrrp! Ninth Street. Now up stoop go.
Hot is brass bannister. No touch, janitor says. Cold in
winter. Hall inside—No! No! Not this one! Not this!
Funny! Old hall from way then, Brownsville pushed right
in. Old cellar hall. Got it, Ninth Street back. Now keep.
Don't let go. Baby carriages under the stair here. Milk-
stink on 'em. Now go. First floor, see the steps, see the
toilets. Bloop! Slipped, slipped down. Gee! Baby carriages.
She's waiting. Upstairs. Fourth floor, waiting. Now go!
Bing! One, two, three, four— Aaa, shit—slipped! Baby
carriages. Milk stink pulls, pulls me back. This time,
jump! All the way up! One jump all the way! One, two,
go—! Wrong! It's wrong! Wrong hallway! No! No! No

cellar door. Not in my house. Not open! Not open! Like
—Like I just smelled. Street open. Street—open-stink,
where they're digging. Aaa! (He ground his teeth in sudden
fury) I'm going up! I'm going up anyway! You won't stop
me! YOU WON'T! I'll hold it! Now! (His fingers pinched
his nose till it hurt) Now I'll go! What—!

The crunch of heels upon the gravel. Terror! His eyes
snapped open. Dwarfed between the huge gas tanks, his
father rounded the path. Eyes downcast as always, he
hurried, jangling the empty grey bottles in their trays.
Louder, louder, nearer, they seemed to clank in David's
heart as well. With every step his father took, the breath
in his own body became more labored, more suffocating.
At the wagon he paused, lifted sombre eyes to heave the
trays on board. Their gaze met. The first tray hung poised
a split second before it came to rest.

"What's the matter?"

David began to weep.

"What's the matter?" His voice sharpened to a sudden
edge. "Speak!"

"The—the bottles there—" he stammered—"They took
them."

"What?" He leaned in, swiftly swept the ice aside,
looked up again in stormy surprise. "Who took them?"

He quailed. "T-Two men."

"Who? Stop your slobbering!"

"Two men. A big one and a short one. And they—
Hennesy they said. Hennesy."

"Hennesy?" He cocked his head, his frown darkening.
"Where did they say they worked?"

"They didn't say!"

"Were you on the wagon?" His lips thinned, voice
changed pitch in mid-word, the signs of gathering wrath.

"Yes! I was here! Papa, I was here!" The words gushed,
being prepared. "They came and they said you knew
them, and I thought you knew them. And they took—"

"And you let them? Cursed fool!" He slammed the
last tray in the wagon, sprang after it. "Which way did
they go?"

"That w-way! Around the corner!"

"Paid yourself again!" he snarled. "Giddap! Giddap!
Billy!" He snatched the whip out of the socket, lashed
the horse. Stung, the beast plunged forward. The wheels

ground against the curb. "Giddap!" Again the whip. Hooves rang out in a pounding, powerful gallop. The wagon lurched, careened around the corner on creaking axle, empty bottles banging in their boxes. His father, jaws working in fury, eyes blazing, swept the street with one glance. It was empty, sunlit and empty. "Where are they?" he muttered through writhing lips. "Ah, to lay my hands on them!"

No sign of them anywhere, though he scoured every building and hallway. They were gone. The horse galloped on. But at the very next intersection, two men on the left strolled out of an alley—A glimpse of empty milk bottles in their hands!

"They?" he snapped eagerly.

"They!"

"Aah!" His suppressed cry rattled exultantly in his throat. "Giddap, Billy! Giddap!" He dragged savagely at the left rein. The horse mounted the sidewalk. The wagon heeled over, shifting its cargo with a roar.

"Cheesit, Augie!" the stocky one yelled out suddenly. "He's after us!"

They broke into a clumsy run, the shorter one lagging. The wagon gained. With a hoarse cry of "Let 'im have it, Wally!" the lean one slowed down momentarily, drew back his arm. The heavy bottle arched toward them hung in the sun, shattered like a bomb before the horse. He reared, flung his head sideways, nostrils crimson, wild eyes rolling. A second later, another bottle flew in the air, fell short, smashed on the ground. Again the whip flashed down.

"Now I'll get you!" His father gnashed his teeth. "Now I'll get you!" And David knew they were doomed.

The charging horse bore down on them. At the corner, with only a few yards between them and the wagon, both men as if by a common impulse, shoved each other in opposite directions. His father turned after the stockier running on the sidewalk. A moment more, the horse was abreast. One yank at the reins and the reins were flung at David. "Hold, you!" Whip in hand, his father leaped from the rolling wagon into the street. The fugitive, trapped before a stable door that wouldn't open, spun about, crouched savagely at bay.

"Waddayuh chasin' me fuh?" His yellow teeth were

bared, the round eyes now slits of fear and fury.

"Hanh!" His father's snarl was almost like laughter, but the grinding of his teeth creaked like a strong cable stretching. "Yuhv'll take my milk!"

"Me? Waddaye shittin' about? I never seen it."

"An' de bottles you t'rew?" He seemed merely to be toying with the man. David knew the answers didn't matter. He grew faint, waiting for the end.

"Yea! I t'rew 'em!" The other was blustering savagely. "An de nex' time watch out who de fuck yer chas—"

Swish! The hiss of the whip cut off his words; the long, stiff thong curled over his shoulder, whacked!

"Owoo!" he howled with pain and fury. "Yuh Jew bastard! You hit me?" He flung himself at David's father, arms thrashing.

"Hanh!" Again that mad cry of mirth. One long, rigid arm shot out, thrust his kicking, flailing adversary back like a ram—while the whip lashed out in the other. Again! Again it fell! It sickened David watching it. He screamed. Suddenly with a sharp crack the whip snapped. His father flung it aside. And as the other, howling with rage, charged in to tackle, he drew up his fist, clenched it like a sledge, and grunting with the effort, crashed it down on his neck.

"Uh!" A small, almost infantile groan broke from the man's open mouth. Then he crumpled, slid down David's father's legs and fell sideways to the ground. Once more he stirred, the cap slipping from his head. The vague, sparse strands of his hair sank leisurely to one side as if on a hinge, revealing the splotched yellow scalp. He lay still.

For a moment longer, David's father towered above him, rage billowing from him, shimmering in sunlight almost, like an aura; then with a last, fierce glance about the empty streets, scooped up the broken whip, stalked to the wagon, leaped in, and leaning out flogged the horse with the end of the rein. The beast bounded forward. Swiftly they left the street, turned south, mingled with the gathering traffic.

The minutes passed in horrible silence. Little by little, his father's dark face grew grey, the fierce blaze in his eyes clouding. In his trembling hands, the reins began to shake out in tiny ripples. His hoarse breath grew louder, rushing through his burred throat in short violent gasps that set his jaw quivering each time as if on springs. In Brownsville was the last time David had seen him look that way. It recalled all the old horror.

"You!" He said at last, and his words were so harsh and guttural, they barely took form. "False son! You, the cause!"

His hand moved. Like the fangs of a snake the brass-buckled ends of the reins bit twice into David's shoulder. He never winced. He hardly even felt them, so frozen with terror he was.

"Say anything to your mother," the strangled voice went on, "and I'll beat you to death! Hear me?"

"Yes, papa."

Amid a crowd of trams and autos, they moved slowly toward Ninth Street.

IV

NOT another word had been spoken. The wagon rumbled over the cobbled car-tracks, wheeled around, drew up beside the curb.

"Get off, dunce!" His father's voice had cleared, was sharp again; his color was beginning to return. "Now remember what I said—be silent!"

Mutely, David climbed down the wagon.

"And don't get lost!" he flung down at him. "Straight to the cheder!"

"Yes, papa." He could feel the stupidity of his own gaze.

"Unh!" he grunted disgustedly. "Hurry now!" Then he clucked to the horse and the wagon clattered north again.

With stunned, shuffling gait, David crossed the street, plodded toward the cheder.

—Mustn't tell her! Mustn't tell! Ow!

How could he contain it! He had but to prolong the wink of his eyes a moment longer and the horrible scenes of that hour flared across his eyelids as on a screen—The ghastly flickering of stolid gas-tanks, cobbles, trenches,

distance, the malevolent streets, the black arc of the whip
still lingering in air though the whip had landed, the
vicious face contorted, and the hand, the hand uplifted.
In the meaningless sounds of the street, he could still
hear the scuffing of their feet, his father's grunt, the thud
of his fist, the howls of rage and pain. The fearful images
would not be shaken, but clung to his mind as though
soldered there. Something had happened! Something had
happened! Even Ninth Street, his own familiar Ninth
Street was warped, haunted by something he could feel;
but perceive with no sense. Faces he had seen so many
times he scarcely ever glanced at any more were twisted
into secret shadows, smeared, flattened, whorled, grotesque
grief and smirking never before revealed. The cheder corridor as he passed through it, scribble of chalk glimmering
on the wall, linoleum battered into traps, seemed un-
level, weird and endless. He caught himself fighting the
old fear of hallways; his step suddenly quickened. Saw-
toothed, bizarre with inlayed wedges of light and shadow,
the cheder yard, gray wash-poles aslant in heavy light,
fences leaning, chipped, red walls, walls sodden with sun,
the hacked sky. Unreal. The cheder itself, whispers in
sudden gloom, knotted figures, cracked benches, the long
table, the inane, perpetual drone, fantastic forms, perspectives. Unreal.

Something, something had happened. He sat dumbly
down, watched the others a moment, then turned away.
Their bickering and their chatter had lost dimension;
nothing was left but a grey and vacuous idiocy, a world
bewitched and hollow. It was as though he heard all
sounds through a yawn or with water in his ears, as though
he saw all things through a tumbler. When would it burst,
this globe about his senses?

If only he had run home first, if only he had told his
mother.

Time dragged on. The cheder filled up. Fortunately for
him he had come early—he would read soon, escape.
Remotely he heard his name called as if through a wall.
He rose, shuffled to the bench as though his will alone
were dragging the whole clog of his body, sat down before
the table.

"You look somewhat pale," the rabbi said quizzically

as he flattened out the book, "Do you feel squeamish today? Ha?"

"No."

"Well, why weren't you waiting your turn on the bench?"

"I didn't know."

"That's news!" He lifted his brows sarcastically, "Well, begin! Haazinu ha shawmayim veadabairaw."

"Haazinu ha shawmayim veadabairaw, vtishma haawretz emri fi." Whirling among the heavy characters on the page, two bodies grappled and strove—He stumbled.

"What ails you? You're somewhat blind today."

Without answering, he went on, "Yaarof kamawtawr l-l-likhiy tizol k-k-katal imrawsi." The letters crowded, parted, deployed—lamp-posts, cobbles, graveled lanes, lanterns on mounds of earth. Whips in air. Time after time he stuttered, halted, corrected himself, went on. The rabbi had begun tapping his pointer slightly as he moved it along.

"Some little deed you've done, today, ha?" He lowered his tilted, bushy face to David's level, and stared with a suspicious grin into his eyes—Tobacco reek. Sweat. Matted nostrils under red, speck-stippled nose. The moist drab gums of false teeth. Revolting. David drew back.

"One deed but a good one, no? No?" His voice rose. "Answer! Are you dumb?"

"No," sullenly. "Didn't do anything."

"Then why do you read like a plaster golem? Ha? Look at me! Lift the hasps of your eyes."

He glanced up at the angry face for a fleeting second, glanced down.

"Fire strike you!" His thumb shot the leaf over viciously. "Read further!"

David waited till the page settled and then with all his powers, fixed on the letters. The effort seemed to drain him of every ounce of strength, and even despite his efforts, he halted and floundered frequently. His head sank lower and lower over the book. At last the rabbi slapped him.

"Go now!" He said acridly, "Enough balking for a day! Enough for a year! And when you leave here," his thumb and forefinger curled expoundingly, "take yourself home, sit long in the privy and you'll have a clearer brow."

Hardly attending, David slid off the bench.

"And hear me!" he warned. "Tomorrow and you pray thus, I'll begin currying."

Voices jeered at him as he crossed the cheder. "Smod guy! Cholly ox! Goot fuh yuh, stingy! Strap onnee ass, yuh'll ged! His fodder'll give 'im wit' de w'ip. I seen—"

He turned. Izzy's voice sank to a whisper. He hurried through the door. New quoins of light in the cheder yard still patterned the old unreality. At the top of the wooden stairs, the long hallway was empty and full of murky shadows. (—Get on your mark! Get se-e-et! Go!—) He raced through it, reached the streetlight with prickling scalp. —(Shittin' fraid-cat, me! Scared now. Never was. And him—Hate him! Stinky mouth! Hate 'em all! Mama, now! Mama—)

Already in the shelter of her arms, he began running along the pavement towards his house. (—Hope he ain't home! Hope, hope he ain't!)

He had jogged to within a few yards of his doorway, when a loud confused cry overhead brought him to a halt. He glanced up. With a fat bosom flopping against the ledge of the second floor window a woman was screaming excitedly down at the street. "Beetrice! Beetrice! Horry op!" She craned dangerously out of the window as though she were trying to look into her own doorway. And presently a half-grown girl, pigtails and ribbons flying behind her, came running out. David stared at them in wonder.

"Where is 'e, Mama?" The girl reached the sidewalk and was screaming up.

"Dere! Zeh! Look!" The woman shrilled down. "Sebm fawdy six in de red house!"

"Where? I can' see!"

"Dort! Oy! Look! De toiteh fluh!"

In open mouthed fixity, the girl stared at the house across the street. "Yea!" She squealed. "I see 'im! I see 'im, Mama!"

"Noo! Catch 'im. Ron! Ron op!"

A small crowd had gathered, children and grownups. Kushy's face was among them. "Hey, watsuh maddeh? Zug, vuss is?"

"He's dere! He's dere on dat house!" the girl babbled and pointed.

"Who?"

"The kinerry! My modder's!" And urged by the shrill voice of her mother upstairs, she began running across the street. "He got out from the cage! I'll give a rewuhd!"

She had no sooner gone inside when suddenly from a niche on the wall of the same house, a bright yellow bird dove down, fluttered uncertainly, then skimmed across the street and landed on the scroll-work of the house next to David's. It perched there a moment while the street gaped up at it, and then it flew up to the roof.

"Whee! Yuh see 'im!" The crowd grew excited. "Oy a fegel! Kent fly so good! Ketch 'im! She'll give a rewuhd!"

"My roof!" One of the boys plucked his cap off and dashed for the doorway. "I'll gid 'im wid my hat!"

"A-key!" Kushy tore after him. "A rewuhd!"

"A-key!" A third followed.

"A-key!" A fourth disappeared inside.

A few seconds later, the girl with the pig-tails stuck her head out of the window.

"He flew away!" voices in the crowd bawled up at her. "On de roof across the street!"

"He flew away, Mama!" she screamed.

"I saw already," the answer shot back. "He shull drop dead!"

Mother and daughter drew their heads in. On the sidewalk necks craned awhile searching the sky. No bird appeared.

"Dey'll never get 'im. Naaa!"

"A nechtige tug!" The small crowd drifted slowly apart.

—Mama!

He woke from his revery.

—Dumb ox, me! Hurry up!

He ran up the stoop, but at the doorway hesitated, peered in. Again the roots of his hair prickled. He could not bring himself to enter the darkness. All the old fears lurked there again. Why had they returned? Angered to the point of tears at his own cowardice, he paced restlessly back and forth across the stoop, now listening for a sound in the hallway, now peering up and down the street for some familiar face. At last he heard a door slam dully inside as though from an upper floor. He leapt into the hallway, scrambled frantically up the stairs. Between the first and second floors he neared the bulky figure of a woman, squeezed past her and up—still listening to the other's dwindling footsteps. On the fourth floor, he threw himself breathlessly at the door— It was locked!

"Mama!" he screamed.

"You, David?" Her startled voice.

The enormous relief! "Yes, mama, open it!" The foot he had drawn back to kick at the door in his fury and terror sank again to the floor.

"Wait!" Her voice had a hurried sound. "I'll open it in a moment."

What was she doing? And as if in answer, he heard a loud splash of water followed by a flurry of tinkling drops. She had been taking a bath in the washtub. She was getting out now. A chair creaked as though she had stepped on it, then the pad of her bare feet on the floor. "Just one little second more," she implored.

"Awrigh' " he called to her.

Silence. Feet moving off, returning. The door opened. And as if the light that widened with it were a wedge, the foggy, tormenting globe about his senses split open and dissolved—hue and contour, sound and scent focused.

"Mama!"

"I didn't mean to keep you waiting." She was still barefooted. Her faded yellow bathrobe, darkened by waterstains clung to breast and thigh. "But I hurried as fast as I could." From glistening brown hair, water still streamed down on the towel across her shoulder. The wonted pallor of smooth throat and face was flushed and beaded with water. "What are you staring at?" She smiled, pulled the bathrobe tighter and shut the door behind him.

"I didn't care if I waited." He smiled with her. He could almost feel his jarred spirit settle softly in its grooves again.

"But you did storm the door with all the old fury," she laughed. And pressing her dripping hair against her bosom, she stooped down and kissed him. The warm, faintly soap-scented humidity of her body, ineffably sweet. "I'm so relieved to see you again."

Where was his father? Behind her the bedroom door was open. No one lay on the bed. Not in. Beatitude flawless.

"You're still wet!" he giggled suddenly. "Even the floor!"

"Yes. I must mop that dry." She caught up the wet, dripping twist of her hair in the towel. "Half the tub is on the floor. I vaulted out in such haste. I don't know why I get so frightened about you—especially if I think you are." As she spoke, she bent sideways, dipped an arm in the tub to pull the stoppers out. The soapy water sucked and gurgled. Against the window-light, her body showed shadowy outlines, hip and knee lending pink to the yellow. "Did you see many sights on the wagon?"

He shook his head violently.

"No?" Her smile faded. "Why such drooping lips?"

"I hate it! I hate it!" It was all he could do to keep from bursting into tears.

"Why?" She looked at him in surprise. "What happened?"

"Nothing. (—*Mustn't tell. Mustn't!*) Didn't like it, that's all."

"Timid little heart! I know. But tomorrow you won't have to go—even if that other man doesn't return, someone else will take that route."

"Never?"

"Never, what? Go?"

"Yes."

"No, never." She sat down, towel a comical turban about her head. "Come here."

He smiled diffidently and went to her. "You look funny."

"Do I?" she chuckled and helped him to her knee. The comfort of being against her breast outstripped the farthest-flung pain. "You don't like being a milkman?"

"No."

"Nor a milkman's helper?"

"No!"

"What would you like to be?"

"I don't know."

She laughed. How the ear teased for that rippling, sinuous sound. "This morning in the butcher-shop I heard a woman say that her son was going to be a great doctor. Hmm! I thought, how blessed your life is! And how old is your son, the butcher asked. Seven, she answered. The butcher nearly missed the bone he was chopping. And here you're eight and still you haven't told me. But you won't have to go along with the wagon any more—— Want some milk? The new yeast cookies you like?" She rubbed her moist brow against his lips. "With the raisins inside?"

"Awrigh'!" he yielded. "But not now." The closeness of her body was too rare to be relinquished so soon.

"Awhrri'," she repeated after him, and so drolly he laughed. "But let me get up."

"No!"

"But I've got to get dressed," she begged. "This shift is clammier than a well-stone. Yes?" She rose; reluctantly he slid from her knee. "I'll get you the milk and cookies first."

He watched her go to the bread-box, open it, draw out several honey-colored cookies, place them on a plate and then take a half-filled quart of milk from the ice-box—

—Wagon! They! Ow!

A shudder ran through him.

—Forget!

She filled a glass, set the cookies and milk on the table.

"You eat them while I dress," she coaxed. "There are more of both if you want them." And uncoiling the towel about her head went into the bedroom.

He sat down, munched the raisined crispness slowly, stared eagerly at the bedroom door waiting for her to come out.

"What time is it now, David?" Her voice rose above the rustling of the garments.

He stared up at the clock on the shelf. "It's ten—eleven minutes after two."

"*After* two?"

"Yes."

"He'll get no sleep this afternoon either."

—He!

"That double collection keeps him—as if he didn't work hard enough as it is. But he ought to be home soon."

—Soon! Home!

The mashed lump of food lay inertly in his mouth.

"Do you remember the time you couldn't tell time?" Her voice went on after a pause. "You told it by whistles. And once you saved calendar leaves—where are they now?"

—He! See him! No! No! Go down! Quick, before he comes!

He gulped down the half-chewed cud, shoved the re-

mainder of the cooky in his pocket and drank the milk
down in noisy haste.

—Take another. She'll ask.

He dropped another cooky into his pocket. "I'm going
down stairs, mama."

"What!" Her voice was surprised.

"Can I?"

"Have you finished so soon?" She came out of the
bedroom. Her dress, hovering between round upstretched
arms, "How did you—" settled like a cloud about her
head, "manage so soon?" sank below throat, armpits,
square scalloped, petticoat. His face was radiant. Her
eyes searched the table.

"I was hungry."

"Well," she lifted the long nape of hair from her neck.
"That's the quickest you've ever eaten. Were they good?"

"Yes." He was already edging toward the door.

"You rush in and rush out as though the coachman
wouldn't wait. But don't stay too long."

"No."

She smoothed down her dress, crouched, kissed him.
"What a fitful one you are! Be up before supper?"

"Yes."

"Take care of yourself in the street, won't you?"

"Yes." He opened the door, shut himself into the gloom
of the hallway.

—Ain't so afraid. Funny, forgot. But hurry . . .

V

IN THE street again, he fled across the gutter to the
side shaded now by houses, and began walking west toward Avenue C. His eyes, peering in all directions to
catch sight of his father before he himself was seen, spied
Izzy dashing out of the cheder hallway. He didn't want
to talk to him. That taunt about the whip still rankled. He
flattened against a store window as Izzy hurried east to-

ward Avenue D, but their glances met; Izzy's sharp eyes
recognized him.

"Hey!" His voice had a novel, friendly note in it.
"W'y'ntcha say sompt'n? W'ea's de geng?"

"I didn' see 'em." He thawed cautiously.

"C'mon, let's find 'em." Izzy briskly took his arm. "Wonner w'ea Kushy is?"

"Dintcha fighd 'im?" He permitted himself to be led.

"Naa! He's a lodda boloney! D'ja fodder gib yuh wid
de w'ip?"

"No! Did he gid de nickel?"

"Naa! Id wuzn'a nickel—jus' like I tol' 'im— He wuz
mad yaw fodder—oh boy!"

"No, he wuzn't." Why did Izzy persist in changing the
subject? "W'a wuz id?"

"W'a'? De nickel? Iyin, like I said."

"Oh!"

"N' de rebbeh god mad on yuh good."

"Yea." Irritably.

"Yuh bedder gib'm poinduhs," he advised. "He ga' me
a smack onna puss, lousy bassid! An' he bussid one on
Srooly—Bang! He's dumb. Betcha million dollehs dey're
all on Evenyeh D."

They rounded the corner— There they all were, sitting
on the curb.

"See? I tol' ye." Izzy shot ahead, shaking David completely. "Hey, Geng!"

"Hey, Izzy!" they chorused.

"Led a reggiluh guy sid donn, will yuh?"

"Led 'im sid donn!" they ordered, and shoving against
each other made room for him beside Kushy.

Stranded, David hesitantly approached and stood up
behind them.

"So w'ea wuz yuh?" Kushy asked.

"I went wid my modder." Izzy basked in their gaze.
"An' we bought shoes—best kind onnuh Eas' Side. Waid'll
yuh see 'em. Wid buttons 'n' flat toes—for kickin' a food-
ball. He wanned t'ree dollehs, bod my modder tol' me I
shull say, Peeuh! Wod lousy shoes! So we god 'em fuh
two. An' nen I went tuh cheder."

"I like bedder poinds," contention broke out from some
point on the line. "Give a bedder kick inna hole!"

"Yea! Ha! Ha!" they chortled, acknowledging the wisdom of the choice.

"Can't gid yuh foot oud," countered Izzy calmly. "So wod's de good?"

"I like bedder rubbehs," another differed—a nonentity this time near the end of the rank. "Kin run beddeh."

"Rubbehs! Yuh greenhunn!" Izzy staggered him with sarcasm first and then finished him off with precision, "Sneakiss, dope! Gid nails righd t'rough 'em—righd t'rough de boddem—'Member, Kushy," he suddenly guffawed, "w'en I tol yuh he said blitz—inna cheder? Rubbehs guzz on shoes, greenhunn!"

"Aaa! Wiseguy!"

"W'ea wuz yiz?" Izzy ignored the slur.

"We?" Kushy paused importantly. "We seen a kinerry." A select few snickered as if at a veiled jest.

"W'a kinerry?"

"G'wan tell 'im," someone urged.

"I wuz dere too!" another put in.

"Waid!" Kushy hastily cautioned them. "My brudder!" And leaning out so he could view both wings, "Hey youz kids, gid odda hea. G'wan!"

"Naa!" The six year olds at either wing protested.

"G'wan!" The older ones blustered. "Skidoo!"

"Street ain' yours!" stubbornly.

"Wanna ged a lam onnuh eye?"

"I'll tell mama," one of the juniors threatened.

"I'll give yuh *now!*" Kushy half-rose.

Sulkily, they slid along the curb a few feet away from the rest.

"So w'ad kinerry?" from Izzy.

They drew closer.

"Yuh know Schloimee Salmonowitz wot lives in sebn-fawdee-fi'?"

"Wad he had de mockee wid de bendij on his head?"

"Yea!"

"Yea, he wuz in my cheder. So wot?"

"So Sadie Salmonowitz came running downstairs 'n' hollerin', My modder's kinerry, my modder's kinerry flied away! I'll give a rewuhd!"

"Yuh god de rewuhd?" Izzy asked eagerly. "How moch?"

"Waid a second. An' den we seen 'im on sebn-fawdy-six, across de stritt an' ziz! He gives a fly back an' zip! op to duh roof—"

"My house!" another voice chimed in. "He flew—"

"Shod op!" Kushy snatched back the thread of his narrative. "Schmeelkee's house he flew. So we all grabbed our hats an' runned inna duh hall. Yuh catch 'em wid a hat—like dot!" Without warning he plucked his neighbor's cap from his head and pitched it spinning into the gutter.

"Ha-a! Ha-a! He-e! He-e!" Clacking like nine-pins before a heavy bowl of mirth they tumbled about the sidewalk. "He-e! He-e! Ha-a! Ha-a! Ha-a!"

"Cud id oud, wise guy!" Grinning at the clever prank, the owner rose to retrieve it. Immediately all buttocks crammed together, squeezing him out of his seat. Returned, he flung himself between the packed usurpers and after much scuffing, cursing, butting and pushing, regained, if not his own place, at least one as desirable.

"So dot's de joke?" inquired Izzy contemptuously when the new equilibrium was finally restored.

"Naa!" crowed Kushy and one or two more. "Dat ain' de joke!"

"So w'od?"

"So we runned opstai's to de roof. An' Schmeelkee fell on his leg, duh dope—"

"Wanna see wea I cut?" Schmeelkee's stocking went down, revealing a newly scabbed skin. "Righd on duh bone!"

"Den wod?"

"So wa-a-aid a minid," drawled Kushy delighted at Izzy's nettled tone. "So we wen' op—quiet! We didn' make no noise cause we didn' wanna scare de kinerry. An' we god on de roof, an' we walked aroun' an we looked— He musta flied away!"

"But we seen annudder kinerry!" Schmeelkee boiled over.

"Woddayuh mean?"

"Sh!" Kushy looked to see whether the juniors on either wing still kept their distance. "So we snuck ovuh by duh air-sheff—yuh know w'ea is between sebn-fifty-one an' sebn-fawdy-nine?"

"Yea."

Absorption stilled their fidgeting. All eyes converged on Kushy. David too leaned closer.

"An' we all gave a look—An' yuh know wod we seen? Hee! Hee! We seen a lady washin' huhself inna washtub! Hee! Hee!"

—*Washtub!* (David grew rigid)

"Wod lady?" Izzy asked.

"Don' know. Couldn't see good huh face."

"So wadjuh see?"

"Ev'yting! Oh, boy! Big tids stickin' oud in frund!" His descriptive hands, molding the air, dragged other hands along with them as though all were tethered to the same excitement. "She was sittin' in duh wawduh!"

—*She! Mine! Aaa, mine!*

The rush of shame set his cheeks and ears blazing like flame before a bellows, drove blood like a plunger against the roof of his skull. He stood with feet mortised to the spot, knees sagging, quivering.

"So den?" Izzy spurred.

"So den, she jomps up an nen we seen ev'yting—!"

"Big bush under duh belly!" The others jumbled voice with gestures. "Fat ass, we seen! Big—Wuh! Wadda kinerry! Wee! An' duh hull knish! All de hairs!"

"Yea? No kiddin'?"

"Sure!"

"Didja watch?"

"No. She gave a look righd ad us."

"She didn' look, I tol' yuh!"

"She did!"

"She didn'!"

"She did! Wod she jump oud for!"

"So?"

"So we run down-stairs—Wee! Wod a kinerry we seen!"

—Aaa! Lousy son of a bitch! Murder 'em! K-Kick 'em! Kill 'em! G-go 'way'—Yuh gonna cry!

"W'a fluh—Yee, wish I wuz dere. W'ea! Tell us—Led's go—"

Like flying hail against his nakedness their sharp cries stunned and flayed him. Blind with loathing, he reeled away—unnoticed.

(—Ow! Ow! Don't let 'em see! Don't let 'em know. Ow!) The hot tears sprang to his eyes, the more scalding for resistance. He twisted about, yanked his head down, and began running to the corner.

—Aaa! Mama! Mine it was! Should have kicked 'em, kicked 'em and run. Go back! Kick em! Kick 'em in the belly. G'wan, you coward! Coward! Coward! Coward! Hate 'em! All! All! Everybody! Shouldn't have gone over. Never go over again! Never talk to them even! Hate 'em! And she—Why did she let them look. Shades, why didn't she pull them? Ain't none! Ain't none! And she let me look at her! Mad at her! Ow! Don't let 'em see me crying! Cry baby! Cry baby!

He stumbled blindly across the street, flung himself into the hallway. The obscure stairs. At last he reached his own floor.

—Scared. Don't care. Scared before. Scared all the time.

—Got to stop crying. She'll ask why. What'll I say? From the roof they saw you. No, no, don't say anything —roof they. Roof . . . Roof? Never was . . up there . . . I wonder? . . .

He stared in breathless irresolution from his own doorway to the roof-door overhead. The clean, untrodden flight of stairs that led up, beckoned even as they forbade; temptingly the light swarmed down through the glass of the roof-housing, silent, untenanted light; evoking in his mind and superimposing an image of the snow he had once vaulted into and an image of the light he had once climbed. Here was a better haven than either, a more durable purity. Why had he never thought of it before? He had only to conquer his cowardice, and that solitude and that radiance were his. But quickly, he must go quickly, before someone came out. He mounted the stairs that even underfoot felt differently, as though the unworn mica in them sparkled through the soles—and stopped at the door. Only a catch held it back; it could be lifted. He tugged it with crooked finger. It flew up suddenly— Panic stricken, he watched the heavy door swing away from his hand, squeak leisurely and on reluctant hinges into the sky. (—Down! Run down!) He threw a frightened glance over his shoulder. (—No! Coward! Stay right here! G'wan! G'wan out! It's light! What're you scared of?) He lifted a tentative unsteady foot over the high threshold. (—Ow!) The red-painted sheet-iron crackled under his

soles with a terrifying report. (—Go back! Run! No!
Won't! G'wan, make a noise! Who cares? G'wan coward!)
Breath bound in his lungs, he swung the snickering door
back into place. It stayed closed.

—Gee!

He sighed tremulously, lifted his head, and with body
pivoting on fixed feet, gazed about him.

The immense heavens of July, the burnished, the shining fathom upon fathom. Too pure the zenith was, too
pure for the flawed and flinching eye; the eye sowed it
with linty darkness, sowed it with spores and ripples of
shadow drifting. (—Even up here dark follows, but only
a little bit) And to the west, the blinding whorl of the sun,
the disk and trumpet, triple-trumpet blaring light. He
blinked, dropped his eyes and looked about him. Quiet.
Odor of ashes, the cold subterranean breath of chimneys.
(—Even up here cellar follows, but only a little bit) And
about were roof-tops, tarred and red and sunlit and red,
roof-tops to the scarred horizon. Flocks of pigeons
wheeled. Where they flew in lower air, they hung like
a poised and never-raveling smoke; nearer at hand and
higher, they glittered like rippling water in the sun.
Quiet. Sunlight on brow and far off plating the sides of
spires and water-towers and chimney pots and the golden
cliffs of the streets. To the east the bridges, fragile in
powdery light.

—Gee! Alone . . . Ain't so scared.

VI

WHEN he came down from the roof a little while later,
he crept down a few steps toward the floor below his
own. He would stamp up just before he entered his
house, stamp toward his door. It would make his coming
home seem more natural. He did so.

His mother looked strange when he entered—so strange
that for a moment, he thought his ruse had failed, he
thought himself discovered. But another glance reassured

him, and yet while it reassured him on one score troubled him vaguely on another. It wasn't awareness or alertness or suspicion that was the cause of that glow in her features, that calm, but something else, something he scarcely ever remembered seeing before—an obscure lassitude, a profound and incomprehensible contentment. What was it? What made the hand that had placed a finger across her lips, warning him that he had made too much noise, come down so slowly and with such peculiar, self-conscious grace as though her whole body found a relish in the very movement of her limbs, and relishing, lingered. It touched a chord of memory within himself, touched it with finger tips—Some thing he had done, felt? What? The wisp of a stir within his being faded before the mind could fasten on it. It was baffling. He looked about the kitchen. The bedroom door was closed—his father was asleep. And on the wash-tub lay a bulky package, the strings cut, but the heavy brown paper still covering it; and beside it, crossing each other, a new white handled whip and the butt of the old broken black one. He felt his legs stiffen, brace against the sudden undertow of terror. He turned away. His mother had lowered the finger from her lips and greeted him. (But where were the outstretched arms she always met him with?) And then she smiled. (But was that smile for him or for that inner languor that suffused and harmonized her spirit?) His eyes darted to the parcel and the whips on the washtub and then returned to her—questioningly. She seemed to avoid his query, and asked instead:

"Why is your nose so sunburned? Where have you been?"

The wonder that her singular appearance had produced within himself almost lowered his guard. He came within a breath of telling her the truth—but stopped himself in time. "On the sidewalk." His eyes wavered between her waist and the linoleum. "We were all sitting. It was hot."

"Your father's bought a new whip," she smiled. "Is that what you wanted to ask me?"

"N-no."

"Oh, no? I thought you were just dying to ask me if

you could have the broken one. Perhaps Albert will give—"

But he was already shaking his head. (It was hard not to be violent, not to be vehement all the time. Sometimes the hoops of caution almost snapped.)

"What's that?" he pointed to the parcel. "Can I look?"

"Why, of course! But I warn you," she laughed, as he went over to the wash-tub, "this time it's really a big surprise!"

There was an old overtone in her words, but he was too experienced now to ask, "Is it for me?" Instead, he merely lifted the heavy wrapping-paper flaps—and stared and blinked and stared again! At his back he heard her expectant laughter. Before him on a shield-shaped wooden plaque, two magnificent horns curved out and up, pale yellow to the ebony tips. So wide was the span between them, he could almost have stretched his arms out on either side, before he could touch them. Though they lay there inertly, their bases solidly fastened to the dark wood, there pulsed from them still a suggestion of terrific power, a power that even while they lay motionless made the breast ache as though they were ever imminent, ever charging.

"And those?" her voice was bright with amusement. "Do you know what those are?"

He gaped at her. "A—a c-cow," he stuttered. "In pictures I saw them. And—and when Aunt Bertha took me to the moving pitchers."

"A cow, but a he-cow!" she laughed. "A bull. I don't know whether you ever saw one even as an infant in Austria. They were monstrous—walls of flesh and strength."

"Did he buy it?"

"Why yes, of course. When he bought the whip."

"Oh! Is that why he got it?"

"Why yes, it reminded him of the time when he took care of cattle. You see," she explained, "When your grandfather—his father was overseer of the baron's yeast factory, he put Albert in charge of the cattle. They fed them on mash—but you've already heard him speak of that."

"What's he going to do with them?" he asked after a pause.

"Hang them up of course. In the front-room." Her eyes wandered to the picture of the corn flowers on the wall. "He couldn't find a nail strong enough."

He was silent. Somehow he couldn't quite believe that it was for memory's sake only that his father had bought this trophy. Somehow looking at the horns, guessing the enormous strength of the beast who must have owned them, there seemed to be another reason. He couldn't quite fathom it though. But why was it that two things so remote from each other seemed to have become firmly coupled in his mind? It was as though the horns lying on the wash-tub had bridged them, as though one tip pierced one image and one tip the other—that man outstretched on the sidewalk, that mysterious look of repose in his mother's face when he had come in. Why? Why did he think of them at one and the same time? He couldn't tell. He sensed only that in the horns, in the poised power of them lay a threat, a challenge he must answer, he must meet. But he didn't know how.

VII

WHEN David thought of the roof the next morning, he thought of it with so peculiarly selfish a joy that it kept him from thinking any further. The roof, that precinct in the sky, that silent balcony on the pinnacle of turmoil, demanded that what thoughts one had be had there. He culled them, sorted out what he would think when he got up there—he would allow them to blossom once he had climbed up the stairs. And a little while later he was there. What sounds from the street, what voices drifted up the air-shafts, only made his solitude more real, the detachment of his reveries more delightful.

He had found an old, weather-beaten box lying in the shady side of the roof-stair housing and he had been sitting there some time watching his thoughts uncurl when the creak of a door somewhere startled him. His first thought was that Izzy or Kushy were coming up again in order to see what they had seen before. And listening to the tread of feet on the squawking tin, he sat there rigidly, gritting his teeth in fury. What right had they to come up again, to torment him after he had found a little peace? Would they drive him out of every place he went, every retreat? He wouldn't let them! He wouldn't let them look down his air-shaft again. He'd fight, he'd scratch, he'd kick! Hidden behind the shed he listened a moment longer. Footsteps were followed by another sound—a hollow scuffing noise as of feet scraping up a fence. Then the tread again, but now no longer on the tin. Who was it? He heard a fluttering whirr. Faint taps. The slight, taut snapping of a stretched string. That couldn't be them. What was it? Cautiously he peeped around the edge of the shed—

On the high lean-to that covered the stairway of the next roof but one, stood a boy, kite-string in hand, spindle rattling at his feet, and in the air a short distance from him, a rag-tailed, crimson kite ducked and soared. His blond hair, only a shade less fair than his brow, hung over his brow like a gold claw. He was snub-nosed; his cheeks had a faint flush and his eyes were blue. Teeth over lip, head lifted into light, he watched his kite intently, now paying out string, now jogging it to newer heights. It swayed slowly, tacking into upper air; there it steadied and drew away with sagging glint of string.

Watching him, David felt a bond of kinship growing up between them. They were both alone on the roof, both inhabitants of the same realm. That was a bond between them. But David could tell by looking at him, that the other had come up to the roof out of assurance—this was only another phase of his life. David himself had come up tentatively, timidly, because there was no other place to go. He suddenly began wishing he could know this carefree, confident stranger. But he had never seen his face before—that blond hair, those blue eyes didn't belong to Ninth Street. How could he begin? Mentally he went over the various ways of striking up an acquaintance. He wished that he had something to offer him—the cookies he had thrown away yesterday or a bit of string. Longingly, he watched him.

With one hand poised as though the string's steadiness

depended on his balance, he felt behind him for the sloping floor under his feet and then sat down. He leaned back contentedly, whistling short fitful notes. David couldn't make up his mind whether he ought to come out of hiding or content himself with merely watching the kite. He watched the kite. And suddenly stared—

It was hard to tell what street they were nearer to, Eleventh or Twelfth but he could see them clearly. There were two, perhaps three boys, and with bodies bent low, they were crawling over the roofs, now emerging now ducking behind chimney pots and skylights. Another few seconds and they were under the hanging arc of the kite-cord—although far below it. He glanced sharply at the owner of the kite. Unaware of any danger, he lay sprawled back, still whistling up at the sky. When David looked back to the distant ones, they had already risen from hands and knees and were vigorously twirling something in the air.

"Pssst!" He leaped out of hiding. "Pssst!" Not daring to speak, he made frantic motions of dragging in the kite-cord.

"W'at?" The other scrambled to his feet. "W'atsa matter?" And when David pointed vehemently in the direction of the distant marauders, "Cheesis! Dey're sling-shootin' it!" he shouted excitedly. "Cheesis!" And as fast as his hands could go, began yanking in the line.

The slings had been thrown. Both missed, fell, doubling back on the strings they trailed. They flung them up again. But as the kite came sailing home, it rose higher and higher—further from their range. At last the owner rested, babbling exultantly.

"Cheesis! See 'em! Dere dey go! Hidin' back o' dat! Bot' of 'em! Didn' get it dough. Lousy micks, nearly slung it! Waaa!" he screeched, thumbing his nose at the two distant figures. "Ya Irish mutts! Waid'll I git ya, I'll rap de piss odda ye!"

What abuse the others bawled back in reply was too faint to hear, but David could see them wagging their hands under their chins.

"Ha! Ha! Look at 'em!" the blond one yelled over to him. "See w'at dey're doin'? Dey t'ink I'm a Jew! See 'em! Dopy mutts! Dopy mutts," he yodeled again. "Dopy mutts!" And then glancing at his feet. "Chee! Looka my

kite-cord—all twissed up! Hey, c'mon over, will ya?
C'mon, give us a hand."

David shook his head.

"Wottsa madder, can'tcha talk?" The other stared at
him.

Nodding vigorously, David pointed down to the roof at
his feet.

The other grinned, face lighting up as though he understood. "C'mon," he whispered throatily, head hooking
the air. "It's easy!"

—Better not.

There was something hazardous about climbing over
the wall on a roof, especially with the deep pit of the
air-shaft near at hand. The thought made one dizzy.

"Go over dat way," the other urged.

(—Ain't scared. Ain't gonna be!) He tiptoed breathlessly across the crackling tin, climbed over the low wall
onto the second roof. Another wall and the blue eyes
gazed curiously down at him over the edge of the shed.

"Who ye scared o'?"

"Nott'n. I live on de top-fluh. I did'n' wan' my modder
sh'd hea' me."

"Oh. Wouldn' she letcha stay hea?"

"No. She'll make me comm donn."

"C'mon up hea' den. Nobody c'n see ye."

"So hoddy yuh go?"

"Hop up on 'at liddle winder. Den dese big bolts. See
'em?"

David assayed them. The other, one eye on his kite, lent
a helping hand. "Sit onna noospaper," he invited when
David had climbed up; "Hol' me kite will ye an' I'll git
me cord onna spool."

"Yea."

"Don' leggo of it." He gave the string into David's keeping. "It's got some pull."

"Gee!" The tug on his hand was almost alive. "It
flies!"

The other laughed. "Sure it flies. Yuh c'n sit down wid
it." He squatted down himself, began undoing the snarl of
string at his feet. "De lousy micks! Look wat dey made
me do! G'wan sit down!"

"Don' your modder care if yuh come op hea?"

"She? Naw! She woiks!"

"Oh! W'ea's yuh foddeh?"

"I ain't got none. Me old man usetuh woik on de rail-ro'. But he wuz squeezed between two trains when I wuz liddle an' we lived in Paterson. Wot's yuh name?"

"Davy. Davy Schearl."

"My name's Leo Dugovka. I'm a Polish-American. You're a Jew, ain'tcha?"

"Y-Yea."

"Say, wuz yew wit' dem kids w'at wuz runnin' on de roof yestiddy?"

"No I wuzn't," vehemently.

"I'll knock dere block off if I ketch 'em nex' time. Dey nearly made de plaster fall down."

"Yea," David's heart warmed to Leo's. "Y'oughta gib'm. Gib'm good!"

"Jist waid'll I gid 'em." Leo worked rapidly at the spindle. "I'll bust 'em one."

"I never seen yuh in dis block. Yuh livin' hea long?"

"Naa, we usen't to live hea, but me ol' lady got a job in 'at big bank on sixt' and Avenee C—yuh know wit dem swell w'ite stones an' gold ledders—Foist National."

"Yea," said David wonderingly. "Wit' iron bars in id 'n' dat big clock. Does she woik wid all dat money?"

"Yea, she cleans all de desks an' awffices 'n' ev'yt'ing."

"Oh? So who gives yuh to eat?"

"I takes it myself?"

"Gee!" David breathed in the enormous freedom. "Yuh gonna comm up hea alluh time?"

"Naw! I hangs out on wes' elevent'. Dat's w'ea we lived 'fore we moved. It's a mick block, only some of de Hogan's alley kids is in de All Saints Camp."

"Oh!" disappointedly. "Gee, dat's far, wes' elebn't."

"Yea, but I got skates."

"Skates, gee!" There was no end to Leo's blessings—no father, almost no mother, skates.

"Git dere in a minute wit' 'em. You got a pair?"

"No."

"Wyntcha git a pair an' hang out wit' me."

"I can't."

"Aintcha yer ol' man livin'?"

"Yea, but he wouldn' buy."

"Wyntcha ast yer ol' lady."

"She can't."

"Chees! Jews never buys nutt'n fer deyr kids."

David searched the horizon for something to fill in the awkward pause. "Dey ain' dere now, doze—doze micks," he ventured.

"Don' worry! Dere jis layin' low, you watch!" He squinted at the distant roofs. "But I ain' gonna let it out dough."

"No." He was relieved that the topic had changed. "How much cost a kite?"

"Dat one's on'y two cents. Butcha gotta git a lodda cord wid it, er ye can't fly it."

"Kentcha fly wit' cotton?"

"Naw! It busts. I had a big kite oncet—twicet as big as dis one—an' wot a pull on it—an' it busted wid even red cord. Wuz way, out over St. Jame's Parochial on Twelft' an' Avenee C—yuh c'n see de cross—See it?"

"Yea."

"Wuz full o' messages an' den it went an' busted. Lost nearly all me cord too—got twissed on de roofs."

"Why yuh god id?" David gazed out at the distant spire outlined against the hazy western blue. "Dat funny cross ev'y place?"

"Funny?" Leo's voice was nettled. "Wot's funny about it?"

"Not funny—I didn' mean!" He was quick to mollify. "I mean w'y yuh god id?"

"Crosses is holy." Leo instructed him severely, "All of 'em. Christ, our Savior, died on one o' dem."

"Oh! (Savior! What?) I didn' know?"

"Sure, even if yuh wears 'em, dey bring yuh luck. When me ol' lady had her appendixitis cut out, she had one o' dem under her piller ev'y night, an' dat's w'y she got better."

"Gee!"

"Yea an' ev'y' time I goes swimmin' in de Hudson I always cross meself t'ree times—like dat. Den yuh kin Johnny-high-dive all yuh wants an' yuh'll never hit bottom—didn'tcha know dat?" And when David looked blank. "Yuh see dis?" As if to clinch his argument, he undid a button on his shirt, reached in and drew out what looked like a square piece of leather on a string. "Know what dat is?"

He scrutinized it, shook his head. Something had been stamped on it in gold—a picture perhaps—but too faded now to make out. "Maybe a man an' a liddle lady," he ventured. "I can't see so good."

"A man and a lady!" Leo turned his head aside to crow. "Oh boy, wot Jews don' know! Dat's a scapiller, see? An' dat's a pitcher o' de holy Mudder an' Chil'. Cheez! Doncha know de Woigin Mary w'en yuh sees 'er?"

"No," guiltily.

"Cheez!" incredulously, and then lifting the bit of leather to examine it more closely, "It's gittin' rubbed off, I guess." He slipped it back under his shirt. "Dat's cawz I goes swimmin' in it all de time in de river."

"An' yuh ain' ascared o' nottin' w'en yuh god dat on?"

"Naw! I tol' ye!"

"Chee!" David sighed and gazed at Leo's chest half in awe, half in envy.

—*Not afraid! Leo wasn't afraid!*

"Hey, look out for dat kite!" Leo relieved him hastily of the string. "Yuh don' wanna led it dive like dat, it'll smack a roof!"

—*Not afraid!*

VIII

THE hour that had passed had been one of the most blissful in David's life. He had never wanted to be any-one's friend until this moment, and now he would have given anything to be Leo's. The longer he heard him speak, the longer he watched him, the more he be-came convinced that Leo belonged to a rarer, bolder, carefree world. There was a glamour about him. He did what he pleased and when he pleased. He was not only free of parents, but he also wore something about his neck that made him almost god-like. Sitting next to him, David's one concern had been how to in-gratiate himself, how to keep Leo amused, keep him

from remembering that time was passing. Whenever Leo
had laughed, David had felt his own bosom swell up with
joy; even when Leo had jeered at him he felt grateful. It
was right that Leo should jeer at him. Leo was a superior
being; his laugh was just. When Leo had asked him
whether Jews wore amulets on their persons, David had
described the "Tzitzos" that some Jewish boys wore under
their shirts, and the "Tfilin", the little leather boxes, he
had seen men strap around their arms and brows in the
synagogue—had described them, hoping that Leo would
laugh. He did. And even when Leo had said of the
"Mezuzeh", the little metal-covered scroll that all Jews
tacked on the door-posts above their thresholds—"Oh!
Izzat wotchuh call em? Miss oozer? Me ol' lady tore
one o' dem off de door w'en we moved in, and I busted
it, an' cheez! It wuz all full o' Chinee on liddle terlit
paper—all aroun' an' aroun'." David had not been hurt.
He had felt a slight qualm of guilt, yes, guilt because he
was betraying all the Jews in his house who had
Mezuzehs above their doors; but if Leo thought it was
funny, then it was funny and it didn't matter. He had
even added lamely that the only thing Jews wore around
their necks were camphor balls against measles, merely
to hear the intoxicating sound of Leo's derisive laugh. But
at last, Time would have his way. The sun had risen to
the zenith and Leo began drawing in the kite-cord. Resentfully, David eyed the approaching kite.

"Yuh ain' gonna fly no maw?" he asked hoping against
hope.

"Naw, I'm goin' down."

David hoped he would be invited. He wasn't. "Wy'ntcha comm t'morreh again?" he urged.

"I'm goin't' elevent', I tol' yuh."

His answer was like a pang. He was slipping away.
He might never see him again! "Wish I had skates!" he
said fervently. "Chee! I wish I had skates!" And suddenly a new thought struck him. "Wot time yuh commin' home? Dont'cha comm home on twelve a'clock an'
eat?"

"Naw. I buys a couple o' franks on a roll fer a jit."

The last shred of hope. Leo's freedom was unattain-
able. David could feel himself drooping. "So I ain' gonna
see yuh?" he asked miserably.

"Hodda ya wan' me to know." Leo had begun climbing down the shed.

"I'll ged yuh somm cake—" David followed him down. "Big hunks if yuh comm up hea tomorreh."

"Naw!"

"Can't I comm witchuh? I c'n walk."

But his clinging to Leo only tended to make him more unfriendly. "G'wan! I don' wancher hanging' aroun' me. Ye ain't big enough."

"Yes I am!"

"Betcha y'ain't even ten."

"Sure I am!" He lied eagerly. "I'm goin' on eleb'n."

"Well, I'm goin' on twelve. Ye ain't got skates anyway." He opened the roof-door, impatiently. "Better go acrost now, 'cause I'm goin down." And as he stepped down, "So long!" And abruptly shut the roof-door behind him."

"So long!" he called through the metal-covered door. "So long, Leo!" And could have wept the next moment. A little while he stood staring at the door, and then mournfully crossed over the roofs and sat down on the box. Without Leo, the roof had suddenly become vacant, had lost its appeal. Nor was sitting on the box comfortable any longer—he could feel its hard edges now, biting into his thighs. But a kind of inertia engendered by loss kept him where he was, and he leaned back broodily against the skylight. Skates. That was the real reason why he had lost Leo—because he lacked them. He could almost see the gulf between himself and Leo widening with Leo's flying skates. And he had liked Leo so much, even if he was a goy, had liked him better than anyone in the whole block. If only he had a pair of skates! There was very little chance though. A penny a day his mother gave him; that made two on Tuesday; three on Wednesday. It would take forever, and one needed dollars and dollars. If he had a pair of skates he could leave the hated boys on his block behind him; he could go to Leo's block, to Central Park, as Leo said he did. That park with the trees, where he went with Aunt Bertha, that white museum—Aunt Bertha! Her candy store! She must have skates in her candy store! She might even have an old pair that she would give him for nothing! Why hadn't he thought of that before? He'd go now. No, he couldn't go now. There was luncheon and cheder. He'd go to-morrow. Oh, wait till Leo saw him with his skates! He hurried joyfully down the stairs.

IX

WITHOUT telling his mother where he was going he had started out early that morning for Aunt Bertha's candy store. It had been a long walk, but high hopes had buoyed him up. And now he saw a few blocks away the gilded mortar and pestle above a certain drugstore window. That was Kane Street. His breast began pounding feverishly as he drew near.

What if she didn't have any skates. No! She must have! He turned the corner, walked east. A few houses and there was the candy store. He'd look into the window first. Jumping up eagerly on the iron scrolls of the cellar railing beside the store window, he pressed his nose against the glass, scrutinized the display. A wild, garish clutter of Indian bonnets, notebooks, pencil boxes, pasteboard females, American flags, uncut strips of battleships and ball players—but no skates for his flitting eyes to light upon. Hope wavered. No, they must be inside. Aunt Bertha would be foolish to keep anything so valuable in the window.

He peered in through a crevice in the chaos. Seated behind the counter, one hand poising a dripping roll above a coffee cup, Aunt Bertha had turned her head toward the rear of the store and was bawling at someone inside. David could hear her voice coming through the doorway. He got down from the rail, sidled around the edge of the window and went in—

"Sluggards! Bedbugs foul!" she shrilled unaware of his entrance. "Esther! Polly! Will you get up! Or shall I spit my lungs out at you! Quick, stinking heifers, you hear me! No?"

Aunt Bertha had changed since David had seen her

last. Uncorseted, she looked fatter now, frowsier. The last remnant of tidiness in her appearance had vanished. Her heavy breasts, sagging visibly against her blouse, stained by fruit juice and chocolate, flopped slovenly from side to side. Fibres of her raffia-course red hair twined her moist throat. But her face was strangely thin and taut as though a weight where her apron bulged were dragging the skin down. "Wait!" she continued. "Wait till your father comes. Hi! He'll rend you with his teeth! Stinking sluts, it's almost nine!" She turned. "Vell?" and recognizing him. "David!" The hectic light in her eyes melted into pleasure. "David! My little bon-bon! You?"

"Yea!"

"Come here!" she spread fat arms like branches. "Let me give you a kiss, my honey-comb! I haven't seen you in—how long? And Mama, why doesn't she come? And how is your father?" Her eyes opened fiercely. "Still mad?" She submerged him in a fat embrace that reeked of perspiration flavored with coffee.

"Mama is all right." He squirmed free. "Papa too."

"What are you doing here? Did you come alone? All this long way?"

"Yes, I—"

"Want some candy? Ha! Ha! I know you, sly one!" She reached into a case. "Hea, I giff you a pineepple vit' emmend. Do I speak English better?"

"Yea." He pocketed them.

"End a liddle suddeh vuddeh?"

"No, I don't want it." He answered in Yiddish. For some reason he found himself preferring his aunt's native speech to English.

"And so early!" She rattled on admiringly. "Not like my two wenches, sluggish turds! And you're younger than they. If only you were mine instead of— Cattle!" She broke off furiously. "Selfish, mouldering hussies! All they know is to snore and guzzle! I'll husk them out of bed now, God help me!" But just as she started heavily for the doorway, a man stepped into the store.

"Hello! Hello!" He called loudly. "What are you scurrying off for? Because I came in?"

"No-o! God forbid!" she exclaimed with mock vehemence. "How fares a Jew?"

"How fares it with all Jews? A bare living. Can you spare me a thousand guilders?"

"Ha! Ha! What a jester! The only green-rinds I ever see are what I peel from cucumbers." And turning to David. "Go in, sweet one! Tell them I'll sacrifice them for the sake of heathens if they don't get up! That's my sister's only one," she explained.

"Comely," admitted the other.

David hesitated, "You want me to go in?"

"Yes! Yes! Perhaps you'll shame the sows into rising."

"Your fledgelings are still in the nest?"

"And what else?" disgustedly. "Lazy as cats. Go right in, my bright."

Reluctantly, David squeezed past her, and casting a last vain glance at the jumbled shelves, pushed the spring door forward and went in. Beyond the narrow passageway, cramped even closer by the stumpy mottled columns on pasteboard boxes carelessly piled, the kitchen opened up with a stale reek of unwashed frying pans. The wooden table in the center was bare except for a half-filled bottle of ketchup with a rakish cap. Pots, one in another, still squatted on the gas-stove. From a corner of the stove-tray under the burners, coffee dripped to a puddle on the floor. The sink was stacked with dishes, and beside it on the washtub a bag-full of rolls lay spilled all over. Splayed newspapers, crumpled garments, shoes, stockings, hung from the chairs or littered the floor. There were three doors, all closed, one on either side and one with a broom against it opening on the yard.

—Gee! Dirty . . . . Which one?

A giggle at his left. He approached cautiously.

"Is she commin'?" A guarded voice inside.

"Sh!"

"Hey," he called out in a non-committal voice, "Yuh momma wants you sh'd ged op!"

"Who're you?" Challengingly from the other side.

"It's me, Davy."

"Davy who?"

"Davy Schearl, Tanta Boita's nephew."

"Oh! So open de daw."

He pushed it back—The clinging stench of dried urine. Lit by a small window that gave upon the squalid grey bricks of an airshaft, the room was gloomy. Only after a few seconds had passed did the features of the two heads that pronged the grey, mussed coverlets separate from the murk.

"It's him!" A voice from the pillow.

"So wodda yuh wan'?" He finally distinguished the voice as Esther's.

"I tol' yuh," he repeated. "Yuh momma wants yuh sh'd get op. She tol' me I shul tell yuh." The message delivered, he began to retreat.

"Comm beck!" Imperiously. "Dope! Wodda yuh wan' in duh staw I asked."

"N-nott'n."

"So waddaye comm hea fuh?" Polly demanded suspiciously. "Kendy?"

"No, I didn'. I jost comm to see Tanta Boita."

"Aaa, he's full of hoss-cops—C'mon, Polly!" Esther was the one nearest the wall. "Ged out!" She sat up.

Polly clung to the covers. "Ged oud yuhself foist."

"Yuh bedder! Yuh hoid w'ad mama said."

"So led 'er say." Peevishly.

"I ain' gonna clean de kitchen by myself," Esther stood up on the bed. "You'll ged!"

"Don' cross over me. Id's hard luck."

"I will if yuh don' ged out!"

"You jus' try—go over by my feet—"

But even as she spoke, Esther jumped over her.

"Lousy bestia!" Polly screeched. And as her sister jounced with unsure footing on the bed, she clutched at the hem of her nightgown and yanked her back. Esther tumbled heavily against the wall.

"Ow! Rotten louse!" Esther screamed in return. "Yuh hoit my head." And swooping down on the coverlets, flung them back. "Yeee!" she squawled as Polly, taken by surprise lay for an instant with nightgown above naked navel, "Yeee! Free show! Free show!"

"Free show, yuhself!" Furiously, Polly clawed at the other's nightgown. "Yuh stinkin' 'fraid cat! Shame! Shame! Free show!" Immediately four bare thighs kicked, squirmed and locked, and the two sisters rolled about in bed, slapping each other and shrieking. After a minute of this, the disheveled Esther, with a last vicious slap, at the other, broke loose, leapt from the bed and squealing rushed past David into the kitchen.

"I'll moider you—yuh rotten stinker!" Polly screamed after her. "I'll break yuh head!" she rolled out of bed as well.

"Yea, I double dare you!" Quivering with spite, Esther bent fingers into claws.

"I'll tell mama on you! I'll tell 'er watchuh done!"

"I ain' gonna go down witchoo." Her sister spat. "Just fer dat, you go yuhself."

"So don't. I'll tell him too!"

"I'll kill yuh!"

"Yea! Yuh know w'ot Polly does?" Esther wheeled on him. "She pees in bed every night! Dat's w'at she does! My fodder has to give her a pee-pot twelve a'clock every night—"

"I don't!"

"Yuh do! Dere!"

"Now I'll never take yuh down, yuh lousy fraid-cat. Never! Never!"

"So don't!"

"An' I hope de biggest moider boogey man tears yuh ass out."

"Piss-in-bed!" Esther taunted stubbornly. "Piss in bed!"

"An he'll comm, Booh!" Polly pawed the air, eyes bulging in mimic fright. "Booh! Like de Mask-man in de serial! Wooh!"

"Aaa, shoddop!" Esther flinched. "Mama'll take me down."

"Yea!" her sister gloated. "Stinkin' fraid-cat! Who'll stay in de staw?"

"You!"

"Yuh should live so!"

"So I'll pee in de sink." Esther threatened.

"Wid de dishes in id! G'wan, I dare yuh! An' yuh know w'ot Mama'll give yuh w'en I tell 'er."

"So I'll waid! Aaa! He'll go down!" she shrilled in sudden triumph. "Mbaa!" her tongue flicked out. "Mbaa! Davy'll go down wit' me!"

"Yea? Waid'll I tell Sophie Seigel an' Yeddie Katz you took a boy down in de toilet and let 'im look. Waid'll I tell!"

"Sticks and stones c'n break my bones, but woids can nevuh hoit me-e!" Esther sang malevolently. "I ain'gonna led 'im look. C'mon, Davy! Waid'll I ged my shoes on."

"Don' go!" Polly turned on him fiercely. "Or I'll give yuh!"

"An' I'll give you!" Esther viciously hooked feet into shoes. "Such a bust, yuh'll go flyin'! C'mon, Davey!"

"Waddayuh wan'?" He looked from one to the other with a stunned, incredulous stare.

"I'll give yuh kendy," Esther wheedled.

"Yuh will not!" Polly interposed.

"Who's askin' you, Piss-in-bed?" She seized David's arm. "C'mon, I'll show yuh w'ea tuh take me."

"W'ea yuh goin'?" He held back.

"Downstairs inna terlit, dope! Only number one. Srooo!" She sucked in her breath sharply. "Hurry op! I'll give yuh anyt'ing inna store."

"Don'tcha do it!" Polly exhorted him. "She won't give yuh nott'n! I'll give yuh!"

"I will so!" Esther was already dragging him after her.

"Leggo!" He resisted her tug. "I don't want—" But she had said anything! A vision of bright-wheeled skates rose before his eyes. "Awri'." He followed her.

"Shame! Shame!" Polly yapped at their heels. "Ev'y-body knows yuh name. He's goin' in yuh terlit!"

Cringing with embarrassment, he hurried across the threshold to Esther's side.

"Shoddop! Piss-in-bed! Mind yuh own beeswax!" She slammed the door in her sister's face. "Over dis way."

A short flight of wooden steps led down into the muggy yard, and a little to the side of them, another flight of stone dropped into the cellar. At the sight of the nether gloom, his heart began a dull, labored pounding.

"Didntcha know our terlit was inna cella'?" she preceded him down.

"Yea, but I fuhgod." He shrank back a moment at the cellar door.

"Stay close!" she warned.

He followed warily. The corrupt damp of sunless earth. Her loose shoes scuffed before him into dissolving dark. On either side of him glimmered the dull-grey, once-white-washed cellar bins, smelling of wet coal, rotting wood, varnish, burlap. Only her footsteps guided him now; her body had vanished. The spiny comb of fear serried his cheek and neck and shoulders.

—It's all right! All right! Somebody's with you. But when is she—Ow!

His groping hands ran into her.

"Wait a secon', will yuh?" she whispered irritably.

They had come mid-way.

"Stay hea." A door-knob rattled. He saw a door swing open—A tiny, sickly-grey window, matted with cobwebs, themselves befouled with stringy grime, cast a wan gleam on a filth-streaked flush bowl. In the darkness overhead, the gurgle and suck of a water-box. The dull, flat dank of excrement, stagnant water, decay. "You stay righd hea in de daw!" she said. "An' don' go 'way or I'll moider you—Srooo!" Her sharp breath whistled. She fumbled with the broken seat.

"Can I stay outside?"

"No!" Her cry was almost desperate as she plumped down. "Stay in de daw. You c'n look—" The hiss and splash. "Ooh!" Prolonged, relieved. "You ain' god a sister?"

"No." He straddled the threshold.

"You scared in de cella'?"

"Yea."

"Toin aroun'!"

"Don' wanna!"

"You're crazy. Boys ain't supposed t' be scared."

"You tol' me y'd give anyt'ing?"

"So waddayuh wan'?" In the vault-like silence the water roared as she flushed the bowl.

"Yuh god skates?"

"Skates?" She brushed hastily past him toward the yard-light, "C'mon. We ain't god no skates."

"Yuh ain'? Old ones?"

"We ain' god no kind." They climbed into the new clarity of the yard. "Wadduh t'ink dis is?" her voice grew bolder. "A two-winder kendy staw? An' if I had 'em I wouldn' give yuh. Skates cost money."

"So yuh ain' god?" Like a last tug at the clogged pulley of hope. "Even busted ones?"

"Naaa!" Derisively.

Despair sapped the spring of his eager tread. Her smudged ankles flickered past him up the stairs.

"Hey, Polly!" He heard her squeal as she burst into the kitchen, "Hey, Polly—!"

"Giddaddihea, stinker!" The other's voice snapped.

"Yuh know wot he wants?" Esther pointed a mocking finger at him as he entered.

"W'a?"

"Skates! Eee! Hee! Hee! Skates he wants!"

"Skates!" Mirth infected Polly. "Waddaa boob! We ain' god skates."

"An' now I don' have to give 'im nott'n!" Esther exulted. "If he wants wot we ain' got, so——"

"Aha!" Aunt Bertha's red head pried into the doorway. "God be praised! Blessed is His holy name!" She cast her eyes up with exaggerated fervor. "You're both up! And at the same time? Ai, yi, yi! How comes it?"

The other two grimaced sullenly.

"And now the kitchen, the filthy botch you left last night! Coarse rumps! Do I have to do everything? When will I get my shopping done?"

"Aaa! Don' holler!" Esther's tart reply.

"Cholera in your belly!" Aunt Bertha punned promptly. "Hurry up, I say! Coffee's on the stove." She glanced behind her. "Come out, David, honey! Come out of that mire." She pulled her head back hurriedly.

"Aaa, kiss my axle," Polly glowered. "You ain' my modduh!" And snappishly to David. "G'wan, yuh lummox! Gid odda hea!"

Chagrined, routed, he hurried through the corridor, finding a little relief in escaping from the kitchen.

"Skates!" Their jeers followed him. "Dopey Benny!"

He came out into the store. Aunt Bertha, her bulky rear blocking the aisle, her breasts flattened against the counter was stooping over, handing a stick of licorice to a child on the other side.

"Oy!" She groaned, straightening up as she collected the penny. "Oy!" And to David. "Come here, my light. You don't know what a help you've been to me by getting them out of bed. Have you ever laid eyes on such bedraggled, shameless dawdlers? They're too lazy to stick a hand in cold water, they are. And I must sweat and smile." She took him in her arms. "Would you like what I gave that little boy just now—ligvitch? Ha? It's as black as a harness."

"No." He freed himself. "You haven't got any skates, have you Aunt Bertha?"

"Skates? What would I do with skates, child? And in this little dungheap? I can't sell five-cent pistols or even horns with the red, white and blue, so how could I sell skates? Wouldn't you rather have ice-cream? It is very good and cold."

"No."

"A little halvah? Crackers? Come, sit down awhile."

"No, I'm going home."

"But you just came."

"I have to go."

"Ach!" she cried impatiently. "Let me look at you awhile—No? Take this penny then," she reached into her apron. "Buy what I haven't got."

"Thanks, Aunt Bertha."

"Come see me again and you'll have another. Sweet child!" She kissed him. "Greet your mother for me!"

"Yes."

"Keep hale!"

X

SPIT someone?

He glanced up and backward overhead. To the north and south the cogged spindle of the sky was an even stone-grey.

—Dope! Ain't spit. Hurry up!

Umbrellas appeared. The black shopping bags of hurrying housewives took on a dew-sprent glaze. Inside their box-like newstands, obscure dealers tilted up shelves above the papers. As the drizzle thickened the dull façades of houses grew even drabber, the contents of misty shop-windows indeterminate. A dense, soggy dreariness absorbed all things, drained all colors to darkness, melted singleness, muddied division—only the tracks of the horse-cars still glinted in the black gutter as whitely as before. He felt disgusted with himself.

—Wet on my shirt, hair, gee! Two blocks yet. Giddap!

Rain had coated sidewalk and gutter with a slimy film.

On flattened tread, he jogged cautiously homeward, ducking under awnings when he could, skirting the jutting stoops. Not too drenched, he reached his corner.

"Run! Run! Sugar baby! Run! Run! Sugar baby!" Sheltered from the downpour, children in the dry covert of hallways relayed the cry—a mocking gauntlet for those who hurried in the rain. There were several such bantams snugly crowing in his own doorway. One or two of the faces belonged to those who had sat on the curb while Kushy had told about the canary. Resentfully, he fixed his eyes before him and ran up the iron stairs of the stoop. He wasn't going to talk to them at all. But as he was about to enter the hallway one of them stepped in his path—

"Hey, you're Davy aintcha?"

"Yea." He looked up sullenly. "Waddayuh wan'?"

"Dey's a kid lookin' fuh yuh."

"Yea," another chimed in. "W'it' skates he had."

"Fuh me? A kid w'it' skates?" His heart bounded with incredulous joy. Sudden warmth gushed through every vein. "Fuh me?"

"Yea."

"Leo? Did he say he wuz Leo?"

"Leo, yea; futt flaw, sebm futty fi'. He's a goy."

"So wad he wan'?" eagerly.

"He says comm op righd away."

"Me?"

"Yea, he wuz jost lookin'—"

But David had already leaped down the stairs and was sprinting through the rain toward Leo's house. Up the stoop he went, proudly, as though Leo's call had saturated the fabric of his spirit with a tingling, toughening glow, as though his being were pursed into a new shape of assurance. Here also children crowded the hallway, but he brushed by them without a word or a moment's hesitation. He was Leo's friend! And he climbed the obscure stairs without a wisp of fear. At the top floor, he stopped, looked about—all the shadowy doors were closed.

"Hey Leo!" he sang out, and the boldness of his own voice surprised him. "Hey Leo, w'ea d'yuh live?"

He heard an answering voice and almost immediately after, a door splayed out a fan of light.

"C'mon in." Leo stepped out.

"Leo!" David would have hugged him if he dared. "Yuh called me?"

"Yea, it begun to rain, so I come back. Didn' wanna get me skates all rusty."

"Gee, I'm glad I comm home!" David followed him into the kitchen.

"I wuz just wipin' 'em." Leo sat down on a chair, picked up an oily rag at his feet and began vigorously polishing the various parts.

"Yuh all alone." He found a seat against the wall.

"Sure."

"Hoddy yuh ged in yuh house?"

"W'it' a key, hodja t'ink?"

"Gee!" admiringly. "Yuh god a key of yuh own 'n' ev'y t'ing?"

" 'Course. See dat shine?" He lifted the gleaming skate.

"Gee, you know how."

"Yuh do dis ev'y day, dey never get rusty on ye."

"No. But look w'ad I brung ye, Leo." Heart leaping with delight he held out the two candies.

"Gee!" Leo hopped up with alacrity. "W'ot kind?"

"A emmend an' pineapple."

"Oh, boy! Bot' of 'em fuh me?"

"Yea." He found himself regretting he had not accepted the other tid-bits his aunt had offered him.

"Yer a nice guy!" Leo set the chocolates on the table. "W'edja git 'em?"

"Aintcha gonna ead 'em?" He asked eagerly.

"Naw, I'm savin' 'em fuh later. I wanna eat sumpt'n else foist."

"Oh! My a'nt ga' me 'em—Gee! I fuhgod tuh tell yuh. She owns a kendy staw."

"No kiddin'! W'ea does she live?"

"Wey down in Kane Stritt. But *you* c'n go easy—yuh god skates."

"Sure let's go dere sometimes—maybe we c'n cop a whole box of jelly beans. D'ja get any gum drops?"

"No," self-reproachfully. "I coulda—Gee!"

"Dey're good." Leo had put down the skates and gone over to the bread box on a shelf beside the sink. "Me fuh sumpt'n t' eat." He drew out a loaf of bread. "Want some?"

"I ain' so hungry." He felt suddenly shy. "Id's oily yed."

"Wot of it?" He began undoing the printed waxed-paper about the bread. "I eats w'en I wants tuh."

"Awri'." Leo's independence was contagious.

"Got sumpt'n good too," he promised, going over to the ice-box. "Sumpt'n we don' have ev'y day."

While Leo ferreted among the dishes, David stole blissful glances about him. It gave him a snug, adventurous feeling to be alone in a whole house with someone so resourceful as Leo. There were no parents to interfere, no orders to obey—nothing. Only they two, living in a separate world of their own. Nor were goyish kitchens so different from Jewish ones. Like his own, this too was a cubical room with stove, sink and washtubs flush against the walls. And the walls were green, and the white curtains, hanging from taut strings across the window-frames, sere with too much washing, and the flowered linoleum, scuffed like his own. Both were equally scrubbed and tidy, but where David's kitchen had a warm tang to its cleanliness, Leo's had a chill, flat odor of soap. That was all the difference between them, except perhaps for a certain picture in the shadowy corner at the further end of the room—a picture that for all of David's staring would not take on a reasonable shape because the light was too dim.

"Is she got a reggiler big canny staw?" Kneeling before the ice-box, Leo had been buttering bread. And now he pushed several objects from a large platter onto a small one. "Ice-cream poller too?" He arose.

"My aunt? Naa. She god just a—" He broke off, gaped at what Leo had placed on the table. In one of the plates was a stack of buttered bread, but on the other, a heap of strange pink creatures, all legs, claws, bodies—"Wod's dat?"

"Dese?" Leo snickered at his surprise. "Don'tcha know wat dis is? Dem's crabs."

"Cre—? Oh, crebs! Dey wuz green-like, w'en I seen 'em in a box on Second Evenyeh—"

"Yea, but dey a'ways gits red w'en ye berl 'em. Dey're real good! Gonna eat some?"

"Naa!" His stomach shrank.

"Didntcha ever eat 'em?"

"Naa! Jews can't."

"Cheez! Jew's can't eat nutt'n." He picked up one of the monsters. "Lucky I ain' a Jew."

"No." David agreed vaguely. But for the first time since he had met Leo, he rejoiced in his own tenets. "Hoddayuh ead?"

"Easy!" Leo snapped off a scarlet claw. "Jist bite into 'em, see?" He did.

"Gee!" David marveled.

"Here's some bread an' budder," Leo offered him a slab. "Yuh c'n eat *dat*, cantchuh? It's on'y American bread."

"Yea." David eyed it curiously on accepting it. Unlike his own bread, this slice was neither drab-grey nor brown, but dough-pale and soft as paste under the finger tips. Where the crust on the bread his mother bought was stiff and thick as card-board, this had a pliant yielding skin, thin as the thriftiest potato paring or the strip one un- wound from a paper lead-pencil. And the butter—he tasted it—salt! He had never eaten salt butter before. However, pulpy and briny though the first mouthful was, there was nothing actually repulsive about it—

"We c'n eat anyt'ing we wants," Leo informed him sucking at a crushed red pincer. "Anyt'ing wot's good."

"Yea?" While he rolled the soggy cud about in his cheek, his eyes had lighted on the picture again, and again were baffled with shadow.

—A man. What? Can't be.

"An' I et ev'y kind o' bread dey is," Leo continued proudly. "Aitalian bread-sticks, Dutch pummernickel, Jew rye—even watchuh call 'em, matziz—matches—" He snickered. "Dey're nuttin but big crackers—D'ja ever eat real spigeddi?"

"No, wod's dat?"

"De wops eat it just like pitaters. An' boy ain' it good!" He rubbed his belly. "Could eat a whole pailful by me- self. We usetuh live nex' door to de Aglorini's—dey was Aitalian—"

—Like my picture too—in my house—with the flowers. Is something else if you know. Have to know or you can't see.—

"An' Lily Aglorini usetuh bring in a big dishful fuh me and de ol' lady. Dat wuz w'en me ol' lady give 'em cakes when she woiked in a ressarran'. On'y wot cheese dey put in—Holy Chee! No wonner guineas c'n faht wit' gollic bombs!"

—A man, for sure now. Has to be. Only his guts are stickin' out. Burning. Gee what a crazy picture. Even mine ain't so. But get mad if I ask—

"Wisht me ol' lady could make real Aitalian spigeddi—Hey!" He demanded abruptly. "Wotcha lookin' at?"

"N-nott'n!" David dropped guilty eyes. "W'ad's-" (—Don't, don't ask him!) "Gee!" He felt the shooting warmth of his own flush and stopped confusedly. (—Dope! Next time listen!)

"Wot's wot?" he demanded staring at him with a wide-mouthed, suspended grin.

"A—yea!" Again, as on the roof, he found a convenient switch. "But I don' know hodda say. My modder, she says it— on'y id's Jewish." He grinned deprecatingly.

"Well, say it!" impatiently.

"W'ad's a orr—a orrghaneest? Dat's how she says id."

"A awginis', yuh mean! Awginis'—Sure! We got one in our choich. He plays a awgin."

"Yea?"

"Dey looks like pianers, on'y dey w'istles—up on top, see? Got long pipes an' t'ings. Didtcha know dat?"

"I didn't know fuh sure—on'y in Jewish."

"Yea, dat's wot it is. Anyhow, who wuz talkin' about choich?"

"Nobody!" With apologetic haste, "Spigeddeh yuh said."

"Yea!" offendedly.

"D'yuh go skatin' in de windertime, too?"

"Naw, wadda gink!" Leo struck at the lure. "How c'n yuh go skatin' in de winter time wit' snow on' de groun'? Yuh skate on slyin' ponds den. Dja ever make one a whole block long?" He expanded again. "We did—me and Patsy McCardy an' Buster Tuttle—it went all de way from Elevent' to Stevens Street."

"Gee!" David relaxed again.

"An' Lily Aglorini tries to slide on it an' bang!" The crab shell cut a red arc. "Right on her can! Wow! She went a whole block wit' her legs stickin' up innee air."

—Guts like a chicken, open. And he's holding them. Whiskers he's got, or no?

"An' den de hawse falls on it and de cop trows ashes

on it. But didn' me and Patsy kid de shoit off her 'cause
she wuz wearin' red drawers."

—Don't look any more, that's all!

But Leo had flicked his gaze over his shoulder. "Oh!"
He asked in resentful surprise. "Is zat all yuh tryin' to
look at?"

"No I wuzn' tryin'! Hones'!—"

"Yes, yuh wuz, don' tell me," disgustedly. "At's twicet
now yuh wuzn' even listenin'!"

"I didn't mean—" He hung his head.

"Well, go on!" The crab crunched under exasperated
teeth. "Take a good look at it, will yuh!"

"Kin I?"

"Dat's w'at its fuh! Course yuh c'n!"

He slid apologetically from the chair, walked over.
"Oh, now I see," He gazed up at it intently. "It ain' w'at
I t'ought." The man *was* bearded, but instead of holding
his bowels in his hand, he was pointing at his breast in
which the red heart was exposed and luminous.

"Wadjuh t'ink it wuz?"

"Couldn' see good," evasively.

"Dintcha ever see dat befaw?"

"No."

"'At's Jesus an' de Sacred Heart."

"Oh! What makes it?"

"Makes wot?"

"He's all light inside."

"Well 'at's 'cause he's so holy."

"Oh," David suddenly understood. "Like him, too!" He
stared in fascination at the picture. "De man my rabbi
told me about—he had it!"

"Had w'a'?" Leo drew abreast of him to look up.

"Dot light over dere!"

"Couldnda had dat," Leo asserted dogmatically. "Dat's
Christchin light—it's way bigger. Bigger den Jew light."

David had turned around to face Leo, but now he
stopped, stared at the opposite wall. Directly above his
chair all this time the same bearded figure had been hanging. Only this time David recognized him. He was made
of flesh-tinted porcelain, and with what looked like baby's
diaper around his loins, hung from a glazed black cross.
"Dat's him?"

"Sure! Yuh seen *him* befaw, dintcha?"

"Some place, yea. But I didn' know he wuz righd over me." With a feeling of dread he eyed the crucifix. "Oncet I seen him in a 'Talian funeral store. He's a'ways wit' nails, ain't he?"

"Yea." Leo took another slice of bread.

"But I didn' know dat wuz a—You ain' gonna git mad, will yuh if I ast you?"

"Naw!" And a second crab. "Ast me!"

"W'y is dat dish on his head busted over dere?" He pointed to the crucifix. "An it ain' busted over—hea." He pointed now to the picture.

"Ha! Ha!" he guffawed through a mouthful of food. "Aintcha de sap, dough! Dat ain' a dish; dat's a halo! Dintcha ever see a halo? It's made ouda light! An dat ain' a dish, neider," pointing to the figure on the cross, "dat's his crown o' t'orns—sharper'n pins wot de Jews stuck on him."

"Jews?" David repeated, horrified and incredulous.

"Sure. Jews is de Chris'-killers. Dey put 'im up dere."

"No?"

"Sure, youse!"

"Gee! W'en?"

"Long ago. T'ousan's o' years."

"Oh!" There was a little comfort in remoteness. "I didn' know." A hundred other questions clamored at his tongue, but fearful of further revelations, he stifled them. "Gee! He's light inside and out, ain' he?" was all he dared offer.

Without bothering to answer, Leo licked his fingers and reached for the candy. "Ummm! Ammonds! Oh boy, bet I could put about ten o' dese in me mout' at oncet. D' yuh ged 'em ev'ytime yuh go dere?"

"I don' go dere."

"Yuh don'? Cheez, I'd go dere ev'y day if me a'nt owned a canny staw!"

"It's too far." He was answering because he knew Leo expected an answer, but within him, something strange was happening, something that swelled against his sides and bosom, that made his palms damp and clinging, his speech muffled and reluctant as in drowsiness.

"Wot of it?" Leo sucked the fragments from his teeth. "Grab a hitch on a wagon w'y dontcha?"

"Didn't see none." He wondered how Leo had failed to hear the pounding of his heart.

"Didn't see none!" he snorted incredulously. "On Avenue D—dat's w'ea yuh went—dintcha?"

"Yea." The strangeness was grown almost as palpable as phlegm to his breathing. Terrific desire seemed to sicken him. He must ask! He must ask!

"Well, wudja go dis time fuh?"

"Skates. I taught maybe—" his voice trailed off.

"Didn' she have 'em?"

"No." He found himself resenting the thorny brightness of Leo's voice—a brightness that kept pricking him always out of a passionate yet monstrous lethargy.

"Make 'er buy 'em faw ye den. Dat's wud I'd do. She'd gid 'em cheaper 'n you—"

"Leo!"

"W'a?"

"C-can you gibme—" A slow finger rose and pointed "G-gib me—one o'— one o'—" He couldn't finish.

"One o' wa-a-a?" Leo clapped hand to chest in sharp surprise.

"Yea." He felt giddy.

"Me scappiler? Cheesis, yuh mus' be nuts! W'at de hell d'ye wan' 'at for?"

"I jos' wan' id."

"Are you tryin' to git funny er sumpt'n." Suspiciously.

"No!" He shook his head vehemently. "No!"

"Well, yer a Jew, aintcha?"

"Yea, bud I—"

"Well, youse can't wear 'em—dontcha know dat? Dey're fer Cat'licks."

"Oh!"

"Ain't got one anyhow—nutt'n 'cep' a busted rosary, me ol' lady foun' in a ressarint."

"Wot's dot—rosary—" eagerly. "Can I have?"

"G'wan, will yuh! Are yuh bugs or sumpt'n?"

"I c'n giv yuh a lodda cakes an' canny—even my penny —See?" He displayed it.

"Naw! It ain't mine an' it costs way more'n dat. Cheez! If I'd aknown you wuz such a pain inna can I wouldna let yuh come up hea."

"I didn' know." He could feel his lips quivering.

"Aw yuh never know!" There was a harsh silence.

"Yuh wan' me tuh go donn?" His voice was desolate.

"Aw yuh c'n stay hea." Leo growled. "But stop bein' a pain inna prat, willyuh?"

"Awrigh'," humbly, "I won' ask no more."

"Is yer a'nt stingy too?" Leo irritably ignored the apology.

"No." He thrust desire and disappointment from him and gave all his attention to Leo. "She gi's me anyt'ing."

"Well why don'tchuh do like I said—ast her to buy a pair of skates and den sell 'em to ye on trust, or sumpt'n."

"Maybe I'll ask her nex' time."

"Sure. Go dere every day till she gizem tuh yuh, dat's de trick."

"I don' like id."

"Wot, astin' her?"

"No. Her kids. Dey ain' her real kids."

"Step-kids yuh mean."

"Yea."

"Wotsa matter wid 'em? Snotty or sumpt'n? W'yncha gib'm a poke innie eye?"

"Dere bigger'n me. An' dey holler on yuh an' ev'yt'ing."

"Yuh ain' scared of 'em are yuh? Don' let 'em bull-doze yuh!"

"I ain' so scared, but dere doity an' wants yuh tuh go donn in de cella' wit' 'em an' ev'yt'ing."

"Cellar?" Leo grew interested. "W'yntcha say dey wuz goils."

"Yea, I don' like 'em."

"D'ja go down?" Grinning avidly he bent forward.

"Yea."

"Yuh did? Wadja do—no shittin' now!"

"Do?" David was becoming troubled. "Nutt'n."

"Nutt'n!" Leo gasped incredulously.

"No. She ast me to stay inna terlit an' she peed."

"Yuh didn' do nutt'n an' dey ast yer to come down de cella' wid 'em?"

"On'y one of 'em ast me." Confusedly he fought off Leo's insistence.

"Oh!" he crowed, "Wot a sap!"

" 'Cause, she said she'd gib me anyt'ing."

"Wee, an' yuh didn' ast 'er?"

"I wanned skates—a old pair," he beat a lame retreat. "I t'ought maybe she had."

"Oh, boy, wot a goof! Yuh said yuh wuz ten yea's old. Oh, boy! She letcha see it?"

"W'a?" He refused even to himself that he guessed.

"Aw! don' make believe yuh didn' know—" his legs spread. "De crack!"

"Dey wuz fight'n in bed," he confessed reluctantly, and then stopped, wishing he had never begun.

"Well, wot about it?" Leo exacted the last scruple.

"Nutt'n. Dey wuz just kickin' wit—wit deir legs, and so—so I seen it."

"Chee!" Leo sighed, "No drawz?"

"No."

"How big 're dey?"

"Bigger'n me—about so moch."

"Bigger'n me?"

"No."

"Jist me size—oh boy! Wa' wuz ye scared of, yuh sap! Dey ain't yuh real cousins. Oh boy, if me an' Patsy was dere—oh boy! Wish he wuzn' in de camp. Oncet we took Lily Aglorini up me house on elevent', an' we makes believe we wus takin' de exercise up de playgroun' in St. Joseph's —bendin', yuh know? An' we bends 'er over a chair an' takes 'er drawz down—oh boy! Hey! Le's go dere, you'n' me—waddaye say? I like Jew-goils!"

"Yuh mean yuh wanna do—yuh wanna play—" David shrank back.

"Sure, c'mon, le's bot' go now!"

"Naa!" His cry was startled, "I don' wanna!"

"Watsa madder—ain't dey dere now?"

"N-no. But I—I have to go home righd away." He had slid off his chair. "Id's dinner time."

"Well, after den—after yuh eat!"

"I have tuh go t' cheder after."

"Wot's dat?"

"W'ea yuh loin Hebrew—from a rabbi."

"Cantcha duck it?"

"He'll comm to my house."

"C'mon anyways, 'fore yuh go t'dat place."

Again that warping globe of unreality sphered his senses. Again the world sagged, shifted, Leo with it—a stranger. Why did he trust anything, anyone? "I don' wanna," he finally muttered.

"Waa! I t'ought yuh wuz me pal!" Leo sneered in ugly disgust. "Is zat de kind of a guy y'are?"

David stared sullenly at the floor.

"I'll tell yuh wot," the voice was eager again. "Yuh wanna loin t' skate, dontcha! Dontcha?"

"Y-Yea."

"Well, I'll loin yuh—right away too. I'll lenja mine w'en we goes over dere—one skate apiece."

"Naa! I'm goin' down."

"Aw, yuh sheen—C'mon I'll give yuh some o' me checkers—got a whole bunch o' crownies. Look, you don' have t' do nutt'n if yuh don' wanna. Us'll go togedder, but you kin stay outside. I ain' gonna do nutt'n—jes' give 'em a feel."

"I don' wanna." David was at the door.

"Yuh stingy kike! Yuh wan' it all yerself, dontchuh? Well, don't hang aroun' me no maw, 'er I'll bust ye one! Hey!" As David opened the door. "Wait a secon'!" He grabbed his arm. "C'mon back!" He dragged David in. "C'mon! I'll tell yuh wot I'll give yuh—"

"I don' wan' nutt'n!"

"Jis' wait! Jis' wait!" Still calling to David, he dragged a chair across the kitchen to a dish-closet above the pantry, climbed up on the pantry ledge, and reaching over his head, drew down a dusty wooden box, which he dropped on the table as he climbed down. In shape it resembled the chalk boxes in school and even had the same kind of sliding cover. But it couldn't be a chalk box, for David had just enough time to glimpse the word God printed in bold, black letters—though curiously enough the letters were printed right above a large, black fish. But before he could bend closer to spell out the smaller letters under the fish, Leo, with a "Hea's wotchuh wanted," had whipped the cover off. Inside lay a jumble of trinkets, rings, lockets, cameos. Leo fumbled among them. "Yea, yuh see dis?" He pulled out a broken string of two-sized black beads near one end of which a tiny cross dangled with a gold figure raised upon it like the one on the wall. "Dat's de busted rosary me ol' lady foun', dere's on'y a coupla beads missin'. I'll give it tuh yuh. Come on it's real holy."

David stared at it fascinated, "C'n I touch id?"

"Sure yuh c'n, go on."

."Does id do like de one around' yer neck?"

"Course it does! An' it's way, way holier."

"An' yuh'll gib me id?"

"Sure I will—fer keeps! If you take me over witchuh t'morrer it's all yourn. Waddaye say, is it a go?"

Head swimming, he stared at the definite, unwinking beads. "It's a-a go." He wavered.

"Atta baby!" Leo whirled the beads enthusiastically. "Look! you don' have t'do nutt'n'—jis' lay putso like I tol' yuh. Dey ain' yer real cousins—wadda you care— oh boy! W'eadja say yuh took 'er?"

"I didn' take her—she took me." Now that he had consented dread gripped him in earnest.

"S'all de same—w'ea?"

"In de cella'—huh cella'—unner de staw w'ea dere's a terlit."

"We'll take 'er dere too huh?"

"Butchuh have t'go troo de staw."

"W'a? Cantchuh sneak in troo de outside?"

"De staw?"

"No de cella'."

"I don' know."

"Sure ye c'n! Door's open I bet— Wot time we goin?"

"W'ad time yuh wan'?"

"In de mawnin—oily—ten o'clock. How's zat? I'll meetcha front o' yer stoop wit' me skates. Awright?"

"Awri'," he consented dully. "I'm goin' donn now."

"Wot's yer hurry?"

"I have tuh. I have tuh go home."

"Well, so long den! An' don' fergit—ten o'clock."

"No—ten o'clock."

He went out, the door closing on Leo's final chuckle. And he groped toward the dim stairs and descended. Hope and fear and confusion had drained him of thought. His mind was numb and suspended now, as though he were drowsy with cold. Without word, without image, he sensed again the past and the future converging on the morrow. And either he found a solvent for his fears or he was lost. He walked into the dreary rain as into an omen. . . .

XI

HIGH morning.

His nervous gaze wandered from frosted window to clock and returned to the window—

"Turn, turn, turn, little mill-wheel," her voice barely more articulate than a hum, sounded curiously distant now. "Work is no play, the hours steal away little mill-wheel." With only her legs hanging in the kitchen—the slack soles of worn house-slippers curving down from bare heels—his mother sat on the sill wiping the outside of the pane. Under the vigorous strokes of the rag the snowy shores of cleaning powder parted rapidly from a channel to a gulf. And in the widening clarity first her throat appeared, straight between lifted chin and old blue dress, and then her face, pale and multiplaned and last her brown hair catching the sun in a thin haze of gold. "Turn, turn, turn, little mill-wheel. . . ."

—Wish she came in! Get scared when she sits like that. Fourth floor too—way, way, down! If she—! Ooh! Don't! And that window it was. Can see the roof from here. Yes, there where they—Son-of-a-bitch!—there where they looked.

Irritably, he shifted his gaze to the other window, which was open and looked out on the street. The sky above the housetops, rinsed and cloudless after rain, mocked him with its serenity. In the street, too far below the window to be seen, the flood of turmoil had risen with the morning and a babel of noises and voices poured over the sill as over a dike. The air was exceptionally cool. Between the drawn curtains of an open window across the street, a woman was combing a little girl's hair with a square black comb. The latter winced every time the comb sank, her thin squeals skimming above the intricate crests of the surging din of the street.

—Louse-comb. Hurts. Sticks in your head . . . wonder if—wonder if—! Late now, but dassent look out. If he's waitin'—But can't be there any more. Must have went. Sure! Now is—? Nearly ha' past eleven. Ten, he said. Must have went. Ha' past eleven and ha' past eleven and all is well . . . Where? Watchman then, in book. Three A, yea. Clock. Someplace had. Hickory dickory, dock. Clock. Never had. But—wheel—what? Once . . . Once I . . . Say again and remember. Hickory, dickory—crazy! Why do they say? Hickory, dickory, wickory, chickory. In the coffee. In a white box for eight cents with yellow sides. In a box. Box. Yesterday. God it said and holier than Jew-light with the coal. So who cares? But that fish, why was that fish? Couldn't read all the little letters. Wish I could. Bet it tells. The beads made you lucky, he said. Don't have to be scared of nothing. Gee if I had!—but don't want it, that's all. Ain't going. And that funny dream I had when he gave me it. How? Forgetting it already. Roof we were with a ladder. And he climbs up on the sun —zip one two three. Round ball. Round ball shining— Where did I say, see? Round ball and he busted it off with a cobble and puts it in the pail. And I ate it then. Better than sponge cake. Better than I ever ate. Wonder what it's made of—Nothing, dope! Dreams. Just was dreaming—

The squealing window stalled his fitful revery.

"There!" His mother sighed with relief as she ducked under the sash. "Now all it lacks is another good rain to ruin it."

His gaze followed hers. Spotless now, the panes betrayed no more of their presence than a jeweled breath —except where tiny flaws spiraled inexplicable hues into warping rarities.

"They're all clean," he said with emphatic reassurance. "You don't have to sit outside any more."

"So they are," she washed her hands under the tap. "I'll hang my curtains up now." And reaching for the towel. "You don't intend to go down today, do you?" Her smile was perplexed.

"Yes, I do!" he protested warily. "But later, maybe."

"Do you know," she unfurled the curtain, "you've been acting of late almost the way you did in Brownsville when you clung to my side like pitch. And how you feared that short flight of stairs! That can't be troubling you now?"

"No." He suddenly felt cross with her for cornering him. "There's nothing to do down stairs. I told you."

"What's happened to all your friends." Her rapid hand wound the curtain string about a nail. "Have they all moved?"

"I don't know—don't like them anyway."

"Ach!" Despairingly. "The skein the cat's played with is easier to unravel than my son. Yesterday it rained from noon till nightfall—you flew up and down those stairs like a butter-churn. And after supper, between Albert's bed-time and yours you sat there beside that window as fidgety as a bird—only more silent. I saw you!" She lifted a mildly admonishing finger. "Now what's the trouble? What is it?"

"Nothing!" He pouted moodily. "Nothing's the matter." But his brain was already at work martialing the excuse.

"I know there is," she insisted gravely. "This morning you woke when I did—seven—and yesterday too. But yesterday you would have spurned your breakfast if I had let you in your eagerness to go down. To-day—Now what is it?" A faint impatience colored her tone.

"Nothing." He shook her off.

"Won't you tell your mother?"

"It's just a boy." He *had* to answer now. "He—he wants to hit me. He said he would if he caught me. That's all."

"A boy? Who?"

"A big boy—Kushy—his name is. Yesterday, they said there was a nickel in the cellar on Tenth Street. And they all ran over and tried to get it up. And Kushy said he didn't get it up because I pushed him."

"Well?"

"So he and his partner want to hit me."

"Oh, is that all? Well, that's easily remedied."

"Why?" The momentary satisfaction with himself changed into uneasiness. "What are you going to do?"

"I'll go downstairs with you."

"No!"

"Why, of course I will. I'm not going to let anyone coop you up here all day. You just point them out to me and I'll—"

"No, you can't do that," he interrupted her desperately.

"If you come down and you talk to them, they'll call me 'fraid-cat'!"

"What does that mean?"

"It's a cat that's afraid."

"Well, aren't you?" she laughed. "Aren't you just a little afraid?"

"I wouldn't be if they weren't so big." He tried to deepen the channel of digression. "You ought to see how big they are. And there's two of them."

"That's all the more reason I ought to go down with you."

"But I don't want to go down!" Emphatically. "I want to stay here."

"You're just pretending."

"No, I'm not! I'm hungry."

"I offered you cake and an apple," she reminded him—"Only a little while ago when I began cleaning."

"I wasn't hungry then."

"Ach!" she scoffed, glancing at the clock. "You're like those large bright flies in Austria that can fly backwards and forwards or hover in the air as though pinned there. And what will you do after you're fed—stay here till the Messiah comes?"

"No. I'll run to the cheder then, and play in the yard and wait for the rabbi."

"I wonder if you're telling the truth?"

"I am too." His injured gaze held steady.

"Well." She sighed. "What would you like—a jelly omelette?"

"Yum! Yum!"

"Very well then." She smiled fondly. "As long as I can get you to eat, I feel safe—That's our only sign." Her breasts heaved, nostrils dilating suddenly. "But why do I sigh?" And going to the china closet drew out several dishes. "I think washing windows makes me do that. It always reminds me of Brownsville and that window with the scrawls and faces on it. I wonder if they've cleaned it yet?" She went to the ice-box. "Is it only a year and a half now since we moved out? It seems further away than five cents will take one." And she fell silent, cracking the eggs against the edge of the bowl.

—Gee lucky for me I thought. Can fool her any time.

She don't know. So I won't get that black thing in the box. So who cares!

The gas-stove popped softly under the match. Lifting a frying pan from its hook on the wall, she set it on the grate—but a moment later pushed it to one side as though she had changed her mind, and walked to the street-window.

—Hope he ain't! Hope he ain't yet. (His startled thought overtook hers)

"Good!" she exclaimed triumphantly and pulled her head in. "I struck it just right. Sometimes I do believe in premonitions."

—Aaa! Wish his horse fell or something!

"Now I can feed all both my men," she laughed. "This is a rare pleasure!" And she hurried back to the ice-box.

He stiffened, ears straining above the rapid beating of eggs. Presently, he heard it, deliberate, hollow, near at hand. The knob turned—The harsh, weather-darkened face.

"I'm prepared for you!" she said cheerfully. "To the second."

Cheeks distended in a short customary puff, he dropped his cap on the wash-tub, leaned his new whip against it. David glanced toward the stove. His mother had dropped the old broken one between the stove and the wall. His father went to the sink and began washing his hands.

"Tired?" She asked as she poured the golden foam into the hissing skillet.

"No."

"Jelly omelette and dried peas, will that please you?" He nodded.

"Is he still out?"

"That's why I'm late again." He wiped his hands. "Till tomorrow."

"Ach! I'll be so glad when he returns."

He met her gaze with dark impassive eyes, slumped down into a chair. "How is it the heir is home?" His thin lips twitched, warping the flat cheek.

—Don't! Don't tell him! Ow! (But he dared not even look at her imploringly)

"Oh!" she said lightly. "There's someone after him. One of the bigger boys in the street."

—Aaa! She went and told him. Hate her!

His father's incurious gaze turned from her face to David's like a slow spoke. "Why?"

"Something about money in a cellar. They were all trying to get it up—how I don't know. But the other— what did you call him?"

"Kushy," sullenly.

"Yes. This Kushy claimed he pushed him just when he lifted it—the money. Isn't that the way it goes? Wouldn't you know the usual childish quarrel?" She bent over the stove. "Only if it's over money, it's not so childish, I guess."

"A cellar?" The hardening of his voice was barely perceptible. "When?"

—Ow! He thinks I told!

"Yesterday, you said, didn't you, David?" Her back was turned. "You don't mind if we have the coffee I brewed this morning?"

"Yes," David's scared eyes rose to the gloomy pressure of his father's. "I—I just said yesterday."

His lean jaw had tightened. Drooping eye-lashes banked his smouldering anger. "What else?"

And though David knew the question was directed at himself—

"Why that's all!" His mother laughed, as though surprised at her husband's interest. "Except that I offered to go down into the street with him, since the other had threatened to strike him." She brought the omelette and coffee pot to the table. "But he refused—said they'd call him—what?—frait-katz." And surveying the spread. "Have I got everything here I want? Water, yes. Dear God!" She exclaimed as she went to the sink. "Isn't it time I learned to speak English?"

—Knows it wasn't! (David steeled himself) Knows it wasn't yesterday! Knows I lied!

But, "Hmph!" his father grunted, relaxing. "He's big enough to take care of himself." There was a strange, veiled look of satisfaction on his face.

"What if they're bigger than he is, Albert?" Protesting mildly, she set the dewy, glass pitcher on the table. "You know, they—"

"Still," his father interrupted her, "if they're too much for you, tell them I'll take the horsewhip to them if they touch you." And glancing up at her, began slicing the bread. "Just to scare them." He added.

"Yes." She sat down uncertainly. "But there's no use kindling a feud out of a threat—especially an urchin's threat."

He made no reply. And during the interval while food was being passed—

—Took my part. Gee! (Mechanically, David lifted his fork) She told him and he knows I lied and he took my part. What did I—fooled him maybe? Naaa! How he looked at me—

"You know," his mother tilted her smile meditatively, "it's almost seven years since I came off that ship, and I've never quarreled with anyone yet. I wouldn't like to start now."

"It would be miraculous if you did." His voice was level. "Your life has been as sealed as a nun's."

"Not quite so sheltered, Albert." She looked faintly piqued. "Compared to yours, yes. But pushcart peddlers when I do my marketing—ach!—they deal out words as sharp as mustard-plasters—more than they do onions or carrots. . . . There's nothing like a pushcart peddler."

—Sure he knows. Bet a million. In the wagon he was then. Just when Kushy got up. And she told him it was yesterday. And he wouldn't say—

"But what I mean is how shall I answer one of these native shrews if she shakes the clapper of her tongue at me in English? Cheh! Cheh! Cheh! They chatter and hiss like a sieve full of ashes."

Thin as a shadow or a breath on water, a rare smile slackened his father's face. "Merely cheh, cheh back at her in Yiddish."

"But I'd feel so humiliated," she laughed.

"Then don't answer her at all. Grow red and march off with your head in the air."

"Ach!" She looked at him curiously. "That's too easy. But if I had worked in a shop the way Bertha had, I could have known by now—What a smoke comes out of *her* mouth."

"Smoke indeed! It blinds you." His lips barely curled.

"Does it? To me, especially since she has the candy store, she sounds like running water—"

"A muddy spatter."

"Or sand. I was going to—"

"In one's teeth."

"You're witty to-day." Her curiosity seemed permanently fixed in her face.

His jaw tightened again and he reached for his coffee.

—Is he my friend? No. Can't be. 'Course he ain't. But why if— Oh! He knows I lied. That's— Dope! Eat! They'll see!

"And you speak so well, because you learned among goyim?"

"In part. But when I ate in beer-saloons to save money for your passage, I used to listen to the others—In beer saloons they speak loudly. And one day I grew bold enough to answer one who was drunk. And he thought I was too. Then I knew I had made a beginning."

"Good kosher food they gave you." Her look had changed to quiet sympathy.

"When you spend fifteen cents a day to keep the breath in your body, you get over asking if the rabbi's blessed your meat."

"I'm glad you had a stronger stomach than him who ate the duck-dinner so cheaply. And wrote home about it—and died of it."

"Humph!"

"Will you have time for a nap to-day?" Reaching over she patted his hand—as rare a gesture as his smile.

His face darkened. He cleared his throat. "I still have an hour."

David slid from his chair. "Can I go down now, mama?"

"Wait, I still have a pear to give you."

"Can't I eat it when I go down?"

"And you feel safe now?" She went to the ice-box.

"Yes." He glanced hurriedly at his father.

"And you're sure you don't want me to watch awhile at the window?" She slipped the chilled, glossy fruit into his hand. "Until you've found out whether this Kushy is there or not?"

"No. I'll just run to the cheder." And as his mother bent down to kiss him—

"Keep out of mischief," the barest overtone hardened his father's voice. "Hear me?"

"Yes, papa." Once more their glances grazed. He reached out for the knob.

"And don't forget to eat your pear," she reminded him. "It's as sweet as—" her voice blurred with the closing door.

He hurried down the stairs, and reaching the street glanced about hastily. No sign of Leo anywhere. Good, that was a relief! He would go to the cheder now and stay in the cheder yard till the rabbi came. He swerved around his father's milk wagon, crossed the gutter obliquely and turned west—

The sudden whirr of wheels behind him—now louder on the side-walk now roaring momentarily over the hollow buckle of a coal chute—

"Hey you!"

There was no need to turn.

Leo, cap in hand, angry mouth open in flushed face, hooked about him, braked his course with a grinding skate, eagle-spread to a stop. Standing on his skates, he looked almost full grown, his bright blonde head towering above David's.

"Yuh runnin' away aintcha?" His snub nose crinkled into an angry sneer. "W'yntcha tell me yuh didn' wanna go—'stid o' makin' me hang aroun' here all day!"

"I didn't say I didn' wanna go." David looked up, smiling placatingly.

"Well, w'yntcha come down? Wotcha waitin' fuh? Yuh noo we said ten o'clock."

"I had to stay upstehs till my fodder came—Yuh see? Dot's his wagon." He pointed to it, hoping Leo would supply the connection he knew didn't exist.

"Well, wot of it?" After a glance.

"Nott'n. But my modder wuz sick, so I had to stay—"

"Aw, bullshit! Yuh know yuh lyin'!"

"No, I ain'!"

"Awri'! c'mon if yuh comin'. Be'faw yuh have to go to dat udder joint—w'utever yuh calls it."

"I can't. I have to go dere now. Wonna pear?"

"Wot!" Leo ignored the proffered fruit. "After ye sez yuh wuz goin'? Don' try t' back out on me or I'll take me skates off an' beltchuh one. Listen! I ain' gonna do nutt'n! I tol' yuh I wuzn'—wotcha scared of?"

"My a'nt's dere too," he countered feebly. "In de kendy staw. She'll know."

"How'z she gonna git wise, yuh sap? We'll duck 'er,

dontcha see? Git 'er down de cella' w'en nobuddy's lookin'. We won't try it if she's watchin'! C'mon! I'm gonna give yuh one o' me skates." And drawing out his skate-key, he slipped down to the curb. "Sit down, will ye? Yuh know wot I got fer ye, dontcha? Sit down!" And as David crouched down beside him. "Iz zat fer me?" He reached for the pear.

"Yea."

"Looks like a good one." He licked his lips.

"Yuh god id witchuh?"

"W'a'?" Between mouthfuls. "Yuh mean de ros'ry? Sure, w'eadja tink it was, up de house?" Leaning sidewise he drew a few beads from his pocket. "See 'em? Dere yours, don't fergit." And thrusting them back, busied himself with the left skate—kicked it free. "G'wan, now, put dis on. I'll loin yuh how to go—don't git scared. Give us yer hoof. Like dat, see?" The strap tightened below David's ankles, next the clamps gripped his sole. "Shove with yer udder foot—watch me. Now slide! 'At's it! Atta baby. Let's go! 'At's it!" He flung the fruit-core into the gutter, headed toward Avenue D. "We'll git dere in a minute wit' a good hitch—wait'll yuh see."

"Gee!" The new freedom of motion was exhilarating. "Gee, id's fun!"

"W'at'd I tell ye!" he urged jubilantly, "Go on, I tell ye, it's easy as pie—Hey, you'll loin real fast!"

They rounded the corner, Leo still barking encouragement.

XII

LAUGHING, jabbering breathlessly, they had been hauled within two blocks of Kane Street when the wagon turned from their route. They let go. The gilded mortar and pestle loomed up—so near! Sobered in an instant, David lagged behind.

"Dontcha wann jos' skate back now?"

"Naw!" Leo exploded eagerly. "Wotcha t'ink we came hea fuh? Nex' block, ain' it?"

"No," listlessly. "It's de one after, but I—"

"C'mon den." Leo forged ahead. "C'mon, will ye!"

There was nothing to do but follow. His blood, which a moment before had been chiming in bright abandon, deepened its stress, weighted its rhythm to an ominous tolling. They reached the corner they were to turn—

"Hey, Leo," David plucked at his sleeve, "w'en yuh gonna gimme it?"

"W'a'?" impatiently.

"Dat ros'ry, watchuh called it, in yuh pocket?"

"Aw, w'en we gits dere!" Leo waved him off vehemently. "Wadda-yuh worryin' about? Show us de joint foist, will ye?"

"On dis side." He led the way cautiously. "See w'ea de ices barrels is—by de daw?"

"Yea," Leo scrutinized the terrain, "It's jist a liddle dump, ain' it? W'ea did ye—Wow!" His voice dropped in suppressed elation. "Didn' I tell ye? Dere's de steps under de staw right like I t'ought!" He nudged David abruptly. "Foller me, will ye."

Heart-beat rising to a panicky thumping, David trailed him across the street. It seemed odd to him that those standing on the stoop or passing by were not aware of his growing terror.

"Take de strap off." Leo kneeled to undo his own.

"Watchuh gonna do?" Crouching beside him, David undid the buckle with clammy fingers.

"Nutt'n! Don' git scared!" His whisper sounded strange against the loud background of the street. "Let's gitcher clamp." He unloosened it, arose with both skates in his hand. "C'n ye see anybody in de staw?"

"Can't see good f'om hea."

"Well, sneak over dis way. Jeez! don' be dumb. Keep goin'."

From his momentary vantage, David squinted hurriedly into the shady doorway across the sunlit gutter. "My a'nt's dere!" He whispered, quickening his step. "An I t'ink it's Polly."

"Dey's *two* goils dere!" Leo countered sharply as they passed. "I seen 'em meself stannin' in front."

"Yea, but I don' know de odder one."

"An she wuzn't dere, wot's 'er name? De one dat went down witcha? No? Well, let's walk back." They retraced their steps.

"No. Couldn't see 'er anyhow. We better go back."

"Aw hol' yer hosses, will ye! Can't chuh wait here a minute till she shows up?" Disgruntled, he flung himself back at the railing beside a stoop. "You'll have lots o' time, wotcha worryin' about—Hey, duck! Duck, will ye!" He pushed the startled David behind him. "Dey're comin' out! Stay dere or dey'll see ye!" And after a few seconds, "Cheez, dat wuz close, but dey're goin' de udder way now. Awright." He stepped to one side, giving David room to view them. "W'ich one is her sister?"

"De skinny one," David stared furtively after the two girls. "Dat's Polly in de yeller dress wit' dat black ma'ket bag."

"Wot about dem, huh?" Leo's blue eyes widened signif-icantly. "W'en dey come back."

"Naa!" He drew away. "I don't know 'em—de odder one."

"Aw, balls!" Leo see-sawed between anger and ardor. "You ain' game fer nutt'n, dat's wot! C'mon, Le's take anudder look. Maybe dat Est'er goil is in dere now." He dragged David past the store again. No sign of her. There was only Aunt Bertha sitting behind the counter reading a newspaper. "Aw, Jesus, wot luck!"

"Yuh see, Est'er ain' dere." David felt that he could argue more boldly now. "An' if we stay hea, de kids an' ev'rybody'll be watchin' us."

"Aw, de hell wit' 'em! De street's free, ain' it? Who's gonna stop me from walkin' here, I'd like t' know." Never-theless his lower lip drooped disappointedly. "She lives in de back, don' she?"

"Yea," he offered the information eagerly. "In de back o' de staw. Yuh have t' go troo w'ea my a'nt is sittin', an' yuh can't do dat."

But his advice, instead of convincing Leo of the fu-tility of all further effort merely spurred him one. "I can't, huh?" was his defiant answer. "Well, watch me! C'mon!" He stepped off the curb.

"Wotchuh gonna do?" He hung back in consternation.

"Jist don't let dat fat dame see ye," Leo took his arm confidingly, "An do wot I say, get me?" They stopped before the stoop of the next house west of the candy store. "Now w'en nobody's lookin', sneak over to dat cella' and duck down. I'll lay out, see?"

"Naaa!"

"G'wan! Be a nice guy." He became even more confiding, "Yuh want dat ros'ry, dontcha? Well, you giz down—I comes after yuh. I'll give it t'ye right dere."

"Den wotcha gonna do?"

"Den we giz inta de yard." His candor was painstaking. "An' if she's dere, all right, an' if she ain' dere all right— I gives it t'ye anyway. An' we goes home."

"An dat's de last?"

"Honest t' Gawd! Now g'wan, sneak over."

With a scared glance about, David sidled to the cellar stairs beneath the store window.

"Duck!" Leo's side-mouthed signal.

He slipped down the steps. A moment later, Leo followed, brushed past him toward the closed door.

"Hope t' shit it opens." He leaned against it. "Yea!" in subdued triumph as the door swung back.

The sudden draft through the cellar bore with it the familiar dank. At the opposite end of the corridor of the dark, the oblong of light was narrow—the door slightly ajar. "C'mon," Leo whispered stealthily. "Don' make no noise."

"Yuh gonna gimme id now?" He wavered at the threshold.

"Sure! Soon as we gits in de yard." He shut the door again as David stepped into the clinging dark. "Don' make no noise, will ye? Wea's de shit-house?"

"Over by dere." The seamless dark swallowed the pointing hand. "Dere's a daw. Waddayuh—"

"Sh! Folly me. Maybe she's in it."

"She don' never comm down by huhself."

"Let's look anyways."

He groped after. . . A bar of murk in a wall of gloom. "Iz zat it?"

"Yea."

A pause. "No one's dere."

"No."

"Hey, hoddy ye say it again?" Leo's breath was warm on his cheek. "Dem Jewish woids I ast yuh on de hitch? "Wa?"

"Yuh know! Shine—shine?"

"Shine maidel," grudgingly.

"Yea! Shine maidel! Shine maidel. An' de udder. Took —tookis, ain' it?"

"Yea."

"Le's go."

They moved forward. Where the wedge of brightness pried the narrowly-opened door, Leo stopped, peered out into the yard. "She live up dere w'ea dem steps is?"

"Yea."

"Hea take dis, will yuh—'faw we giz out." A skate clicked faintly as he thrust the strap into David's hands.

"W—waddayuh wan' I shuh do?" David held it off as if it had become dangerous.

"Nutt'n. Don' do nutt'n." Leo urged reassuringly, "Jis' come out wit me and make believe you takin' it off— make a noise, see? If she's in de back, jis' say I'm yuh frien' an I lets yuh use me skates an' ev'yting. An' nen I'll talk to 'er."

"An' nen yuh'll gimme it?"

"Didn' I say I would? C'mon." He glanced boldly around at the gaping windows. "Nobody's watchin'." And both climbed up into the brilliant yard.

"Now!" He whispered, dropping to one knee and drag- ging David down beside him. "Like yuh jis' come—a lotta noise. G'wan!" He clashed his skate on the ground. "Yea! Gee!" His voice rose in loud, pretended bluster. "Can I beatchoo? Wow! Anytime! Two blocks? Wut's two blocks. I'll race yuh ten—Say sumpt'n fer Chris' sake!"

"Yea! Yea!" David contributed quaveringly. "Ten blocks, yuh can't. Yea! Yea!"

"G'wan I c'n too!" His bragging grew even louder. "Wad- dayuh wanna bet! A dolla'? Le's see yer dough—" The click of the latch in the door. "Sure I c'n. Run ye ragged—"

Midway up in the widening groove of the doorway, two eyes peered out. A loose pigtail swung into sun. Esther, picture-magazine in hand, looked out startled and angry.

"You!" To David. "Waddayuh doin' in my yod."

"N-nutt'n, I—"

"Hello, Kid!" Leo pleasant and unfeazed.

"Shott op!" Indignantly. "I'll tell my modder on— Ma—!"

"Hey!" Leo's quick cry cut her short. "Wait a secon'

will ye?" And when she paused to pout. "Dis guy's yuh cousin ain' he?"

"So wadda you wan'?"

"Well," in grieved surprise. "Can't he come into yaw yard?"

"No, he *can't*". She thrust her head out emphatically. "W'y didn't he come troo de front? Mama!"

"I'll tell yuh." Leo strove desperately to engage her. "Give us a chanct, will ye?"

"W'a'?" in contemptuous disbelief.

"It's like dis," Leo drew near the steps, lowered his voice confidentially. "He's too bashful."

"Wot's he bashful about?"

"Yuh see," he grinned up at her, winked. "He had to do sumpt'n, dat's all—you know wot!"

"I don' know wot." Appeased somewhat, she was still emphatic.

"Dintcha Davy? Yuh had to go t' de terlit."

"Yea I had tuh." David followed the lead. "I had tuh go."

"Ye see?" Leo rested his case soberly. "Dat's why."

"So wyntcha comm beck to duh frond?" Suspicion still lingered in her face.

"Aw!" Leo flipped an admiring grin up at her. "He says he had a real good-looker fer a cousin. So I says I don' believe it. So he says I'll show 'er t'ye. Boy!" His confirmation was intense. "Oh boy!"

"Pooh!" Shut eyes and tossed pig-tails. "Smott alick."

"Sure he did, dintcha, Davy?"

"Yea," He grinned uneasily at the ground.

"See? So I says if she's a real good-looker like you says I'll let 'er use me skates."

"So who wants yuh skates."

"Yuh don'?" He swung an injured look at David, "Wadja say she did fer?"

"I—"

"He says to me," his crestfallen voice blocked David's. "He says she wants t'loin, so I says, awright—if she's a real good-looker I'll loin 'er. Cheez! Wot a guy! I t'oughtcha wuz me frien'."

"Aaaa! Yuh a lodda hoss-cops!" Esther's disbelief wavered—She smiled. "Yuh bedder ged oud, 'faw I tell my modder on ye."

"Now I know w'y y'ast me t'come hea." Leo still clung fast to his resentment at David. "Yuh jis' wanned t' lend me skates to's yuh could come up hea easier, dat's all. Yer a fine guy! I'm goin'!" He moved in no particular direction.

"Who's skates are dey?" She took a step down the wooden stairs. "Yaw's?"

"Sure dey're mine. Ball-bearin's' n' ev'yting. Go like lightnin'. Yuh wanna loin?"

"Wat's yuh name?"

"Leo—uh—Leo Ginzboig."

"You ain' a Jew!"

"Who ain'!" In his vehemence he still had time to dart a triumphant glance at David. "Cantcha tell by me name?"

"Aaa, yuh a lia'," she giggled.

"W'at d'ye wanna bet? Dontcha believe a guy?"

"Yea, g'wan!"

"I can't talk so good 'cause we alw'ys lived over on de Wes' side. But I c'n say sumpt'n. Wanna hea' me?"

"Yea!" derisively.

"Shine maidel, dere! Dat's wutchoo are. see? Tookis! Mm! Oh boy! Ain' dat good."

"Oooh! W'otchoo said!"

"Tookis. Wud of it?"

"Eee!" Her shrill squeal was more delighted than shocked.

"Hey, woddy yuh say." Leo became earnest. "W'y d'ntcha come down into de yard an' skate?"

"Naa, I can't."

"Dontcha wanna loin?"

"Naa!"

"Sure yuh do! I'll loin yuh in one lesson. C'mon!"

"Naa, can't skate hea." She threw a glance over her shoulder. "My modder'll call me."

"Well, you c'n go up if she wants yuh," Leo suggested generously. "Nobody's gonna stop ye."

"Yea," her eyes sought the windows overhead. "Bot ev'ybody c'n look."

"Oh, I see! Yea. Well w'y dontcha come outside, see? We'll wait fer ye in de street—nobody'll watch yuh." And when he saw that she was wavering, he indicated David and himself arrogantly. "Us two is goin' outside, see? We'll wait fer ye acrosst de street. Waddayuh say?"

"Mmm!"

"Den we skates yuh aroun' de block—w'ea nobody knows us. Wotchuh scared of? C'mon, 'faw he has t' go t' dat place."

"W'a' place?"

"You know—wadduh yuh call it, Davy?"

"Yuh mean cheder?"

"Yea."

"Bot *you* don' go dere!" she jeered.

"Well, *he* does." Leo grinned. "So yuh better shoot! C'mon Davy!" Linking his arm into David's, "We'll be waitin' fuh yuh outside across de street, don' fergit!"

A coy giggle was the only response they got.

XIII

"CHEEZIS, kid!" Leo whispered excitedly as they plunged into the gloom. "We got' er goin'—W'y'd'ntcha tell us she had tits on 'er?"

"Yuh gonna gimme it now?" In the reeling of his mind, only one thing held out hope of steadfastness.

"Aw take yer time, will ye!" Leo rebuffed him impetuously. "You'll git it, watchuh worryin' about? I don' wanchuh backin' out on me soon as yuh grabs it— Cheeziz!" he marveled. "You're nuts, ye know? Dont'cha wanna give 'er a feel 'er nutt'n?"

"No!" The darkness hid the revulsion of his features if not of his voice.

"Oh, boy, watch me den!" He pulled the door back cautiously. "Wait'll we gets 'er down—oh boy! Give us it now, will ye." As they stepped out he snatched the skate from David's slackening fingers. "And stay hea a secon', see!—I'll lay chickee." He crept warily up the stairs. ',C'mon!" A peremptory hand curved upward.

David ran up the stairs, joined him as he sneaked away from the store. Together, they crossed the street.

"Wait fer 'er here." He stepped under the shadow of an awning. "See 'er yet?" His head bobbed from side to side in his eagerness. "Jesus, if she don' come out I'm gonna beat de piss outa— W'eas me skate key? Le's walk past—Naw! Wonder w'en dat udder liddle—dat sister o' hers 'll come back? Better go dat way w'en she comes out—so's we don' run into— Hey!" His hand's quick thrust jarred the inert David. "Dat's her! She sees us! C'mon!"

Esther stood in the doorway. With a single sly wag of his head, Leo made for the west corner, went a short distance, turned abruptly and hurried across the street. David trailed him.

She approached with a casual, leisurely air.

"C'mon, kid!" He went to meet her. "Let's git dese on."

"I don't think I wanna." She tilted her nose indifferently.

"Sure yuh do." He swamped her with enthusiasm, "Waid'll yuh feel dat wind blowin' aroun' ye w'en' yuh goin' fas'—right up yer drawz."

"Aaa, hee, hee!" she snickered, shaking off his ardor. "Shot up, you!"

"Sit down on dat stoop, will ye?" he drawled masterfully, at the same time pushing her against the steps behind her. "So's a guy c'n put 'em on fer ye!"

"I don' wanna!" she squealed, kicking her legs out in gratified protest. "Yuh gonna lemme fall—I know!"

"G'wan, who's gonna letcha fall!" He throttled the coy jerking of her foot, rested it on his knee. "Hol' still, will yuh! I gotta pull 'at skate in a liddle." The skate-key dropped beside him to the pavement. "Wait a secon'!" Head cocked, facing Esther, he bent sideways almost to the ground, picked it up, dropped it again—

"Oooh!" she squealed reproachfully. "Stop dot!" Both hands snatched the curtain of her dress tight below her knees. "Yuh doidy!"

"Who me?" Leo straightened innocently. "I wuz jis' lookin' fer me skate-key."

"Yuh wuz not—you!"

"Aw, hey! Cantcha b'lieve a guy—? Give us yer udder leg, will yuh, yer seein' t'ings." And as he tightened the clamps of the other skate. "Gonna lemme put me key in yer lock?"

"Wadje say?" She leaned forward.

"I says, d'ye care if I put me key in yer lock?"

Her eyes bulged. "Aw!" she shrieked, flinging herself

back. "Watchoo said!" And giggled behind her palms and yanked her dress down again. "Shott up!"

"Wat'd I say?" unflinchingly.

"*You* know!" Her two pigtails rayed out from her vigorously wagging head. "Shame on you!"

"Aw! Hey, Davy," he smirked significantly. "Wot'd I say?"

"I don' know." David returned his gaze apathetically.

"Dere y'are! I wuz jis' talkin' about me skate-key— Come on!" He scrambled to his feet. "Give us yer hands."

"Eee!"

"Co-om o-on!" He lifted her to her feet, and— "Whoo!" as the skates slid under her. "Gotchuh w'ea I wantchuh." He grabbed her below buttock and breast, steadying her. "Oh boy!"

"Leggo!" She thrust him back, lost balance and, "Eee!" held on to him. "Dey'll see!"

"Awri', don' git leary!" Leo became the grave instructor. "Jis' take Davy and me's shoulder, see?" He pushed the unwilling David to the other side. "Dat's it! Hol' onna us!"

"Slow now!" she warned, "Or I won't—"

"Yea! Yea! We'll take it easy! C'mon, wake up, Davy! Giddap!" And as both began trotting. "Dat's it! Atta baby! I'll hol' yuh if yer goin' on yer—you know—oh boy! Gid otta de way, kid." He brushed a boy from the path. "Liddle bassid can't stop us, kin he! Atta kid! Aintchoo goin' dough. Gittin' any wind up der yet. Atta kid!" He plied her with short yelps of flattery and encouragement.

As they neared the corner, Esther's shrieks grew shriller and shriller, Leo's cries more ardent, his supporting arm lower and more lingering. To the left of them, David, aware she was hardly holding him, jogged on in silence, listening with dull apprehension to their jangled excited cries. At the corner, Leo halted them breathlessly—

"Ain' dat fun?"

"Yea, ooh!"

"Yuh wanna go faster?"

"No-o!" provocatively.

"Sure ye do— Hey, Davy!" with sudden solicitude. "Yer all plugged out, aintcha?"

"Me? Uh—"

"Sure y'are!"

"He ain' so big like you." Esther seconded him. "I can't hold so good."

"Yea." Leo agreed, and solemnly, "Yuh better stay right hea, Davy, an' wait fer us. I'll pull her meself."

"Awri'," sullenly.

"Naa, let 'im comm too," Esther repented her rashness.

"G'wan!" He grabbed her hand. "He don' wanna! Whe-e-e!" He sirened like a fire-engine, pawed the ground. "Hol' fast!" And before she could tear from his grasp he was off—Esther squalling rapturously after.

XIV

DAZED with a kind of listless desolation, he watched them speed toward the opposite corner, saw Esther whirled round and grabbed, and then both spin screeching out of sight. He slumped as though his own gathering foreboding dragged him down, slouched aimlessly to the curb and sat down.

—I know . . . I know . . . I know . . . (Like a heavy stone pried half out of its clinging socket of earth, sluggish thought stirred and settled again) I know . . . I know . . . They're going to. So . . . Don't care. I know.

Incurious eyes glided over the shallow glare of the street, caught on slight snags of significance, dwelled, returned, dwelled, shuttle-like. There were several boys across the street, playing for steel marbles which they rolled beside the curb. They played with the large ones, the twentiers, and paid each other off with small ones, as big as steel beads. He watched them awhile, and then his mind returned to its own misery.

—Getting scared . . .

—Wonder where they are? Could have gone all around the block already. Twice. Two blocks, even. Went away, maybe? Naa staying there. I know. Hope they never come— Will though . . .

—Getting scared . . .

—Shut up! I ain't! So if he gets her—down there—

what? What'll I do? I'll ask. Just ask, that's all. I'll say, give it to me, them lucky beads, c'mon! You said you would before. And now he'll give it to me. Has to. Then what? Go someplace else. So I'll go. And I'll take them, yea. And I'll look in and I'll let them down slow, slow, that's right— Gee! And if I get it so it'll be all right. I'l do it all the time, so it will be all right.

—A twentier I'll try to get—a twentier-light. It was bigger the first time, a quarter-big-light. But even if it's a twentier, I'll be glad. Even if it's only a tenner-light, I'll be glad. Could get it light. He said like his. In and out. Wonder how big his is. Didn't ask. But never have to be scared even if it's only a tenner-light. And have to watch out too—don't lose them. Where'll I put? Lots of places. Could hide them on roof. Top of chimney where no one looks. Yea—but! Fall in, maybe. Gee! And hee! Lady finds them in the stove. Look! Ooh! What! A cross! Oy! Gevalt, like my aunt says. Naa. Better in the house. Under the bed—no. Mama cleans. Then where then . . . behind looking—yea! Big looking glass on the floor. Every time I looked, yea, could remember—

"Talk like I said!" The sharp undertone meshed with no cog in the humming street.

He started, turned around.

"Hullo, Davy!" Leo, boldly impassive, now carried the skates. Esther beside him lifted guilty eyes from the ground, squirmed, scratched painstakingly under a pig-tail. "I tolju he wuz sleepin'. He's a'ways sleepin', aintcha Davy?"

She giggled.

David rose, watched them uneasily.

"We had some skate, didn' we Esther?" Leo prompted her.

"Yea." And as if by rote. "Yurra good ronner."

"Sure I am." Exuberantly. "But y'oughta see me w'en I'm goin' real good! An' c'n she skate, Davy! Wait'll you see 'er do a spread eagle—way out, dat way!"

"Shottop!" She blushed, shuffled.

There was a pause.

"Uh—I gotta go, Esther." Abruptly he took David's arm.

"Aintcha—? Aintcha—?" David was startled. "Wea yuh goin'?" Automatically, he fell into step as though he had been braced against a body charging at him and been missed. "Home, yuh goin'?"

"Naw!" Leo led him two or three paces off, and with elaborate modesty whispered loudly in his ear. "I gotta take a piss."

"Oh!"

"See I tol' 'er dat!" Leo hissed the last words, nudged him. "See!" And called back noncommittally. "Yuh goin' in de staw, aintcha Esther."

"I don' know," she shrugged in huffy indifference.

"C'mo-on," he drawled at her and smirked when he saw her melting, winked. "Le's go, Davy!" His urgent hand hurried David toward the store again. "Here she comes after us!"

Out of the corner of his eye when he turned, David glimpsed her leisurely trailing behind them. Reaching the cellar steps, they halted, Leo glancing around under the guise of fumbling with his skates. A few houses away Esther too had stopped and was watching them with a queer, mixed simper—as though she were flaunting her vacancy.

"Don' watch 'er!" Leo snapped. "Hop down!"

Frightened now to the very core, sure of the approaching crisis, David stumbled down the steps. Before he reached the bottom, Leo's feet came pattering after, and Leo with a "Hurry up!" threw back the door. Together, they entered. The door swung to. In the rank gloom nothing had changed but the notch of light bitten from the further dark, which was wider.

"Cheezis!" Leo's clashing skates heightened the exultation of his voice. "Tol' yuh I'd git 'er goin'! Didn' I? Didn' I? Oh, boy! Wut we didn' do aroun' at corner'! Did I feel 'er! Oh, boy! Looka—" hastily. "You don' know nutt'n about it, see? Don' fergit now—I'm jis' takin' a piss!"

"Y-yea."

"Oh, boy! oh, boy!" His restless feet patted the earthen floor. "Wait'll she gits down here."

(Ask him now!) "Yuh—are yuh—?"

But as though the dark were a medium for his thought —"Yea! Yea!" Leo interrupted him irritably. "Cantcha wait'll she gits down! Cheez, I fergot!" He hurried past the toilet. "Lemme try some of dese daws faw she

comes—see if dey—" And yanked at one after another
of the grey doors of the storage-bins. "Oh, boy!" As one
swung open. "Lot's o' room in hea. See dat?" He motioned
for David to draw closer. "Lot's o' room ain' it?" There
was a small, clear space between the doorway and the
shapeless black masses of furniture piled high in the rear.

"Now one fer you!" He clawed the doors across the
murky alley, found another that opened. "Now if some-
buddy comes, see, you gits in hea—her ol' lady er
sumpt'n. Soon as ye hear 'em you go psst! an' duck! See?
But stay near dat daw so's yuh c'n see 'em faw dey sees
you—den duck an' psst! Catch on? An' nen we're safe
—all of us!" He glanced at the open doorway. "W'ea de
hell is she? An' looka, w'en she comes down wotever I
says, jis say yea, see? An' look dumb, dat's all, jis' look
dumb! An' I'll give it t'ye like I said—jus w'en she
comes. Now don' fergit." He motioned to the cellar bin,
"Dat's w'ea you runs, if—Sh!"

Both had heard it—the scrape of feet outside.

"Lay low!" Leo shoved him before him into the bin,
shut the door, "Sh!" He peeped out through a crack in
the doorway. "Who de hell is it?"

Strumming silence. Only the sound of their breath in
the blackness. Behind him the hard edges, knobs, of piled
furniture, and higher something yielding, sack or mat-
tress. Confused and formless memories. Again the scrape
of feet, cautious and approaching.

"Wonner if—cheezis, must be her! Hol' me skates!"
He pushed the door open a few inches wider, knifed
through and ran on tip-toe toward the yard-light.

Watching him through the bin-door, David froze in terror.

"Hey, c'mon!" Leo had flattened himself into the
shadow behind the door-jamb. "C'mon down, will ye.
We're hea." A pause. "C'mon kid." Again the persuasive
drawl. "You know me-e."

Feet scuffed outside, descended slowly into the oblong
of light. A short dress. Esther.

"No, I ain' gonna!" She balked on the last step.

"Awri' listen den! I wanna tell yuh sumpt'n."

"So tell me hea!" She peered into the dark.

"Look, yuh don' wan' me t'yell or nutt'n, do ye? Or
go outside w'ea ev'ybuddy c'n see us?"

"Hea den. I'll stay righd hea." She stepped down, toed the plank of the sill. "Now tell me."

"Aw, I can't tell ye hea!" Leo sounded both hurt and despairing. "Give us a chanst, will ye? Listen!" He took her arm. "We don' want dat sap back dere t' hea' wut I say—Hey, Davy!" Peremptorily. "Come out o' dere, will ye!"

David sneaked from the bin, edged closer.

"W'ea wuz he?" Esther eyed him furtively.

"Jis' inna back. Jis' inna back!" Leo pulled her toward him. "Now you stay hea." He turned to David severely. "I wanna talk t' Esther—Jis', a secon' Esther, dat's all!"

She followed Leo in. They brushed past David on the way, and floating by him, their faces in the murky air were staring and pale. Where the deeper gloom near the toilet half-dissolved them—

"No maw!" sharply from Esther.

"Ye ain' scared, are ye?" Himself wavering in the dark, Leo's husky voice was distinct. "Wit' me witchuh?"

"Aw!" irresolutely.

"Well, listen . . . now I wuz gonna . . . Whee! Oh, boy!"

"Stop!" Her loud hiss. "Tell me, or I'm goin' out!"

"Listen den. See dat bin? Waid'll I show ye." The door creaked faintly.

"Yea," suspiciously.

"Well, I sez t' him, yuh know who dat bin b'longs tuh? It b'longs t' Esther's ol' lady. She tol' me, I sez, see?

"So?"

"Den he sez, wot's inside? So I sez, wodjuh t'ink—candy!"

She tittered.

"Ain' he a sap!" Leo's amused snort joined her eagerly. "An' den I sez yuh know wut me an' Esther's gonna do? We're gonna sneak in an' find some—yuh know, chawklits, gum drops. He sez, yuh gonna gimme some? Sure I sez if we finds some— Weew! Esther!"

"Don'!" half-heartedly. "Yuh didn'!"

"Yes, I did! I did so! An' I sez lay chickee fer us— Mm! will ye— Eww!"

A silence.

"No!" protestingly. "So w'at?"

"So I sez . . . lay chickee fer us . . . an! . . . an! . . . so he sez . . ."

"Ooh!"

"He'll lay chick . . . Weew . . . Kid! Waddayuh say?"
A mumbling, A rustling . . .

"He'll watch. It's better in dere den hea'. Can't see us!"

"Uh!"

"Wait a secon'! I wanna git me skates. Hey Davy!"
Quick-footed, breathless he loomed from dark to half-
light. "Gonna git de candy like I tol' yuh. Hea!" As he
grabbed the skates from David's fist, his other hand flew
to his side. "Take it! Now lay putso!"

The slight rattle of a small heap suddenly grown in his
palm. *Them!* A shudder ran through him.

"Don' fergit!" Leo's voice sped off. "Till we comes!"

Stealthy gurgles, hissings, mutterings.

"C'mo-on!"

The bin-door creaked. Feet shuffled. Faint whines. And
the door creaked again, clicked. Only the barest of whispers now, stirrings blending with the dark's hum.

—Mine! It's mine! (The jerky throbbing of his blood
reiterated) Mine! I got it. Big-little-big-little-little-little-
big-busted. Gee! Him hanging— What!

A thin squeal seeped through door and dark. Esther's.

—Aaa! (Disgust filled him. He stumbled toward the
yard-light) By light go, can't hear! Right ones? (A sudden qualm of doubt. He scrutinized them) Yes, right
ones! Same! Didn't fool me. Out of the box with God.
Mine! (Convulsive fingers crushed them) Don't care! Ain't
scared! If I can make it! Ooh, if I can make it! Never
be scared! Never! Go on! No, wait! No, now! Where?

Darting eyes fastened on the snug niche behind the
open door. He squeezed in, pulled the door back as far
as it would go, and enclosed as in a cell, he squatted
first, then stretched his legs out altogether and leaned his
cheek against the slim airy bar of light cut twice by the
hinges.

—Hurry up! Look where it's dark, real dark . . .
Look. . . . No . . . No good. See too much yet, stops
it. Then shut then. Same thing. Like he said. It's inside
and it's out. Like him with the light-guts. Now keep. How
big did I—? Twentier I said. But not now. First you
have to get it. After it's a twentier. Like the light in the
hall, when I seen it. Gee, how I peed— Hurry up! So
now you're standing on them—only alone. Nobody else is

akey now. It's going to be all mine. Quarter I thought then
—bigger it was. But it's round, so better twentier. So shut
up! You're standing on them—you said that already.
On your knees. Feel how they were? How—burn—like.
Began to hurt just before Kushy wanted to fight and
papa came. Hurry up! Down, look down! Can you see?
Maybe. Nearly can't. But—Look! G'wan now! G'wan! 'Fore
it goes! Let it down! One is—is a little bead. Real easy!
Two is little bead. Faster! This—little. This—little This—
faster. And that—him now—right over it. Long enough?
Gee. Hope so! Right over!

Past drifting bubbles of grey and icy needles of grey,
below a mousetrap, a cogwheel, below a step and a
dwarf with a sack upon his back, past trampled snow
and glass doors shutting, below the gleam on a turning
knob and bird upon a lawn, sank the beads, gold figure
on the cross swinging slowly, revolving, sank into massive
gloom. At the floor of the vast pit of silence glimmered the round light, pulsed and glimmered like a coin.

—Touch it! Touch it! Drop!

And was gone!

—Aaa! Where? Where? Look harder! Bend closer! Get
it again! Again!

And would not reappear.

"I'm gonna get it," almost audibly. *"I am!"*

His teeth gritted, head quivering in such desperate
rage, the blood whirred in his ears. Like a tightened knot,
his body hardened, hands clenched, breath dammed and
stifled within him. He fished.

"I am!"

Now saliva drooled unheeded from his lips. Pent breath
pressed veins in anguished bulges against his throat. His
nostrils flickered scooping vainly at the air. And still he
sought the depths, strangling. Then darkness, swirling
and savage, caught him up like a wind of stone, pitched
him spinning among palpable drum-beats, engulfed
him in a brawling welter of ruined shapes—that parted
—and he plunged down a wailing fathomless shaft. A
streak of flame—and screaming nothingness.

The tortured breast rebelled, sucked up air in a
squealing gasp. He collapsed against the bin behind him,
leaned there with whirling senses . . . Slowly the

roaring shadows quieted. Cloudy air displaced the giddy dark like a fixed despair.

—Lost it . . . (Leaden-slow his thought) Lost it . . . Covered up all. . . . Cellar-floor dirty . . . Like the nickel then . . . Gone. Gone. . . .

A sound in the yard outside. Inertia's thick buffer about the mind muffled it. Again. He listened. The hiss of shoes, sleathily on the stone outside the door approaching. He sat bolt upright, staring at the crack between door and jamb.

—Who? Can't call!

Pricked ears sifted the depths of the shadowy corridor where Esther and Leo were— All was hushed.

—Hope they hear! Hope! Hope! Gee! Ow! Be still!

The steps drew nearer—Unblinking eyes glued against the bar of light, he stuffed the beads in his pocket, crowded back against the corner, dropped his jaw to breathe in silence. The careful steps drew nearer. For the briefest instant like a figure in a cramped panel, Polly, lips thrust out in scared curiosity, paused in the crack of light and vanished. Soft footfalls behind the door, she appeared again in the murky frame between him and the door-edge. He saw her advance into the cellar, lift herself on tip-toe and cock her head from side to side, listening—

Murmurs beyond. A muffled giggle.

—Aaa (He clenched his teeth against the inner fury) Why didn't they keep still! Polly had heard them!

"No! No maw!" Louder, "Leggo!" The unseen door banged open.

"Aw, hey!"

"No! Lemme oud!" A scuffling. "Lemmeee—Unh!" As though someone had butted her, Esther's cry ended in a terrified grunt. "Polly!"

"Eee!" her sister squealed. "You!"

For a moment all three seemed to have lost their tongues.

"Aw, it's only yer sister, ain' it?" Leo bolstered up a shaky voice with a clash of skates.

"Yuh wuz wit' him in dere!" Polly's voice was a mixture of gloating and disbelief.

"I wuzn'!" Esther's shrill cry rose furiously. "I'll give yuh in a minute!"

"I seen yuh! I seen yuh! I knew yuh wouldn' comm donn by yuhself. Waid'll I tell!"

"Hey, wait a secon'," Leo hastily took control. "Wea's Davy? He'll tell yuh wot we wuz doin'? Hey Davy! We wuz playin' a trick on him, see? He's in dere! Betcha million!" A bin-door creaked. "Hey Davy!" A pause. "W'ea de hell—"

"Aaa, Davy!" Polly sneered venomously. "Yuh cowid! Don't blame it on sommbody else, 'cause yuh can't fool *me!*"

"Who's tryin' t' blame it on somebody else!" Leo was nettled. "He's hea I tell yuh—someplace. Hey Davy!"

"He is!" Esther maintained stormily. "He wuz wit' us!"

"Hey, Davy! C'm out wea'ver y'are! C'mon." His voice rang through the cellar. "I'll bust ye one! Come on out!"

Shrunken with guilt and terror, David crammed himself deeper into the corner.

"He musta run away, de liddle bastid— Hey Davy!" He bellowed. "Ooo, waid'll I gitchoo!"

"Aaa, shod op!" Contemptuously from Polly. "Stop makin' believe!"

"Waddayuh lookin' at me faw?" Esther stormily.

"You know w'at!" Her sister answered significantly. "You know w'at."

"W'at!"

"Snot! Yuh wuz playin' bad in dat place wit' him! Dat's watchoo wuz doin'! Wit' dat bum! Yuh t'ink I don' know?"

"I wuz not!" Esther screamed.

"Yuh wuz!"

"Who's a bum?" Leo's voice bullying.

"Who else? You! You took her in dere, yuh rotten bum!"

"Don' call me a bum!"

"I will so—yuh rotten bum!"

"I'll slap yuh one, yuh stinkin' sheeny!"

"Me! Wotta you? Ooo!" Her voice trailed off into horrified comprehension. "Oooh, w'en I tell—He's a goy too! Yuh doity Crischin, ged oud f'om my cella'—faw I call my modder. Ged oud!"

"Yuh mudder's ass! Call 'er, I dare ye! I'll rap de two o' yiz!"

"You leave her alone!" Esther turned on him fiercely. "Ged odda you! Go on! Ged oud!"

"Aw, shet up!" He was stung. "Ye wuz in dere yeself —w'ut're ye takin' her side fer?"

"Ooo! Hooo!" Esther burst into a loud betrayed wail. "Ged oud! Waaa!"

"Ged oud, yuh doity Crischin!" Polly's screech swelled above her sister's bawling. "Doity bum, ged oud!"

"Aw righ'—" mockingly. "Keep yer drawz on! G'wan fight it out yerself." His voice retreated.

"Doity bum!"

"Sswt!" He whistled jeeringly from a distance. "Tell 'er wut I wuz doin', kid. Yuh jew hewhs! We wuz hidin' de balonee! Yaaa! Sheenies! Brrt!" He trumpeted. "Sheenies!" Skates clashed. The door slammed.

"Oooh! Hooo!" Esther's sobbing filled the cellar.

"Yuh oughta cry, yuh doity t'ing!" Polly lashed at her. "Good fuh yuh! Comm down wit' dat goyish bum in de cella'!"

"Y-y' ain' gonna t-tell." Esther whined brokenly. "He made me! I didn' wanna go!"

"Made yuh!" scornfully. "Mama said yuh wuz in de back o' de staw. Yuh didn't have t' comm down—if yuh didn' wanna! I'm gonna tell!"

"No!" Her sister lifted a frantic wail. "Didn' I stop him f'om hittin' yuh? Didn' I? Poppa'll kill me if yuh tell 'im! You know!"

"So led 'im!" Stonily. "Den yuh won' go wit' goys no maw. Yuh always callin' me piss-in-bed, anyway! So dere!"

"I'll never call yuh again, Polly! Never! Never in all my life!"

"Yea, pooh! I b'lieve yuh!"

"I won't! I won't!"

"Lemme go!"

"Don't tell! Ow!"

"Lemme go!"

David, petrified in his niche of darkness saw her drag the screaming Esther after her toward the cellar door.

"Don't tell! Don't tell!"

"Lemme go! Yuh hea?" Polly seized the door-knob for support, wrenched her other hand free. "I *am* gonna—"

"Eee!" Esther screamed. "Look! Look!"

"Wa?" In spite of herself.

"It's him! Him! Davy!"

He had scrambled to his feet, cowering—

"He made me! He brung him!"

Cornered, he tensed for an opening.

"You!" Esther screamed. "Now I'm gonna give yuh—rotten liddle bestitt! It's your fault!" And suddenly she struck out with both hands, caught him flush on the cheeks, clawed.

With a gasp of pain, he ducked under her arms, butted past her. She pursued, squalling with rage, collared him again, pounded his back and head. As if in a nightmare, he struggled, silently in the dark to tear himself free.

"Mama!" Polly's scream at the other end. "Mama!"

"Polly!" Esther's hold loosened. "Polly! Wait, Polly!" She flew after her sister. "Wait! Don't tell! Don't tell! Polly! Polly!"

Her frenzied cry ringing in his ears, he flung himself at the street door, raced up the cellar stairs. Without caring whether any one marked him or not, he leaped out into the street and fled in horror toward Avenue D.

XV

HE HAD run and run, and now his own breath stabbed his lungs like a knife and his legs grew so heavy, they seemed to lift the sidewalk with them. Tottering with exhaustion, he dropped into a panicky, stumbling walk, clawed at his stockings, gasping so hoarsely, people turned to stare. Only one thought in the screaming chaos of terror and revulsion his mind had fallen into remained unbroken: To reach the cheder—to lose himself among the rest.

—Like I never came! Like I never came!

Now he ran, now he walked, now he ran again. And always the single goal before him—the cheder yard, the carefree din of the cheder. And always the single burden:

—Like I never came! Like I never came!

Fourth Street. In the flat smear of houses, he descried, or thought he did, the edge of his own on Ninth. It quickened his flagging legs, quelled somewhat the tumult and the fierce yapping pack within him and behind.

—Near house; Don't go. Go round. But tired, all tired out. No! Go round! Go round!

At Seventh, he cut west, entered Avenue C, and at Ninth, turned East again, dragging his faltering legs cheder-ward. He must hold gnashing memory at bay. He must! He must! He'd scream if he didn't forget! A furtive glance at his house as he reached the cheder entrance. He slipped into the hallway, hurried through.

The cheder yard. Haven! Haven at last! Several of the rabbi's pupils were there. Loiterers, late-comers, elfin and voluble, they squatted or sprawled in the dazzling sun, or propped idle, wagging heads against the blank wall of the strict cube which was the cheder. His heart sprang out to them; tears of deliverance lifted so brimming high in his eyes a breath would have spilled them. He had always been one of them, always been there, never been away. Silently, fears relaxing in the steeping tide of gratitude, he came down the wooden steps, approached. They looked up—

"Yaw last!", said Izzy, languid and scrupulous.

He grinned ingratiatingly. "Yea."

"Aftuh me!" Solly severely.

"Aftuh me!" Schloimee.

"Aftuh me!" Zuck, Lefty, Benny, Simkee decreed.

"Awri!" He was only too glad to be lorded over— the token of their accepting him, the token of their letting him share their precious aimlessness, innocence, laughter. "Yea, I'm last. I'm last." And finding a place against the cheder wall, he squatted down. He focused his whole being upon them. He would not think now. He would only listen, only forget.

Solly was speaking—in his voice an immense and mournful yearning. "Wisht I had a chair like dat!"

"Me too! Yea! Wisht I had t'ree chairs, like dat."

Their amens were also mournful as if little hope inspired them.

"So yuh don't have to gib'm all, do yuh?" Izzy fought back despair. "If yuh don' wanna play fuh 'em, waddayuh wanna give 'im all, if yuh god so moch?"

"Cauthye I wanthyloo, dayuth w'y'." Benny was obdurate. Benny was also afflicted with a lateral emission—no word he uttered ever succeeded in reaching his lips, but instead splashed out through his missing teeth. But David was only too glad that Benny spoke so thickly. It meant that he had to concentrate all his faculties on what he said. In trying to divine Benny's meaning, one could forget all else. "If I blyibm duh ywully ylyod, den he wonthye hilyt me so moyuch, myaytlybe."

"Yea, he geds a lodda hits," sober Simkee reminded the rest. "De rebbeh never knows w'at he's tuckin' aboud."

"Dat's righ'!" Izzy tacked into sympathy. "We know yuh gid hit a lot, Benny, bot one poinder ain' gonna make no differ'nce, is id? How moch yuh god?"

"A ylod."

"How moch?"

"Thwenny thlyeb'm."

"Twennyy seb'm!" they echoed marveling. "He's god 'nuff fuh a mont'!"

"So if yuh gib'm twenny-six?" Izzy persisted. "Won' he drop dead anyways? Nobody ever grab'm twenny-six! Only Hoish w'en he won 'em aftuh Wildy swiped 'em. Let's see 'em!"

After a moment of hesitation, Benny opened several buttons on his shirt, drew out a bundle of sticks neatly tied with a string, and displayed them fondly. They were sharpened at one end and were of the same length and color as pointers—though not quite so straight.

Necks were craning. Some sighed. Some gasped. Within David surge after surge of gratitude beat about his heart. Oh, he was glad to be among them! To forget!

"Like real poinde's!"

"C'n yuh bend 'em?"

" 'N yuh cut 'em all outchuh self?"

"Gee, I wish I had dot kin' o' chair!"

And as Benny was about to stow them away in his bosom again—

"Aintcha gonna give us one?" Izzy pleaded, "Look, I god de match! Led's smoke one—jos' one—will yuh, Benny."

"Nyo!"

"Aaa, don't be a stingy louse!" they clamored.

Benny hesitated. "Lyuh gonniyl yuledth mhe sthmhoke tdew?"

"Sure! We'll letcha smoke all yuh want!"

"Wadyuh t'ink!"

"Dlyust one." He relented and drew a single reed out of the bound sheaf.

Izzy seized it jubilantly. "Now watch!" he admonished them. "Like a steamboat it's gonna give." And striking the match on the stone between his legs, applied it to one end of the reed, meanwhile sucking at the other. The former glowed, the latter yielded a sere, aromatic smoke.

"Gee!" they saucer-eyed. "Give a look, he's real smokin'!"

"Wad'd I tell yuh!" Izzy's features spread out in triumph. "I know dem chairs. Dey makes a noise w'en yuh sid on 'em. Crrk! Crrrk! Don' dey Benny?"

"Lyea. Dlyon' flyegedl, I'm fylyoist t' stlmook."

"Next aftuh Benny!"

"Next aftuh Simkee!"

"Me! I'm nex' aftuh—!"

"You! Hoddy huh gid like—!"

"G'wan!"

"Wadda noif! Hooz nex', Izzy?"

After much wrangling, turns were assigned.

Being near them, hearing the erratic spatter of their voices, yielding to their flickering moods was like basking in a hectic familiar oblivion. Their squabbling, their stridence drowned memory; that tireless tossing of their bodies, their whirring gestures, jerky antics stitched a fluctuant, tough, ever-renewing veil between himself and terror. David forgot. He was one of them.

Someone—it was Srooly—came out of the cheder, and once outside the door, squinted at them in surprise. "De cop'll getchoo!"

"Yea!" they sneered. "He ain't a'scared o' us! Ha! Ha! Haw! Haw!"

Still squinting, Srooly approached. "Watcha smokin'?"

"Cantchuh see, cock-eye Mulligan? A cigah!"

He bent closer. "It's a stick, liar!"

"Sure! It's a smoke-stick an' id could be fuh a poinder. Bud we didn' wanna."

"Uh! So hoddy yuh go?"

"Like dot." Lefty, whose turn it was, enlightened him

with a billow of smoke. "Dere's liddle holes in id, all de way t'roo!"

"Give us a puff," Srooly asked.

"Id's mine," Izzy announced. And no one contesting his claim, "I'm gonna dinch it an' smook somm maw lader—aftuh Lefty finishes."

"Give us a puff befaw."

"Fuh somm o' yuh flies I will."

"Wise-guy! Yuh givin' Lefty a smook fuh nutt'n."

"So wot? Don' smook den!"

"Aaa! Kipp it!"

"Puh! Who wants yuh flies!"

"Awri!" said Srooly. "I'll give yuh one."

"Give!"

Srooly brought out a smallish, square vial, squinted thoughtfully at the flies inside. "Most o' 'em I jos' caught in de gobbidj by Seven-twenty. On'y de big ones I take."

"Hurry op, Lefty!"

"Aaa, waid a secon', I jos' god id!" Lefty puffed vigorously.

"Hey! I fuhgod!" Srooly suddenly remembered. "Huz nex'? Yuh bedder go in, de rebbeh says. Cause on'y Moishe is dere."

"Me!" Schloimee rose. "Waid fer us, will ye, geng. Don' forged!" He went off.

Srooly held the vial up to the light. Grey horseflies, glittering blue-bottles crawled and fell on the glassy sides. "Dey's a old geezer in de cheder, yuh know?"

"Wit' whiskers like de rebbeh!" The rest informed him. "We theleen 'im faw lyow dyihl. He's loinin' de guys."

"Naa, he ain' loinin' de guys," said Srooly. "He's jost sittin' an' lookin'."

"So watz'e want?"

"Cow shid I know?" Srooly shrugged. "De Rebbeh wanzuh show off, dat's all. An' now—Hch! Hch! Hch! Moish is readin' an' he's dumb like anyt'ing. Hch! Hch! De rebbeh's gonna be med on him."

"Aw' yaw dumb too," said Izzy cuttingly.

"So he sh'd worry," the rest consoled themselves. "De rebbeh never hits w'en sommbody's lookin'!"

"Yea—? He stuck me in de ass wid de poinder—under de table! So de udder old geezer shouldn't see!"

"Ppprr!" Lefty surrendered the inch-long reed to Izzy. "Hea! Id's gedden hod!"

"Give us de fly now if yuh want id."

"Wad kind d'yuh want? De shiny or de hawsfly?"

"De haws! Dey fighd bedder."

Tilting the vial up, Srooly spilled two or three flies into his palm, stuffed back into the neck all but one and this he gave to Izzy. In return, the stumpy reed was handed over. The horse-fly, wing-stripped, crawled impotently about on Izzy's hand.

"Now I'll show yuh hoddeh smook!" Srooly put the bit of reed to his mouth. "Watch a real, reggilieh smooker —like I loined f'om my fodder! Watch!" and sucked with such abandon the ember at the other end sparkled— "M'lya!" Sudden pain contorted his face. "Luddle luddle! Ow! Id boins like fiah! Ow!" He threw the stub down. "Mplyaw!"

"Yeee! Look o' him dance!" Glee filled them. They howled with mirth.

"Oooo! My dung! Ow!" Frantically he licked the sides of the glass bottle—"Ooo, id's hod!"

"Lummox!" they jeered.

"Dot's watchuh ged fuh bein' a hog!"

"Wadyl pulyly stho hodth!"

"Aa, shod up!" Srooly was almost in tears. "I'll feel you off, see if I don'. All o' yuh! Waid'll I ged my big brudder aftuh yuh—lousy bestitts!" He walked off, tongue in the wind.

"Big smooker!" They howled after him. "Fot brains! Yaaa! Good fer yuh! Yaaa!"

When their hoots, cat-calls, capers had subsided—"Who yuh gonna give id?" Lefty asked.

"T' Choloimis on de foist step." Izzy waved farewell to the fly in his palm. "Bye! Bye! Buzzicoo!"

"Naa, don' give id t' him—he's fat a'reddy. Give id t' Baby Moider by de fence!"

"Naa!" Zucky urged, "Schreck-dreck by de daw—he's de best spider in de woild."

"No, I ain'!" Izzy would not be overruled. "Choloimis 'z' de biggest so Choloimis geds id."

He rose. They followed him noisily across the yard.

—*No! No! No!* (Without stirring, he stared fixedly after them) *No! No! You forgot! You forgot!*

"Don't scare 'im! Don' shake his house! Sh! Stholop yuh plyushin!" They trooped down the cellar steps. From below the level of the yard, as from underground, their stealthy voices rose. "C'n yuh see 'im? Yea! See 'im in his hole dere? See? He' thyl waitlyn!"

—Ow! (Like a stopper blown or a plug, the terrific jar of awakened terror) The cellar! The cellar! The cellar! Told her now! She, Polly! Aunt Bertha, she told! Knows! Long ago! Long ago! She knows! What? What's she going to do? What? No! No! Don't tell, Aunt Bertha! Don't tell! Don't! No! No! No! Ow, Mama! Mama!

Shrill from the cellar, their voices rose:

"Dere! Look! Look! T'row it now! Easy don' bust id! Look o' him! He's walkin' roun'. Whee! Dere he comes! Dere he comes! Lyow! He glyabth 'im! Fight! Fight! Gib'm, haws-fly! In de kishkis—nudder one! C'mon, Choloimis! Yowee! Tie 'im op! He's god 'im! Wid de legs! Waddye big wungl! Pullin' him! Pullin' him! Hully Muzziz! Look! In de hole! Bye! Bye! Buzzicoo! Yea! Yea!" Excited voices fused into a treble dirge. "Bye! Bye! Buzzicoo! Yea Spider! Yea!"

The cheder door swung open. With a hunted expression on their faces, Schloimee and Moish came hurrying out, and a moment later, the rabbi, red lips visible in the glossy black beard, corners down-curved into a threatening frown.

"Where are they?" He crimped blunt brows at David. "There? Below? In that black chaos?"

Grafted to terror, the mind, wrested away, tore terror with it. He couldn't speak.

"What ails you? Are you gagging? Speak!"

"Th-they're down there!" He stammered.

"So!" He intoned viciously. "When I'm through with them, even death will spurn them!" And lifting his head, he bellowed across the yard. "Clods! Bleak and eternal! Come out of that pit, you hear me? Come out before a rain of stripes drowns you there!"

Hasty, startled cries below, scufflings, scuffings. They pellmelled up the cellar-steps, halted in a cluster, shamefaced and cowed. He surveyed them. "Mice!" His voice was withering. "Mice! Who gnaws at the Torah next?"

"Me." Zuck shuffled forward warily.

"You?" Disgustedly. "What is this? Have all the plaster

golems in the cheder connived to read in relays? Hanh?
Will you torture me like the heathen god? Or what?"
His sour gaze swept them, alighted on David. "You! Come
in!"

"Me?" He started.

"On whom does my gaze end? Get up!" And once more
to the others. "Let the rest of you sit here in an agony!
But sit!" He shook a violent finger, and then crooked it
at David.

He had scrambled to his feet and hurried to the rabbi's
side. For the first time since he had entered the cheder,
the perilous task of reading when the rabbi was angry
suddenly became welcome to him. Any anxiety, any disquiet was inviting if it could stem or shunt the fierce
rush of this terror.

"Only one more!" As he entered, the rabbi addressed
someone inside. "Be patient, Reb Schulim! Would you
leave me in disgrace, nor hear at least one limber tongue?
Hanh? Surely, you wouldn't."

Trailing behind, David peered past him toward the light.
In the swirling sepia that always seemed to fill the cheder
after the glare of the yard, he could distinguish no one.
But when he waded to the window, risen like a square,
variegated rock above the sifting dusk, the wavering outlines of a man drifted out of the dim corner beside the
rabbi's chair. The figure was seated, hunched over a cane.
The wan gleam on his grey beard was like a whisper
from light to shadow.

The rabbi chuckled, apologetically, drew up his chair:
"When I can pierce stiff brass with a hair of my head,
then I'll pierce their skulls with wisdom. American Esaus,
all of them! But this, Reb Schulim, this is a true Yiddish
child."

Reb Schulim's only reply was to clear his throat.

David slid over the bench, and while the rabbi pinched
the pages, the dusk lifted, and he peeped shyly up at the
stranger. He was old, Reb Schulim, hawk-beaked. Although
his lipless mouth in the grey beard looked stretched and
grim, his eyes, his dark eyes in their intricate pouches
were liquid, strangely sorrowful and attentive. Unlike the
rabbi, he was neat, wore a black coat of thin, rusty cloth,
and instead of an oily brown straw, a wide black hat
crumpled the skull cap at the back of his pink and silver-

grizzled pate. He hawked incessantly which made David glance up again and again only to be caught in the mournful quietude of those eyes. They affected him strangely.

"He's a curious child." Reb Schulim's voice was husky and deliberate. "His look is hungry and unquiet."

"You've struck it, Reb Schulim!" The rabbi spread hairy fingers on the page—kept them spread. "Sometimes he prays like lightning, sometimes an imp flies into his head and he can't see a word. Today I know he'll pray. Here's something to make him." As though it were hinged to the book, he lifted his hand, but only enough for Reb Schulim to read—not David. "Do you remember I told you once—?"

Reb Schulim puckered his lips, cleared his throat, lifted grave, benign eyes to David's face, but made no answer.

"I'd start him in chumish," the rabbi wheeled the book around. "But I see his mother so rarely. I've never asked her—Listen!" He took his hand away from the page. "Begin, my David!"

The type was small. The thrill of apprehension that ran through him seemed to flutter the characters before him. He focused on them, condensing their blur. "Bishnas mos ha melech Uzuyahu—!" And stopped and stared. The number on top of the page was sixty-eight. The edge of the book was blue.

"What's the matter?" Rare tolerance softened the rabbi's voice. "Why do you wait?"

"It's—It's him!" Past radiance threw a last parting beam into the depths of his mind. "That one!"

"Which one? Who?"

"That man! Th-that man you said! Isaiah! He said—he said he saw God and it—and it was light!" Excitement clogged his tongue.

"Well, Reb Schulim!" The rabbi's swarthy brow canted in triumph. "One glance was all he needed, and that was months and months ago! This!" His blunt finger drummed on David's brow. "This has an iron wit! No?" His black beard seemed to shake out sparks of satisfaction.

Reb Schulim tapped his cane against the bench. "A cherished seedling of Judah. Indeed!"

"Now all of it!" The rabbi settled down to business. "Begin once more."

"Beshnas mos hamelech Uzuyahu vaereh es adonoi

yoshaiv al kesai rom venesaw veshulav melayim es hahayhel Serafim omdim memal lo." Not as a drone this time, like syllables pulled from a drab and tedious reel, but again as it was at first, a chant, a hymn, as though a soaring presence behind the words pulsed and stressed a meaning. A cadence like a flock of pigeons, vast, heaven-filling, swept and wheeled, glittered, darkened, kindled again, like wind over prairies. "Shaish kenawfayim shash kenawfayim leahod. Beshtyim yehase fanav uveshtayim." The words, forms of immense grandeur behind a cloudy screen, overwhelmed him—"Yehase raglov uveshtayim yeofaif—"

"As though, he knew what he read," Reb Schulim's husky speech. "That young voice pipes to my heart!"

"If I weren't sure—indeed, if I didn't know him, I'd think he understood!"

David had paused. The rabbi sat back, hands locked on his belly.

"Vekaraw se el se vamar—"

The head of the cane clicked against the table; a shadow glided over the page. Leaning forward with out-stretched arm, Reb Schulim patted David's cheek with chill fingers.

"Blessed is your mother, my son!"

(-*Mother!*) "Kadosh, Kadosh, Kadosh adonoi tse-vawos." The words blurred. A howl of terror beat down all majesty. (-*Mother!*) "Mlo hol haeretz h-vo-do—" He stumbled. (-*Mother!*)

"What is it?" The rabbi's fingers unbraided upon his paunch and stretched out as if to seize.

"Va-va- yaw-yaw noo-noo-" (-*Mother!*) Without an-swering, he suddenly burst into tears.

"Hold! What is it?" His hasty hand clicked David's chin up. "What makes you weep?"

Reb Schulim's large compassionate eyes were also on him: "Reb Yidel, I tell you he does understand."

David sobbed brokenly.

"Come, answer!" Perplexity made the rabbi urgent. "One word only!"

"My-my mother!" he wept.

"Your mother—well?" Sudden alarm quickened his speech. "What of her? Speak! What's happened!"

"She—she's!—"

"Yes! Well!"

He did not know what it was that compelled him to say it, but it was compulsion greater than he could withstand. "She's dead!" He burst into a loud wail.

"Dead? Dead? When? What are you saying!"

"Yes! Ooh!"

"Shah! Wait!" The rabbi stemmed his own confusion. "I saw her here. Why! Only—! What—! When did she die, I ask you?"

"Long ago! Long ago!" His head rocked in the abandon of his misery.

"Hanh? Long? Speak again!"

"Long ago!"

"But how could that be? How? I've seen her. She brought you here! She paid me! Tell me, what is long ago?"

"That—that's my aunt!"

"Your—!" The breath jarred audibly against his throat. "But—but you called her mother! I heard you! She told me she was."

"She just says she is! Owooh! Just says! Just says! To everyone! Wants me to call her too—" A gust of grief blew his voice from him.

"Aha!" In suspicious sarcasm. "What kind of a yarn are you telling? How do you know? Who told you?"

"My aunt—my aunt told me!"

"Which aunt? How many are there?"

"Yesterday!" He wept. "No. Not—not yesterday. When you wanted to—to hit me. Then. That—that day, when I c-couldn't read. She owns a candy st-store. She told me."

"On that day—Monday?"

"Y-yes!"

"And she told you? The other one?"

"Yes! Owooh! She owns a c-candy-store."

"Ai, evil!"

"Foolish woman!" Reb Schulim chided sadly. "To reveal this to a child."

"Pheh, foolish!" The rabbi spat disgustedly. "Sweet sister, the hussy! What business of hers was it? Squirming tongue! The gallows is due her! No?"

Reb Schulim sighed, shook David gently: "Come, my child! Dry your tears! If it was long ago—then long ago already was too late for your weeping. Come! She no longer has ears where she lies there. God commanded it."

"Well, where's your nose-rag?" The rabbi patted irritably among David's pockets. "The gallows! Here!" He drew it out. "Blow!" And as he pinched David's nose clean. "You don't remember her then, do you? When did she die?"

"No! I don't—I don't know. She didn't tell me."

His brow knit in fresh perplexity. "Well, why aren't you with your father? Where's he?"

"I—I don't know!"

"Hmpph! Did she say anything about him?"

"She s-said he was a- a-"

"What?"

"I forgot! I forgot how to say it." He wept.

"Then think! Think. What was he, a tailor, a butcher, a peddler, what?"

"No. He was— He was— He played—"

"Played? A musician? Played what?"

"A— A— Like a piano. A—A organ!" He blurted out.

"An organ? An organ! Reb Schulim, do you see land?"

"I think I see what is seen first, Reb Yidel. The spire."

"Mmm! Why aren't you with him?" His voice was cautious.

"Because—because he's in Eu—Europe."

"And?"

"And he plays in—in a— She says he plays in a ch-church. A church!"

"Woe me!" He slumped back against his chair. "I foresaw it! You hear, Reb Schulim? When he said an organ-player, I—I knew! Oh!" his face lighted up. "Is that what you meant when you said spire—a church?"

"Only that."

"Ha, Reb Schulim, would God I had your wisdom! And what do you think now?"

Reb Schulim gravely flattened his grey beard against his coat. "There's truth in an old jest."

"That a bastard is wise?"

Reb Schulim hawked, hawked again more violently, spat under the table. For a second or two, the only sound in the room was the smeary scrape of his foot on the floor. "Let us hope they saw to it he was made a Jew."

"I'll do more than hope." With a righteous scowl, the rabbi scratched the blunt end of the pointer among the

sparse hairs of his underlip. "I'll do more!" He regarded
David fixedly. "Er—David, mine, tell me this one thing
more. Did she, that everlasting slut, that candy store muck-
raker, your aunt, did she tell you where—in what land
your mother met the-er-the organ-player?"

"She-she—yes— She said."

"Where?"

"In where there was— there was c-corn."

"Where?" His brows drew together in ragged ridges.

"Where corn was grow-growing. She said. Where corn
was. They went there. She told me like—like that they
went."

"Oy!" The rabbi sounded as though he were strangling.
"Enough! Enough! Thank God you're here, Reb Schulim!
Else who would have believed me! Ai! Yi! Yi! Yi! Can
you picture so foul, so degraded a she who would tell
this to a child so young!"

"A vile, unbridled tongue!"

"Ach! Pheh!" the rabbi spat over the edge of the table.
"The gallows I say! A black, uncanny death! But you—"
he turned abruptly to David. "Go now! Weep no more!
And hear me: Say nothing—nothing to anyone! Understand? Not a word."

"Yes." He hung his head in misery.

"Go!" Hasty fingers fluttered before him. David slid
from the bench, turned, feeling their eyes pursuing him,
and stumbled toward the door.

The yard. They were still lolling against the cheder
wall.

"Hooray! Hully Muzzis!" Izzy's aggrieved voice greeted
him. "He's oud a'ready! Hooray!"

David hurried toward the wooden stairs.

"Hey, look, Iz, he's cryin'!"

"An' jos' my nex' too!"

"Waddee hitchuh fuh? Hey!"

"Hey watsa madder!"

The corridor muffled their cries. He fled through to
the street. One wild glance at his house and he scurried
west. A strange chaotic sensation was taking hold of
him—a tumultuous, giddy freedom, a cruel caprice that
made him want to caper, to skip, to claw at his hands,
to pinch himself until he screamed. A secret wanton
laughter kept arising to his lips, but never issued, gurgled

in his throat instead with a gurgle of pain. He wanted to smirk at the people whom he neared, wanted to jeer, bray, whistle, double-thumb his nose—but dared not until they had passed. He rattled the loose spheres on the stanchions of stoops, struck the tassels of the awnings, set the chains before the cellars swinging, kicked the ash-cans.

"Fugimbestit! Fugimbestit!" The pressure of his frenzy, too great to be contained seethed from his lips. "You! You! Watchuh lookin'! Yoop! Don' step on de black line! Bing! Don' step on de black line. Ain't I ain't! Ain't I! Pooh fuh you too 'lilulibuh! Don' step on de black line! I'm sommbody else. I'm somebody else—*else*—ELSE! Dot's who I am. Hoo! Hoo! Johnny Cake! Blt! Dat's fuh you! Blyoh! Stinker! Look out fuh de fox. Fox; fix fux, look out! Don' step on de black line. Yoop! Take a skip! In de box! Yoop! Yoop! Two yoops! Yoop! Hi! Hop, skip an' a yoop! Hi! Funny! Ow! Owoo!"

At Avenue C, he ran blindly north.

"Yoop! All busted lines. Here all busted. Watch oud! Watch oud! Hey, busted sidewalk, lousy, busted sidewalk, w'y yuh busted? Makes double jumps! Triple jumps! Fawple jumps. Fipple jumps. Yoop! Yoop! Triple! Fipple! Fipple! Kipple! Is a cake! Johnny cake! Why yuh busted? Touch a crack, touch a cella', touch a cella', touch a devil. He, black buggerunner! Busts it! Hee, yee! Va y'hee! V y'hee, wee, wee. Wee. Wee. Pee, pee! Pee, pee, tee tee! Yoop! sh! So watchuh lookin'? Make me step on it. Don' count, devil, 'cause— Pee, pee, dere! Blya! Pee, pee, yea, gotta. Sommtime gotta. Gonna now! Naa! Yea! Gonna now. Take id oud! See! Look! Look! All de goils. Sh! Shattop! Wot I care. See! Hea id comes. Double dare yuh stop me. Double—"

He stepped to the curb.

"Izz wit! Zzz! Lager beeuh comms f'om—He said, Goy, sonn'va bitch! Goy sonn'vabitch! Leo sonn'vabitch! He said! Zzz! Ha! Piss higher! Look o' my bow! Who cares! Ooh bedder! One bott'n, two bott'n! C'n jump now! Higher. Yoop! Yoop! Hi—"

Tenth Street. The car-tracks. To the east the panel of the river, shore and hazy sky.

"It follows! Run to elebent'. Run, run, Johnny cake! Yoop! Look o' me ev'ybody! Watch me! No, no! Not me! Him! Him—me! Me—Him. Watchuh lookin'? Fuhgim-

bestit, it's him! He fooled him! Ol' smoke-mout'-stink! He
fooled him, ol' geezer. Wuz'n me. Him! He did it! I ain'! I
ain' even! So tell. Can't tell on me. I ain'. So tell! Tell her!
Tell Tanta Berta! Tell my modder! I ain'! Yoop! Look o'
me-no-him-go! Look o' him! Him! Him! Weewuth!
Weeewuth! Ain' even tiad! Ain' even me! Elebent, a'reddy!
Follers me it, water. Follers no me-him! Watchuh foller'n fuh? Lousy, bestitt, copycat river! Skidoo! Mind yuh
own lousy biz! Beat it den, beat it, lousy! Beat, Beat it!
Beat it! Yoop, Yowooh!"

He ran screaming northward. . . .

XVI

THREADING his way among the hordes of children,
hurdles of baby carriages, darting tricycles and skate-
wheel skooters that cluttered the sidewalks of Avenue B,
the squat, untidy, Jew waddled northward on weak and
flabby hams. He stooped slightly as he walked. Seen from
the front, a glossy black beard hung suspended from a
brown straw hat; the arms that were locked behind his
buttocks furled both sides of his dull alpaca coat revealing a greasy insufficient vest that lapsed before reaching
his belt; upon the spotted broad expanse of vest a broad
watchchain stretched across the wide paunch, barely spanning the gap from pocket to pocket; between the vest and
the belt, soiled, wrinkled shirt tails cropped out in a
foliated ledge of linen. Seen from the side, baggy pants
of indeterminate somberness swept upward and outward
in a soft curve, bracket wise to the overhanging shirt.
Slant sun-light on his rear, alternate upon the worn-smooth,
almost-lacquered cheeks and cylinders of his pants teetered
with his teetering limbs and ricocheted. And he walked
northward threading his way.

Arrived at the corner of Sixth Street and Avenue B,
he stopped to let an automobile pass, and made good the
few seconds he whiled away by drawing out his watch.
Under the pressure of thick and oily thumb, the case

snapped open like a gold, obedient bivalve. He glanced at the face. Ten minutes to six. Hi! (He sighed mentally) Over an hour before sunset. There was time. There was time. None would gather in the synagogue before seven. There was time to spare. And he squeezed the gold lips clicking over the glint of white. But as he brought the watch near his vest pocket, his head snapped back, jarring his brown straw hat over his eye-brows and he sneezed. Shaken fingers missed the slit in the cloth. The time-piece bounced off his paunch and swung out on its gold chain like a pendulum. He cursed in Yiddish, clutched at it, hauled it in and thrust it rudely back into its place. And then retreating a step from the curb, bowed himself, and pinching his nostrils trumpeted their contents into the gutter. The mucus spattered into the dust like livid fleur-de-lis. He reached for his gray handkerchief, buttoned his coat, (it was cool for July) and stepped forward again.

Yi! Yi! Yi! He mused bitterly as his rambling fingers investigated the dryness of his beard. Nothing had gone right with him this day. Nothing. Unfortunate Jew! Was he not an unfortunate Jew? Dear God! Dear God! To sneeze when he holds a watch in his hand. Hi! Hi! Hi! True, it was chained to his person. But what if it was? Does the heart know that? The foolish heart! How it leaps with fright like a colt! And then finds out. A curse on it! On what, the heart? No, not the heart, the watch! No, not the watch either. Hi! Hi! Hi! He was getting stupid with his years. Not the watch, the event. A curse on the event! By all means! Hi-i! An evil day! And this morning when he crossed the gutter, engrossed in bad news (truly, he cause of it all, he reassured himself) engrossed him! Where was his brain that moment? Engrossed, he had caught his walking stick in the eye of a sewer-cover. May it be ground to a powder! Caught and broken it above the ferrule. And a dollar and thirty cents he had paid for it not so long ago, a dollar and thirty cents. From Labele Rifka's, his cousin, and would it not be meet in the eyes of the Almighty that death befell Labele for selling him a broom-straw for a dollar and thirty cents? For that price, God would surely nod in assent. Broken it above the ferrule. And the brats had stood about him and laughed. . . .

A curse on them! He glared about him at the children

and half grown boys and girls who crowded the stoops
and overflowed into the sidewalks and gutter. The devil
take them! What was going to become of Yiddish youth?
What would become of this new breed? These Americans!
This sidewalk-and-gutter generation? He knew them all
and they were all alike—brazen, selfish, unbridled. Where
was piety and observance? Where was learning, veneration
of parents, deference to the old? In the earth! Deep in
the earth! On ball playing their minds dwelt, on skates,
on kites, on marbles, on gambling for the cardboard pictures, and the older ones, on dancing, and the ferocious
jangle of horns and strings and jigging with their feet.
And God? Forgotten, forgotten wholly. Ask one who
Mendel Beiliss is? Ask one, did he shed goyish blood for
the Passover? Would they know? Could they answer?
Vagabonds! Snipes! Jiggers with their feet! Corrupt generation! Schmielike, his own grandchild, lifting a nickel
from his purse. (Ah, but he fetched him a few sterling
whacks when he caught him. A few, but good ones.) And
his wooden pointers stolen from his cheder. And those
brats in the street laughing when he broke his walking
stick. An ageing man and they had jeered at him. And
that lout especially, may he break his bones before the
rest; asking him if he had lost a ball, in the foul water
below. He, a rabbi, an ageing man. Hi! Hi! May a tumor
in his belly and a tumor in his head grow to be as big as
that ball. Mocking an ageing man. Yiddish youth! Turd-
worth. Exactly so was his own boyhood in Vilna, in Russ-
Poland. Ex-a-actly so-o! Others went sliding on sleds. Not
he. Others slid on the ice with the goyim. Not he. They
stuck pins into each other in the cheder. Not he. Hi! He
had scarcely ever laughed even in his youth. Pogroms.
Poverty. What was there to laugh at? Reb R'fuhl was his
rabbi then. That was a rabbi! No random cuff did you get
from him when he was vexed. No mild pinch on the jowl.
Ha, no! When he was angered, he flogged, and when he
flogged he took their pants down and spread the flap of
their drawers—and all so slowly and with what sweet
words. Hi! Ha! Ha! That was a sight to behold! They
remembered it those young ones. Not the watery discipline
that he enforced. That's what was ruining this generation—
watery discipline. Hi! And he, himself a rabbi now, he had
held the culprit's legs while the straps sank into the white

uttocks. There was a kind of pleasure then in hearing
another howl, in watching another beaten, seeing the
naked flesh squirm and writhe and the crack of the buttocks tighten under the biting thongs. A kind of pleasure,
but it had passed now, dulled with over-use he supposed.
Hi! Hi! . . .

An evil day. . . .

And at noon, he had quarreled with Ruchel, his daughter, over the chicanery of her husband, Avrum, the butcher. Cold-storage liver he was selling and palming it off
for fresh. A snide generation. Why should the children be
better than their fathers? No sanctity anywhere, no faith.
It's kosher, she said. Ruchel his daughter, his thorn. It
tastes just as good. In food there should be some trust, he
had answered. If you were selling walking sticks sell the
flawed, the warped, the brittle. Say nothing, tell nothing.
But what enters the mouth, there you must betray no
trust. If you're selling "treifes" say it is "treife" and men
will hold you a man. If you're selling cold-storage for
fresh—But it's kosher, she had said. Of course it's kosher,
he had answered. Liver is kosher till it rots. It needs no
washing before the third day. No salting. Even a goy
knows that. Hi! Hi! My daughter, my daughter! It's good.
It tastes good you say. There was a Jew traveling toward
Odessa and he ate in an inn without knowing what he
ate. Good beef he called it. Savory gravy. And they told
him—what? They told him it was horsemeat. And hi-hi-hi
my daughter—it tastes good. And how far is the step
from cold storage meat to meat not kosher and how far
is the step from meat not kosher to pig's flesh? Hi! Hi!
Hi! My daughter! You'll drive me into the deep earth with
the weight of shame. May your head drop off from your
shoulders, and your husband's head beside it. My daughter . . .

Hi . . . An evil day. . . .

And in the afternoon, Reb Schulim had come to his
heder, Reb Schulim, his townsman, to review learning.
And had reviewed not learning but a long procession of
dumbskulls, stutterers, louts half blind with too much
loitering in cellars. A black fate had let the best ones
lead first, and the best had scattered before Reb Schulim
came and only the dullards were left to shame him. A
good rabbi, Reb Yidel, he must have thought—Hmmmm-

m-m! h-m-m—h-m-m-m! A good rabbi! Not one has h[e]
taught to utter three words one upon the other withou[t]
fumbling. Not one could speak the tongue without [a]
snuffle or a snort—except this child, David, this bastard[.]
God have pity on him, a goy's spawn, a church organist'[s]
Hi! Hi! And it is strange that true Yiddish children o[f]
pious parents should prove such God-forsaken dolts an[d]
this one-only half-a-jew—perhaps not (I could have foun[d]
out then and there, but—) circumcised—an iron wit[h]
God's ways. Hidden. A pitiful story and a triple curs[e]
befall the aunt, sister, slut, who revealed it. I say th[e]
gallows, Haman's gibbet, high . . .

Hm-m-m-m! Evil day! . . .

Then why do you go? Reb Yidel, why do you go[?]
Would it not be better on a day like this not to be th[e]
bearer of evil tidings? Accursed, calamitous day! Woul[d]
it not to be safer to turn and stride back toward th[e]
synagogue. They may not understand. Should they accus[e]
you of breeding hatred, call you augur-nosed, are yo[u]
prepared? Should they mock at you and scorn you an[d]
say, Reb Yidel, your nose is in every wind like the spoke[s]
of a wheel, have you a remedy? Have you an answer[?]
None. But I am an upright man, and someone must tel[l]
them. Shall the child know and they not know he knows[.]
Is he truly a Jew, this David? Shall the foul sister go un[-]
spared? Someone must warn them, advise. And I vowed[.]
I vowed. Hi! Hi! Hi! Alas! Foreboding! . . .

Grimacing so violently his black beard twitched i[n]
several places simultaneously, twitched and caught th[e]
sunlight in a skein of drawn pitch, pin-point glints an[d]
iridescence, the dumpy, ageing Jew stopped at the corne[r]
of Avenue C and Ninth Street, looked west into the su[n]
when he meant to go east, and opened the trigger-tau[t]
button on his dull alpaca coat. Relieved from strain, th[e]
cloth crumpled against his arms in flutings. The curtain[s]
drawn, the grease spots on his vest glistened in vitreou[s]
tableau. Beaked thumb and forefinger pecked among hi[s]
pockets, drew out a torn bit of paper, unfolded it.

"Seven-fifty-one," he muttered after scanning the Hebre[w]
characters. "Fourth floor. Perhaps this corner of Avenu[e]
D. Perhaps the other. Pray God I put it down correctly.["]

He replaced the scrap of paper, turned and strode eas[t]
through the familiar street. Abreast of his cheder doorway[,]

he felt the old bleak stir of recognition, glanced into the hallway and crossed the street. Head cocked, he scanned the house numbers increasing one after the other.

"Seven-fifty-one." His lips formed the words silently. "Fourth floor." He added mentally. And taking a deep, sighing breath against the stairs he had to climb, climbed the stoop, entered the hallway and mounted the shadowy stairs.

Winded, stertorous, perturbed, he reached the top and brightest landing, and with heaving paunch, eyed the Mizzuzahs, some still bright, some painted over, above the several doors. And knocked at the nearest one.

"Who is it?" The sharp female voice behind the panels inquired in Yiddish.

"Does the Mrs. Schearl live here?" He asked, knowing somehow that she didn't.

"No." A heavy busted, bare-armed woman opened the door. "She lives there. That door in the front. That door."

His eyes swept from the coarse-grained red skin of her throat to the door her finger pointed at. He nodded, not surprised that she kept her own door opened, watching him inquisitively. And knocked again.

"Oh! David! David! Is it you?" A voice of immense eagerness called out to him. "Is it closed? I've been waiting—"

"This is I—Reb Yidel Pankower," he said as the door opened.

XVII

WISH I had a potsee, a potsee. Could go slower. Go slower. Look around. See if to see. Look around. An exhaustion beyond anything he had ever felt; a weariness the vastest rest could never match. He was so tired his very thought seemed a function of his breathing, as though the mind were so spent it needed the impulse of breath to clear the word away, else it echoed in stagnance.

He dragged tottering rebellious legs toward the car tracks of Tenth.

—Take longer if I had a potsee. Longer, lots longer. And kick it here, so it goes there. And there, and there, and kick it there, so it goes here. And here and follow it. And follow it where it went. And if it went away, go away. Go with it. And if it comes back, come back. Ow! Mama! Mama! Tired all out! Ow! Mama! Should have gone away. Anyway. Away. Forty-one Street, said. Big house. Forty-one street River was. And Thirty Street River was. And was and it followed. And train and it followed. And he said it goes. Goes where? Br-Bronx, Bronx Park, he said. Is animals, he said with the package. Lots and trees. Lots. Then it comes back. Five cents. Have to come back always. Go home. Never get lost no more. No more. Know number. Never. Slow. Go slower. Car-tracks. Ow! Too near! Too near already. Ow! Ow!

With all the horror of one tottering over an abyss, he stared at the cobbles, the gleaming tracks.

—Stay here! Go back! Stay here! Ow! What'll I do? Where'll I go? Mama! Mama! Stay here till fifty wagons; take a step. Fifty autos; take a step. Fifty—Tired! Tired all out. Can't wait! Can't wait no more. Don't let him hit me, Mama, I'm crossing! I'm crossing, Mama! Ow! Getting near! Getting near! Where's a potsee? A potsee. Garbage cans look. Ain't out yet. Flies he found. Cellar. Them! Ow! A potsee! A potsee! Something. Find! Find!

Nerveless fingers fumbled numbly in his pockets.

—Pencil. No good. Break off gold and rubber. Step on—No good! No good! What? Cord when I thought kite. What'd I go up for? Why! Why! Canary! Ow! Lousy! Lousy son-of-a-! Back pocket . . . Them! It's them! No good shitten them! Kick! Throw away! Tear! Shitten, goy-beads! Tear! Kick for a potsee! Gwan! They'll see, but they'll see! Don't care! Ow! Getting near! Getting near! My lamppost, Ninth! Oh, Mama, Mama, don't let him hit me! I'm going round! I'm going round! Oooh, look every place! Look every place!

Only his own face met him, a pale oval, and dark, fear-struck, staring eyes, that slid low along the windows of stores, snapped from glass to glass, mingled with the enemas, ointment-jars, green globes of the drug-store—snapped off—mingled with the baby clothes, button-heaps, underwear of the drygoods store—snapped off—with the cans of paint, steel tools, frying pans, clothes-lines of the hardware store—snapped off. A variegated pallor, but pallor always, a motley fear, but fear. Or he was not.

—On the windows how I go. Can see and ain't. Can see and ain't. And when I ain't, where? In between them if I stopped, where? Ain't nobody. No place. Stand here then. BE nobody. Always. Nobody'd see. Nobody'd know. Always. Always No. Carry—yes—carry a looking glass. Teenchy weenchy one, like in pocket-book, Mama's. Yea. Yea. Yea. Stay by house. Be nobody. Can't see. Wait for her. Be nobody and she comes down. Take it! Take looking-glass out, Look! Mama! Mama! Here I am! Mama, I was hiding! Here I am! But if Papa came. Zip, take away! Ain't! Ain't no place! Ow! Crazy! Near! I'm near! Ow!

His eyes glazing with panic, he crept toward his house, and as he went, grasped at every rail and post within reach—not to steady himself, though he was faint, but to retard. And always he went forward, as though an ineluctable power tore him from the moorings he clutched.

A boy stood leaning against the brass bannister on the top step of the stoop. He held in his hands the torn tissue of a burst red balloon which he sucked and twisted into tiny crimson bubbles. As David, fainting with terror, dragged himself up the stone stairs, the other nipped at a moist, new-made sphere. It popped. He grinned blithely.

"Yuh see how I ead 'em? One bit!"

David stopped, stared at him unseeingly. In the trance that locked his mind only one sensation guttered with a bare significance. The chill of the tarnished railing under his palm, the chill and the memory of its lustre and the flat taint of its corruption.

"Now, I'll make a real big one!" said the boy. "Watch me!" The stretched red rubber hollowed into a small antre in his mouth, was engulfed, twisted, revealed. "See dot! In one bite!"

Pop!

Despair. . .

XVIII

"FAH a penny, ices, Mrs! Fah a penny, ices! Fah a penny, ices, Mrs!"

The grimy six-year-old who had just come in, rapped on the marble counter with his copper.

"Fah a penny, ices, Mrs!"

But neither the slight, long-nosed owner of the store, gnawing bitterly at his sallow mustache, nor his slovenly, red-haired wife glaring at him, nor their pimpled, frightened daughter in the rear moved to do his bidding.

"Fah a penny, ices, Mrs! Hey!"

Another six-year-old came into the store.

"Yuh gonna gimme a suck, Mutkeh?"

"Dey dowanna gib *me* even!" Mutkeh turned to his friend with an injured look.

"Let's go t' Solly's. Yea?"

"Noo!" muttered the owner in Yiddish. "Are you going to give it to him or will you let him clamor there all evening."

"Boils and pepper, that's what I'll give him!" she crossed her arms defiantly. (The six-year-olds looked hurt.) "Can't *you* do it? Are you dead?"

"I won't!" His small peevish jaw shot as far forward as its teeth would allow. "Let the whole store be burnt to the ground! I won't!"

"Then be burned with it!" She spat at him. "I need you and your penny business! A candy-store he saddled me with—good husband! Polly, go give it to him."

Sullenly, red underlip curled out like a scarlet snail-shell, Polly left off pinching the sides of her dress and came out into the front. There she lifted the rusty lid of the can floating in the half-melted ice of the tub, ladled out the pale-yellow, smoking, crystalline mush into a paper cup and handed it to the boy. The two children went out. And as the girl retreated to the rear of the store, her mother nodded at her vindictively—

"And you had to tell him, ha? Foul-piss-in-bed! After I warned you not to!"

"You ain' my moddeh," Polly mumbled in English.

"I'll give you something in a minute," her stepmother unlocked her arms, "You think you're safe because your father's here?"

"Leave her alone!" her husband interfered resentfully. "Do you think she's wrong maybe? Had it been your own flesh and blood, you would have been there in a wink, no? You'd have watched. You wouldn't have sat in front on your fat hole, while that Esau scum handled my poor daughter——"

"Be a scape-goat for dogs!" her voice rose in a brow-beating stormy scream. "And for rats! And for snakes! Can I watch everything? The store! The customers! The salesmen! The kitchen! And your stinking daughters as well! Isn't it enough you've given me a candy-store to age me, and with a candy-store loaded my belly with one of yours—Here!" She lifted the chocolate-stained, mounded apron as though she meant to throw it at him. "And besides all this, you ask me to watch those filthy hussies! If they don't even listen to me, how can I watch them. Aren't they old enough! Don't they know enough! And that one in the kitchen where she pretends to weep—a wench of twelve! Let her choke there! And you—you don't deserve to have the earth cover you! Telling me to watch them! And if you want to know something else, you'll make no more fuss about it, but you'll go into the kitchen and eat your supper!" Gasping breathlessly, she stopped.

"Yes?" Though he groped for words, it wasn't fury that halted his speech, but a kind of invincible stubbornness that kept laboriously intrenching itself deeper and deeper. "Supper—me—you ask—me—to eat? Your zest —and may your zest—for life—be as little all your life —as I—as mine is for food! Supper—after what's happened! Woe to you! But this once—I—You won't straddle me like a—a good horse! No! This—you—this once you won't ride——"

"Kiss my arse!" She broke in on him again. "Riding you! I'm not ridden, ha? Oh what a fool you are—choking over it! As if it's never happened before that two brats should be playing like animals. Is she maimed! Has he snatched it from her—the prize? Won't it heal before she's married?"

"How do you know? Do you know how big he was? What has he wrought? Did you even look to see?"

"Look? Yes!" she suddenly snorted mockingly. "I looked! Her drawers were dirty—as they always are! Why don't you go inside and look at her yourself!"

"Go break a blood vessel!" he muttered.

"Brats at play and he's worrying! About what, God knows—the future, marriage, suitors. They'll explore her before they'll marry her, is that it? Oh, idiot! Do you want a suitor for her? Blow your nose—she'll have a tall one!"

His small frame stiffened. Blood flared in his sallow face.

"That's how your mother answered your father, ha? Over your sister, Genya, ha? And exactly the same way—a goy! It's a family trait by now! To you it's nothing!" The spurt of anger that had driven his words failed him suddenly. He retreated.

"Burn like a candle!" She advanced upon him furiously. "Will you vomit up past shame! A secret I told you, you dare mock me with? I'll give you something to make your world keel over!"

His back against the glass doors of the toy closet, he had lifted his arms defensively. "Go away! Let me alone! If you'll swill refreshments at my funeral, I'll swill them at yours!"

"Be slaughtered by a chinaman!" She turned her back on him contemptuously. "Manikin! I don't hear you any more! Go talk to my buttocks!"

"All right! All right!" He swayed impotently. "Let it be as you say. My just one! My righteous! Let it be as you say. But him, that little rogue with the big eyes, he goes scot-free, ha? That's dealing justly, ha? A nephew is dearer to you than the daughters I brought you. But remember there's a God in heaven—He'll judge you for this!"

"Did I say he ought to go unpunished?" She wheeled around again. "Did I? I told you I'd tell Genya in the morning. With the first light of day I'll tell her. What more do you want? Would you like Albert to know? Would nothing else suit you but that? How many times have I told you what a maniac he is? Haven't you even seen it for yourself? He'd tear that child limb from limb! Is that what you want? Well you won't get it! And now go inside and eat! Go inside as I tell you and stop hammering the samovar—daughter! daughter! Or God help me you'll have pangs and hemorrhoids for an appetizer!"

Completely cowed and yet too stubborn to move, he stood there muttering while she glared at him. "Genya. . . . Good! Good! She with her light hand and soft voice. Yeh! Yeh!" He nodded bitterly. "She'll never lift either against him. She'll talk to him, that's what she'll do— fondle him. And with that he'll be punished—words. With words after what he's done to my Esther. All right! All right! If that's the kind of treatment I get—good. . . Good! Good! But I'm not satisfied—know that! I'm not satisfied."

"Will you go in?"

He turned to go. But as he turned, a woman entered the store.

"Hello, Mrs. Sternowitz!"

"Hello!"

"And Mr. Sternowitz! I didn't see you. How fares it?"

"Fair."

"Only fair? Tt! Tt! Well, give me for two cents hair-pins. You sell three packages for two cents, no?"

"Yes."

Mrs. Sternowitz turned and waddled heavily toward the rear of the store; Polly, her mouth still hanging, stepped sullenly to one side. As she fumbled among the boxes stacked on the shelves, fumbled and sighed laboriously, and muttered about the dark, her husband watched her, flexing and unflexing nervous hands. Suddenly he clenched his fist, and while his wife's back was still turned to him, sidled toward the front of the store, brushed by the puzzled woman at the counter and slunk out. Polly gaped after him. Her step-mother, all unaware, lifted haphazardly now one lid of a box, now another. The customer laughed.

"What's the matter with your husband?" she asked.

"Ach!" Mrs. Sternowitz threw casually over her shoulder. "God alone knows what's ailing him. His nose has fallen to the ground and he won't pick it up."

"That's the way with men," the woman chuckled. "You'll be lying in soon, no?"

"Too soon. Oh! Here it is! A new box?" She dragged it out. "These have something between their legs, these hairpins, cha! cha! Another new variety." She broke off abruptly, her questioning glance flicking from daughter to customer. "Where is he? Nathan!"

"That's why I asked you." The woman still smiled. "It looked to me as though he fled."

"Fled?" She stood stock-still. "Where?"

"There. Toward Alden Avenue I think. What is it?"

But Mrs. Sternowitz had already flung back the counter lid, and with a frightened yet furious expression was hurrying toward the door. She ran out on the sidewalk, stared eastward frantically, ran a few steps, came rushing back.

"I don't see him! I don't see him!" she spluttered, pinching frantically at her neck and dragging at the flesh. "He's tricked me! He's off—to Genya's!" She turned furiously on her daughter. "Why didn't you tell me he was sneaking off, you little snake!" She lifted her hand to strike, but thought better of it. "Ai!" She threw the box of hairpins down on the counter, and began fumbling desperately with her apron strings. And while the other woman stared at her in alarm, shouted garbled, flurried injunctions at Polly.

"Go call Esther!" She threw the apron from her at last and stooped down to button her shoes. "Hurry! Hurry! Call her out! Quick! Oh, if I get my hands on him! Oh, God help him. Quick! Oh, if I get him! Quick! Call her! You two mind the store. Call Mrs. Zimmerman if I don't get back soon! Watch the cash drawers! Hurry, do you hear? He can't have gone far! I'll get him! I'll make a scene in the middle of the street. I'll drag him back by the hair! Hurry! Watch! The two-faced—" She rushed out of the store.

The other woman looked after her in amazement and then turned to Polly. "What's the matter with your mother?"

"I don't know," was the morose answer. And then she went to the back of the store, threw open the kitchen door and screamed at someone inside.

"C'mon out, Esther! Poppa wen' away! Momma wen' away! Comm out! Comm on! Yuh hev t' watch!"

XIX

AT THE second landing of the unlit' hallway, the harsh stench of disinfectants rasped the grain of his nostrils. Behind that doorway where the voices of children filtered through, Mrs. Glantz's brood had the measles. Upward and beyond it, wearily, wearily. And at the turn of the stairs, the narrow, crusted, wire-embedded window was open. He loitered again, stared down. In the greying yard below, a lean, grey cat leaped at the fence, missed the top and clawed its way up with intent and silent power. And he upward also, wearily.

—Her fault. Hers. Ain't mine. No it ain't. It ain't. Ask anybody. Take a step and ask. Is it mine? Bannister-sticks, is it mine? Mine is . . . Mine ain't . . . Mine is . . . Mine ain't. Mine is . . . Mine ain't . . . There! See! Chinky shows! Her fault. She said about him. Didn't she? She told it to Aunt Bertha. Her fault. If she liked a goy, so I liked. There! She made me. How did I know? It's all her fault and I'm going to tell too. Blame it on her. Yours Mama! Yours! Go on! Go on! Next! Next floor! Mama! Mama! Owoo!

And leaving the third landing where the stale reek of cabbage and sour cream filled the uncertain light, a low whimper forced its way through his lips and echoed with an alien treble in the hollow silence. And upward, clammy palms clinging to the bannisters and squealing in thin reluctance as they slid. And again the turn of the stairs and the open window framing a soft clarity with the new height. Across the alley, a face between curtains grimaced, tilted back; crooking fingers plucked the collar off.

—Stop hollerin'! Stop! You, inside, stop! Don't know. They don't know. Who told them? Tell me, who could've? Well, tell me? There! See! Polly didn't tell—Esther wouldn't let her. She ran after her. But maybe she didn't catch. She did! She didn't. She did! But even if—so what?

Aunt Bertha wouldn't tell. Aunt Bertha likes me. See? Aunt Bertha wouldn't tell on me for a million, zillion dollars. Don't she hate Papa? Didn't she want me 'stead of them? Didn't she? So she wouldn't tell. Gee, ooh, God! 'Course she wouldn't tell. So what? What am I scared of? (He leaned against the bannister in an ecstasy of hope) Nobody knows! Oooh, God, make nobody know! Go on then! Make believe nothing happened. Gee, nothing-but —but him. Rabbi? Aaa, he forgets. Sure he does! All the time. What's he got to remember for? Go on, gee, God! Go on! But—but where were you? It's way late. Me? Where was I? Got lost, that's what. Way in the other side of Avenue A. Why? Thought it was the other side. That's where I was. Go on! Oooh, God! Wish I broke a leg. Ow! Don't! Yea! Sh!

The pale blue light of the transom obliquely overhead.

—Nobody—in?

He crept to his doorway, stiff ankle-joints cracking like gun-shots. A blur of voices behind the door.

—Sh! Who? Who's there?

Pent breath trembling in his bosom, he leaned nearer, leaned nearer and poised for flight.

Someone laughed.

—Who? She? Mama? Yes! *Yes!*

Again, out of a mumble of voices, again the laugh— strained, nervous, but a laugh. Hope clutched at it.

—She! Laugh is hers! She don't know! Don't know nothing! Wouldn't laugh if she knew. No! No! Don't know! Can go!

His brain flew open as though a light were swung into it—

—Nobody knows! Can go!

Yet his whole being shied in terror when he reached out his hand for the door knob—

The door that clicked open, clicked shut upon their voices. And—

"David! David, child! Where have you been?"

"Mama! Mama!" But not soon enough could he fling himself into her bosom, not deep enough nest his eyes there before he saw in a blur of vision the bearded figure before the table.

"Mama! Mama! Mama!"

Only the sheltering valley between her breasts muffled

his scream of fear to her heart. Convulsive, unerring hands flew up to her neck, sought and clasped the one upright pillar of this ruin.

"Hush! Hush! Hush child! Have no fear!" Her body rocked him.

And at his back, his father's voice, morose, sardonic, "Yes, hush him! Comfort him! Comfort him!"

"Poor frightened one!" Her words came to him from her bosom and lips. "His heart is beating like a thief's. Where have you been, life? I'm dead with anxiety! Why didn't you come home?"

"Lost!" he moaned. "I was lost on Avenue A."

"Ach!" She clasped him to her again. "Because you told a strange tale?"

"I was just making believe! I was just making believe!"

"Were you?" Behind him his father's cryptic voice. "Were you indeed!"

He could feel his mother start. The heart beneath his ear begun to pound heavily.

"Hi! Yi! Yi! Yi! Yi!" From another corner of the room, the rabbi's dolorous groan broke up into a train of sighs. "I see I have wrought badly coming here. No?" He paused, but none answered his question. Instead,

"Stop your whining, you!" his father snapped.

"But what was I to do?" The rabbi launched himself again. His voice, so uncommonly unctuous and placating, sounded strange to David's ears despite his misery. "Had he been a dullard, a plaster golem, such as only the King of the Universe with his holy and bounteous hand knows how to bestow on me, would I have believed him? Psh! I would have said—Bah! Ox-brained idiot, away with this drool! And then and there would I have fetched him such a cuff on the jowls, his children's children would have cried aloud! Hear me, friend Schearl, he would have flown from me like a toe-nail from a shear! But no!" His voice heightened, deepened, grew rich with huskiness. "In my cheder he was as a crown in among rubbish, as a seraph among Esau's goyim! How could I help but believe him? A yarn so incredible had to be true. No? His father a goy, an organ-grinder—an organ player in a church! His mother dead! She met him among the corn—"

"What!" Both voices, but with what different tones!

"I said among the corn. You, Mrs. Schearl, his aunt! What! The like will not be heard again till the Messiah is a bride-groom. Speak! No?"

Again that silence and then as though the silence were creaking with its own strain, the ominous grating sound of a stretched cable, his father's grinding teeth. Under his ear, the heavy beat of the heart tripped, fluttered, hammered raggedly. The stricken catch of the quick breath in her throat was like the audible sublimate of his own terror.

"But uh—uh—now it's a jest, no? Uh—ah, what! A jest!" His hurried nails could be heard harrying his beard. "Not-eh-ah-poo! Not a doubt!" Stumbling at first, his speech began to tumble, growing more flustered as it grew heartier. "It's your child now. No! It's your child! Always! What's there to be disturbed about? Ha? A jest! A tale of a—of a hunter and a wild bear! Understand? Something to laugh at! Ha! Ha—hey, scamp, there! You won't gull me again! What these imps can't invent! Ha! Ha! A jest, no?"

"Yes! Yes!" Her alarmed voice.

"Hmph!" Savagely from her husband. "You agree readily! Where did he get this story? Let him speak! Where did he? Was it Bertha, that red cow? Who?"

David moaned, grasped his mother closer.

"Let him alone, Albert!"

"You say so, do you? We'll find out!"

"But uh—you won't hold it against me—uh—I mean that I told you. May God requite me if I came here trying to meddle, to stir up rancor. Yes! May I wither where I sit! Hear me! Not a jot did I care to pry! Let the feet grow where they list, I cared not! Not I! But I thought here am I his rabbi, and I thought it's my duty to tell you—at least that you might know that he knew—and in what way he was made aware."

"It's all right!" She unclasped one arm. "I beg you don't be disturbed."

"Well then, good! Good! Ha! I must go! The Synagogue! It grows late." The creak of his chair and scrape of his feet filled the pause as he rose. "Then you're not angered with me?"

"No! No! Not at all!"

"Good-night then, good-night." Hastily. "May God bestow you an appetite for supper. I shan't trouble you again. If you wish I'll start him on Chumish soon—a rare thing for one who has spent so little time in a cheder. Good-night to you all."

"Good-night!"

"Hi-yi-yi-yi-yi-! Life is a blind cast. A blind caper in the dark. Good-night! Hi-i! Yi! Yi! Evil day!"

The latch ground. The door opened, creaked, closed on his hi-yi-ing footsteps. And of the silence that followed the beating of her heart condensed the anguish into intervals. And then his father's voice, vibrant with contempt—

"The old fool! The blind old nag! But this once he wrought better than he knew!"

He felt his mother's thighs and shoulders stiffen. "What do you mean?" she asked.

"I'll tell you in a moment," he answered ominously. "No, on second thought I won't need to tell you at all. It will tell itself. Answer me this: Where was my father when I married you?"

"Do you need ask me? You know that yourself—he was dead."

"Yes, I know it," was his significant retort. And his voice tightening suspiciously. "You saw my mother?"

"Of course! What's come over you, Albert?"

"Of course!" he repeated in slow contempt. "Why do you smirk at me with that blank, befuddled look? I mean did you see her before I brought her to you myself?"

"What is it you want, Albert?"

"An answer without guile," he snapped. "You know what I'm talking about! I know you too well. Did she come to you alone? In secret? Well? I'm waiting!"

As though her body were compelled to follow the waverings of an immense irresolution, she swayed back and forth, and David with her. And at last quietly: "If you must know—she did."

"Ha!" The table slid along the floor. "I knew it! Oh, I know her nature! And she told you, didn't she? And she warned you! Of me! Of what I had done?"

"There was nothing said of that—!"

"Nothing? Nothing of what? How can you be so simple?"

"Nothing!" she repeated desperately. "Stop tormenting me, Albert!"

"You wouldn't have said nothing." He pursued her relentlessly. "You would have asked me, what? What I had done? She told you!"

His mother was silent.

"She told you! Is your tongue trapped in silence? Speak!"

"Ach—!" and stopped. Only David heard the wild beating of her heart. "Not now! Not with him here!"

"Now!" he snarled.

"She did." Her voice was wrung from her. "And she told me I ought not to marry you. But what difference—"

"She did! And the rest? The others? Who else!"

"Why are you so eager to hear?"

"Who else?"

"Father and mother. Bertha." Her voice had become labored. "The others know. I never told you because I—"

"They knew!" he interrupted her with bitter triumph. "They knew all the time! Then why did they let you marry me? Why did *you* marry me?"

"Why? Because no one believed her. Who could?"

"Oh!" sarcastically. "Is that it? That was quickly thought of! It was easy to shut your minds. But she swore it was true, didn't she? She must have, hating me afterwards as she did. Didn't she tell you that my father and I had quarreled that morning, that he struck me, and I vowed I would repay him? There was a peasant watching us from afar. Didn't she tell you that? He said I could have prevented it. I could have seized the stick when the bull wrenched it from my father's hand. When he lay on the ground in the pen. But I never lifted a finger! I let him be gored! Didn't she tell you that?"

"Yes! But, Albert, Albert! She was like a woman gone mad! I didn't believe it then and I don't believe it now! Let's stop now, please! Can't we talk about it later?"

"Now that it's all become clear to me you want to stop, is that it?"

"And why is it suddenly so clear?" her tone held a sharp insistence. "What is so clear to you? What are you trying to prove?"

"You ask me?" ominously. "You dare ask me?"

"I do! What do you mean?"

"Oh, the gall of your kind! How long do you think you'll hide it! Will I be lulled and gulled forever? Must I tell you? Must I blurt it out! My sin balances another? Is that enough for you?"

"Albert!" her stunned outcry.

"Don't call to me!" he snarled. "I'll say it again—they had to get rid of you!"

"Albert!"

"Albert!" He spat back at her. "Whose is he? The one you're holding in your arms! Ha? How should he be named?"

"You're mad! Dear God! What's happened to you?"

"Mad, eh? Mad then, but not a cheat! Come! What are you waiting for? Unmask yourself! I've been unmasked to you for years. All these years you said nothing. You pretended to know nothing. Why? You knew why! I would have asked you what I've just asked you now! I would have said why did they let you marry me. There must have been something wrong. I would have known! I would have told you. But now, speak! Speak out with a great voice! Why fear? You know who I am! That red cow betrayed you, didn't she? I'll settle with her too. But don't think there was no stir in this silence. All these years my blood told me! Whispered to me whenever I looked at him, nudged me, told me he wasn't mine! From the very moment I saw him in your arms out of the ship, I guessed. I guessed!"

"And you believe a child's fantasy?" She spoke with a fixed flat voice of one staggered by the incredible. "The babbling? The wandering of a child?"

"No! No!" he bit back with a fierce sarcasm. "Not a bit of it. Not a word. How could I? It's muddled of course. But did you want a commentary. Let him speak again. It might be clearer."

"I've thought you strange, Albert, and even mad but that was pride and that made you pitiful. But now I see you're quite, quite mad! Albert!" She suddenly cried out as if her cry would waken him. "Albert! Do you know what you're saying!"

"A comedienne to the end." He paused, drew in the sharp breath of one marveling—"Hmph! How you sustain it! Not a tremor! Not a sign of betrayal! But answer me this!" His voice thinned to a probe. "Here! Here's a

chance to show me my madness. Where is his birth
certificate? Ha? Where is it? Why have they never sent
it?"

"That? Was it because of that one single thing your
blood warned you so much? Why, dear God, they wrote
you—my own father did. They had looked for it everywhere and never found it—lost! The confusion of departure! What other reason could there be?"

"Yes! Yes! What else could it be? But we—we know
why it stayed lost, don't we? It was better unfound! After
all, was I there to see him born? Was I even there to see you
bearing him? No! I was in America—on their money,
notice! The ticket they bought me. Why were they so
eager to get rid of me? Why such haste, and I not married more than a month?"

"Why? Can't you see for yourself? There were nine
in my family. Servants, others, outsiders began to know.
They had hoped I would follow you soon. There was no
money at home. The store was failing. The sons weren't
grown yet. You couldn't send for me—"

"Oh, stop! Stop! I know all that! Who is it they began
to know of—you or me?"

"Do you still persist? Of you, of course! Your mother
went around telling everyone."

"And they were ashamed, eh? I see! But now I'll tell
you my version. Here I am in America sweating for your
passport, starving myself. You see? Thousands of miles
away. Alone. Never writing to anyone only to you. Now!
He's born a month or two too soon to be mine—perhaps
more. You wait that time. That month or two, and then,
why then exactly on the head of the hour you write me—
I have a son! A joy! Fortune! I have a son. Ha! But when
you came across, the doctors were too knowing. Fool your
husband, they said. You were frightened. Seventeen
months were too few for one so grown. Twenty-one then!
Twenty-one they might believe, and twenty-one of course
I thought he was. There you are! Wasn't that it? I haven't
forgotten. My memory's good. An organist, eh? A goy,
God help you! Ah! It's clear! But my blood! My blood I
say warned me!"

"You're mad! There's no other word!"

"So? But good enough for your kind. That's what they
reasoned back home—the old, praying glutton and his

wife—Did you know an organist? Well, why don't you answer?"

"I—oh, Albert, let me alone!" She moved David about frantically under her arms. "Let me alone in God's name! You've heaped enough shame on me for nothing. It's more than I can bear. You're distraught! Let's not talk about it anymore! Later! Tomorrow! I've suffered twice for this now."

"Twice! Ha!" He laughed. "You've a gift for blurting things out! Then you knew an organist?"

"You claim I did!" Her voice went suddenly stony.

"Did you? Say it."

"I did then. But that was—"

"You did! You did!" His words rang out again. "It fits! It matches! Why look! Look up there! Look! The green corn—taller than a man! It struck your fancy, didn't it? Why, of course it would! The dense corn high above your heads, eh? The summer trysts! But I—I married in November! Ha! Ha!—Sh! Don't speak! Not a word! You'll be ludicrous, you're so confounded!"

"And you believe? And you believe? This that you're saying! Can you believe it?"

"Anhr! Do I believe the sun? Why I've sensed it for years I tell you! I've stubbed my feet against it at every turn and tread. It's been in my way, tangled me! And do you know how? Haven't you ever seen it? Then why do weeks and weeks go by and I'm no man at all? No man as other men are? You know of what I speak! You ought to, having known others! I've been poisoned by a guess! Corruption has haunted me. I've sensed it! I've known it! Do you understand? And it's been true!"

She rose. And David still in her arms, still clasping her neck, dared not breathe nor whimper in his terror, dared not lift his eyes from the shelter of her breast. And his father's voice, nearer now, broke like a rod of stiff, metallic words across his back.

"Hold him tightly! He's yours!"

She answered, a kind of cold deliberate pity in her voice. "And now, now that you know what you think you know, the corruption's drained. Is that how you are? The fog is split. Why didn't you tell me sooner what clouded you? I would have freed you sooner."

"And now like any discovered cheat you'll mock me, eh?"

"I'm not mocking you, Albert. I'm just asking you to tell me exactly what it is you want."

"I want," his teeth ground into his words. "Never to see that brat again."

She sucked in her breath as if making a last attempt. "You're driving me mad, Albert! He's your son! Your son! Oh, God! He's yours. What if I knew another man long before I met you—! It was long ago, I swear to you! Can he, must he be his? He's yours!"

"I'll never believe you! Never! Never!"

"Why then I'll go!"

"Go. I'll caper! I'll dance on the roofs! I'll be rid of it! Be rid of it, I tell you! The nights in the milk wagon! The thoughts! The torment! The stables—hitching the horse. The other men! The torment! I'll be rid of it! His—"

But as though answering his suppressed scream of exaltation, noises in the hallway, wrangling, angry, confused, battered like turbulent waves against the door. He stopped as though struck. About David's legs the clasp of his mother's arms tightened protectingly. Again the cries threatening, reproachful and a stamp and shuffling of feet. A sharp crack at the door, Flung open, it banged against a chair.

"Now let me go! I'm here! I'm going to speak!"

He knew the voice! One wild glance he threw over his shoulder—Aunt Bertha grappling with her husband seemed less strange to him now than that the light of the kitchen had grown so grey. With a whimper of despair, he clutched at his mother's neck, buried his face frenziedly into the crook of her throat. And she, bewildered—

"Nathan! You? Bertha! What is it? You look so frantic!"

"I—I am angry!" Uncle Nathan gasped tormentedly. "I have much—!"

"It's nothing!" Aunt Bertha beat his words down. "My man is a fool! Look at him! He's gone crazy!"

"Let me speak! Will you let me speak!"

"Be strangled first!" She flew at him venomously. "He wants—do you know what he wants? Can't you guess? What does a Jew want? Money. He's come to borrow money! And why does he want money? To make a bigger store. Nothing else! He's out of his head! I'll tell you what happened to him. He dreamt last night the police came and stripped off his boots, the way they did his bankrupt grandfather in Vilna. It's gone to his head. He's frightened. His wits are in a foam. Ask him where he is now. He couldn't answer you. I'm sure he couldn't. And how are you, Albert! It's a fair brace of months since I have seen you! You ought to visit us sometimes, see our little store, and vast variety of bon-bons. Cheh! Cheh! Und heva suddeh-wawdeh!"

David's father made no answer.

And lightly as though she expected none. "And why are you holding him in your arms, Genya?"

"Just to—just to feel his weight," his mother replied unsteadily. "And he is heavy!" She bent over to put him down.

"No, Mama!" he whispered, clinging to her. "No, Mama!"

"Only a moment, beloved! I can't hold you in my arms so long. You're too heavy!" She set him on his feet. "There! Once he gets up, he won't come down." And still keeping her trembling hand on his shoulder, she turned to Nathan. "Money? Why—?" She laughed confusedly. "I think the world's gone mad! What makes you come to us of all people? Are you in your right senses, Nathan?"

Fixing his glowering, harassed eyes on David, Nathan opened his mouth to speak—

"Of course!" Aunt Bertha outstripped him. "Of course, you haven't any money." She dug her elbow viciously into her husband's ribs. "That's what I told him. To the very words! Didn't I?"

Almost giddy with terror and guilt, David had dodged behind his mother. At her side stood his father, arms folded across his chest, aloof, nostrils still slowly flaring in the ebb and flow of passion. In the greying light, his face looked like stone, only the nostrils and the crooked vein on his brow alive. Then he uncrossed his arms. His dense, smoldering eyes traveled from face to face, brushed David's who jerked his head away in panic, traveled on and returned, cleaving there. Without turning to look, David knew himself regarded, so palpable was that gaze, so like a pressure. Enveloping him, it seemed to sap him from without. He grew dizzy, reached out numb hands

for his mother's dress, hung there faintly. His father shifted
his gaze. And as though he had been struggling under
water until this moment, David gulped down breath,
heard sounds again, voices.

"And you won't sit down?" His mother was asking
solicitously. "You're tired, both of you. I can see it. Why,
supper for two more would take no longer. Please stay!"

"No! No! Thanks, sister!" Aunt Bertha was positive.
"But if he would go hunting for rusty horseshoes before
he's had his supper, why he can wait a little longer—
I'm as tired as he is. And I warned him!"

"I'm sorry we can't help you, Nathan. You know we would
if we had it! Oh! It's all so mixed! I'm confused! Why!"
She laughed ruefully. "If it weren't so absurd, Nathan,
it would be flattering that you should think we had any
money."

Biting his lips, Uncle Nathan stared at the floor, swayed
as if he might fall. "I have nothing to say." he answered
dully. "She's said it all."

"You see?" There was a note of triumph in Aunt
Bertha's voice. "He's ashamed of himself now. But now
I like him!" She began nudging him toward the door.
"Now he's my man and as good a man as ever ate prunes
with his meat. Come, good heart! Mrs. Zimmerman is
waiting— My customers will think I'm burying you."

"You've a cunning way!" He answered, shaking her off
sullenly. "You've clogged my chimney well! But you wait!
You'll laugh in convulsion yet!"

"Come! Come!" She gave him a push toward the door.
"Hoist up your nose! That venture you want money for
can wait!"

Uncle Nathan wrested his arm away, shook a desperate, baffled finger at his wife. "A curse on you and your
money and your whole story! I'll stay! I'll speak!"

Aunt Bertha ignored him, opened the door. "Good night,
sister! Forgive him! He's always been a good husband,
but to-night— You know how men are! When they're a
little unstrung, they revel in it. Come, you!"

Cowering behind his mother, David watched Aunt Bertha
drag her stubborn husband toward the door. Their going
would be no deliverance—one doom postponed, another
waiting. There could be no less terror if they stayed, or if
they went. Whatever way the mind turned it faced only

fear. This he had escaped. Aunt Bertha had saved him. But his father! His father again! Their going abandoned him to that fury! But—

"Wait!"

For the first time since they had come, his father spoke. And now he uncrossed his arms and stalked suddenly to the door.

"Wait!" He gripped Uncle Nathan's shoulder, towered above him. "Come back!"

"What do you want of my man!" Aunt Bertha snapped in angry surprise. "You let him alone. He's distraught enough without you troubling him. Come, Nathan!" She redoubled her tugging at the other shoulder.

"It's you who should let him alone!" her brother-in-law growled dangerously. "You and your cursed deceit! Come in, Nathan!"

Staring amazed from face to face, Uncle Nathan could muster no more than a bewildered grunt.

"I say let him go!" Aunt Bertha shrieked furiously. "Wild beast, take your paws off!"

"When I'm done!"

"Albert! Albert!" his mother's frightened voice. "What are you doing! Let him alone!"

"No! No! Not till he's spoken!"

For a moment, half in the thickening light of the kitchen, half in the gloom of the corridor, they wrestled for him, Uncle Nathan's pale, alarmed face, bobbing back and forth between them, and all three struggling figures, shadowy, unreal as nightmare. A moment longer, and with one vicious yank, David's father pulled them back into the room, and with such force, the other man pitched forward, his hat flying to the floor. He slammed the door.

"Listen to me, Nathan!" He drummed his stiff hand against the other man's chest. "You came here to say something, now say it. Stifle that she-ass and her guile! Say it! It isn't money!"

"N-nothing! Nothing! So help me, G-God!" Before the thrust of the other's hand, Uncle Nathan fell back against his wife. "Bertha told you everything! May evil befall me if she didn't! A store! I wanted! I saw! That was all! No, Bertha?"

"You fool!" She spat at her husband. "Didn't I warn

you not to come here! Didn't I tell you you'd groan and remember? I've a good mind to—What do you want of him?" She wheeled furiously on her brother-in-law. "You let him alone, ungovernable beast! Do you hear? He's come for money and nothing else! How many times do you want to be told? I don't have to endure any more of your rages! Remember that!"

"Hold your tongue!" His father was beginning to quiver. "You treacherous cow! I know you of old. I know what you've already done. Speak, Nathan!" He smashed his fist down on the wash tub. "Don't let her trick you! Speak! Whatever it is! Have no fear of me! Only the truth! I have reasons! It may do me good to hear!"

"What's he saying?" Aunt Bertha's eyes bulged. "What new insanity gripes him!"

"Albert, I beg of you!" his mother had seized her husband's arm. "If you've any quarrel, it's with me. Let the man alone. He's told you all."

"Has he? So you think! Or pretend, maybe! But I know better! I have eyes! I have seen! Will you speak?" Wrath stretched him to his full height. Teeth bared, he advanced, dwarfing the other man who cowered.

"I-I've already s-said everything," his lips trembling, Uncle Nathan reached behind him for the door. "I must leave! Bertha! Come!"

But David's father had rammed his palm against the door.

"You'll wait! You hear me? You'll wait till you answer me one thing! And you'll answer it!"

"W-what do you want?"

"Why, when you opened your mouth to speak—Before that she-ass brayed you out of words and will—Why did you stare at him?" He hammered the air in David's direction. "Why that look? What was it you were trying to say about him?"

"I—I have nothing to say. I didn't look at him. Let me alone in God's will. Genya! Bertha! Don't let him quarrel with me."

"Albert! Albert! Stop torturing the man!"

"A curse on you! You fiend!" Aunt Bertha tried to squeeze in between them "You madman! Let him alone!"

He flung her viciously aside. "And you, will you tell me what he did? Or do you want my fury to burst—!"

"Oh! Oh! Woe me! Woe me!" Aunt Bertha filled the room with a loud gasping and lament. "Woe me! Did you see what he did? He threw me? And me with a child in my belly. Monster! Mad dog! It's not drawers you've ripped this time. It's a child you've destroyed! On your head my miscarriage. Oh you'll pay for this! May they hang you. May you—"

"Not if you had twins would it trouble me. Your breed is well destroyed. But I will find out what he did. That brat there! I'm waiting!" His voice became strangled. "I tell you I'm at the end of my patience!"

Uncle Nathan began to sag as though about to faint.

"He—uh—uh— oy! oy! He—!"

"Not a word!" Aunt Bertha screamed. "Open that door or I'll shriek for help! Let us out!"

They faced each other in a silence so awful it seemed as if the very room would burst with the tension of it.

Blind with terror, unnoticed by any, David had already reeled toward the stove. (—*It's there! It's there!*) A tortured, anguished voice babbled within him. (—*It's there! She put it there! It's there!*) Groping, tottering hands reached into the dark niche between the stove and the wall—

"Speak!" In the shrunken, shadowy room, his father had become all voice, and his voice struck with the brunt of thunder.

"Bertha!" Uncle Nathan wailed. "Save me! Save me, Bertha! He's going to strike! Bertha! Bertha!"

"Help!" she screamed. "Let go the door! Help! Help! Call! Genya, throw up the window! Help!"

"Albert! Albert! Have mercy!"

"Speak!" Above their screaming, the horrible gritting of his teeth.

"I— I— uh—he— it was he— uh. Oh, Bertha! Noth—"

"Anh!" That insensate snarl. The shadowy arm drew back. "You—!"

"Papa!"

The bent arm hung in air, hung motionless. The writhing face above it turned.

"Papa!" In the swirling, crumbling, darkened mind, that one compulsion rallied the body and the brain like a standard. A dream? No, not a dream. Not a dream nor the memory of a dream. An act, ordained, foreseen, inevitable as this very moment, a channel of expertness, imbued for ages, reiterated for ages, familiar as breath.

He approached. The rest stood spellbound.

"I— It was me, papa—"

"David! Child!" His mother sprang toward him. "What have you got in your hand!"

But before she could reach him, he had lifted the broken whip into his father's curling fingers.

"David!" She seized him, drew him out of danger. "A whip! Near him! What are you doing!"

"This?" The lids dropped over his father's consuming eyes. "Why do you—? Why is this given? You know what happened to this? Is it your fate you're begging for?"

"I— I— Please, papa!"

"You shan't touch him! You hear me, Albert! I won't endure it!" All entreaty, all timidity had vanished, in its stead a fierce resolve. She bowed over David like a ledge of rock. "Whatever he's done or anyone thinks he's done, you shan't touch him!"

"Band against the alien, the stranger!" His father's voice was hollow and perilous, "But let me hear him!"

"Say nothing, child!" Aunt Bertha's warning cry.

But he was already speaking. And the words he spoke were like staggering burdens he bore up a great steep where his own sighs battered him, where he floundered in his own tears.

"I was—I was on—the roof. Papa! I was on the roof! And there was a b-boy. A big one—and—and he had a kite—k-kite, they called it. Kite—goes h-higher than r-roofs—it goes—"

"What are you talking about!" His father ground. "Stop your candle-gutter! Hurry!"

"I'm—I'm—" He gasped for breath.

"God's fool!" Aunt Bertha rasped under her breath. "My man! My man! May earth gape for you this very hour! You see what you've wrought!"

"Me?" Uncle Nathan groaned. "My fault? How did I—"

"So—s-somebody—wanted to take it. The k-kite. And I called. And I said—look out! Look out! So I—I was his friend. Leo. He had skates and then—Ow! Papa! Papa! And we went to Aunt Bertha's. And we got Polly on the other side—in the yard. He got her—And he gave her the skates. And then, ow! Ow! He took her in—in the cellar. And he—he—"

"He what!" The implacable voice was like a goad.

"I don't know! Ow! He p-played—he played—bad!"

"Anh!"

"Don't you come near him!" his mother screamed. "Don't you dare! That's enough, child! Hush! That's enough!"

"H-he did! Not me, Papa! Papa, not me! I didn't! Ow! Papa! Papa!" He clung frenziedly to his mother.

"That's hers! Her spawn! Mark me! Hers!" He seemed to be stifling in a wild insane joy. "Not mine! Not a jot of me! Bertha, cow! Not mine! You, Nathan! Rouse your sheep-wits! Your mate's betrayed my wife! Do you know it? Blabbed her secret! Told him whose he was. An organist somewhere. How I harbored a goy's get! A rake! A rogue's! His and hers! But not mine! I knew it! I knew it all the time! And now I'm driving her out! Her and him, the brat! Let him beat her in time to come. But I'm free! He's no part of me! I'm free!"

"He's mad!" The other two whispered hoarsely and shrank away.

"Hear me!" He was slavering at the mouth. "I nurtured him! Three years I throttled surmise, I was the beast of burden! Good fortune I never met! Happiness never! Joy never! And—and that was right! Why should I meet anything but misfortune! That was right! I was tainted. I was bridled with another's sin. But for that—for all that suffering I have one privilege! Who will deny me? Who? One privilege! To wreak! To quench! Once!"

And before anyone could move, he had lunged forward at David's mother.

"Ow! Papa! Papa! Don't!"

Those steel fingers closed like a crunching trap on David's shoulders—yanked him out of her hands. And the whip! The whip in air! And—

"Ow! Ow! Papa! Ow!"

Bit like a brand across his back. Again! Again! And he fell howling to the floor.

His mother screamed. He felt himself grabbed, pulled to his feet, dragged away. And now his aunt was screaming, Uncle Nathan's hoarse outcry swelling the tumult. In the shadows, figures swayed, grappled—And suddenly his father's voice, exultant, possessed, hypnotic—

"What's that? That! Look! Look at the floor! There! Who disbelieves me now? Look what's lying there! There where he fell! A sign! A sign I tell you! Who doubts? A sign!"

"Unh!" Uncle Nathan grunted as though in sudden pain.

"Woe me!" Aunt Bertha gasped in horror. "It's—! What! No!"

Terror impinging on terror, David squirmed about in his mother's arms—looked down—

There, stretched from the green square to the white square of the checkered linoleum lay the black beads— the gold cross framed in the glimmering, wan glaze. Horror magnified the figure on it. He screamed.

"Papa! Papa! Leo—he gave them! That boy! It fell out! Papa!" His words were lost in the uproar.

"God's own hand! A sign! A witness!" his father was raving, whirling the whip in his flying arms. A proof of my word! The truth! Another's! A goy's! A cross! A sign of filth! Let me strangle him! Let me rid the world of a sin!"

"Put him out! Genya! Put him out! David! David! Him! Hurry! Let him run!" Aunt Bertha and Uncle Nathan were grappling with his father. "Hurry! Out!"

"No! No!" his mother's frenzied cry.

"Hurry! I say! Hurry! Help! We can't hold him!" Uncle Nathan had been shaken off. With knees bent, Aunt Bertha was hanging like a dead weight from his father's whip-hand. "He'll slay him," she shrieked. "He'll trample on him as he let his father be trampled on. Hurry, Genya!"

Screaming, his mother sprang toward the door—threw it open— "Run! Run down! Run! Run!"

She thrust him from her, slammed the door after him. He could hear the thud her body flung against it. With a wild shriek he plunged toward the stairs—

On the whole floor and even on the one below it, doors had been opened. Spears of gas-lamps crisscrossed in the unlit hallway. Gaping, craning faces peered out, listening, exclaiming, reporting to others behind them—

"Hey, boychick! Vus is? A fight! Hey vot's de maddeh? Hooz hollerin'? Leibeleh! Dun' go op! You hea' vot I say. Dun go op! Oy! Cull a cop! Tek keh! Quick! Vehzee runnin'? Hey, boychick!"

A reeling smear of words, twitching gestures, fractured lights, features, a flickering gauntlet of tumult and dismay. He never answered, but plunged down. None stopped him. Only a miracle saved him from crashing down the dark steps. And now the voices were above him, and he heard feet trampling on the stairs, and now all noises merged to a flurried humming and now almost unheard—his down-drumming feet had reached the hallway—

Blue light in the door-frame.

Arms up and gasping like a runner to the tape—

The street.

The street. He dared to breathe. And stumbled to the sidewalk and stood there, stood there.

XX

DUSK. Storelight and lamplight condensed—too early for assertion. The casual, canceled stir and snarling of distance. And on the sidewalks, men and women striding with too certain a gait, and in the gutter, children crossing, calling, not yet conceding the dark's dominion. The world dim-featured in mouldering light, floating, faceted and without dimension. For a moment the wild threshing of voices, bodies, the screams, the fury in the pent and shrunken kitchen split their bands in the brain, flew out to the darkened east, the flagging west beyond the elevated, the steep immensity of twilight that dyed the air above the housetops. For a moment, the rare coolness of a July evening dissolved all agony in a wind as light as with the passing of a wand. And suddenly there was space even between the hedges of stone and suddenly there was quiet even in the fret of cities. And there was time, inviolable even to terror, time to watch the smudged and cluttered russet in the west beckon to the night to cover it. A moment, but a moment only, then he whimpered and ran.

—Can't! Ow! Can't! Can't run! Can't! Hurts! Hurts! Ow! Mama! Legs! Mama!

He had no more than reached the corner when every racked fibre in his body screamed out in exhaustion. Each time his foot fell was like a plunger through his skull. On buckling legs, he crossed Avenue D, stopped, wobbling with faintness, rubbed his thighs.

—Can't go! Can't! Hurt! Ow! Mama! Mama!

Fearfully, he peered over his shoulder, eyes traveling upward. From the first to the third floor of his house, the lighted kitchens behind bedrooms cast their dull stain on the windows—one dusky brass, one fawn, one murky grey. A column of drab yet reassuring light—except his own on the fourth floor, still sullen, aloof and dark. He caught his breath in a new onslaught of terror. Waves of fear serried his breast and back—

—Ain't not yet! Ow! Fighting yet! Him! What's he doing! Mama! Mama! He's hitting! Ow! Can't run! Some place! Stay here! Find! Watch! Wait till— Wait! Wait! Scared! Hide! Some place . . . Where?

A short distance to his left, the closed dairy store between Ninth and Tenth was unlit. He stumbled toward it. Behind the barricade of milk cans chained to the cellar-railing, he crouched down on the store-step, fixed lifted, imploring eyes to his windows. Dark, still dark. Baleful, unrelenting, they hid yet betrayed the fury and disaster behind them. He moaned, bit his fingers in agony, stared about him with a wild, tortured gaze.

Across the street the bar of green light in the photography shop blazed out. People passed, leisurely, self-absorbed, and as they entered the radius of the light, it fixed them momentarily in caustic, carrion-green. None marked him there, but drifted by with too buoyant and too aimless a gait for his own misery, drifted by with bloated corroded faces, as if heaved in the swell of a weedy glare, as if lolling undersea. Too sick to endure it, he looked away, looked up.

—Dark yet up. Dark . . . First, second, third is light. Mine Dark. Dark mine only. Papa stop. Stop! Stop, papa. Light it now. Ain't mad no more. Light it, mama. Now! One, two, three, now! One, two, three, now! Now! Aaa! Ain't! Ain't! Ow! Run away, mama! Don't let him! Run away! Here! Here I am! Run! Mama! Mama! Mama!

He whimpered.

A man, paunched, slow-footed, his bulky body rolling

on baggy unbending knees drew near. Opposite David, he turned a slow head toward the light, palmed a strange, corrupt-purple splotch on his jowls, pinched his under lip and lumbered on.

—With the whip. The busted one. Here he hit too. Him like from wagon. And I gave it. Won't bust no more. If he—Don't let him! Don't let him! Run in! Bedroom! Hold door. Tight! Don't let go! Aunt Bertha! Uncle! You too! Hold it! Fast! Don't let him hit her! Hold it! Ow! Mama! Stop! Stop, papa! Please! Ow! Look! Is—dark—dark yet. Dark.

Beside him on the ground floor of the same house where he sat concealed, a window squawked, whirred open. And a man's voice in sing-song harangue:

"Aaa, dawn be a wise-guy! Hooz tuckin' f'om vinnin'! A dollar 'n' sexty fife gestern! A thuler 'n' sompt'n' —ova hadee cends—Sonday! An' Monday night in back f'om Hymen's taileh-shop, rummy, *tuh* sevendy. Oy, yuh sh'd die. An' I sez if yuh ken give a good dill, Abe, yuh sheoll dill in jail auraddy! An' if I luz again, a fire sol dich bald urtreffen!" The voice retreated.

—If it lights, so what? What'll I do? He'll ask me. What'll I do? What? What? Papa, nothing. I wanted . . . I wanted. What? The—The—on the floor. Beads. Fell out—pocket. What for you—? Ow! Papa, I don't know What? Why? He'll look. He'll say. Ball. Ball I wanted Ball? He'll say—ball? Yes. Ball. In my head. Ow! I can't tell. Must! In my head seen. Was. In the corner. By milk-stink baby carriages. White. Wasn't scared. What? What? What? Yes. Wasn't scared. How I seen one once, when—When? Sword in the fire. Tenth Street. Ask the rabbi. Sword. In the crack light and he laughed. When I read that he—Fire. Light. When I read. Always scared till then—and they made me. Goyim by river. And They—So had. So lost. Wanted back, Papa! Papa! Wanted back. And he said yes. Leo. Like inside-outside guts burning. And he said would. Come out of box. Said God on—Wait, Papa! Papa! Don't hit! Don't! Ow! Didn't want a big one, only twentier. Littler even. Only nickel-big. Down under fished—like when—Ow! That's why, Papa! That's why! Didn't—Ow! Ain't! Ain't! Ain't lit yet! What'll I do? Ain't lit yet!

They had gathered across the street before the house

beside the barber shop on the corner, boys, nimble, nervous and shrill. And one stood threateningly on the stoop while the rest crouched tensely on the curb—

"Wolf, are yuh ready?"

"I'm geddin' ouda bed!"

"Wolf, are yuh ready?"

"I'm goin' t' de sink!"

"Wolf, are yuh ready?"

"I'm washin' op mine face—"

With precious, mincing gait, two women approached, scanning with dead caressing flutter the dead faces of the men who passed them. Their cheeks in the vitriolic glare of the photography-shop window were flinty yet sagging; green light glazed the velvet powder, scummed the hectic rouge, livid over lurid. One, the nearest, swelling her bosom to the figment strand she lifted from it, sent a glancing beam at David from casual polished, putrescent eyes. They sauntered on trailing a languid wake of flesh and perfume, redolent for all the ten foot gap between them, emphasizing by denying their corruption.

—Milk—stink here too. Where? Cans, because. Milk —stink big cans. What's that—there by—cellar? What? Sword it—No! Don't care! Don't care! Mama! Mama!

"Wolf are yuh ready?"

"I'm putt'n' on my shoes—"

—If she runs, runs away. Don't look for me. Can't see. If she—like she said. Never see her again. Take, me, mama! Don't run away! Mama! Here I am, Mama! By cans I'm hiding! By store! Dark yet—is dark. Dark always! She went already. Didn't look! Don't want to find me! Never! Never! She went! She went! Ow! Look someplace else! Look! Look someplace! Sword by cans! No, ain't. Forgot! He forgot. Store-spoon, milk-spoon. Why! Ow! Mama! Mama! Ain't light! Never! Never!

"Wolf, are yuh ready?"

"I'm pudd'n on my drawz—"

"No fair! Hey, yuh pud on de drawz a'reddy!"

"Awri'! So I'm pudd'n' on my shoit!"

"Wolf, are—"

The clatter of a horse-car drowned them out. And from the window beside him loud and sudden laughter—

"A bluff, ha? Nisht by Mudjkih! Ha! Ha! Ha! Ha! Ven 'Erry says a full-house is a full—"

—If it was—! If it was a sword. So what? You're scared. Ain't not! You're scared! I ain't! I ain't! I ain't! Yes, you know because it ain't. Double dare me? Double dare me? You know it ain't? Could! Even if it ain't a sword, could go in the crack. Where it splashes, hold cup like where you held sword. You're scared. Triple dare me? Somebody'll see. Let 'em! Don't care! Can't get it out. Anyway. Cans too heavy—Can too. Empty. I triple dare you? Wait! Aaaa, knew you was scared. Wait! Three waits! No more! No more! Only three waits. No more! (He was muttering aloud now) "Yuh gonna lighd winder? Winder! Winder! Yuh gonna lighd winder?"

"Wolf, are yuh ready?"

"I'm tieingk op mine shoe-laces!"

—Winder, secon' chance! Yuh gonna lighd winder? I'll go! I'll go! Winder! Mama! Mama! I'll go!

He had risen to his feet. Once more his anguished eyes beseeched the window, and then a fit of horrible rage convulsed him and he writhed and beat the wall beside him. Seconds passed. The fit left him and he tasted the salt blood on his bitten lip and peered with a new, strange feeling of craftiness up and down the greenish street.

Humanity. On feet, on crutches, in carts and cars. The ice-vendor. The waffle-wagon. Human voices, motion, seething, throbbing, bawling, honking horns and whistling. Troubling the far clusters of street lamps, setting store-lights guttering with their passing bodies like a wind. He shuddered, looked near at hand. Across the street, the wolf was crouching, ready to spring; the boys that baited him, twitched warily, giggled nervously at each cry. In the photography-shop, the enlarged pictures of age gazed out at him, mummified and horrible. From wall and side-walk, lamplight and mercury vapor had crowded the gloaming into night; above the streets the hollow cobalt air dissolved heaven's difference with the roof tops. No one was watching him.

In hatred this time, in challenge, his eyes stabbed the window. Dark. He defied it.

Stealthily, he sidled to the nearest milk-can, took hold of the cover and handle. Under his palms, the metal was cold, the heavy can unwieldy, a shifting steely glimmer under his eyes. He leaned against it—harder. It

budged, sounded hollow. Again he braced himself, thrust—
Clank!

Wedged between the shoulder of the can and the
cellar grill, the long, grey, milk-dipper clattered to the
ground. He stooped to pick it up—

"Tadam, padam, pam! Thew! Thew! He had to get
under, get out and get under—" With a jaunty, swagger-
ing stride and nasal hum and toothy whistle, a tall, square-
shouldered man drew abreast. "To fix up his little machine!"
Between cap and black shirt, frosty green-blue eyes winked
down at David, turned away, and passing, left their chill
fire lingering in the air. "Pam! Pam! Prra! To fix up his
little machine!"

The coast was clear now. Across the street, the children were shrieking with excitement. David picked up the
dipper, crept out of the store entrance, and with the scoop
of the dipper under his armpit, long, flat handle in his
hand, he slunk quickly toward Tenth Street—

"Wolf are yuh ready!" their voices pursued him.

"I'm co-o-o--o-omin'—down—duh—st-o-o-op!"

—Goin'! I'm goin', winder! Winder! Winder! I'm goin'!
Uphill, the faint slope, steep to aching legs, he ran,
avoiding the careless glance of the few who noticed.
Tenth Street. A street car crossed the Avenue, going
west. The river wind blew straight and salt between a
flume of houses. He swung sharply into it, entered the
river-block, dimlit, vacant. Ahead of him, like a barrier,
the one beer-saloon, swinging door clamped in a vise of
light, the mottled stained-glass window bulging with a
shoddy glow.

—Somebody'll see.

He skulked in the shadows against the rough wall of
the iron-works, crept forward. In the ebb of river-wind,
the faint bitter flat beer spread round him. Gone in the
quick neaping of wind—A man knuckles to mustache,
flung back the swing-door—whirred reiteration of bar
and mirror, bottles, figures, aprons—David slunk past him
into deeper shadow.

And now the old wagon-yard, the lifted thicket of
tongues; the empty stables, splintered runways, chalked
doors, the broken windows holding still their glass like
fangs in the sash, exhaling manure-damp, rank. The last
street lamp droning in a cyst of light. The gloomy, massive

warehouse, and beyond it, the strewn chaos of the dump heap stretching to the river. He stopped. And where a shadowy cove sank between warehouse wall and dump heap, retreated.

—Yuh dared me . . . Yuh double-dared me . . . Now I gotta.

The tracks lay before him—not in double rows now but in a single yoke. For where he stood was just beyond the fork of the switch, and the last glitter on the tines lapsed into rust and rust into cobbles and cobbles merged with the shadowy dock and the river.

—Scared! Scared! Scared! Don't look!

He plucked his gaze away, tossed frenzied eyes about him. To the left, the chipped brick wall of the warehouse shut off the west and humanity, to the right and behind him, the ledge of the dump heap rose; before him land's end and the glitter on the rails.

—Yuh dared me . . . Yuh double-dared me . . . Now I gotta. I gotta make it come out.

The small sputter of words in his brain seemed no longer his own, no longer cramped by skull, but detached from him, the core of his surroundings. And he heard them again as though all space had compelled them and were shattered in the framing, and they boomed in his ears, vast, delayed and alien.

—Double-dared me! Now I gotta! Double-dared me! *Now I gotta make it come out.*

XXI

INSIDE the Royal Warehouse, located on the East River and Tenth Street, Bill Whitney, an old man with a massive body, short-wind and stiff, rheumatic legs, toiled up the stairway to the first floor. In his left hand, he held a lantern, which in his absent-mindedness, he jogged from time to time to hear the gurgle of its fuel. In his right hand, clacking on the bannister at each upward reach of his arm, he held a key—the key he turned the clocks

with on every floor of the building—the proof of his
watch and wakefulness. As he climbed the swart stairs,
stained with every upward step by shallow, rocking lanter-
light, he muttered, and this he did not so much to popu-
late the silence with ephemeral, figment selves, but to
follow the links of his own, slow thinking, which when he
failed to hear, he lost:

"And wut? Haw! Ye looked down—and—sss! By Gawd
if there waren't the dirt-rud under ye. And. Ha! Ha! Haw!
No wheels. Them pedals were there—now waren't they?
Saw 'em as clear—as clear—but the wheels gone—nowhere. By Gawd, thinks I— Now by Gawst, ain't it queer?
Old Ruf Gilman a'standin' there, a'standin' and a'gappin'.
Jest a'standin' and a'gappin' as plain— And the whiskers
he growed afore the winter . . . By the well with the
white housing. A'savin' his terbaccer juice till he had nigh
a cupful . . . Whawmmmmm! Went plumb through the
snaw in the winter . . ."

> Resounded, surged and resounded, like
> ever swelling breakers:
> —Double! Double! Double dared me!
> Where there's light in the crack,
> yuh dared me. Now I gotta.

In the blue, smoky light of Callahan's beer-saloon, Callahan, the pale fattish bar-keep jammed the dripping beer-
tap closed and leaned over the bar and snickered. Husky
O'Toole—he, the broad-shouldered one with the sky-blue
eyes—dominated those before the bar (among them, a
hunchback on crutches with a surly crimp to his mouth,
and a weazened coal-heaver with a sooty face and bright
eye-balls) and dwarfed them. While he spoke they had listened, grinning avidly. Now he threw down the last finger
of whiskey, nodded to the bar-tender, thinned his thin
lips and looked about.

"Priddy wise mug!" Callahan prompted filling his glass.

"Well." O'Toole puffed out his chest. "He comes up fer
air, see? He's troo. Now, I says, now I'll tell yuh
sompt'n about cunt— He's still stannin' by de fawge,
see, wit' his wrench in his han'. An I says, yuh like
udder t'ings, dontcha? Waddayuh mean, he says. Well, I
says, yuh got religion, aintcha? Yea, he says. An' I says,
yuh play de ponies, dontcha? Yea, he says. An' yuh like
yer booze, dontcha? Sure, he says. Well I says, none o'

dem fer me! Waddayuh mean, he says. Well, I says, yuh c'n keep yer religion, I says. Shit on de pope, I says— I wuz jis' makin' it hot—an' t'hell witcher ponies I says— I bets on a good one sometimes, but I wuzn' tellin' him—an' w'en it comes t' booze I says, shove it up yer ass! Cunt fer me, ev'ytime I says. See, ev'ytime!"

They guffawed. "Yer a card!" said the coal heaver. "Yer a good lad!—"

> *As though he had struck the enormous bell*
> *of the very heart of silence, he*
> *stared round in horror.*

"Gaw blimy, mate!" Jim Haig, oiler on the British tramp *Eastern Greyhound*, (now opposite the Cherry Street pier) leaned over the port rail to spit. "I ain't 'ed any fish 'n' chips since the day I left 'ome. W'y ain't a critter thought of openin' a 'omely place in New York—Coney Island fer instance. Loads o' prawfit. Taik a big cod now—"

> *Now! Now I gotta. In the crack,*
> *remember. In the crack be born.*

"Harrh! There's nights I'd take my bible-oath, these stairs uz higher." On the first floor, Bill Whitney stopped gazed out of the window that faced the East River. "Stinkin' heap out there!" And lifting eyes above the stove-in, enameled pots, cracked washtubs, urinals that glimmered in the back snarl, stared at the dark river striped by the gliding lights of a boat, shifted his gaze to the farther shore where scattered, lighted windows in factories, mills were caught like sparks in blocks of soot, and moved his eyes again to the south-east, to the beaded bridge. Over momentary, purple blossoms, down the soft incline, the far train slid like a trickle of gold. Behind and before, sparse auto headlights, belated or heralding dew on the bough of the night. "And George a'gappin' and me a'hollerin' and a'techin the ground with the toe of my boot and no wheels under me. Ha! Ha! Mmm! Wut cain't a man dream of in his sleep . . . A wheel . . . A bike . . ." He turned away seeking the clock. "And I ain't been on one . . . not sence . . . more'n thirty-five . . . forty years. Not since I uz a little shaver . . ."

> *Clammy fingers traced the sharp edge of*
> *the dipper's scoop. Before his eyes*
> *the glitter on the car tracks whisked . . .*
> *reversed . . . whisked . . .*

"Say, listen O'Toole dere's a couple o' coozies in de back." The bar-keep pointed with the beer knife. "Jist yer speed!"

"Balls!" Terse O'Toole retorted. "Wudjah tink I jist took de bull-durham sack off me pecker fer—nuttin'? I twisted all de pipes I wanna we'en I'm pissin'!"

"No splinters in dese boxes, dough. Honest, O'Toole! Real clean—"

"Let 'im finish, will ye!" the hunchback interrupted sourly. "O'Toole don' have to buy his gash."

"Well, he says, yea. An' I says yea. An' all de time dere wuz Steve an' Kelly unner de goiders belly-achin'—Hey trow us a rivet. An' I sez—"

    —*Nobody's commin'!*

Klang! Klang! Klang! Klang! Klang!

The flat buniony foot of Dan MacIntyre the motorman pounded the bell. Directly in front of the clamorous car and in the tracks, the vendor of halvah, candied-peanuts, leechee nuts, jellied fruits, dawdled, pushing his push-cart leisurely. Dan MacIntyre was enraged. Wasn't he blocks and blocks behind his leader? Hadn't his conductor been slow as shit on the bell? Wouldn't he get a hell of a bawling out from Jerry, the starter on Avenue A? And here was this lousy dago blocking traffic. He'd like to smack the piss out of him, he would. He pounded the bell instead.

Leisurely, leisurely, the Armenian pedlar steered his cart out of the way. But before he cleared the tracks, he lifted up his clenched fist, high and pleasantly. In the tight crotch of his forefingers, a dirty thumb peeped out. A fig for you, O MacIntyre.

"God damn yuh!" He roared as he passed. "God blast yuh!"

    —*So go! So go! So go!*
     But he stood as still and rigid as
     if frozen to the wall, frozen fingers
     clutching the dipper.

"An' hawnest t'Gawd, Mimi, darlin'." The Family Entrance to Callahan's lay through a wide alley way lit by a red lamp in the rear. Within, under the branching, tendriled chandelier of alum-bronze, alone before a table beside a pink wall with roach-brown mouldings, Mary, the crockery-cheeked, humid-eyed swayed and spoke, her voice being maudlin, soused and reedy. Mimi, the crockery-cheeked, crockery-eyed, a smudged blonde with straw-colored hair like a subway seat, slumped and listened. "I was that young an' innercent, an' hawnest t' Gawd, that straight, I brought it t' the cashier, I did. And, Eeee! she screams and ducks under the register, Eeee! Throw it away, yuh boob! But what wuz I t'know—I wuz on'y fifteen w'en I wuz a bus-goil. They left it on a plate—waa, the mugs there is in de woild—an' I thought it wuz one o' them things yuh put on yer finger w'en ye git a cut—"

"A cut, didja say, Mary, dea'?" The crockery cheeks cracked into lines.

"Yea a cut— a cu— Wee! Hee! Hee! Hee! Hee! Mimi, darlin' you're comical! Wee! Hee! Hee! He! But I wuz that young an' innercent till he come along. Wee! Hee! Hee! Hawnes' t' Gawd I wuz. I could piss troo a beer-bottle then—"

Out of the shadows now, out on the dimlit, vacant
street, he stepped down from the broken
curb-stone to the cobbles. For all
his peering, listening, starting, he
was blind as a sleep-walker, he was
deaf. Only the steely glitter on the
tracks was in his eyes, fixed there like
a brand, drawing him with cables as
tough as steel. A few steps more and
he was there, standing between the
tracks, straddling the sunken rail.
He braced his legs to spring, held
his breath. And now the wavering point
of the dipper's handle found the long,
dark, grinning lips, scraped, and
like a sword in a scabbard—

"Oy, Schmaihe, goy! Vot luck! Vot luck! You should only croak!"

"Cha! Cha! Cha! Dot's how I play mit cods!"

"Bitt him vit a flush! Ai, yi, yi!"

"I bet he vuz mit a niggerteh last night!"

"He rode a dock t' luzno maw jock—jeck I shidda said. Cha! Cha!"

"He's a poet, dis guy!"

"A putz!"

"Vus dere a hura mezda, Morr's?"

"Sharrop, bummer! Mine Clara is insite!"

Plunged! And he was running! Running!

"Nutt'n'? No, I says, nutt'n'. But every time I sees a pretty cunt come walkin' up de street, I says, wit' a mean shaft an' a sweet pair o' knockers, Jesus, O'Toole, I says, dere's a mare I'd radder lay den lay on. See wot I mean? Git a bed under den a bet on. Git me?"

"Haw! Haw! Haw! Bejeeziz!"

"Ya! Ha! He tella him, you know? He lika de fica stretta!"

They looked down at the lime-streaked, overalled wop condescendingly, and—

"Aw, bulloney," he says, "Yeah, I says. An' booze, I says, my booze is wut I c'n suck out of a nice tit, I says. Lallal'mmm, I says. An' w'en it comes t' prayin', I says, c'n yuh tell me anyt'ing bedder t' pray over den over dat one!" O'Toole hastily topped the laugh with a wave of his hand. "Yer an at'eist, yuh fuck, he hollers. A fuckin' at'eist I says— An' all de time dere wuz Steve and Kelly unner de goiders hollerin', hey trow us a riv—"

Running! But no light overtook him,
no blaze of intolerable flame. Only
in his ears, the hollow click of iron
lingered. Hollow, vain. Almost within
the saloon-light, he slowed down, sobbed
aloud, looked behind him—

"But who'd a thunk it?" Bill Whitney mounted the stairs again. "By Gawd, who'd a thunk it? The weeks I'd held that spike for 'im . . . Weeks . . . And he druv and never a miss . . . Drunk? Naw, he warn't drunk that mornin'. Sober as a parson. Sober. A'swingin' of the twelve pound like a clock. Mebbe it was me that nudged it, mebbe it war me . . . By Gawd, I knowed it. A feelin' I had seein' that black sledge in the air. Afore it come down, I knowed it. A hull damned country-side it might of slid into. And it had to be me . . . Wut? It wuz to be? That cast around my leg? A pig's tit! It wuz to—"

Like a dipped metal flag or a gro-
tesque armored head scrutinizing the
cobbles, the dull-gleaming dipper's
scoop stuck out from between the rail,
leaning sideways.

—Didn't. Didn't go in. Ain't lit. Go back.
He turned—slowly.
—No—body's—look—

"Bawl? Say, did I bawl? Wot else'd a kid've done w'en her mont'ly don' show up—Say! But I'll get even with you, I said, I'll make a prick out of you too, like you done t' me. You wait! You can't get away with that. G'wan, he said, ye little free-hole, he called me. Wott're ye after? Some dough? Well, I ain't got it. That's all! Now quit hangin' aroun' me or I'll s-smack ye one! He said."

"Where d'ja get it?"

"I borreed it—it wuzn't much. She called herself a m-mid-wife. I went by m-meself. My old-huhu—my old l-lady n-never—O Jesus!" Tears rilled the glaze.

"Say—toin off de tap, Mary, f'Gawd's sake!"

"Aw! Sh-hu-hu-shut up! Can't I b-bawl if I—I—uh-huuh—G-go p-peddle yer h-hump, h-he says—"

"But not hea', Mary, f'r the lova Pete. We all gets knocked up sometimes—"

—Horry op! Horry op back!

"They'll betray us!" Into the Tenth Street Crosstown car, slowing down at Avenue A, the voice of the pale, gilt-spectacled, fanatic face rang out above all other sounds: above the oozy and yearning "Open the door to Jesus" of the Salvation Army singing in the park; above the words of the fat woman swaying in the car as she said, "So the doctor said cut out all meat if you don't want gall-stones. So I cut out all meat, but once in a while I fried a little boloney with eggs—how I love it!" Above the muttering of the old gray-bearded Jewish peddlar (he rocked his baby carriage on which pretzels lay stacked like quoits on the upright sticks) "Founder of the universe, why have you tethered me to this machine? Founder of the universe, will I ever earn more than water for my buckwheat? Founder of the universe!" Above the even enthusiasm of the kindly faced American woman: "And do you know, you can go all the way up inside her for twenty-five cents. For only twenty-five cents, mind you! Every American man, woman and child ought to go up inside her, it's a thrilling experience. The Statue of Liberty is—"

—He stole up to the dipper warily,
on tip—

"Shet up, down 'ere, yuh bull-faced harps, I says, wait'll
I'm troo! Cunt, I says, hot er snotty 'zuh same t' me. Dis
gets 'em hot. Dis gets em hot I sez. One look at me, I
says, an yuh c'n put dat rivet in yer ice-box—t'ings 'll
keep! Yuh reams 'em out with dat he says—kinda snotty
like. Shit no, I says I boins 'em out. W'y dontcha trow it
t'dem, he ays, dey're yellin' fer a rivet. Aaa, I don' wanna
bust de fuckin' goider I says. Yer pretty good, he says.
Good, I says, didja ever see dat new tawch boinin' troo a
goider er a flange er any fuck'n' hunka iron—de spa'ks
wot goes shootin' down—? Didja? Well dat's de way 'I
comes. Dey tol' me so. An' all de time dere wuz Steve
and Kelly unner de goiders havin' a shit-hemorrage an'
yellin' hey, t'row—"

> *toe, warily, glancing over his*
> *shoulders, on tip-toe, over serried*
> *cobbles, cautious—*

"Wuz t' be. And by Gawd it might hev gone out when
I went to bed a' suckin' of it. By Gawd it hed no call t' be
burnin'. . . . Wuz to be—Meerschaum, genuwine. Thankee
I said. Thankee Miz Taylor. And I stood on the back-
stairs with the ice-tongs. Thankee and thank the Doctor
. . . Boston, the year I—Haw, by Gawd. And the hull damn
sheet afire. And Kate ascreamin' beside me . . . Gawd damn
it! It hadn't ought to 'a' done it . . . A'lookin' at me still
now . . . A'stretchin' of her neck in the white room . . .
in the hospital—"

> *As though his own tread might shake the*
> *slanting handle loose from its perch*
> *beneath the ground. And now, and—*

"Why not? She asks me. Pullin' loaded dice on Lefty.
The rat! He can't get away with that y'know. I know, Mag,
I said. It'd do my heart good to see a knife in his lousy
guts—only I gotta better idee. What? She asks me. Spill it.
Spill it is right, I says t' her. I know a druggist-felleh, I
said, good friend o' mine. O yea, she looks at me kinda
funny. Croak him with a dose o'—No! I said. No poison.
Listen Mag. Throw a racket up at your joint, will ye? Give
him an invite. He'll come. And then let me fix him a
drink. And I winks at her. Dintcha ever hear o' the Span-
ish Fly—"

> *over it now, he crouched,*
> *stretched out a hand to*

"They'll betray us!" Above all these voices, the speaker's voice rose. "In 1789, in 1848, in 1871, in 1905, he who has anything to save will enslave us anew! Or if not enslave will desert us when the red cock crows! Only the laboring poor, only the masses embittered, bewildered, betrayed, in the day when the red cock crows, can free us!"

> *lift the dipper free. A sense almost*
> *palpable, as of a leashed and imminent*
> *and awful force.*

"You're de woist fuckin' liar I ever seen he sez an' ducks over de goiders."

> *focused on his hand across the hair-*
> *breadth*

"Yuh god mor'n a pair o' sem'ns?"

> *gap between his fingers and the*
> *scoop. He drew*

"It's the snug ones who'll preach it wuz to be."

> *back, straightened. Carefully bal—*

"So I dropped it in when he was dancin'—O hee! Hee! Mimi! A healthy dose I—"

> *anced on his left, advance—*

"Yeah. I sez, take your pants off."

> *ed his right foot—*
> *Crritlkt!*
> *—What?*
> *He stared at the river, sprang away*
> *from the rail and dove into the shad-*
> *ows.*

"Didja hear 'im, Mack? De goggle-eyed yid an' his red cock?"

> *The river? That sound! That sound*
> *had come from there. All his senses*
> *stretched toward the dock, grappled with*
> *the hush and the shadow. Empty . . . ?*

"Swell it out well with batter. Mate, it's a bloomin' goldmine! It's a cert! Christ knows how many chaps can be fed off of one bloody cod—"

> *Yes . . . empty. Only his hollow nos-*
> *trils sifted out the stir in the*
> *quiet; The wandering river-wind seamed*
> *with thin scent of salt*

"An' he near went crazy! Mimi I tell ye, we near bust, watchin—"

decay, flecked with clinging coal-tar—
Crrritlkt!

"Can't, he sez, I got a tin-belly."

—It's— Oh— It's—it's! Papa. Nearly
like. It's—nearly like his teeth.
Nothing . . . A barge on a slack hauser or
a gunwale against the dock chirping
because a

"I'll raise it."

boat was passing.
—Papa like nearly.
Or a door tittering to and fro in the wind.

"Heaz a can-opener fer ye I sez."

Nothing. He crept back.

"Hemm. These last durn stairs."

And was there, over the rail. The
splendor shrouded in the earth, the
titan, dormant in his lair, disdain-
ful. And his eyes

"Runnin' hee! hee! hee! Across the lots hee! hee! jerkin' off."

lifted

"An' I picks up a rivet in de tongs an' I sez—"

and there was the last crossing of
Tenth Street, the last cross—

"Heazuh a flowuh fer ye, yeller-belly, shove it up yer ass!"

ing, and beyond, beyond the elevateds,

"How many times'll your red cock crow, Pete, befaw y' gives up? T'ree?"

as in the pit of the west, the last

"Yee! hee! hee! Mary, joikin'—"

smudge of rose, staining the stem of

"Nawthin' t' do but climb—"

the trembling, jagged

"Show culluh if yuh god beddeh!"

chalice of the night-taut stone with

"An' I t'rows de fuck'n' rivet."

the lees of day. And his toe crooked into
the dipper as into a stirrup. It
grated, stirred, slid, and—

"Dere's a star fer yeh! Watch it! T'ree Kings I god. Dey came on huzzbeck! Yee! Hee Hee! Mary! Nawthin' to do

but wait fer day light and go home. To a red cock
crowin'. Over a statue of. A jerkin'. Cod. Clang! Clang!
Oy! Machine! Liberty! Revolt! Redeem!"

> Power
>
> *Power! Power like a paw, titanic power,*
> *ripped through the earth and slammed*
> *against his body and shackled him*
> *where he stood. Power! Incredible,*
> *barbaric power! A blast, a siren of light*
> *within him, rending, quaking, fusing his*
> *brain and blood to a fountain of flame,*
> *vast rockets in a searing spray! Power!*
> *The hawk of radiance raking him with*
> *talons of fire, battering his skull with*
> *a beak of fire, braying his body with*
> *pinions of intolerable light. And he*
> *writhed without motion in the clutch of*
> *a fatal glory, and his brain swelled*
> *and dilated till it dwarfed the galaxies*
> *in a bubble of refulgence—Recoiled, the*
> *last screaming nerve clawing for survival.*
> *He kicked—once. Terrific rams of dark-*
> *ness collided; out of their shock space*
> *toppled into havoc. A thin scream wobbled*
> *through the spirals of oblivion, fell like*
> *a brand on water, his-s-s-s-ed—*

"W'at?

        "W'ut?

                "Va-at?

                        "Gaw blimey!

                "W'atsa da ma'?"

The street paused. Eyes, a myriad of eyes, gay or
sunken, rheumy, yellow or clear, slant, blood-shot, hard,
boozy or bright swerved from their tasks, their play, from
faces, newspapers, dishes, cards, seidels, valves, sewing
machines, swerved and converged. While at the foot of
Tenth Street, a quaking splendor dissolved the cobbles, the
grimy structures, bleary stables, the dump-heap, river and
sky into a single cymbal-clash of light. Between the livid
jaws of the rail, the dipper twisted and bounced, consumed in roaring radiance, candescent—

                "Hey!"

"Jesus!"

"Give a look! Id's rain—

"Shawt soicit, Mack—"

"Mary, w'at's goin'—"

"Schloimee, a blitz like—"

"Hey mate!"

On Avenue D, a long burst of flame spurted from underground, growled as if the veil of earth were splitting. People were hurrying now, children scooting past them, screeching. On Avenue C, the lights of the trolley-car waned and wavered. The motorman cursed, feeling the power drain. In the Royal Warehouse, the blinking watchman tugged at the jammed and stubborn window. The shriveled coal-heaver leaned unsteadily from between the swinging door—blinked, squinted in pain, and—

"Holy Mother O' God! Look! Will yiz!"

"Wot?"

"There's a guy layin' there! Burrhnin'!"

"Naw! Where!"

"Gawd damn the winder!"

"It's on Tent' Street! Look!"

"O'Toole!"

The street was filled with running men, faces carved and ghostly in the fierce light. They shouted hoarsely. The trolley-car crawled forward. Up above a window slammed open.

"Christ, it's a kid!"

"Yea!"

"Don't touch 'im!"

"Who's got a stick!"

"A stick!"

"A stick, fer Jesus sake!"

"Mike! The shovel! Where's yer fuck'n' shov—"

"Back in Call—"

"Oy sis a kind—"

"Get Pete's crutch! Hey Pete!"

"Aaa! Who touched yer hump, yuh gimpty fu—"

"Do sompt'n! Meester! Meester!"

"Yuh crummy bastard, I saw yuh sneakin'—" The hunchback whirled, swung away on his crutches. "Fuck yiz!"

"Oy! Oy vai! Oy vai! Oy vai!"

"Git a cop!"

"An embillance—go cull-oy!"

"Don't touch 'im!"

"Bambino! Madre mia!"

"Mary. It's jus' a kid!"

"Helftz! Helftz! Helftz Yeedin! Rotivit!"

A throng ever thickening had gathered, confused, paralyzed, babbling. They squinted at the light, at the outstretched figure in the heart of the light, tossed their arms, pointed, clawed at their cheeks, shoved, shouted, moaned—

"Hi! Hi down there! Hi!" A voice bawled down from the height. "Look out below! Look out!"

The crowd shrank back from the warehouse.

W-w-whack!

"It's a—"

"You take it!"

Grab it!"

"Gimme dat fuck'n' broom!"

"Watch yerself, O'Toole!"

"Oy, a good men! Got should—"

"Oooo! De pore little kid, Mimi!"

"He's gonna do it!"

"Look oud!

"Dunt touch!"

The man in the black shirt, tip-toed guardedly to the rails. His eyes, screwed tight against the awful glare, he squinted over his raised shoulder.

"Shove 'im away!"

"Go easy!"

"Look odda!"

"Atta boy!"

"Oy Gottinyoo!"

The worn, blackened broom straws wedged between the child's shoulder and the cobbles. A twist of the handle. The child rolled over on his face.

"Give 'im anudder shove!"

"At's it! Git 'im away!"

"Quick! Quick!"

Once more the broom straws rammed the outstretched figure. He slid along the cobbles, cleared the tracks. Someone on the other side grabbed his arm, lifted him, carried him to the curb. The crowd swirled about in a dense, tight eddy.

"Oy! Givalt!"

     "Gib'm air!"

          "Is 'e boined?"

"Bennee stay by me!"

       "*Is* 'e boined! Look at his shoe!"

   "Oy, de pooh mama! De pooh mama!"

         "Who's kid?"

"Don' know, Mack!"

    "Huz pushin'?"

"Jesus! Take 'im to a drug-store."

     "Naa, woik on 'im right here. I woiked in a power house!"

     "Do sompt'n! Do sompt'n!"

The writhing dipper was now almost consumed. Before the flaring light, the weird white-lipped, staring faces of the milling throng wheeled from chalk to soot and soot to chalk again—like masks of flame that charred and were rekindled; and all their frantic, gnarling bodies cut a carting splay of huge, impinging shadow, on dump-heap, warehouse, river and street—

Klang! The trolley drew up.

"Oyeee! Ers toit! Ers to-i-t! Oye-e-e-e!" A woman screamed, gagged, fainted.

"Hey! Ketch 'er!"

    "Schleps aveck!"

      "Wat d' hell'd she do dat fer—"

    "Vawdeh!"

They dragged her away on scuffing heels to one side.

    "Shit!" The motorman had jumped down from the car and seized the broom—

     "Fan 'er vid de het!"

    "Git off me feet, you!"

"At's it! Lean on 'im O'Toole! Push 'im down! At's it! At's it! I woiked in a power house—"

And with the broom straws the motorman flipped the mangled metal from the rail. A quake! As if leviathan leaped for the hook and fell back threshing. And darkness.

Darkness!

They grunted, the masses, stood suddenly mute a moment, for a moment silent, stricken, huddled, crushed by the pounce of ten-fold night. And a voice spoke, strained, shrunken, groping—

"Ey, paizon! She 'sa whita yet—lika you looka da slacka lime alla time! You know?"

Someone shrieked. The fainting woman moaned. The crowd muttered, whispered, seething uneasily in the dark, welcomed the loud newcomers who pierced the dense periphery—

"One side! One side!" Croaking with authority, the stone-grim uniformed one shouldered his way through. "One side!"

"De cops!"

"Dun't step on 'im!"

"Back up youz! Back up! Didja hea' me, Moses? Back up! Beat it! G'wan!" They fell back before the perilous arc of the club. "G'wan before I fan yiz! Back up! Let's see sompt'n' in hea'! Move! Move, I say!" Artificial ire flung the spittle on his lips. "Hey George!" He flung at a burly one. "Give us a hand hea, will yiz!"

"Sure! Git back you! Pete! Git that other side!"

The policeman wheeled round, squatted down beside the black-shirted one. "Don' look boined."

"Jist his shoe."

"How long wuz he on?"

"Christ! I don't know. I came ouda Callahan's an' de foist t'ing I know somebody lams a broom out of a winder, an' I grabs it an' shoves 'im off de fuck'n t'ing—"

"Sh! Must a done it himself— Naa! Dat ain't de way! Lemme have 'im." He pushed the other aside, turned the child over on his face. "Foist aid yuh gits 'em hea." His bulky hands all but encompassed the narrow waist. "Like drownin', see?" He squeezed,

Khir-r-r-r-f! S-s-s-s-.

"I hoid 'im!"

"Yeah!"

"He's meckin' him t' breed!"

"See? Gits de air in 'im."

Khir-r-r-r-f! S-s-s-s.

"Looks like he's gone, do. W'ere de hell's dat ambillance?"

"Vee culled id a'reddy, Ufficeh!"

"Arh!"

"Rap 'im on de feet arficer, I woiked in a power—"

Khir-r-r-r-f! S-s-s-s

"Anybody know 'im? Any o' youz know dis kid?"

The inner and the craning semi-circle muttered blankly. The policeman rested his ear against the child's back.

"Looks like he's done fer, butchuh can't tell—"

Khir-r-r-r-f! S-s-s-s.

"He sez he's dead, Mary."

"Dead!"

"Oy! Toit!"

"Gott sei donk, id's nod mine Elix—"

Khir-r-r-r-f. S-s-s-s.

"Sit im helfin vie a toitin bankis." The squat shirt-sleeved Jew whose tight belt cut his round belly into the letter B turned to the lime-streaked wop—squinted, saw that communication had failed. "It'll help him like cups on a cawps," he translated—and tapped his chest with an ace of spades.

Khi-r-r-r-f. S-s-s-s.

(E-e-e-e. E-e-e-e-.

One ember fanned . . . dulling . . . uncertain)

"Here's the damned thing he threw in, Cap." The motor-man shook off the crowd, held up the thinned and twisted metal.

"Yea! Wot is it?"

"Be damned if I know. Hot! Jesus!"

Khir-r-r-f. S-s-s.

(E-e-e-e-e.

Like the red pupil of the eye of darkness, the ember dilated, spun like a pinwheel, expanding, expanding, till at the very core, a white flaw rent the scarlet tissue and spread, engulfed the margin like a stain—)

"Five hundred an' fifty volts. What a wallop!"

"He's cooked, yuh t'ink?"

"Yea. Jesus! What else!"

"Unh!" The policeman was grunting now with his efforts.

Kh-i-r-r-r-f! S-s-s-s.

"Hey, Meester, maybe he fell on id—

De iron—"

"Sure, dot's righd!"

"Id's f'om de compeny de fault!"

"Ass, how could he fall on it, fer the love O Jesus!" The motor-man turned on them savagely.

"He could! Id's easy!"

"Id vuz stink—stick—sticken oud!"

"He'll sue, dun' vorry!"
"Back up, youz!"
Khi-r-r-r-f! S-s-s.
(*Eee-e-e-e*
And in the white, frosty light within
the red iris, a small figure slanted
through a desolate street, crack-paved,
rut-guttered, slanted and passed, and
overhead the taut, wintry wires whined
on their crosses—
E-e-e-e-e.
They whined, spanning the earth and sky.
—Go-d-d-b! Go-o-o-ob! G-o-o-b! G'bye! . . .)
"Makin' a case fer a shyster. C'n yuh beat it!"
"Ha-a-ha! Hunh!"
"I'm late. Dere it is." The motorman dropped the
gnarled and blackened dipper beside the curb.
"An Irisher chuchim!"
"Ain't it a dirty shame—"
"Noo vud den!"
"Wat's happened, chief?"
"Dere give a look!"
"Let's git troo dere!"
"Unh!"
Kh-i-r-r-r-f! S-s-s-s.
(*—G'by-e-e. Mis-s-s-l-e. M-s-ter. Hi-i-i-i.*
Wo-o-o-d.
And a man in a tugboat, hair under
arm-pits, hung from a pole among the
wires, his white undershirt glittering.
He grinned and whistled and with every
note yellow birds flew to the roof.)
"T'ink a shot o' sompt'n' 'll do 'im any good?"
"Nuh! Choke 'im if he's alive."
"Yeh! If hiz alife!"
"W'ea's 'e boined?"
"Dey say id's de feet wid de hen's wid eveytingk."
"Unh!"
Khi-r-r-r-f! S-s-s-s.
(*We-e-e-e-*
The man in the wires stirred. The
Wires twanged brightly. The blithe

*and golden cloud of birds filled the
sky.)*
"Unh!"
*(Klang!
The milk tray jangled. Leaping he
neared. From roof-top to roof-top,
over streets, over alley ways, over
areas and lots, his father soared with
a feathery ease. He set the trays
down, stooped as if searching, paused—)*
"Unh!"
*(A hammer! A hammer! He snarled,
brandished it, it snapped like a whip.
The birds vanished. Horror thickened
the air.)*
"Unh!"
    "He's woikin' hard!"
"Oy! Soll im Gott helfin!"
      "He no waka."
*(Around him now, the cobbles stretched
away. Stretched away in the swirling
dark like the faces of a multitude aghast
and frozen)*
"Unh!"
*(W-e-e-e-e-e-p! Weep! Overhead the
brandished hammer whirred and whistled.
The doors of a hallway slowly opened.
Buoyed up by the dark, a coffin drifted
out, floated down the stoop, and while
confetti rained upon it, bulged and
billowed—)*
"Unh!"
Khi-r-r-r-rf! S-s-s-s-
*(—Zwank! Zwank! Zwank!
The man in the wires writhed and
groaned, his slimy, purple chicken-
guts slipped through his fingers.
David touched his lips. The soot
came off on his hand. Unclean.
Screaming, he turned to flee, seized
a wagon wheel to climb upon it. There
were no spokes—only cogs like a
clock-wheel. He screamed again, beat*

the yellow disk with his fists.)
"Unh!"

Kh-i-r-r-rf! S-s-s-s.
"Didja see it?"
"See it? Way up on twelft'!"
"I could ivin see id in de houz—on de cods."
"Me? I vas stand in basement—fok t'ing mack blind!"
"Five hundred an' fifty volts."

*(As if on hinges, blank, enormous
mirrors arose, swung slowly upward
face to face. Within the facing
glass, vast panels deployed, lifted a
steady wink of opaque pages until
an endless corridor dwindled into
night.)*

"Unh! Looks Jewish t' me."
"Yeah, map o' Jerusalem, all right."
"Poor bastard! Unh!"
"Couldn't see him at foist!"
"Unh!"

Kh-ir-r-rf! S-s-s-s.
*("You!" Above the whine of the
whirling hammer, his father's voice
thundered. "You!"
David wept, approached the glass,
peered in. Not himself was there,
not even in the last and least of
the infinite mirrors, but the cheder
wall, the cheder)*

"Junheezis!"

Kh-i-r-r-rf! S-s-s-s.
*(Wall sunlit, white-washed. "Chadgodya!"
moaned the man in the wires. "One
kid one only kid." And the wall dwindled
and was a square of pavement with a footprint in it—half green, half black,
"I too have trodden there." And
shrank within the mirror, and the
cake of ice melted in the panel beyond. "Eternal years," the voice
wailed, "Not even he.")*

"Unh!"

"Gittin' winded? Want me to try it?"
"Nunh!"

"Look at 'im sweat!"
"Vy not? Soch a coat he's god on!"
"Wot happened, brother?"
"Cheh! He esks yet!"

"Back up, you!"
"Unh!"

Kh-i-r-r-r-f! S-s-s-s.
(And faded, revealing a shoe box full
of calendar leaves, "the red day must
come.")

"Unh! Did he move or sumpt'n?"
"Couldn't see."

(which lapsed into a wooden box with
a sliding cover like the chalk-boxes
in school, whereon a fiery figure
sat astride a fish. "G-e-e-e o-o-o d-e-e-e-!"
The voice spelled out. And shrank and was
a cube of sugar gripped be-)

"Unh!"

Kh-i-r-r-r-f! S-s-s-s.
"Shah! Y'hea id?"
"W'a?"
"Yea! It's commin!"
"Id's commin'!"
"I sees it!"

"Meester Politsman de——"
"Back up, youz!"

A faint jangle seeped through the roar of the crowd.
"Unh!"

(tween the softly glowing tongs. "So
wide we stretch no further——" But when
he sought to peer beyond, suddenly the
mirrors shifted, and——
"Go down!" his father's voice thun-
dered, "Go down!" The mirrors lay
beneath him now; what were the groins
now jutted out in stairs, concentric
ogives, bottomless steps. "Go down!
Go down!" The inexorable voice beat
like a hand upon his back. He
screamed, de——)

Jangle! Angle! Angle! Angle!
"Dere! It's comin'!"
"Look! Look hod dere!"
"Orficer!"
Angle! Jang!
"Christ's about time!"
The crowd split like water before a prow, reformed
in the wake, surged round the ambulance, babbling,
squall—

(scended. Down! Down into darkness,
darkness that tunneled the heart of
darkness, darkness fathomless. Each
step he took, he shrank, grew smaller
with the unseen panels, the graduate
vise descending, passed from stage
to dwindling stage, dwindling. At
each step shed the husks of being,
and himself tapering always downward
in the funnel of the night. And now
a chip—a step-a flake-a step-a shred.
A mote. A pinpoint. And now the seed
of nothing, and nebulous nothing, and
nothing, And he was not. . . .)

ing, stabbing the dark with hands. "Ppprrr!" Lips flickered audibly as the blue-coat rose. With one motion,
palm wiped brow, dug under sweat-stained collar. Softly
bald, the bareheaded, white garbed interne hopped spryly
from the ambulance step, black bag swinging in hand,
wedged whitely through the milling crowd. Conch-like
the mob surrounded, contracted, trailed him within the
circle, umbiliform—

"Lectric shot; Doc!"
"De hospital!"
"Knocked him cold!"
"Shock?"
"'Zee dead?"
"Yea, foolin' aroun' wid de—"
"Shawt soicited it, Doc!"
"Yea, boined!"
"Vee sin id Docteh!"
"Git back, youz!" The officer crouched, snarled, but
never sprang. "I'll spit right in yer puss!"

"Mmm!" The interne pinched the crease of his trousers, pulled them up, and kneel—

"Guess yuh better take 'im witchuh, Doc. Couldn't do a goddam t'ing wit—"

"He's gonna hea' de heart! See?"

(*But*—)

ing beside the beveled curbstone, applied his ear to the narrow breast.

"Shoe's boined. See it, Doc?"

(*the voice still lashed the nothingness*
that was, denying it oblivion. "Now find!
Now find! Now find!" And nothingness
whimpered being dislodged from night,
and would have hidden again. But out
of the darkness, one ember)

"Take it off, will you, let's have a look at it."

(*flowered, one ember in a mirr*—)

"Sure!" Blunt, willing fingers ripped the

(*or, swimming without motion in the*
motion of its light.)

buttons open,

"Hiz gonna look."

(*In a cellar is*)

dragged the shoes off,

(*Coal! In a cellar is*)

tore the stocking down, re—

(*Coal! And it was brighter than the*
pith of lightning and milder than pearl,)

vealing a white puffy ring about the ankle, at

(*And made the darkness dark because*
the dark had culled its radiance for
that jewel. Zwank!)

"Is it boined?"

"Can't see, c'n you?"

which the interne glanced while he drew

"Waddayuh say, Doc?"

a squat blue vial from his bag, grimaced, un-

(*Zwank! Zwank! Nothingness beati-*
fied reached out its hands. Not cold
the ember was. Not scorching. But as
if all eternity's caress were fused and
granted in one instant. Silence)

corked it, expertly tilted it before

*(struck that terrible voice upon the
height, stilled the whirling hammer.
Horror and the night fell away. Ex-
alted, he lifted his head and screamed
to him among the wires— "Whistle,
mister! Whistle!)*

the quiet nostrils. The crowd fell silent, tensely watching.
"Amonya."

"Smells strong!"
"Stinks like in de shool on Yom Kippur."

*(Mister! Whistle! Whistle! Whistle!
Whistle, Mister! Yellow birds!)*

On the dark and broken sidewalk, the limp body gasped,
quivered. The interne lifted him, said sharply to the officer. "Hold his arms! He'll fight!"

"Hey look! Hey look!"
"He's kickin'!"

(Whistle, mister! WHISTLE!")

"W'at's he sayin'?"
"There! Hold him now!"

(A spiked star of pain of consciousness burst within him)

"Mimi! He's awright! He's awright!"
"Yeh?"
"Yea!"
"No kiddin'! No kiddin'!"

"Yeh!"
"Yuh!"
"Yeh!"
"Oi, Gott sei dank!"

XXII

"THERE you are, sonny! There you are!" The interne's
reassuring drawl, reached him through a swirl of broken
images. "You're not hurt. There's nothing to be scared
about."

"Sure!" the policeman was saying beside him.

David opened his eyes. Behind, between them and around them, like a solid wall, the ever-encroaching bodies, voices, faces at all heights, gestures at all heights, all converging upon him, craning, peering, haranguing, pointing him out, discussing him. A nightmare! Deliverance was in the thought. He shut his eyes trying to remember how to wake.

"How does that foot feel, sonny?" The routine, solicitous voice again inquired. "Not bad, eh?"

He was aware for the first time of the cool air on his naked leg, and below it a vague throbbing at the ankle. And once aware, he couldn't shake off the reality of it. Then it wasn't a dream. Where had he been? What done? The light. No light in the windows upstairs . . . His father. His mother. The quarrel. The whip. Aunt Bertha, Nathan, the rabbi, the cellar, Leo, the beads—all swooped upon him, warred for preeminence in his brain. No. It wasn't a dream. He opened his eyes again, hoping reality would refute conviction. No it wasn't a dream. The same two faces leaned over him, the same hedge of humanity focused eyes on his face.

"Looks like he's still too weak," said the interne.

"Yuh goin' t'take him wid ye?"

"No!" Grimacing emphatically, the interne shut the black bag. "Why, he'll be able to walk in less than five minutes. Just as soon as he gets his breath. Where does he live?"

"I don' know. None o' dese guys know— Say, w'ere d'yuh live? Huh? Yuh wanna go home, dontchuh?"

"N-nint' street." He quavered. "S-sebm fawdynine."

"Nint' Street." The crowd reechoed. "Say ufficeh," a coatless man came forward. "Det's on de cunner Even-yuh D."

"I know! I know!" The policeman waved him back with surly hand. "Say, Doc, will ye give us a lift."

"Sure. Just pick him up."

"Yea, ooops! Dere ye go!" Burly arms went under his knees and back, lifted him easily, carried him through the gaping crowd to the ambulance. His head swam again with the motion. He lay slack on a long leather cot between greenish walls, aware of faces whisking by the open doorway, peering in. The interne seated himself at the back, called to the driver. The bell clanged, and as the wagon jolted forward, the policeman mounted the low step in the rear. Behind the ambulance, rolling on rubber-tired wheels on the cobbles, he could hear the voices calling the way. "Nint' Street! Nint' Street!" The throb in his ankle was growing in depth, in dullness of pain, permeating upward like an aching tide within the marrow. What had he done? What had he done? What would they say when they brought him upstairs. His father, what—? He moaned.

"That doesn't hurt you that much, does it?" asked the interne cheerily. "You'll be running around to-morrow."

"Yer better off den I tawt ye'd be, said the policeman behind him. "Cheezis, Doc, I sure figgered he wuz cooked."

"No. The shock went through the lower part. That's what saved him. I don't see why he was out so long anyway. Weak, I guess."

Behind beating hooves and jangling bell, he felt the ambulance round the corner at Avenue D. The policeman turned to look behind him and then squinted sideways at David's foot.

"His shoes wuz boined in front. An' he's got it up on de ankle."

"Narrowest part."

"I see. Dat'll loin yuh a lesson, kid." He disengaged one hand from the ambulance wall to wave a severe finger at David. "Next time I'll lock yiz up. Wot flaw d'yuh live on?"

"T-top flaw."

"Would have t'be," he growled disgustedly. "Next time I will lock yiz up—making me woik, an' takin' de Doc away from a nice pinocle game. Wot dese goddam kids can't t'ink of. Geez!"

The ambulance had rounded the second corner and came to a stop. Grinning, the interne leaped down. Stooping over and grunting as he stooped, the policeman lifted him in his arms again and bore him quickly through the new throng that came streaming around the corner. On the stoop, several children recognized him and bawled excitedly, "It's Davy! It's Davy!" A woman in the gas-lit corridor cradled cheek in palm in terror and backed away. They mounted the stairs, the interne behind them and behind him remnants of the crowd, children of the house, following eagerly at a wary distance, jabbering, calling to him, "Watsa maddeh? Watsa maddeh, Davy?" Doors opened on the landings. Familiar heads poked out. Familiar voices shrilled at others across the hallway. "It's him! F'om opstehs. Veh de fighd voz!" As they neared the top the policeman had begun breathing heavily, shedding thick hot breath on David's cheek, grunting, the lines on his scowling, tough, red face deep with exertion.

The top floor. David's eyes flashed to the transom. It was lit. They were in. What would they say? He moaned again in terror.

"Where is it?" the red face before him puffed.

"Over—over dere!" he quavered weakly.

The door. The arm under his knees slid forward. Beefy knuckles rapped, sought the knob. Before an answer came, the door, nudged forward by his own thighs, swung open.

Before him stood his mother, looking tense and startled, her hand resting on his father's shoulders, and below seated, his father, cheek on fist, eyes lifted, sourly glowering, affronted, questioning with taut and whiplike stare. The others were gone. It seemed to David that whole ages passed in the instant they regarded each other frozen in their attitudes. And then just as the policeman began to speak, his mother's hand flew to her breast, she gasped in horror, her face went agonizingly white, contorted, and she screamed. His father threw his chair back, sprang to his feet. His eyes bulged, his jaw dropped, he blanched.

For the briefest moment David felt a shrill, wild surge of triumph whip within him, triumph that his father stood slack-mouthed, finger-clawing, stooped, and then the room suddenly darkened and revolved. He crumpled inertly against the cradling arms.

"David! David!" His mother's screams pierced the reeling blur. "David! David! Beloved! What is it? What's happened?"

"Take it easy, missiz! Take it easy!" He could feel the policeman's elbow thrust out warding her off. "Give us a chanst, will yuh! He ain't hoit! He ain't a bit hoit! Hey Doc!"

The interne had stepped between them and David staring weakly through the sickening murk before his eyes, saw him pushing her resolutely away. "Now! Now! Don't get him excited, lady! It's bad! It's bad for him! You're frightening him! Understand? Nicht ver—Schlect! Verstehen sie?"

"David! My child!" Unhearing, she still moaned, frantically, hysterically, one hand reached out to him, the other clutching her hair. "Your foot! What is it, child! What is it darling?"

"Put him down on the bed!" The interne motioned impatiently to the bed-room. "And listen, Mister, will you ask her to stop screaming. There's nothing to worry about! The child is in no danger! Just weak!"

"Genya!" his father started as if he were jarred. "Genya!" He exclaimed in Yiddish. "Stop it! Stop it! He says nothing's wrong. Stop it!"

From outside the door, the bolder ones in the crowd of neighbors that jammed the hallway had overflowed into the kitchen and were stationing themselves silently or volubly along the walls. Some as they jabbered pointed accusingly at David's father and wagged their heads significantly. And as David was borne into the bedroom, he heard one whisper in Yiddish, "A quarrel! They were quarreling to death!" In the utterly welcome half-darkness of the bed-room he was stretched out on the bed. His mother, still moaning, had followed, and behind her his restraining hand upon her shoulder came the interne. Behind them the upright, squirming bodies, pale, contorted faces of neighbors clogged the doorway. A gust of fury made him clench his hands convulsively. Why didn't they go away? All of them! Why didn't they stop pointing at him?

"I was just this minute going down!" his mother was wringing her hands and weeping, "Just this minute I was going down to find you! What is it darling? Does it hurt you? Tell me—"

"Aw, Missiz!" the policeman flapped his hands in disgust. "He's all right. Be reasonable, will yiz! Just a liddle boined, dat's all. Just a liddle boined. Cantchuh see dere's nutt'n' wrong wid 'im!"

She stared at him uncomprehendingly.

"Schreckts ach nisht! Schreckts ach nisht!" The chorus of women in the doorway translated raggedly. "Sis im goor nisht geshehen! S' goor nisht geferlich!"

"Dat's it, you tell her!" The policeman shouldered his way through the door.

The interne had undressed him, pulled the covers down and tucked him in. The smooth sheets felt cool on his throbbing foot.

"Now!" He straightened, turned decisively to David's mother. "You can't help him by crying, lady. If you want to help him go make him some tea. A lot of it."

"Kein gefahr?" she asked dully, disbelievingly.

"Yes! Yes! That's right!" he answered impatiently. "Kein gefahr! Now make him some tea."

"Teh, Mrs. Schearl," a woman in the doorway came forward. "Geh macht eem teh!"

"Teh?"

"Yes! Teh!" the interne repeated. "Quick! Schnell! Yes?"

She turned numbly. The woman offered to help her. They went out.

"Well, how's the kid?" the interne grinned down at him. "Feel good?"

"Y-yeh."

"That's the boy! You'll be all right in a little while."

He turned to leave. A fattish, bare-armed woman stood at his shoulder. David recognized her. She lived on the same floor.

"Ducktuh!" she whispered hurriedly. "Yuh shoulda seen vod a fighd dere vus heyuh!" She contracted, rocked. "Oy-yoy! Yoy-u-yoy! Him, dat man, his faddeh, he vus hittin' eem! Terrible! A terrhible men! En' dere vus heyuh his cozzins—oder huh cozzins—I don' know! En' dey vus fighdingk. Oy-yoy-yoy! Vid scrimms! Vid holleringk! Pwwweeyoy! En' den dey chessed de boy all oud f'om de house. En den dey chessed de odder two pipples! En' vee vus listeningk, en' dis man vos crying. Ah'm khrezzy! Ah'm khrezzy! I dun know vod I do! I dun' know vod I said! He ses. Ah'm khrezzy! En' he vus cryingk! Oy!"

"Is that so?" the interne said indifferently.

"Id vus terrhible! Terrhible! En' Ducktuh," she patted his arm. "Maybe you could tell me fah vy my liddle Elix dun eat? I give him eggks vid milk vid kulleh gedillehs. En he don' vonna eat nottingk. Vod sh'd I do?"

"I don't know?" He brushed by her. "You'd better see a doctor."

"Oy bist du a chuchim!" she spat after him in Yiddish. "Does the breath of your mouth cost you something?"

His mother returned. Her hair was disheveled. Tears

still stained her cheek though she had stopped crying. "You'll have some tea in a minute, darling." A tremulous gasp of after-weeping shook her. "Does your foot hurt very much?"

"N-no," he lied.

"They told me you were at the car-tracks," she shuddered. "How did you come there? You might have been— Oh! God forbid! What made you go? What made you do it?"

"I don't—I don't know," he answered. And the answer was true. He couldn't tell now why he had gone, except that something had forced him, something that was clear then and inevitable, but that every passing minute made more inarticulate. "I don't know, mama."

She groaned softly, sat down on the bed. The fat woman with the bare arms touched her shoulders and leaned over her.

"Poor Mrs. Schearl!" she said with grating, provocative pity. "Poor Mrs. Schearl! Why ask him? Don't you know? Our bleeding, faithful mother's heart they think nothing of wringing. Nothing! Woe you! Woe me! Before we see them grown, how many tears we shed! Oy-yoy-yoy! Measureless. So our children bring us suffering. So our men. Alas, our bitter lot! No?" Her see-saw sigh heaved gustily, pitched audibly. She folded her hands on her loose flabby belly and rocked sorrowfully.

His mother made no answer, but gazed fixedly into his eyes.

In the kitchen, he could hear the policeman interrogating his father, and his father answering in a dazed, unsteady voice. That sense of triumph that David had felt on first being brought in, welled up within him again as he listened to him falter and knew him shaken.

"Yes. Yes," he was saying. "My sawn. Mine. Yes. Awld eight. Eight en'—en' vun mawnt'. He vas bawn in—"

"Wait a minute!" The policeman's voice interrupted him. "Say, Doc, befaw yuh go, tell us, did I do it good. You know—dat foist-aid business. Waddayer say? In case dere's a commendation er sompt'n."

"Sure! Fine! Couldn't have done it better myself."

"T'anks, Doc. An' say, gimme de medical repawt, will uh? Shock? Foolin' aroun' wit' de car-tracks wit—Heh! Heh!—merlicious intent."

"Oh—er—just say, shock . . . caused by . . . short circuiting . . . trolley power—what d'you call it—rail."

"Yea."

"Then—electrical burn . . . on ankle . . . right foot . . . second degree. Got it?"

"Secon' degree, yea."

"Applied artificial respir—"

"Aw Doc, have a heart, will yuh!"

"You want a commendation, don't you?" the interne laughed. "Well anything—first aid. Child revived— I've left a slip for you, Mister. On the table. Carron oil. Smear it around the ankle tonight and tomorrow. The blib ought to be gone in a day or two."

"Yes."

"And if he doesn't feel well tomorrow, take him to the Holy Name Hospital—it's on the slip. But he'll be all right. Well, Lieutenant, I'll see you again."

"Yea. So long, Doc."

The woman who had gone out with David's mother came in balancing a cup of tea. Silently his mother propped him up on the pillows and began feeding him out of the spoon. The hot, sugared tea quickened his blood. He sighed, feeling vitality return, but only enough to know his body's weariness. There were no more cool places between the sheets for his throbbing foot. The women in the doorway had turned their backs to him and were listening to the policeman who was holding forth in the kitchen.

"An' say," his reassuring voice boomed out. "I woiked over 'im, Mister, an' no foolin'! Yuh hoid wot de Doc sez, didntcha? If it wuzn' fer me, dat kid wouldn' be hea. Yessir! People don't appreciate a cop aroun dis neighborhood. But w'en dere in dutch— Say, I seen 'em boined Mister! I'm tellin' yuh. I seen a switchman was so boined —say! He musta fell on de rail. An' nobody knew a t'ing about it. Out dere in de car-barns on a hunner'n fifty-fift' an' Eight' Avenoo. Must a been on dere fer hours. An' de foist t'ing yuh know, his bones was troo de elevated— right down t' de ground—black as zat stove, Mister! Y'had da gadder 'im up in a sheet. Yessir! So he wuz gettin' off easy, dat kid o' yours. But even so if it hadn'ta been fer me— Say, d'yuh wan' all o' dese people in hea?"

"I—I don'—" His father sounded stunned. "I—I—
ou—"

"Sure. C'mon goils. De kid's gotta get some quiet now.
Vaddayuh say? All right, gents."

"Vee know dem," voices objected. "Vee liff heyuh."

"Not hea'," indulgently. "Not all o' yiz. C'mon. Come
a later—one at a time—"

There was a general shuffling of feet, murmured pro-
ests.

"Er fumfit shoin far a bissel geld," sneered the woman
vith the bare arms as she went out. "Gitzeem a krenk!"

"I god Davy's shoes and stockin', Mister," a boy's voice
iped. "He goes to my cheder."

"Atta boy. Just leave 'em hea. C'mon de rest o' yiz.
Dat goes fer you too, Solomon."

Feet went through the doorway, voices dwindled. The
oor was shut.

"Well, I got de place quiet for yuh," said the policeman. "Funny all de trouble dese kids o' ours gives us,
uh? You said it. Geeziz I'm a cop an' I can't keep mine in
ne, bringin' home repawt co'ds dat'd make yer hair toin
rey. Well, my beat's aroun' hea' in case yuh wanna see
e sometime. Walsh is de name." He loomed up in the
oorway. "How're yuh feelin' now, kid? He'll be all right.
ure. He's full o' de devil a'reddy. I'll fan yuh wit' me stick
I catch yuh foolin' aroun' dem tracks again. See? 'Night."
He flicked an open palm, turned and went out.

He had finished his tea. The sudden, flushing surge
f heat that filled the hollows of his tired body drove
tipple of perspiration to his brow and lips. His underwear
lung to him cutting at the crotch. The trough of the bed-
ing where he lay had become humidly warm and un-
omfortable. He wriggled closer to the cooler edge of the
ed where his mother was seated and lay back limply.

"More?" She asked putting the cup down on the window
ill.

"No, mama."

"You've had nothing to eat since the morning, beloved.
You're hungry, aren't you?"

He shook his head. And to ease the throbbing in his
ight foot, slid it furtively from under the covers at her
ack to cool it.

His father stood in the doorway, features dissolved in

the dark. Only the glitter in his eyes was sharply visible
fixed on the puffy gray ankle. His mother turned at his
tread, spied the swollen foot also. Her sucked breath hissed
between pain-puckered lips.

"Poor darling! Poor child!"

His father's hand fell heavily against the door-frame.
"He's written down the name of some medicine for us to
get," he said abruptly. "To smear on his foot."

"Yes?" She half rose. "I'll go get it."

"Sit there!" His peremptory tone lacked force as
though he spoke out of custom, not conviction. "It will
be quicker for me to get it. Your neighbors outside won't
delay *me* with their tongues." But instead of going,
he stood where he was. "He said he'd be better in a day or
two."

She was silent.

"I said he'd be better in a day or two," he repeated.

"Yes. Of course."

"Well?"

"Nothing."

There was a pause. His father cleared his throat. When
he spoke his voice had a peculiar harshness as though he
were at the same time provoking and steeling himself
against a blow.

"It— it's my fault you'd say. Is that it?"

She shook her head wearily. "What use is there to
talk about faults, Albert? None foresaw this. No one alone
brought it on. And if it's faults we must talk about it's
mine as well. I never told you. I let him listen to me
months and months ago. I even drove him downstairs to—
to—"

"To protect him—from me?"

"Yes."

His teeth clicked. His chest rose. The expulsion of his
breath seemed to rock him slightly. "I'll go get it." He
turned heavily out of the doorway.

David listened to his father's dull, unresilient footfall
cross the kitchen floor. The door was opened, closed. A
vague, remote pity stirred within his breast like a wreathing, raveling smoke, tenuously dispersed within his being,
a kind of torpid heart-break he had felt sometimes in
winter awakened deep in the night and hearing that dull
tread descend the stairs.

"Perhaps you'll be hungry in a little while," his mother said persuasively. "After you've rested a bit and we've put the medicine on your foot. And then some milk and a boiled egg. You'd like that?" Her question was sufficiently shored by statement to require no answer. "And then you'll go to sleep and forget it all." She paused. Her dark, unswerving eyes sought his. "Sleepy, beloved?"

"Yes, mama."

He might as well call it sleep. It was only toward sleep that every wink of the eyelids could strike a spark into the cloudy tinder of the dark, kindle out of shadowy corners of the bedroom such myriad and such vivid jets of images—of the glint on tilted beards, of the uneven shine on roller skates, of the dry light on grey stone stoops, of the tapering glitter of rails, of the oily sheen on the night-smooth rivers, of the glow on thin blonde hair, red faces, of the glow on the outstretched, open palms of legions upon legions of hands hurtling toward him. He might as well call it sleep. It was only toward sleep that ears had power to cull again and reassemble the shrill cry, the hoarse voice, the scream of fear, the bells, the thick-breathing, the roar of crowds and all sounds that lay fermenting in the vats of silence and the past. It was only toward sleep one knew himself still lying on the cobbles, felt the cobbles under him, and over him and scudding ever toward him like a black foam, the perpetual blur of shod and running feet, the broken shoes, new shoes, stubby, pointed, caked, polished, buniony, pavement-beveled, lumpish, under skirts, under trousers, shoes, over one and through one, and feel them all and feel, not pain, not terror, but strangest triumph, strangest acquiescence. One might as well call it sleep. He shut his eyes.

AFTERWORD

THIS is the first paperback publication* of Henry Roth's novel, *Call It Sleep*. It seems to me a remarkable book, one of the best novels of our time. I thought so when I first read it, more or less by chance, a few months after its initial publication in New York in December 1934. It remained extraordinarily vivid in my memory; but until recently, no one I met, American or British, seemed to have heard of it, much less to have read it, and it was not until 1956, in Professor Rideout's *The Radical Novel in the United States*, that I came across any reference to it in a critical work. That year, however, was a turning point in the book's history: it was named twice— by Alfred Kazin and Leslie A. Fiedler—in a symposium, "The Most Neglected Books of the Past 25 Years," that appeared in the *American Scholar*. Since then, both Kazin and Fiedler have written about it at length elsewhere, Fiedler notably in his book *Love and Death in the American Novel;* and during the past few years its stature has been increasingly recognized and acclaimed in the United States. It was reissued in New York in 1960, and reading it again in that edition more than confirmed my early opinion of it: I found it even more impressive than I had remembered it.

The history of *Call It Sleep*, then, is seemingly a tale of years of neglect followed by a sudden rediscovery. In fact, the novel by no means did badly on its first publication. The years 1934 and 1935 were grim ones for American publishing, and Henry Roth's publisher, Robert O. Ballou, was driven out of business by the economic hazards of the times within a few months of launching

* The first paperback edition referred to here was published in October, 1964. Critical attention was immediate and enormous beginning with a review on the front page of *The New York Times Book Review* on October 25th by Irving Howe. Since then it has gone through nearly twenty editions with over 1,000,000 copies in print.

Call It Sleep. All the same, it went into two editions and sold 4,000 copies: and it collected a most impressive set of reviews.

Yet I think the book we have rediscovered looks a little different now from what it did in the 'thirties. The 'thirties, in America even more than in England, was the period of socially conscious fiction and of much theorizing about what was called the proletarian novel. Inevitably, *Call It Sleep* was seen as an attempt at a proletarian novel; or it was judged that it would have been a better book if it had been a proletarian novel, as by the reviewer of the Communist weekly, *New Masses,* who wrote: "It is a pity that so many young writers drawn from the proletariat can make no better use of their working-class experience than as material for introspective and febrile novels." Today, despite its setting of urban poverty, it is difficult to see *Call It Sleep* as a proletarian novel in the 'thirties sense at all. It exists in quite another dimension, which Professor Fiedler comes near defining when he applies to it C. M. Doughty's epigram: "The Semites are like to a man sitting in a cloaca to the eyes, and whose brows touch heaven." This very well suggests both the social environment in which Roth's characters exist and the condition of striving in which the central character, David Schearl, has his being.

Call It Sleep, after a short prologue, tells the story of David's life in the slums of New York between the ages of six and nine. David, except in the prologue, is the novel's center of consciousness; but the prologue is important because it establishes the emotional pattern that is to dominate the child's life. It describes the meeting on Ellis Island in 1907 between Albert Schearl, a Polish Jewish immigrant already working in New York as a printer, and the wife and infant son who have followed him to join him in what the epigraph calls ironically the Golden Land. It shows immediately the relation between husband and wife, which for the greater part of the book we see through David's eyes and through its effects on him. The characters, as immigrants, are uprooted and isolated. The father is permanently and radically estranged from the world about him; for him, immigration is a form of banishment. He is proud, bitter, violent, inordinately suspicious; his paranoiac self-regard causes him to lose job after job; and increasingly he turns against his son, who in the end he believes is not his child but a bastard conceived by his wife after his leaving her for America. Warmhearted, sensual, his wife Genya is also isolated, imprisoned in her ignorance of English:

"I know that I myself live on one hundred and twenty-six Boddeh Stritt—"

"Bahday Street," her husband corrected her. "I've told you scores of times."

"Boddeh Stritt," she resumed apologetically. He shrugged. "It's such a strange name—bath street in German. But here I am. I know there is a church on a certain street to my left, the vegetable market is on my right, behind me are the railroad tracks and the broken rocks, and before me, a few blocks away is a certain store window that has a kind of whitewash on it—and faces in the whitewash, the kind children draw. Within this pale is my America, and if I ventured further I should be lost. In fact," she laughed, "were they even to wash that window, I might never find my way home again."

Forced in upon herself by her husband's harshness and coldness towards her, she turns increasingly to the child, who finds in her lap his only sure refuge from the terrors of the New York slums.

The boy himself is isolated by his very childishness and, beyond this, by the emotional relationship, classically Freudian in its pattern, between his parents. *Call It Sleep* must be the most powerful evocation of the terrors of childhood ever written. Lost, bewildered, friendless, the small boy David scuttles through the streets of the Lower East Side like a frightened little animal lost in a jungle inhabited by the larger carnivores. We are spared nothing of the crudeness of cosmopolitan slum life and living. There is, for instance, the horrified boy's initiation into sex by a crippled girl only a little older than himself. The irons on her legs creak as she embraces him. "Between de legs. Who put id in is de poppa. De poppa's god de petzel. Yaw de poppa." And all the terrors the boy experiences in the streets of New York are brought together, symbolized, in his fear of the tenement houses in which he lives, the dark, rat-infested cellars with their overwhelming suggestion of mindless and brutal animality, the sweating stairways to be tremblingly climbed to the topmost apartment, which means warmth and security because his mother is there, and, finally, the roof above, the escape to which is freedom.

Yet though the squalor and filth, the hopelessness and helplessness of slum-life are remorselessly presented and the cacophony never ceases—this must be the *noisiest* novel ever written—*Call It Sleep* does not strike one as primarily a novel of social protest, an exposure novel, like Farrell's *Studs Lonigan,* to which many reviewers of the first edition compared it. Roth's subject is no more poverty and its stultifications than it is Joyce's in *A Portrait of the Artist.* Indeed, there is a sense in which the Schearls are in the slums but not of them. Roth shows this beautifully in his dialogue. He renders with what seems quite horrible fidelity the mutilations of English as spoken by the immigrant slum-dwellers, Jewish, Hungarian, Italian, Irish alike. "My ticher calls id Xmas, bod de kids call id Chrizmas. I'd's a goyish holiday anyways. Wunst I hanged op a stockin' in Brooklyn. Bod mine fodder pud in a eggshells wid terlit paper an' a piece f'om a ol' kendle. So he leffed w'en he seen me. Id ain' no Sendy Klaws, didya know?" David, too, speaks like this when he is speaking English—but not when he is at home with his parents, talking in Yiddish. Then he, and they, speak a remarkably pure English, the English of people of cultivation; and we see them in a wholly new light. In this way, Roth makes us sharply aware, as no other novelist except Willa Cather has done, in a book like *My Antonia,* of the degradation, the diminution in human dignity, that was one aspect of the immigrant's lot as he moved from a society with a traditional culture to another with no culture at all. We feel this with David's parents; we see it, by implication at any rate, at its most striking in the representation of the teacher of Hebrew, Reb Yidel Pankower. Dirty, irascible, a petty sadist, a Dickensian character conducting what appears to be an almost Dickensian parody of religious education—this is certainly part of the truth about him; but it is only part, what one is tempted to call the American truth about him, or the truth in English. The deeper truth is revealed by his discovery of David's caliber. The rabbi belongs to a much older and richer culture than that of the Lower East Side; and it is he who makes the final comment on the Golden Land: "A curse on them! He glared about him at the children and half-grown boys and girls who crowded the stoops and overflowed in the sidewalks and gutters. The devil take them! What was going to become of Yiddish youth? What could become of this new breed? These Americans? This side-walk-and-gutter generation?" With Reb Yidel Pankower we are back with Doughty's "The Semites are like to a man sitting in a cloaca to the eyes, and whose brows touch heaven."

There is another obvious difference between this novel and the American novels of social protest of the 'thirties, of which *Studs Lonigan* may be taken as representative. In those novels, the characters strike one as being wholly conditioned by their economic and cultural circumstances; they are almost excretions of their environment. This is anything but true of Roth's characters. Despite the conditions in which they live, they are dominating figures. This is most obviously so of Albert Schearl: half-mad as he is, he is a tragic figure. And Genya and her sister Bertha exist just as much in the round as feeling, suffering, reacting human beings. They exist as it were as natural forces. Bertha is a very considerable comic creation, but she has her moments of pathos and perception, as when, wanting desperately to be married, to Genya's "Why, Bertha, New York is full of all kinds of men who would want you," she retorts: "Yes! It's also full of all kinds of glib, limber Jewesses who can play the piano."

But the real center of the novel is the boy David, and Roth seems to me to plunge us into a child's mind more directly and more intransigently than any other novelist has done. We experience the child's instantaneous apprehension of his world. Roth captures, too, better, I think, than it has been done in English before, what might be called a child's magical thinking, which is closely allied to the thinking of the poet. With David, we are a long way from either Tom Sawyer or the boy Studs Lonigan; his world is not that of simple fantasy or make-believe but one he creates with the desperate, compulsive imagination of the poet. However grotesquely different the environments in which they lived, he is, it seems to me, of the company of the boy Wordsworth in *The Prelude*. Racked by guilt he cannot understand, obsessed by notions of an incomprehensible God, he has intimations of transfiguration prompted by Reb Yidel Pankower's translation at the Hebrew School of a passage of scripture in which an angel is described as touching the lips of Isaiah with a fiery coal so that he may speak in the presence of God. And the transfiguration is realized at the end of the novel when, fleeing his father's anger both at his possession of a rosary, which he has got for what seem its magical properties, and at his apparently precocious sexual depravity, he runs through the streets at night and pushes the handle of a zinc milk ladle into the slot between the streetcar tracks that carries the live rail. Knocked out by the electric shock that results, as he comes round he has a vision that unifies his fragmented world and, in a sense, reconciles him to his experience of that world. In a mysterious way, the world becomes a whole.

Roth, who was born in 1906, wrote *Call It Sleep* in his middle twenties. Apart from two or three sketches, he has written nothing since. According to the biographical information given in the last American edition of *Call It Sleep*, he now lives with his wife and family at a farm called "Roth's Waterfowl" deep in rural Maine. His father lives near by; his mother, hating the quiet of the country, has remained in East Side New York. He earns his living raising ducks and geese and slaughtering and plucking those raised by other farmers. He also coaches local boys who need help in Latin and mathematics; and his wife teaches in an elementary school in a neighboring town. He is quite cut off from literary life, and the only paper he reads regularly is the *New Statesman*. He has said: "I don't think I'll write again."

More than one can say, one hopes that time will prove him wrong. Even so, to have written *Call It Sleep* is itself enough to make any man's reputation. In it, Roth shows himself a master of the novelist's art, a master of sympathy, humor, detachment and deep poetic insight into the immigrant's lot and into the mind of childhood. Place, time and people are alike uniquely and unforgettably evoked, so that to read *Call It Sleep* is to live it.

WALTER ALLEN

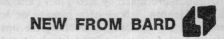